Norstrilia

by

Cordwainer Smith

The NESFA Press
Post Office Box 809
Framingham, MA 01701-0203
1994

First Revised Edition
Third Printing — September 1998

Library of Congress Card Catalog Number: 94-68979
ISBN: 0-915368-61-7

Contents

Acknowledgments

This book, like all NESFA Press books, was put together through the efforts of many volunteers. Frank and Lisa Richards and their company, QuickScan (PO Box 71, Marlow, NH 03456, (603) 446-7307), scanned in the book. Laurie Mann made the contractual arrangements. Mark Olson and Tony Lewis arranged for the cover and introduction, acted as liaisons to the rest of NESFA (now that I live in Pittsburgh, not New England, and I can't do so in person anymore), and helped in a number of ways, both big and little. Mark also arranged for the final printing. George Flynn copyedited the book and compared the text we had to previous book and magazine versions, helping to make our text much better and providing much of the information now found in the appendix. (Alan Elms, who wrote the introduction, also provided information on differences between editions.) Gay Ellen Dennett and Claire Anderson helped choose the cover. David Cherry helped us contact the artist. Merle and Aron Insinga helped with dust jacket design. Thanks to you all.

James A. Mann
Pittsburgh, PA
October 1994

Foreword

Norstrilia is the only SF novel by Dr. Paul Linebarger (Cordwainer Smith). The novel is a part of the rich future history that Smith developed in most of his other stories, that of the Instrumentality of Mankind. It forms an essential, even pivotal, place in that history, bringing together many of the themes Smith explored in other stories and advancing many historical threads.

As Alan Elms explains in detail in his introduction, *Norstrilia* had a complex publishing history. It was published split into two parts for magazine publication (under the titles of "The Boy Who Bought Old Earth" and "The Store of Heart's Desire"). Then it was published as two novels (*The Planet Buyer* and *The Underpeople*). Finally, Ballantine/Del Rey recombined the parts into the novel *Norstrilia*. This edition is the most complete and accurate edition we've been able to put together. It incorporates a number of corrections to the Ballantine/Del Rey editions. It also includes an appendix of material that was part of the previous versions, before they were reformed into *Norstrilia*. Of special interest is the material Smith wrote to bridge the two novels, but which was removed (since it was no longer needed) when they were recombined.

NESFA Press also publishes *The Rediscovery of Man: The Complete Short Science Fiction of Cordwainer Smith* and the *Concordance to Cordwainer Smith*.

Introduction

Alan C. Elms

In the spring of 1957, Paul Linebarger began to imagine the broad outlines of his first (and, as matters would turn out, his only) science fiction novel. Linebarger's earlier published fiction had come to him quickly: two mainstream novels had each been written in a few weeks, and a suspense novel had taken months at most. He had also written several shorter pieces of science fiction, published under the pseudonym of Cordwainer Smith. Though their gestation time is unknown, each had taken Linebarger only a few hours or days to set down on paper.

But his science fiction novel was different. Like the giant sick sheep that it would describe in its early pages, it swelled in size and developed in peculiar directions. Linebarger worked on it in fits and starts, interrupted for long periods by other work, by psychological crises, and by serious physical illness. Several times he began the manuscript again from the beginning. As he changed psychologically, the book changed too. By the time the novel was essentially done, six years after it was begun, Linebarger confessed to his agent that he was going through "one of those morbidly oversensitive periods in which an author does not know whether he has a pile of blah or a minor classic on his hands" (letter to Harry Altshuler, 11 March 1963; Linebarger Collection, Spencer Research Library, University of Kansas).

By now, *Norstrilia* has achieved the status of at least "minor classic" and maybe more. But Paul Linebarger did not live to see it happen. He tried as best he could to get the entire novel into print, but as he acknowledged at one point, it was regarded as "over-length" by potential publishers—about 25% longer than the 60,000 words considered marketable for a science fiction novel at the time. Most of the manuscript's first half appeared in *Galaxy* in early 1964, but *Galaxy* readers were referred to the magazine's sister publication, *Worlds of If Science Fiction,* to find the rest of the story—actually, only pieces of the rest. Pyramid Books bought the whole manuscript for paperback publication, but insisted on publishing it as two apparently self-contained "novels." The first half appeared as *The Planet Buyer* in October 1964, with a two-page "Epilogue and Coda" added by Linebarger to give readers a sense of closure. After writing and rewriting a new introductory section to make the novel's second half stand more or less on its own, Linebarger died in 1966, at age 53. That second half, titled *The Underpeople,* did not appear in book form until 1968; even then, it did not include substantial segments of the remaining manuscript, and it made no direct mention that it was a sequel to *The Planet Buyer.* In 1975, nearly a decade after Linebarger's death, a Ballantine Books paperback reunited the two halves of the manuscript and restored most of the earlier deletions. After another twenty years, this NESFA Press edition finally gives *Norstrilia* its first hardcover American publication.

Even in the butchered format of the magazine and Pyramid Books versions, even with the numerous typographical errors of the Ballantine edition, *Norstrilia* has made its mark. In a perceptive early review of *The Planet Buyer,* Theodore Sturgeon proclaimed, "The Next Great Name Is Smith," and suggested that "If literary historians of the future make of Cordwainer Smith another Tolkien, it will not be too surprising" (*National Review,* June 1, 1965; Sturgeon sent a copy of his review to Linebarger with a note apologizing for its understatement). By 1985, the novel was so cherished by some readers that when a scholar/fan wrote about "touchstone" passages in science fiction, she began with the scene in *Norstrilia* where Rod McBan gets his first sight and smell of the planet Earth (Carol McGuirk, *Fantasy Review,* December 1985. McGuirk also asked rhetorically, "Smith, like every major s-f writer, has his own cadre of admirers—but has his *centrality* in the genre been argued?"). Two years later, a poll asking knowledgeable readers to choose the "All-Time Best Science Fiction Novel" placed *Norstrilia* at number 35, just below Orwell's *1984* and several notches above major works by two of Linebarger's favorite writers, H. G. Wells and Olaf Stapledon (*Locus,* August 1987). When one of the field's most active scholars recently listed a dozen basic works of science fiction that he would assign to an undergraduate class, *Norstrilia* was included along with Le Guin's *Left Hand of Darkness,* Gibson's *Neuromancer,* and other obvious choices (Gary Westfahl, *Science Fiction Eye,* Spring 1994).

Paul Linebarger had not seen his mission in life as writing the Great American Science Fiction Novel. He held a full-time position as Professor of Asiatic Politics at the School of Advanced International Studies of the Johns Hopkins University, and he took his work there seriously. He carried out frequent assignments on the side (or under cover), doing intelligence work around the world for U. S. Army Intelligence and occasionally for the CIA. At times he engaged in speechwriting, ghostwriting, and other tasks for prominent political figures, including Dwight D. Eisenhower and Nelson Rockefeller. Though writing science fiction was much more than a hobby for him (he saw it as essential to his psychological health), the brief periods of time Linebarger was able to find for his fiction lent themselves better to writing short stories than novels. But in 1957 he spent a one-semester sabbatical leave at the Australian National University in Canberra. Amid his teaching and scholarly writing in Australia (plus more off-the-record intelligence work in nearby countries), he had the time and the emotional freedom to think about writing a science fiction novel.

Important aspects of the novel were influenced by his experiences in Australia. Linebarger had been a world traveler from age five. He spent much of his childhood in China and Europe, and he revisited those areas often throughout his life, along with trips to many other countries on every major continent. But Australia felt special to him. It combined aspects of the exotic and of frontier America. Its English-origin settlers displayed a tough but honest code of ethics and a friendly independence that he admired. He told his Australian friends that when he retired he wanted to settle there for the rest of his life. He never got old enough to retire (his university wouldn't consider it until he was at least 55), but he did get back to Australia for one more sabbatical leave a year before he died. In the meantime he returned often to an imagined Australia, in the novel that through most of its gestation was titled *Old North Australia,* then finally *Norstrilia* for short. (In case you're wondering, *Norstrilia* should probably be pronounced Nor-STRILE-ya with an Australian accent—but Linebarger left no instructions, and who knows what that accent will be 15,000 years from now?)

Norstrilia could have been a fairly simple novel about the settlers of another planet who struggle to reproduce and maintain the culture of twentieth-century North Australia. Fairly good science fiction novels have often been written that way: transpose elements of the Roman Empire or Elizabethan England to another planet or a future Earth, then let the history books and the biographies guide your plot and your characters. Linebarger pretends, in *Norstrilia*'s first five pages, that he is indeed telling just such a simple story. But before we've finished reading page 1, we know the story won't be all that simple. As we finish page 2, we know the central protagonist is a very unpredictable fellow. By page 3, the planet Norstrilia begins to sound distinctly unlike old North Australia ever was on Earth—indeed, unlike any part of Earth has ever been.

Paul Linebarger wanted to build the character and values of his Australian friends into a science fiction novel, and to some extent he did. But he had other agendas as well. Among them, these are prominent in *Norstrilia:*

Literary Adaptation

Like other writers before him (e.g., Jack Williamson) and after (e.g., Robert Silverberg), Paul Linebarger often looked to works of great literature for science-fictional ideas. In his short stories he adapted works as diverse as the French romance *Paul et Virginie*, Arthur Rimbaud's poem *Le bateau ivre*, and the traditional Chinese narrative *Quest of the Three Kingdoms*. Linebarger had been reading classic Chinese literature since childhood, in translation and in the original. As his ideas for *Norstrilia* were developing, another Chinese classic came to mind: the hundred-chapter epic *The Journey to the West*. (The most accurate translation now available is Anthony C. Yu's four-volume University of Chicago Press edition. Arthur Waley's partial translation, *Monkey*, is the best-known English version. Another recent adaptation in contemporary terms is Mark Salzman's *The Laughing Sutra*.)

The Journey to the West tells the story of a real seventh-century Buddhist monk and his altogether fantastic monkey bodyguard, who travel to India to look for Buddhist scriptures. Before they attain their goal they must endure, as Anthony Wu summarizes, "a long series of captures and releases of the pilgrims by monsters, demons, animal spirits, and gods in disguise." In *Norstrilia,* Rod McBan begins his journey to Earth in an ironically similar quest—not for scriptures but for ancient postage stamps. He is accompanied by a monkey-protector, and he encounters various monsters or demons (giant spiders and mutated humans), animal spirits (the underpeople), and gods in disguise (the E'telekeli). One of the underpeople, the cat-woman C'mell, may be partly inspired by Kuan-yin, a female Buddha in *The Journey to the West* who organizes assistance for the traveling monk. The monk not only hopes to obtain Buddhist scriptures to take back to China, but also seeks self-enlightenment and, as Anthony Wu says, an answer to "the question of whether all men, or only part of humanity, could attain Buddhahood." Rod McBan does not seek self-enlightenment but he gets it anyway, at the hands of Earth's last clinical psychologist; and, with the encouragement of C'mell, he lends his assistance to an underground (literally!) movement that will ultimately unite people and underpeople, at least at a spiritual level. There may be even more connections between *Norstrilia* and *The Journey to the West,* in both deep structure and detail. But Paul Linebarger was never one to let strict literary parallels spoil a good story, and much of *Norstrilia* wanders far from *The Journey*.

Political Values

Paul Linebarger was an academic political scientist by training and by professional identification, but he was a political activist as well, in

several arenas. He has been inaccurately characterized (e.g., in the Clute/
Nicholls *Science Fiction Encyclopedia*) as a right-winger, and he did
enjoy baiting his more liberal friends with outrageous pronouncements.
But in the American context, he usually occupied the ground between
moderate Republican and moderate Democrat, with a heavy dose of
realpolitik on certain matters of state. In the Chinese context, Linebarger
had grown up with a strong belief in the greatness of Sun Yat-sen and
with a sustained preference for the rule of Chiang Kai-shek over Mao
Tse-tung. Linebarger and his family enjoyed close personal ties with Sun,
with Chiang, and with many prominent members of the Kuomintang.
But according to his colleagues and former students, he was not blind to
the corruptions of the Nationalist Chinese Government of Taiwan. His
real emotional commitment was not to that government but to the welfare
of the Chinese people. In *Norstrilia,* Linebarger delights in devising ex-
amples of interplanetary realpolitik and displaying his expertise in psychological warfare. But his strongest emotional investment there is in the
cause of the underpeople—which for Linebarger did not primarily represent the American civil rights movement, as some have suggested, but
the long struggle of the Chinese masses toward political and personal
freedom. (Again, Linebarger was not trying to construct an exact parallel
to the Chinese struggle in his depiction of the underpeople. He mixes
elements of Chinese history with borrowings from Joan of Arc and other
inspired leaders and martyrs, and emerges with a mythic struggle far
broader and more archetypal than any given political movement on Earth.)

Personal Myth

The name "Rod" may have been chosen as a joking reference to the
magical golden rod wielded by Monkey in *The Journey to the West.* The
name "McBan" probably came from Anthony, one of Linebarger's middle
names. Rod McBan's full name, Roderick Frederick Ronald Arnold William MacArthur McBan the hundred and fifty-first, reflects Linebarger's
ambivalence about his own distended name, Paul Myron Anthony
Linebarger, and that of his father, Paul Myron Wentworth Linebarger.
That's only the beginning of the autobiographical elements built into
Norstrilia.

Starting in his peripatetic childhood, Paul Linebarger had suffered
for decades from a profound psychological isolation. Rod's inability to
"spiek" and "hier" telepathically like others on his planet reflects
Linebarger's strong sense of missing out on the shared feelings of his
peers as he passed often from one country and linguistic context to another. Rod's eventual confrontation with the psychotherapist Catmaster
was mirrored in Linebarger's own life by encounters with several psycho-

therapists. Some gave him temporary relief from his isolation; others left him grateful to be able to live with himself. C'mell may be endowed with characteristics of several desired but somehow forbidden women in his life; we know that she was based in part on the qualities of his favorite cat Melanie, and on his yearnings to be as emotionally close to a human woman as he sometimes felt toward Melanie and his other cats. And Rod's self-effacing cousin Lavinia resembles in certain ways Linebarger's second wife Genevieve, with whom he was satisfied to live out the final years of his life.

Spiritual Stirrings

In those final years, Linebarger's previously unfocused religious feelings intensified. He had grown up nominally Methodist, but had felt little interest in the more spiritual aspects of religion until Genevieve's mother underwent a painful terminal illness. As Linebarger and his wife began to embrace Episcopalianism (a compromise between his Protestant and her Catholic upbringing), the evolving worlds of *Norstrilia* acquired distinct religious undertones and overtones as well. But although Linebarger welcomed the ceremonial and communal aspects of Episcopalianism, his personal beliefs about salvation and the afterlife remained ambiguously unorthodox—as does the religion of the E'telekeli and his underperson disciples.

Science Fiction Tropes

Paul Linebarger enjoyed orchestrating all these elements in *Norstrilia,* but he remained quite aware that he needed to tell an entertaining and reader-involving story. He had been a voracious reader of science fiction since the early days of *Amazing Stories,* building up a major collection of science fiction books in several languages. (He collected stamps, guns, typewriters, and science fiction.) Though he easily pulled elements of world literature into his own work, he was steeped in the science fiction tradition and happily elaborated on it. The accidentally entrepreneurial "Boy Who Bought Old Earth" of *Norstrilia* is at one level making friendly fun of Heinlein's "Man Who Sold the Moon." The underpeople incorporate elements of Dr. Moreau's beast-people and the Time Traveler's Morlocks. But those Wellsian elements barely anticipated Linebarger's far more elaborate development of underpeople society, as well as the society of "true men" on Earth's surface and beyond.

Packing all these tropes, icons, themes, borrowings, and personal myths into one novel was a tall order. Linebarger didn't completely pull it off. At several points the novel is missing transitions or clearly developed motivations; at other points there are minor or major inconsistencies.

(For the reader unfamiliar with the rest of Linebarger's science fiction, even more may seem to be missing. See *The Rediscovery of Man: The Complete Short Science Fiction of Cordwainer Smith,* published by NESFA Press in 1993, for explanations in story form of many otherwise obscure references in *Norstrilia.*) The novel is distinctly episodic—partly as a result of following *The Journey to the West* as a model, partly because of Linebarger's own episodic life, which kept getting in the way of producing a totally unified novel.

But few science fiction novels—indeed, few novels in any genre—display the exuberance of imaginative invention that persists from beginning to end of *Norstrilia.* Sometimes the novel seems to be, as a few critics have complained, "just one damned thing after another." But that's part of its charm as well: the charm of encountering the unexpected, and then the even more unexpected, followed shortly by the wildly improbable and the utterly fantastic—all anchored by the struggling hero Rod and his constantly fascinating companion C'mell. And throughout the novel there is the language of Cordwainer Smith, which Theodore Sturgeon (himself a master of language) described as at times "exalted," at other times "anguished," at still other times "deadly humorous." Before and after Paul Linebarger's early death, many science fiction writers—from Ursula Le Guin to Harlan Ellison to Frederik Pohl, from Algis Budrys to Robert Silverberg to Australia's own Terry Dowling—have tried to write like Cordwainer Smith. But there was only one real Cordwainer Smith. In *Norstrilia* his distinctive voice spieks clearly, and it is a joy for the reader's mind to hier.

Norstrilia

THEME AND PROLOGUE

Story, place and time—these are the essentials.

1

The story is simple. There was a boy who bought the planet Earth. We know that, to our cost. It only happened once, and we have taken pains that it will never happen again. He came to Earth, got what he wanted, and got away alive, in a series of very remarkable adventures. That's the story.

2

The place? That's Old North Australia. What other place could it be? Where else do the farmers pay ten million credits for a handkerchief, five for a bottle of beer? Where else do people lead peaceful lives, untouched by militarism, on a world which is booby-trapped with death and things worse than death. Old North Australia has stroon—the santaclara drug— and more than a thousand other planets clamor for it. But you can get stroon only from Norstrilia—that's what they call it, for short—because it is a virus which grows on enormous, gigantic, misshapen sheep. The sheep were taken from Earth to start a pastoral system; they ended up as the greatest of imaginable treasures. The simple farmers became simple billionaires, but they kept their farming ways. They started tough and they got tougher. People get pretty mean if you rob them and hurt them for almost three thousand years. They get obstinate. They avoid strangers, except for sending out spies and a very occasional tourist. They don't mess with other people, and they're death, death inside out and turned over twice, if you mess with them.

Then one of their kids showed up on Earth and bought it. The whole place, lock, stock and underpeople.

That was a real embarrassment for Earth.

And for Norstrilia, too.

If it had been the two governments, Norstrilia would have collected all the eye-teeth on Earth and sold them back at compound interest. That's the way Norstrilians do business. Or they might have said, "Skip it, cobber. You can keep your wet old ball. We've got a nice dry world of our own." That's the temper they have. Unpredictable.

But a kid had bought Earth, and it was his.

Legally he had the right to pump up the Sunset Ocean, shoot it into space, and sell water all over the inhabited galaxy.

He didn't.

He wanted something else.

The Earth authorities thought it was girls, so they tried to throw girls at him of all shapes, sizes, smells and ages—all the way from young ladies of good family down to dog-derived undergirls who smelled of romance all the time, except for the first five minutes after they had had hot antiseptic showers. But he didn't want girls. He wanted postage stamps.

That baffled both Earth and Norstrilia. The Norstrilians are a hard people from a harsh planet, and they think highly of property. (Why shouldn't they? They have most of it.) A story like this could only have started in Norstrilia.

3

What's Norstrilia like?

Somebody once singsonged it up, like this:

"Grey lay the land, oh. Grey grass from sky to sky. Not near the weir, dear. Not a mountain, low or high—only hills and grey grey. Watch the dappled dimpled twinkles blooming on the star bar.

"That is Norstrilia.

"All the muddy glubbery is gone—all the poverty, the waiting and the pain. People fought their way away, their way away from monstrous forms. People fought for hands and noses, eyes and feet, man and woman. They got it all back again. Back they came from daylight nightmares, centuries when monstrous men, sucking the water around the pools, dreamed of being men again. They found it. Men they were again, again, far away from a horrid *when.*

"The sheep, poor beasties, did not make it. Out of their sickness they distilled immortality for man. Who says research could do it? Research, besmirch! It was a pure accident. Smack up an accident, man, and you've got it made.

"Beige-brown sheep lie on blue-grey grass while the clouds rush past, low overhead, like iron pipes ceilinging the world.

"Take your pick of sick sheep, man, it's the sick that pays. Sneeze me a planet, man, or cough me up a spot of life-forever. If it's barmy there, where the noddies and trolls like you live, it's too right here.

"That's the book, boy.

"If you haven't seen it, you haven't seen Norstrilia. If you did see it, you wouldn't believe it. If you got there, you wouldn't get off alive.

"Mother Hitton's Littul Kittons wait for you down there. Little pets they are, little little little pets. Cute little things, they say. Don't you believe it. No man ever saw them and walked away alive. You won't either. That's the final dash, flash. That's the utter clobber, cobber.

"Charts call the place Old North Australia."

We can suppose that that is what it is like.

4

Time: first century of the Rediscovery of Man.

When C'mell lived.

About the time they polished off Shayol, like wiping an apple on the sleeve.

Long deep into our own time. Fifteen thousand years after the bombs went up and the boom came down on Old Old Earth.

Recent, see?

5

What happens in the story?

Read it.

Who's there?

It starts with Rod McBan—who had the real name of Roderick Frederick Ronald Arnold William MacArthur McBan. But you can't tell a story if you call the main person by a name as long as Roderick Frederick Ronald Arnold William MacArthur McBan. You have to do what his neighbors did—call him Rod McBan. The old ladies always said, "Rod McBan the hundred and fifty-first ..." and then sighed. Flurp a squirt at them, friends. We don't need numbers. We know his family was distinguished. We know the poor kid was born to troubles.

Why shouldn't he have troubles?

He was due to inherit the Station of Doom.

And then he gets around. He crosses all sorts of people. C'mell, the most beautiful of the girlygirls of Earth. Jean-Jacques Vomact, whose family must have preceded the human race. The wild old man at Adaminaby. The trained spiders of Earthport. The Subcommissioner Teadrinker. The Lord Jestocost, whose name is a page in history. The friends of the Ee-telly-kelly, and a queer tankful of friends they were. B'dank, of the cattle-police. The Catmaster. Tostig Amaral, about whom the less said the better. Ruth, in pursuit. C'mell, in flight. The Lady Johanna, laughing.

He gets away.

He *got* away. See, that's the story. Now you don't have to read it.

Except for the details.

They follow.

(He also bought one million women, far too many for any one boy to put to practical use, but it is not altogether certain, reader, that you will be told what he did about them.)

AT THE GATE OF THE GARDEN OF DEATH

Rod McBan faced the day of days. He knew what it was all about, but he could not really feel it. He wondered if they had tranquilized him with half-refined stroon, a product so rare and precious that it was never, never sold off-planet.

He knew that by nightfall he would be laughing and giggling and drooling in one of the Dying Rooms, where the unfit were put away to thin out the human breed, or else he would stand forth as the oldest land-holder on the planet, Chief Heir to the Station of Doom. The farm had been salvaged by his great^{32}-grandfather, and it was called Doom when he first inherited it, but the great^{32}-grandfather had bought an ice-asteroid, crashed it into the farm over the violent objections of his neighbors, and learned clever tricks with artesian wells which kept his grass growing while the neighbors' fields turned from grey-green to blowing dust. The McBans had kept the sarcastic old name for their farming station, the Station of Doom.

By night, Rod knew, the Station would be his.

Or he would be dying, giggling his way to death in the killing place where people laughed and grinned and rollicked about while they died.

He found himself humming a bit of a rhyme that had always been a part of the tradition of Old North Australia:

We kill to live, and die to grow—
That's the way the world must go!

He'd been taught, bone deep, that his own world was a very special world, envied, loved, hated and dreaded across the galaxy. He knew that he was part of a very special people. Other races and kinds of men farmed crops, or raised food, or designed machines, and manufactured weapons. Norstrilians did none of these things. From their dry fields, their sparse wells, their enormous sick sheep, they refined immortality itself.

And sold it for a high, high price.

Rod McBan walked a little way into the yard. His home lay behind him. It was a log cabin built out of Daimoni beams—beams uncuttable, unchangeable, solid beyond all expectations of solidity. They had been

5

purchased as a matched set thirty-odd planet hops away and brought to Old North Australia by photosails. The cabin was a fort which could withstand even major weapons, but it was still a cabin, simple inside and with a front yard of scuffed dust.

The last red bit of dawn was whitening into day.

Rod knew that he could not go far.

He could hear the women out behind the house, the kinswomen who had come to barber and groom him for the triumph—or the other.

They never knew how much he knew. Because of his affliction, they had thought around him for years, counting on his telepathic deafness to be constant. Trouble was, it wasn't; lots of times he heard things which nobody intended him to hear. He even remembered the sad little poem they had about the young people who failed to pass the test for one reason or another and had to go to the Dying House instead of coming forth as Norstrilian citizens and fully recognized subjects of Her-Majesty-the-Queen. (Norstrilians had not had a real queen for some fifteen thousand years, but they were strong on tradition and did not let mere facts boggle them.) How did the little poem run, "This is the house of the long ago..."? In its own gloomy way it was cheerful.

He erased his own footprint from the dust and suddenly he remembered the whole thing. He chanted it softly to himself.

This is the house of the long ago,
Where the old ones murmur an endless woe,
Where the pain of time is an actual pain,
And things once known always come again.
Out in the Garden of Death, our young
Have tasted the valiant taste of fear.
With muscular arm and reckless tongue,
They have won, and lost, and escaped us here.
This is the house of the long ago.
Those who die young do not enter here.
Those living on know that hell is near.
The old ones who suffer have willed it so.
Out in the Garden of Death, the old
Look with awe on the young and bold.

It was all right to say that they looked with awe at the young and bold, but he hadn't met a person yet who did not prefer life to death. He'd heard about people who chose death—of course he had; who hadn't? But the experience was third-hand, fourth-hand, fifth-hand.

He knew that some people had said of him that he would be better off dead, just because he had never learned to communicate telepathically and had to use old spoken words like outworlders or barbarians.

Rod himself certainly didn't think he would be better dead.

Indeed, he sometimes looked at normal people and wondered how they managed to go through life with the constant silly chatter of other people's thoughts running through their minds. In the times that his mind lifted, so that he could hier for a while, he knew that hundreds or thousands of minds rattled in on him with unbearable clarity; he could even hier the minds that thought they had their telepathic shields up. Then, in a little while, the merciful cloud of his handicap came down on his mind again and he had a deep unique privacy which everybody on Old North Australia should have envied.

His computer had said to him once, "The words *hier* and *spiek* are corruptions of the words *hear* and *speak*. They are always pronounced in the second rising tone of voice, as though you were asking a question under the pressure of amusement and alarm, if you say the words with your voice. They refer only to telepathic communication between persons or between persons and underpeople."

"What are underpeople?" he had asked.

"Animals modified to speak, to understand, and usually to look like men. They differ from cerebrocentered robots in that the robots are built around an actual animal mind, but are mechanical and electronic relays, while underpeople are composed entirely of Earth-derived living tissue."

"Why haven't I ever seen one?"

"They are not allowed on Norstrilia at all, unless they are in the service of the defense establishments of the Commonwealth."

"Why are we called a Commonwealth, when all the other places are called worlds or planets?"

"Because you people are subjects of the Queen of England."

"Who is the Queen of England?"

"She was an Earth ruler in the Most Ancient Days, more than fifteen thousand years ago."

"Where is she now?"

"I said," the computer had said, "that it was fifteen thousand years ago."

"I know it," Rod had insisted, "but if there hasn't been any Queen of England for fifteen thousand years, how can we be her subjects?"

"I know the answer in human words," the reply had been from the friendly red machine, "but since it makes no sense to me, I shall have to quote it to you as people told it to me. 'She bloody well might turn up one of these days. Who knows? This is Old North Australia out here among the stars and we can dashed well wait for our own Queen. She might have been off on a trip when Old Old Earth went sour.' " The computer had clucked a few times in its odd ancient voice and had then said hopefully, in its toneless voice, "Could you restate that so that I could program it as part of my memory assembly?"

"It doesn't mean much to me. Next time I can hier other minds thinking I'll try to pick it out of somebody else's head."

That had been about a year ago, and Rod had never run across the answer.

Last night he had asked the computer a more urgent question:

"Will I die tomorrow?"

"Question irrelevant. No answer available."

"Computer!" he had shouted. "You know I love you."

"You say so."

"I started your historical assembly up after repairing you, when that part had been thinkless for hundreds of years."

"Correct."

"I crawled down into this cave and found the *personal* controls, where great[14]-grandfather had left them when they became obsolete."

"Correct."

"I'm going to die tomorrow and you won't even be sorry."

"I did not say that," said the computer.

"Don't you care?"

"I was not programmed for emotion. Since you yourself repaired me, Rod, you ought to know that I am the only all-mechanical computer functioning in this part of the galaxy. I am sure that if I had emotions I would be very sorry indeed. It is an extreme probability, since you are my only companion. But I do not have emotions. I have numbers, facts, language and memory—that is all."

"What is the probability, then, that I will die tomorrow in the Giggle Room?"

"That is not the right name. It is the Dying House."

"All right, then, the Dying House."

"The judgment on you will be a contemporary human judgment based upon emotions. Since I do not know the individuals concerned, I cannot make a prediction of any value at all."

"What do you think is going to happen to me, computer?"

"I do not really think, I respond. I have no input on that topic."

"Do you know anything at all about my life and death tomorrow? I know I can't *spiek* with my mind, but I have to make sounds with my mouth instead. Why should they kill me for that?"

"I do not know the people concerned and therefore I do not know the reasons," the computer had replied, "but I know the history of Old North Australia down to your great[14]-grandfather's time."

"Tell me that, then," Rod had said. He had squatted in the cave which he had discovered, listening to the forgotten set of computer controls which he had repaired, and had heard again the story of Old North Australia as his great[14]-grandfather had understood it. Stripped of personal names and actual dates, it was a simple story.

This morning his life hung on it.

Norstrilia had to thin out its people if it were going to keep its Old Old Earth character and be another Australia, out among the stars. Otherwise the fields would fill up, the deserts turn into apartment houses, the sheep die in cellars under endless kennels for crowded and useless people. No Old North Australian wanted that to happen, when he could keep character, immortality, and wealth—in that particular order of importance. It would be contrary to the character of Norstrilia.

The simple character of Norstrilia was immutable—as immutable as anything out among the stars. This ancient Commonwealth was the only human institution older than the Instrumentality.

The story was simple, the way the computer's clear long-circuited brain had sorted it out.

Take a farmer culture straight off Old Old Earth—Manhome itself.

Put the culture on a remote planet.

Touch it with prosperity and blight it with drought.

Teach it sickness, deformity, hardihood. Make it learn poverty so bad that men sold one child to buy another child the drink of water which would give it an extra day of life while the drills whirred deep into the dry rock, looking for wetness.

Teach that culture thrift, medicine, scholarship, pain, survival.

Give those people the lessons of poverty, war, grief, greed, magnanimity, piety, hope and despair by turn.

Let the culture survive.

Survive disease, deformity, despair, desolation, abandonment.

Then give it the happiest accident in the history of time.

Out of sheep-sickness came infinite riches, the santaclara drug, or stroon, which prolonged human life indefinitely.

Prolonged it—but with queer side effects, so that most Norstrilians preferred to die in a thousand years or so.

Norstrilia was convulsed by the discovery.

So was every other inhabited world.

But the drug could not be synthesized, paralleled, duplicated. It was something which could be obtained only from the sick sheep on the Old North Australian plains.

Robbers and governments tried to steal the drug. Now and then they succeeded, long ago, but they hadn't made it since the time of Rod's great[19]-grandfather.

They had tried to steal the sick sheep.

Several had been taken off the planet. (The Fourth Battle of New Alice, in which half the menfolk of Norstrilia had died beating off the Bright Empire, had led to the loss of two of the sick sheep—one female and one male. The Bright Empire thought it had won. It hadn't. The sheep got well, produced healthy lambs, exuded no more stroon, and died. The Bright Empire had paid four battle fleets for a coldbox full of mutton.) The monopoly remained in Norstrilia.

The Norstrilians exported the santaclara drug, and they put the export on a systematic basis.

They achieved almost infinite riches.

The poorest man on Norstrilia was always richer than the richest man anywhere else, emperors and conquerors included. Every farm hand earned at least a hundred Earth megacredits a day—measured in real money on Old Earth, not in paper which had to travel at a steep arbitrage.

But the Norstrilians made their choice: *the* choice—

To remain themselves.

They taxed themselves back into simplicity.

Luxury goods got a tax of twenty million percent. For the price of fifty palaces on Olympia, you could import a handkerchief into Norstrilia. A pair of shoes, landed, cost the price of a hundred yachts in orbit. All machines were prohibited, except for defense and the drug-gathering. Underpeople were never made on Norstrilia, and imported only by the defense authority for top secret reasons. Old North Australia remained simple, pioneer, fierce, open.

Many families emigrated to enjoy their wealth; they could not return.

But the population problem remained, even with the taxation and simplicity and hard work.

Cut back, then—cut back people if you must.

But how, whom, where? Birth control—beastly. Sterilization—inhuman, unmanly, un-British. (This last was an ancient word meaning *very bad indeed.*)

By families, then. Let the families have the children. Let the Commonwealth test them at sixteen. If they ran under the standards, send them to a happy, happy death.

But what about the families? You can't wipe a family out, not in a conservative farmer society, when the neighbors are folk who have fought and died beside you for a hundred generations. The Rule of Exceptions came. Any family which reached the end of its line could have the last surviving heir reprocessed—up to four times. If he failed, it was the Dying House, and a designated adopted heir from another family took over the name and the estate.

Otherwise their survivors would have gone on, in this century a dozen, in that century twenty. Soon Norstrilia would have been divided into two classes, the sound ones and a privileged class of hereditary freaks. This they could not stand, not while the space around them stank of danger, not when men a hundred worlds away dreamed and died while thinking of how to rob the stroon. They had to be fighters and chose not to be soldiers or emperors. Therefore they *had* to be fit, alert, healthy, clever, simple and moral. They had to be better than any possible enemy or any possible combination of enemies.

They made it.

Old North Australia became the toughest, brightest, simplest world in the galaxy. One by one, without weapons, Norstrilians could tour the other worlds and kill almost anything which attacked them. Governments feared them. Ordinary people hated them or worshipped them. Offworld men eyed their women queerly. The Instrumentality left them alone, or defended them without letting the Norstrilians know they had been defended. (As in the case of Raumsog, who brought his whole world to a death of cancer and volcanoes, because the Golden Ship struck once.)

Norstrilian mothers learned to stand by with dry eyes when their children, unexpectedly drugged if they failed the tests, drooled with pleasure and went giggling away to their deaths.

The space and subspace around Norstrilia became sticky, sparky with the multiplicity of their defenses. Big outdoorsy men sailed tiny fighting craft around the approaches to Old North Australia. When people met them in outports, they always thought that Norstrilians looked simple; the looks were a snare and a delusion. The Norstrilians had been conditioned by thousands of years of unprovoked attack. They looked as simple as sheep but their minds were as subtle as serpents.

And now—Rod McBan.

The last heir, the very last heir, of their proudest old family had been found a half-freak. He was normal enough by Earth standards, but by Norstrilian measure he was inadequate. He was a bad, bad telepath. He could not be counted on to hier. Most of the time other people could not transmit into his mind at all; they could not even read it. All they got was a fiery bubble and a dull fuzz of meaningless sub-sememes, fractions of thought which added up to less than nothing. And on spieking, he was worse. He could not talk with his mind at all. Now and then he transmitted. When he did, the neighbors ran for cover. If it was anger, a bloody screaming roar almost blotted out their consciousnesses with a rage as solid and red as meat hanging in a slaughterhouse. If he was happy, it was worse. His happiness, which he transmitted without knowing it, had the distractiveness of a speed saw cutting into diamond-grained rock. His happiness drilled into people with an initial sense of pleasure, followed rapidly by acute discomfort and the sudden wish that all their own teeth would fall out: the teeth had turned into spinning whorls of raw, unqualified discomfort.

They did not know his biggest personal secret. They suspected that he could hier now and then without being able to control it. They did not know that when he did hier, he could hier everything for miles around with microscopic detail and telescopic range. His telepathic intake, when it did work, went right through other people's mind-shields as though they did not exist. (If some of the women in the farms around the Station of Doom knew what he had accidentally peeped out of their minds, they would have blushed the rest of their lives.) As a result, Rod McBan had a frightful amount of unsorted knowledge which did not quite fit together.

Previous committees had neither awarded him the Station of Doom nor sent him off to the giggle death. They had appreciated his intelligence, his quick wit, his enormous physical strength. But they remained worried about his telepathic handicap. Three times before he had been judged. Three times.

And three times judgment had been suspended.

They had chosen the lesser cruelty and had sent him not to death, but to a new babyhood and a fresh upbringing, hoping that the telepathic capacity of his mind would naturally soar up to the Norstrilian normal.

They had underestimated him.

He knew it.

Thanks to the eavesdropping which he could not control, he understood bits and pieces of what was happening, even though nobody had ever told him the rational whys and hows of the process.

It was a gloomy but composed big boy who gave the dust of his own front yard one last useless kick, who turned back into the cabin, walking right through the main room to the rear door and the back yard, and who greeted his kinswomen politely enough as they, hiding their aching hearts, prepared to dress him up for his trial. They did not want the child to be upset, even though he was as big as a man and showed more composure than did most adult men. They wanted to hide the fearful truth from him. How could they help it?

He already knew.

But he pretended he didn't.

Cordially enough, just scared enough but not too much, he said, "What ho, auntie! Hello, cousin. Morning, Maribel. Here's your sheep.

Curry him up and trim him for the livestock competition. Do I get a ring in my nose or a bow ribbon around my neck?"

One or two of the young ones laughed, but his oldest "aunt"—actually a fourth cousin, married into another family—pointed seriously and calmly at a chair in the yard and said:

"Do sit down, Roderick. This is a serious occasion and we usually do not talk while preparations are going on."

She bit her lower lip and then she added, not as though she wanted to frighten him but because she wanted to impress him:

"The Vice-Chairman will be here today."

("The Vice-Chairman" was the head of the government; there had been no Chairman of the Temporary Commonwealth Government for some thousands of years. Norstrilians did not like posh and they thought that Vice-Chairman was high enough for any one man to go. Besides, it kept the offworlders guessing.)

Rod was not impressed. He had seen the man. It was in one of his rare moments of broad hiering, and he found that the mind of the Vice-Chairman was full of numbers and horses, the results of every horse race for three hundred and twenty years, and the projection forward of six probable horse races in the next two years.

"Yes, auntie," he said.

"Don't bray all the time today. You don't have to use your voice for little things like saying *yes*. Just nod your head. It will make a much better impression."

He started to answer, but gulped and nodded instead.

She sank the comb into his thick yellow hair.

Another one of the women, almost a girl, brought up a small table and a basin. He could tell from her expression that she was spieking to him, but this was one of the times in which he could not hier at all.

The aunt gave his hair a particularly fierce tug just as the girl took his hand. He did not know what she meant to do. He yanked his hand back.

The basin fell off the small table. Only then did he realize that it was merely soapy water for a manicure.

"I am sorry," he said; even to him, his voice sounded like a bray. For a moment he felt the fierce rush of humiliation and self-hate.

They should kill me, he thought... *By the time the sun goes down I'll be in the Giggle Room, laughing and laughing before the medicine makes my brains boil away.*

He had reproached himself.

The two women had said nothing. The aunt had walked away to get some shampoo, and the girl was returning with a pitcher, to refill the basin.

He looked directly into her eyes, and she into his.

"I want you," she said, very clearly, very quietly, and with a smile which seemed inexplicable to him.

"What for?" said he, equally quietly.

"Just you," she said. "I want you for myself. You're going to live."

"You're Lavinia, my cousin," said he, as though discovering it for the first time.

"Sh-h-h," said the girl. "She's coming back."

When the girl had settled down to getting his fingernails really clean, and the aunt had rubbed something like sheep-dip into his hair, Rod began to feel happy. His mood changed from the indifference which he had been pretending to himself. It became a real indifference to his fate, an easy acceptance of the grey sky above him, the dull rolling earth below. He had a fear—a little tiny fear, so small that it might have seemed to be a midget pet in a miniature cage—running around the inside of his thinking. It was not the fear that he would die: somehow he suddenly accepted his chances and remembered how many other people had had to take the same play with fortune. This little fear was something else, the dread that he might not behave himself properly if they did tell him to die.

But then, he thought, I don't have to worry. Negative is never a word— just a hypodermic, so that the first bad news the victim has is his own excited, happy laugh.

With this funny peace of mind, his hiering suddenly lifted.

He could not see the Garden of Death, but he could look into the minds tending it; it was a huge van hidden just beyond the next roll of hills, where they used to keep Old Billy, the eighteen-hundred-ton sheep. He could hear the clatter of voices in the little town eighteen kilometers away. And he could look right into Lavinia's mind.

It was a picture of himself. But what a picture! So grown, so handsome, so brave looking. He had schooled himself not to move when he could hier, so that other people would not realize that his rare telepathic gift had come back to him.

Auntie was spieking to Lavinia without noisy words. "We'll see this pretty boy in his coffin tonight."

Lavinia thought right back, without apology. "No, we won't."

Rod sat impassive in his chair. The two women, their faces grave and silent, went on spieking the argument at each other with their minds.

"How would you know—you're not very old?" spieked auntie.

"He has the oldest station in all of Old North Australia. He has one of the very oldest names. He is—" and even in spieking her thoughts cluttered up, like a stammer—"he is a very nice boy and he's going to be a wonderful man."

"Mark my thought," spieked the auntie again, "I'm telling you that we'll see him in his coffin tonight and that by midnight he'll be on his coffin-ride to the Long Way Out."

Lavinia jumped to her feet. She almost knocked over the basin of water a second time. She moved her throat and mouth to speak words but she just croaked,

"Sorry, Rod. Sorry."

Rod McBan, his face guarded, gave a pleasant, stupid little nod, as though he had no idea of what they had been spieking to each other.

She turned and ran, shout-spieking the loud thought at auntie, "Get somebody else to do his hands. You're heartless, hopeless. Get somebody else to do your corpse washing for you. Not me. Not me."

"What's the matter with her?" said Rod to the auntie, just as though he did not know.

"She's just difficult, that's all. Just difficult. Nerves, I suppose," she added in her croaking spoken words. She could not talk very well, since all her family and friends could spiek and hier with privacy and grace. "We were spieking with each other about what you would be doing to-morrow."

"Where's a priest, auntie?" said Rod.

"A what?"

"A priest, like the old poem has, in the rough rough days before our people found this planet and got our sheep settled down. Everybody knows it.

Here is the place where the priest went mad.
Over there my mother burned.
I cannot show you the house we had.
We lost that slope when the mountain turned.

There's more to it, but that's the part I remember. Isn't a priest a special-ist in how to die? Do we have any around here?"

He watched her mind as she lied to him. As he had spoken, he had a perfectly clear picture of one of their more distant neighbors, a man named Tolliver, who had a very gentle manner; but her words were not about Tolliver at all.

"Some things are men's business," she said, cawing her words. "Any-how, that song isn't about Norstrilia at all. It's about Paradise VII and why we left it. I didn't know you knew it."

In her mind he read, "That boy knows too much."

"Thanks, auntie," said he meekly.

"Come along for the rinse," said she. "We're using an awful lot of real water on you today."

He followed her and he felt more kindly toward her when he saw her think, *Lavinia had the right feelings but she drew the wrong conclusion. He's going to be dead tonight.*

That was too much.

Rod hesitated for a moment, tempering the chords of his oddly attuned mind. Then he let out a tremendous howl of telepathic joy, just to bother the lot of them. It did. They all stopped still. Then they stared at him.

In words the auntie said, "What was that?"

"What?" said he, innocently.

"That noise you spieked. It wasn't meaning."

"Just sort of a sneeze, I suppose. I didn't know I did it." Deep down inside himself he chuckled. He might be on his way to the Hoohoo House, but he would fritter their friskies for them while he went.

It was a dashed silly way to die, he thought all to himself.

And then a strange, crazy, happy idea came to him:

Perhaps they can't kill me. Perhaps I have powers. Powers of my own. Well, we'll soon enough find out.

THE TRIAL

Rod walked across the dusty lot, took three steps up the folding staircase which had been let down from the side of the big trailer van, knocked on the door once as he had been instructed to do, had a green light flash in his face, opened the door, and entered.

It *was* a garden.

The moist, sweet, scent-laden air was like a narcotic. There were bright green plants in profusion. The lights were clear but not bright; their ceiling gave the effect of a penetrating blue, blue sky. He looked around. It was a copy of Old Old Earth. The growths on the green plants were *roses;* he remembered pictures which his computer had showed him. The pictures had not gotten across the idea that they smelled nice at the same time that they looked nice. He wondered if they did that all the time, and then remembered the wet air: wet air always holds smells better than dry air does. At last, almost shyly, he looked up at the three judges.

With real startlement, he saw that one of them was not a Norstrilian at all, but the local Commissioner of the Instrumentality, the Lord Redlady—a thin man with a sharp, inquiring face. The other two were Old Taggart and John Beasley. He knew them, but not well.

"Welcome," said the Lord Redlady, speaking in the funny singsong of a man from Manhome.

"Thank you," said Rod.

"You are Roderick Frederick Ronald Arnold William MacArthur McBan the one hundred and fifty-first?" said Taggart, knowing perfectly well that Rod was that person.

Lord love a duck and lucky me! thought Rod, *I've got my hiering, even in this place!*

"Yes," said the Lord Redlady.

There was silence.

The other two judges looked at the Manhome man; the stranger looked at Rod; Rod stared, and then began to feel sick at the bottom of his stomach.

For the first time in his life, he had met somebody who could penetrate his peculiar perceptual abilities.

At last he thought, "I understand."

The Lord Redlady looked sharply and impatiently at him, as though waiting for a response to that single word "yes."

17

Rod had already answered—telepathically.

At last Old Taggart broke the silence.

"Aren't you going to talk? I asked you your name."

The Lord Redlady held up his hand in a gesture for patience; it was not a gesture which Rod had ever seen before, but he understood it immediately.

He thought telepathically at Rod, "You are watching my thoughts."

"Indeed I am," thought Rod, back at him.

The Lord Redlady clapped a hand to his forehead. "You are hurting me. Did you think you said something?"

With his voice Rod said, "I told you that I was reading your mind."

The Lord Redlady turned to the other two men and spieked to them: "Did either of you hier what he tried to spiek?"

"No." "No." They both thought back at him. "Just noise, loud noise."

"He is a broadbander like myself. And I have been disgraced for it. You know that I am the only Lord of the Instrumentality who has been degraded from the status of Lord to that of Commissioner—"

"Yes," they spieked.

"You know that they could not cure me of shouting and suggested I die?"

"No," they answered.

"You know that the Instrumentality thought I could not bother you here and sent me to your planet on this miserable job, just to get me out of the way?"

"Yes," they answered.

"Then, what do you want to do about him? Don't try to fool him. He knows all about this place already." The Lord Redlady glanced quickly, sympathetically up at Rod, giving him a little phantom smile of encouragement. "Do you want to kill him? To exile him? To turn him loose?"

The other two men fussed around in their minds. Rod could see that they were troubled at the idea he could watch them thinking, when they had thought him a telepathic deaf-mute; they also resisted the Lord Redlady's unmannerly precipitation of the decision. Rod almost felt that he was swimming in the thick wet air, with the smell of roses cloying his nostrils so much that he would never smell anything but roses again, when he became aware of a massive consciousness very near him—a fifth person in the room, whom he had not noticed at all before.

It was an Earth soldier, complete with uniform. The soldier was handsome, erect, tall, formal with a rigid military decorum. He was, furthermore, not human and he had a strange weapon in his left hand.

"What is that?" spieked Rod to the Earthman. The man saw his face, not the thought.

"An underman. A snake-man. The only one on this planet. He will carry you out of here if the decision goes against you."

Beasley cut in, almost angrily. "Here, cut it out. This is a hearing, not a blossoming tea party. Don't clutter all that futt into the air. Keep it formal."

"You want a formal hearing?" said the Lord Redlady. "A formal hearing for a man who knows everything that all of us are thinking? It's foolish."

"In Old North Australia, we always have formal hearings," said old Taggart. With an acuteness of insight born of his own personal danger, Rod saw Taggart all over again for the first time—a careworn poor old man, who had worked a poor farm hard for a thousand years; a farmer, like his ancestors before him; a man rich only in the millions of megacredits which he would never take time to spend; a man of the soil, honorable, careful, formal, righteous, and very just. Such men did not yield to innovation, ever. They fought change.

"Have the hearing then," said the Lord Redlady, "have the hearing if it is your custom, my Mister and Owner Taggart, my Mister and Owner Beasley."

The Norstrilians, appeased, bowed their heads briefly.

Almost shyly, Beasley looked over at the Lord Redlady. "Sir and Commissioner, will you say the words? The good old words. The ones that will help us to find our duty and to do it."

(Rod saw a quick flare of red anger go through the Lord Redlady's mind as the Earth Commissioner thought fiercely to himself, "Why all this fuss about killing one poor boy? Let him go, you dull clutts, or kill him." But the Earthman had not directed the thoughts outward and the two Norstrilians were unaware of his private view of them.)

On the outside, the Lord Redlady remained calm. He used his voice, as Norstrilians did on occasion of great ceremony:

"We are here to hear a man."

"We are here to hear him," they responded.

"We are not to judge or to kill, though this may follow," said he.

"Though this may follow," they responded.

"And where, on Old Old Earth, does man come from?"

They knew the answer by rote and said it heavily together: "This is the way it was on Old Old Earth, and this is the way it shall be among the stars, no matter how far we men may wander:

"The seed of wheat is planted in dark, moist earth; the seed of man in dark, moist flesh. The seed of wheat fights upward to air, sun and space; the stalk, leaves, blossom and grain flourish under the open glare of heaven. The seed of man grows in the salty private ocean of the womb, the sea-darkness remembered by the bodies of his race. The harvest of wheat is collected by the hands of men; the harvest of men is collected by the tenderness of eternity."

"And what does this mean?" chanted the Lord Redlady.

"To look with mercy, to decide with mercy, to kill with mercy, but to make the harvest of man strong and true and good, the way that the harvest of wheat stood high and proud on Old Old Earth."

"And who is here?" he asked.

They both recited Rod's full name.

When they had finished, the Lord Redlady turned to Rod and said, "I am about to utter the ceremonial words, but I promise you that you will not be surprised, no matter what happens. Take it easy, therefore. Easy, easy." Rod was watching the Earthman's mind and the minds of the two Norstrilians. He could see that Beasley and Taggart were befuddled with the ritual of the words, the wetness and scent of the air, and the false blue sky in the top of the van; they did not know what they were going to do. But Rod could also see a sharp, keen triumphant thought forming in the bottom of the Lord Redlady's mind, *I'll get this boy off!* He almost smiled, despite the presence of the snake-man with the rigid smile and the immovable glaring eyes standing just three paces beside him and a little to his rear, so that Rod could only look at him through the corner of his eye.

"Misters and Owners!" said the Lord Redlady.

"Mister Chairman!" they answered.

"Shall I inform the man who is being heard?"

"Inform him!" they chanted.

"Roderick Frederick Ronald Arnold William MacArthur McBan the one hundred and fifty-first!"

"Yes, sir," said Rod.

"Heir-in-trust of the Station of Doom!"

"That's me," said Rod.

"Hear me!" said the Lord Redlady.

"Hear him!" said the other two.

"You have not come here, Child and Citizen Roderick, for us to judge you or to punish you. If these things are to be done, they must be done in another place or time, and they must be done by men other than ourselves. The only concern before this board is the following: should you or should you not be allowed to leave this room safe and free and well, taking into no account your innocence or guilt of matters which might be decided elsewhere, but having regard only for the survival and the safety and the welfare of this given planet? We are not punishing and we are not judging, but we *are* deciding, and what we are deciding is your life. Do you understand? Do you agree?"

Rod nodded mutely, drinking in the wet, rose-scented air and stilling his sudden thirst with the dampness of the atmosphere. If things went wrong now, they did not have very far to go. Not far to go, not with the motionless snake-man standing just beyond his reach. He tried to look at the snake-brain but got nothing out of it except for an unexpected glitter of recognition and defiance.

The Lord Redlady went on, Taggart and Beasley hanging on his words as though they had never heard them before.

"Child and Citizen, you know the rules. We are not to find you wrong or right. No crime is judged here, no offense. Neither is innocence. We are only judging the single question, Should you live or should you not? Do you understand? Do you agree?"

Said Rod, "Yes, sir."

"And how stand you, Child and Citizen?"

"What do you mean?"

"This board is asking you, what is your opinion? Should you live or should you not?"

"I'd like to," said Rod, "but I'm tired of all these childhoods."

"That is not what the board is asking you, Child and Citizen," said the Lord Redlady. "We are asking you, what do you think? Should you live or should you not live?"

"You want me to judge myself?"

"That's it, boy," said Beasley. "You know the rules. Tell them, boy. I said we could count on you."

The sharp friendly neighborly face unexpectedly took on great importance for Rod. He looked at Beasley as though he had never seen the man before. This man was trying to judge him, Rod; and he, Rod, had to help decide on what was to be done with himself. The medicine from the snake-man and the giggle-giggle death, or a walk out into freedom. Rod started to speak and checked himself; he was to speak for Old North Australia. Old North Australia was a tough world, proud of its tough men. No wonder the board gave him a tough decision. Rod made up his mind and he spoke clearly and deliberately:

"I'd say no. Do not let me live. I don't fit. I can't spiek and hier. Nobody knows what my children would be like, but the odds are against them. Except for one thing ..."

"And what, Child and Citizen, is that?" asked the Lord Redlady, while Beasley and Taggart watched as though they were staring at the last five meters of a horse race.

"Look at me carefully, Citizens and Members of the Board," said Rod, finding that in this milieu it was easy to fall into a ceremonious way of talking. "Look at me carefully and do not consider my own happiness, because you are not allowed, by law, to judge that anyhow. Look at my talent—the way I can hier, the big thunderstorm way I can spiek." Rod gathered his mind for a final gamble and as his lips got through talking, he spat his whole mind at them:

anger-anger, rage-red,

blood-red,

fire-fury,

noise, stench, glare, roughness, sourness and hate hate hate,

all the anxiety of a bitter day,

crutts, whelps, pups!

It all poured out at once. The Lord Redlady turned pale and compressed his lips, Old Taggart put his hands over his face, Beasley looked bewildered and nauseated. Beasley then started to belch as calm descended on the room.

In a slightly shaky voice, the Lord Redlady asked,

"And what was that supposed to show, Child and Citizen?"

"In grown-up form, sir, could it be a useful weapon?"

The Lord Redlady looked at the other two. They talked with the tiny expressions on their faces; if they were spieking, Rod could not read it. This last effort had cost him all telepathic input.

"Let's go on," said Taggart.

"Are you ready?" said the Lord Redlady to Rod.

"Yes, sir," said Rod.

"I continue," said the Lord Redlady. "If you understand your own case as we see it, we shall proceed to make a decision and, upon making the decision, to kill you immediately or to set you free no less immediately. Should the latter prove the case, we shall also present you with a small but precious gift, so as to reward you for the courtesy which you will have shown this board, for without courtesy there could be no proper hearing, without the hearing no appropriate decision, and without an appropriate decision there could be neither justice nor safety in the years to come. Do you understand? Do you agree?"

"I suppose so," said Rod.

"Do you really understand? Do you really agree? It is your life which we are talking about," said the Lord Redlady.

"I understand and I agree," said Rod.

"Cover us," said the Lord Redlady.

Rod started to ask *how* when he understood that the command was not directed at him in the least.

The snake-man had come to life and was breathing heavily. He spoke in clear old words, with an odd dropping cadence in each syllable:

"High, my lord, or utter maximum?"

For answer, the Lord Redlady pointed his right arm straight up with the index finger straight at the ceiling. The snake-man hissed and gathered his emotions for an attack. Rod felt his skin go goose-pimply all over, then he felt the hair on the back of his neck rise, finally he felt nothing but an unbearable alertness. If these were the thoughts which the snake-man was sending out of the trailer van, no passerby could possibly eavesdrop on the decision. The startling pressure of raw menace would take care of that instead.

The three members of the board held hands and seemed to be asleep.

The Lord Redlady opened his eyes and shook his head, almost imperceptibly, at the snake-soldier.

The feeling of snake-threat went off. The soldier returned to his immobile position, eyes forward. The members of the board slumped over their table. They did not seem to be able or ready to speak. They looked out of breath. At last Taggart dragged himself to his feet, gasping his message to Rod,

"There's the door, boy. Go. You're a citizen. Free."

Rod started to thank him but the old man held up his right hand:

"Don't thank me. Duty. But remember—not one word, ever. Not one word, ever, about this hearing. Go along."

Rod plunged for the door, lurched through, and was in his own yard. Free.

For a moment he stood in the yard, stunned.

The dear grey sky of Old North Australia rolled low overhead; this was no longer the eerie light of Old Earth, where the heavens were supposed to shine perpetually blue. He sneezed as the dry air caught the tissue of his nostrils. He felt his clothing chill as the moisture evaporated out of it; he did not think whether it was the wetness of the trailer van or his own sweat which had made his shirt so wet. There were a lot of people there, and a lot of light. And the smell of roses was as far away as another life might be.

Lavinia stood near him, weeping.

He started to turn to her, when a collective gasp from the crowd caused him to turn around.

The snake-man had come out of the van. (It was just an old theater van, he realized at last, the kind which he himself had entered a hundred times.) His Earth uniform looked like the acme of wealth and decadence among the dusty coveralls of the men and the poplin dresses of the women. His green complexion looked bright among the tanned faces of the Norstrilians. He saluted Rod.

Rod did not return the salute. He just stared.

Perhaps they had changed their minds and had sent the giggle of death after him.

The soldier held out his hand. There was a wallet of what seemed to be leather, finely chased, of offworld manufacture.

Rod stammered, "It's not mine."

"It—is—not—yours," said the snake-man, "but—it—is—the—things—gift—which—the—people—promised—you—inside.—Take—it—because—I—am—too—dry—out—here."

Rod took it and stuffed it in his pocket. What did a present matter when they had given him life, eyes, daylight, the wind itself?

The snake-soldier watched with flickering eyes. He made no comment, but he saluted and went stiffly back to the van. At the door he turned and looked over the crowd as though he were appraising the easiest way to kill them all. He said nothing, threatened nothing. He opened the door and put himself into the van. There was no sign of who the human inhabitants of the van might be. There must be, thought Rod, some way of getting them in and out of the Garden of Death very secretly and very quietly, because he had lived around the neighborhood a long time and had never had the faintest idea that his own neighbors might sit on a board.

The people were funny. They stood quietly in the yard, waiting for him to make the first move.

He turned stiffly and looked around more deliberately.

Why, it was his neighbors and kinfolk, all of them—McBans, MacArthurs, Passarellis, Schmidts, even the Sanders!

He lifted his hand in greeting to all of them.

Pandemonium broke loose.

They rushed toward him. The women kissed him, the men patted him on the back and shook his hand, the little children began a piping little song about the Station of Doom. He had become the center of a mob which led him to his own kitchen.

Many of the people had begun to cry.

He wondered why. Almost immediately, he understood—

They liked him.

For unfathomable *people* reasons, mixed-up, non-logical human reasons they had wished him well. Even the auntie who had predicted a coffin for him was sniveling without shame, using a corner of her apron to wipe her eyes and nose.

He had gotten tired of people, being a freak himself, but in this moment of trial their goodness, though capricious, flowed over him like a great wave. He let them sit him down in his own kitchen. Among the babble, the weeps, the laughter, the hearty and falsely cheerful relief, he heard a single fugue being repeated again and again: they liked him. He had come back from death: he was their Rod McBan.

Without liquor, it made him drunk. "I can't stand it," he shouted. "I like you all so dashed bloomed crutting much that I could beat the sentimental brains out of the whole crook lot of you ..."

"Isn't that a sweet speech?" murmured an old farm wife nearby.

A policeman, in full uniform, agreed.

The party had started. It lasted three full days, and when it was over there was not a dry eye or a full bottle on the whole Station of Doom.

From time to time he cleared up enough to enjoy his miraculous gift of hiering. He looked through all their minds while they chatted and sang and drank and ate and were as happy as Larry; there was not one of them who had come along vainly. They were truly rejoicing. They loved him. They wished him well. He had his doubts about how long that kind of love would last, but he enjoyed it while it lasted.

Lavinia stayed out of his way the first day; on the second and third days she was gone. They gave him real Norstrilian beer to drink, which they had brought up to one-hundred-and-eight proof by the simple addition of raw spirits. With this, he forgot the Garden of Death, the sweet wet smells, the precise offworld voice of the Lord Redlady, the pretentious blue sky in the ceiling.

He looked in their minds and over and over again he saw the same thing,

"You're our boy. You made it. You're alive. Good luck, Rod, good luck to you, fellow. We didn't have to see you stagger off, giggling and happy, to the house that you would die in."

Had he made it, thought Rod, or was it chance which had done it for him?

ANGER OF THE ONSECK

By the end of the week, the celebration was over. The assorted aunts and cousins had gone back to their farms. The Station of Doom was quiet, and Rod spent the morning making sure that the fieldhands had not neglected the sheep too much during the prolonged party. He found that Daisy, a young three-hundred-ton sheep, had not been turned for two days and had to be relanolized on her ground side before earth canker set in; then he discovered that the nutrient tubes for Tanner, his thousand-ton ram, had become jammed and that the poor sheep was getting a bad case of edema in his gigantic legs. Otherwise things were quiet. Even when he saw Beasley's red pony tethered in his own yard, he had no premonition of trouble.

He went cheerfully into the house, greeting Beasley with an irreverent, "Have a drink on me, Mister and Owner Beasley! Oh, you have one already! Have the next one then, sir!"

"Thanks for the drink, lad, but I came to see you. On business."

"Yes, sir," said Rod. "You're one of my trustees, aren't you?"

"That I am," said Beasley, "but you're in trouble, lad. Real trouble."

Rod smiled at him evenly and calmly. He knew that the older man had to make a big effort to talk with his voice instead of just spieking with his mind; he appreciated the fact that Beasley had come to him personally, instead of talking to the other trustees about him. It was a sign that he, Rod, had passed his ordeal. With genuine composure, Rod declared:

"I've been thinking, sir, this week, that I'd gotten out of trouble."

"What do you mean, Owner McBan?"

"You remember..." Rod did not dare mention the Garden of Death, nor his memory that Beasley had been one of the secret board who had passed him as being fit to live.

Beasley took the cue. "Some things we don't mention, lad, and I see that you have been well taught."

He stopped there and stared at Rod with the expression of a man looking at an unfamiliar corpse before turning it over to identify it. Rod became uneasy with the stare.

"Sit, lad, sit down," said Beasley, commanding Rod in his own house.

Rod sat down on the bench, since Beasley occupied the only chair— Rod's grandfather's huge carved offworld throne. He sat. He did not like

27

being ordered about, but he was sure that Beasley meant him well and was probably strained by the unfamiliar effort of talking with his throat and mouth.

Beasley looked at him again with that peculiar expression, a mixture of sympathy and distaste.

"Get up again, lad, and look round your house to see if there's anybody about."

"There isn't," said Rod. "My Aunt Doris left after I was cleared, the workwoman Eleanor borrowed a cart and went off to the market, and I have only two station hands. They're both out reinfecting Baby. She ran low on her santaclara count."

Normally, the wealth-producing sicknesses of their gigantic half-paralyzed sheep would have engrossed the full attention of any two Norstrilian farmers, without respect to differences in age and grade.

This time, no.

Beasley had something serious and unpleasant on his mind. He looked so pruney and unquiet that Rod felt a real sympathy for the man.

Beasley repeated, "Go have a look, anyhow."

Rod did not argue. Dutifully he went out the back door, looked around the south side of the house, saw no one, walked around the house on the north side, saw no one there either, and reentered the house from the front door. Beasley had not stirred, except to pour a little more bitter ale from his bottle to his glass. Rod met his eyes. Without another word, Rod sat down. If the man was seriously concerned about him (which Rod thought he was), and if the man was reasonably intelligent (which Rod knew he was), the communication was worth waiting for and listening to. Rod was still sustained by the pleasant feeling that his neighbors liked him, a feeling which had come plainly to the surface of their honest Norstrilian faces when he walked back into his own back yard from the van of the Garden of Death.

Beasley said, as though he were speaking of an unfamiliar food or a rare drink, "Boy, this talking has some advantages. If a man doesn't put his ear into it, he can't just pick it up with his mind, can he now?"

Rod thought for a moment. Candidly he spoke, "I'm too young to know for sure, but I never heard of somebody picking up spoken words by hiering them with his mind. It seems to be one or the other. You never talk while you are spieking, do you?"

Beasley nodded. "That's it, then. I have something to tell you which I shouldn't tell you, and yet I have got to tell you, so if I keep my voice blooming low, nobody else will pick it up, will they?"

Rod nodded. "What is it, sir? Is there something wrong with the title to my property?"

Beasley took a drink but kept staring at Rod over the top of the mug while he drank.

"You've got trouble there too, lad, but even though it's bad, it's something I can talk over with you and with the other trustees. This is more personal, in a way. And worse."

"Please, sir! What is it?" cried Rod, almost exasperated by all this mystification.

"The Onseck is after you."

"What's an onseck?" said Rod. "I have never heard of it."

"It's not an it," said Beasley gloomily, "it's a him. Onseck, you know, the chap in the Commonwealth government. The man who keeps the books for the Vice-Chairman. It was Hon. Sec., meaning Honorary Secretary or something else prehistoric, when we first came to this planet, but by now everybody just says Onseck and writes it just the way it sounds. He knows that he can't reverse your hearing in the Garden of Death."

"Nobody could," cried Rod. "It's never been done; everybody knows that."

"They may know it, but there's civil trial."

"How can they give me a civil trial when I haven't had time to change? You yourself know—"

"Never, laddie, never say what Beasley knows or doesn't know. Just say what you think." Even in private, between just the two of them, Beasley did not want to violate the fundamental secrecy of the hearing in the Garden of Death.

"I'm just going to say, Mister and Owner Beasley," said Rod very heatedly, "that a civil trial for general incompetence is something which is applied to an owner only after the neighbors have been complaining for a long time about him. They haven't had the time or the right to complain about me, have they now?"

Beasley kept his hand on the handle of his mug. The use of spoken words tired him. A crown of sweat began to show around the top of his forehead.

"Suppose, lad," said he very solemnly, "that I knew through proper channels something about how you were judged in that van—there! I've said it, me that shouldn't have—and suppose that I knew the Onseck hated a foreign gentleman that might have been in a van like that—"

"The Lord Redlady?" whispered Rod, shocked at last by the fact that Beasley forced himself to talk about the unmentionable.

"Aye," nodded Beasley, his honest face close to breaking into tears, "and suppose that I knew that the Onseck knew you and felt the rule was wrong, all wrong, that you were a freak who would hurt all Norstrilia, what would I do?"

"I don't know," said Rod. "Tell me, perhaps?"

"Never," said Beasley. "I'm an honest man. Get me another drink."

Rod walked over to the cupboard, brought out another bottle of bitter ale, wondering where or when he might have known the Onseck. He had never had much of anything to do with government; his family—first his grandfather, while he lived, and then his aunts and cousins—had taken care of all the official papers and permits and things.

Beasley drank deeply of the ale. "Good ale, this. Hard work, talking, even though it's a fine way to keep a secret, if you're pretty sure nobody can peep our minds."

"I don't know him," said Rod.

"Who?" asked Beasley, momentarily off his trail of thought.

"The Onseck. I don't know any Onseck. I've never been to New Canberra. I've never seen an official, no, nor an offworlder neither, not until I met that foreign gentleman we were talking about. How can the Onseck know me if I don't know him?"

"But you did, laddie. He wasn't Onseck then."

"For sheep's sake, sir," said Rod, "tell me who it is!"

"Never use the Lord's name unless you are talking to the Lord," said Beasley glumly.

"I'm sorry, sir. I apologize. Who was it?"

"Houghton Syme to the hundred-and-forty-ninth," said Beasley.

"We have no neighbor of that name, sir."

"No, we don't," said Beasley hoarsely, as though he had come to the end of his road in imparting secrets.

Rod stared at him, still puzzled.

In the far, far distance, way beyond Pillow Hill, his giant sheep baa'd. That probably meant that Hopper was hoisting her into a new position on her platform, so that she could reach fresh grass.

Beasley brought his face close to Rod's. He whispered, and it was funny to see the hash a normal man made out of whispering when he hadn't even talked with his voice for half a year.

His words had a low, dirty tone to them, as though he were going to tell Rod an extremely filthy story or ask him some personal and most improper question.

"Your life, laddie," he gasped, "I know you've had a rum one. I hate to ask you, but I must. How much do you know of your own life?"

"Oh, that," said Rod easily. "*That.* I don't mind being asked that, even if it is a little wrongo. I have had four childhoods, zero to sixteen each time. My family kept hoping that I would grow up to spiek and hier like everybody else, but I just stayed me. Of course, I wasn't a real baby on the three times they started me over, just sort of an educated idiot the size of a boy sixteen."

"That's it, lad. *But can you remember them, those other lives?*"

"Bits and pieces, sir. Pieces and bits. It didn't hold together—" He checked himself and gasped, "Houghton Syme! Houghton Syme! Old Hot and Simple. Of course I know him. The one-shot boy. I knew him in my first prepper, in my first childhood. We were pretty good friends, but we hated each other anyhow. I was a freak and he was too. I couldn't spiek or hier, and he couldn't take stroon. That meant that I would never get through the Garden of Death—just the Giggle Room and a fine owner's coffin for me. And him—he was worse. He would just get an Old Earth lifetime— a hundred and sixty years or so and then blotto. He must be an oldish man now. Poor chap! How did he get to be Onseck? What power does an Onseck have?"

"Now you have it, laddie. He says he's your friend and that he hates to do it, but he's got to see to it that you are killed. For the good of Norstrilia. He says it's his duty. He got to be Onseck because he was always jawing about his duty and people were a little sorry for him because he was going to die so soon, just one Old Earth lifetime with all the stroon in the universe produced around his feet and him unable to take it—"

"They never cured him, then?"

"Never," said Beasley. "He's an old man now, and bitter. And he's sworn to see you die."

"Can he do it? Being Onseck, I mean."

"He might. He hates that foreign gentleman we were talking about because that offworlder told him he was a provincial fool. He hates you because you will live and he will not. What was it you called him in school?"

"Old Hot and Simple. A boy's joke on his name."

"He's not hot and he's not simple. He's cold and complicated and cruel and unhappy. If we didn't all of us think that he was going to die in a little while, ten or a hundred years or so, we might vote him into a Giggle Room ourselves. For misery and incompetence. But he *is* Onseck and he's after you. I've said it now. I shouldn't have. But when I saw that sly cold face talking about you and trying to declare your board incompetent right while you, laddie, were having an honest binge with your family and neighbors at having gotten through at last—when I saw that white sly face creeping around where you couldn't even see him for a fair fight— then I said to myself, Rod McBan may not be a man officially, but the poor clodding crutt has paid the full price for being a man, so I've told you. I may have taken a chance, and I may have hurt my honor." Beasley sighed. His honest red face was troubled indeed. "I may have hurt my honor, and that's a sore thing here in Norstrilia where a man can live as long as he wants. But I'm glad I did. Besides, my throat is sore with all this talking. Get me another bottle of bitter ale, lad, before I go and get my horse."

Wordlessly Rod got him the ale, and poured it for him with a pleasant nod.

Beasley, uninclined to do any more talking, sipped at the ale. Perhaps, thought Rod, he is hiering around carefully to see if there have been any human minds nearby which might have picked up the telepathic leakage from the conversation.

As Beasley handed back the mug and started to leave with a wordless neighborly nod, Rod could not restrain himself from asking one last question, which he spoke in a hissed whisper. Beasley had gotten his mind so far off the subject of sound talk that he merely stared at Rod. Perhaps, Rod thought, he is asking me to spiek plainly because he has forgotten that I cannot spiek at all. That was the case, because Beasley croaked in a very hoarse voice,

"What is it, lad? Don't make me talk much. My voice is scratching me and my honor is sore within me."

"What should I do, sir? What should I do?"

"Mister and Owner McBan, that's your problem. I'm not you. I wouldn't know."

"But what would you do, sir? Suppose you were me."

Beasley's blue eyes looked over at Pillow Hill for a moment, abstractedly. "Get offplanet. Get off. Go away. For a hundred years or so. Then that man—*him*—he'll be dead in due time and you can come back, fresh as a new-blossomed twinkle."

"But how, sir? How can I do it?"

Beasley patted him on his shoulder, gave him a broad wordless smile, put his foot in his stirrup, sprang into his saddle, and looked down at Rod.

"I wouldn't know, neighbor. But good luck to you, just the same. I've done more than I should. Goodbye."

He slapped his horse gently with his open hand and trotted out of the yard. At the edge of the yard the horse changed to a canter.

Rod stood in his own doorway, utterly alone.

THE OLD BROKEN TREASURES
IN THE GAP

After Beasley left, Rod loped miserably around his farm. He missed his grandfather, who had been living during his first three childhoods, but who had died while Rod was going through a fourth, simulated infancy in an attempt to cure his telepathic handicap. He even missed his Aunt Margot, who had voluntarily gone into Withdrawal at the age of nine hundred and two. There were plenty of cousins and kinsmen from whom he could ask advice; there were the two hands on the farm; there was even the chance that he could go see Mother Hitton herself, because she had once been married to one of his great[11]-uncles. But this time he did not want companionship. There was nothing he could do with people. The Onseck was people too; imagine Old Hot and Simple becoming a power in the land. Rod knew that this was his own fight.

His own.

What had ever been his own before?

Not even his life. He could remember bits about the different boyhoods he had. He even had vague uncomfortable glimpses of seasons of pain—the times they had sent him back to babyhood while leaving him large. That hadn't been his choice. The old man had ordered it or the Vice-Chairman had approved it or Aunt Margot had begged for it. Nobody had asked him much, except to say, "You will agree ..."

He had agreed.

He had been good—so good that he hated them all at times and wondered if they knew he hated them. The hate never lasted, because the real people involved were too well-meaning, too kind, too ambitious for his own sake. He had to love them back.

Trying to think these things over, he loped around his estate on foot.

The big sheep lay on their platforms, forever sick, forever gigantic. Perhaps some of them remembered when they had been lambs, free to run through the sparse grass, free to push their heads through the pliofilm covers of the canals and to help themselves to water when they wanted to drink. Now they weighed hundreds of tons and were fed by feeding machines, watched by guard machines, checked by automatic doctors. They were fed and watered a little through the mouth only because pastoral

33

experience showed that they stayed fatter and lived longer if a semblance of normality was left to them.

His Aunt Doris, who kept house for him, was still away.

His workwoman Eleanor, whom he paid an annual sum larger than many planets paid for their entire armed forces, had delayed her time at market.

The two sheephands, Bill and Hopper, were still out.

And he did not want to talk to them, anyhow.

He wished that he could see the Lord Redlady, that strange offworld man whom he had met in the Garden of Death. The Lord Redlady just looked as though he knew more things than Norstrilians did, as though he came from sharper, crueler, wiser societies than most people in Old North Australia had ever seen.

But you can't ask for a Lord. Particularly not when you have met him only in a secret hearing.

Rod had gotten to the final limits of his own land.

Humphrey's Lawsuit lay beyond—a broad strip of poor land, completely untended, the building-high ribs of long-dead sheep skeletons making weird shadows as the sun began to set. The Humphrey family had been lawing over that land for hundreds of years. Meanwhile it lay waste except for the few authorized public animals which the Commonwealth was allowed to put on any land, public or private.

Rod knew that freedom was only two steps away.

All he had to do was to step over the line and shout with his mind for people. He could do that even though he could not really spiek. A telepathic garble of alarm would bring the orbiting guards down to him in seven or eight minutes. Then he would need only to say,

"I swear off title. I give up Mistership and Ownership. I demand my living from the Commonwealth. Watch me, people, while I repeat."

Three repetitions of this would make him an Official Pauper, with not a care left—no meetings, no land to tend, no accounting to do, nothing but to wander around Old North Australia picking up any job he wanted and quitting it whenever he wanted. It was a good life, a free life, the best the Commonwealth could offer to Squatters and Owners who otherwise lived long centuries of care, responsibility, and honor. It was a fine life—

But no McBan had ever taken it, not even a cousin.

Nor could he.

He went back to the house, miserable. He listened to Eleanor talking with Bill and Hopper while dinner was served—a huge plate of boiled mutton, potatoes, hard-boiled eggs, station-brewed beer out of the keg. (There were planets, he knew, where people never tasted such food from birth to death. There they lived on impregnated pasteboard which was salvaged from the latrines, reimpregnated with nutrients and vitamins, deodorized and sterilized, and issued again the next day.) He knew it was a fine dinner, but he did not care.

How could he talk about the Onseck to these people? Their faces still glowed with pleasure at his having come out the right side of the Garden of Death. They thought he was lucky to be alive, even more lucky to be the most honored heir on the whole planet. Doom was a good place, even if it wasn't the biggest.

Right in the middle of dinner he remembered the gift the snake-soldier had given him. He had put it on the top shelf of his bedroom wall, and with the party and Beasley's visit, he had never opened it.

He bolted down his food and muttered, "I'll be back."

The wallet was there, in his bedroom. The case was beautiful. He took it, opened it.

Inside there was a flat metal disk.

A ticket?

Where to?

He turned it this way and that. It had been telepathically engraved and was probably shouting its entire itinerary into his mind, but he could not hier it.

He held it close to the oil lamp. Sometimes disks like this had old-writing on them, which at least showed the general limits. It would be a private ornithopter up to Menzies Lake at the best, or an airbus fare to New Melbourne and return. He caught the sheen of old-writing. One more tilt, angled to the light, and he had it. "Manhome and return."

Manhome!

Lord have mercy, that was Old Earth itself!

But then, thought Rod, *I'd be running away from the Onseck, and I'd live the rest of my life with all my friends knowing I had run away from Old Hot and Simple. I can't. Somehow I've got to beat Houghton Syme CXLIX. In his own way. And my own way.*

He went back to the table, dropped the rest of the dinner into his stomach as though it were sheep-food pellets, and went to his bedroom early.

For the first time in his life, he slept badly.

And out of the bad sleep, the answer came,

"Ask Hamlet."

Hamlet was not even a man. He was just a talking picture in a cave, but he was wise, he was from Old Earth itself, and he had no friends to whom to give Rod's secrets.

With this idea, Rod turned on his sleeping shelf and went into a deep sleep.

*   *   *

In the morning his Aunt Doris was still not back, so he told the workwoman Eleanor.

"I'll be gone all day. Don't look for me or worry about me."

"What about your lunch, Mister and Owner? You can't run around the station with no tucker."

"Wrap some up, then."

"Where're you going, Mister and Owner, sir, if you can tell me?" There was an unpleasant searching edge in her voice, as though—being the only adult woman present—-she had to check on him as though he were still a child. He didn't like it, but he replied with a frank enough air,

"I'm not leaving the station. Just rambling around. I need to think."

More kindly she said, "You think, then, Rod. Just go right ahead and think. If you ask me, you ought to go live with a family—"

"I know what you've said," he interrupted her. "I'm not making any big decisions today, Eleanor. Just rambling and thinking."

"All right then, Mister and Owner. Ramble around and worry about the ground you're walking on. It's you that get the worries for it. I'm glad my daddy took the official pauper words. We used to be rich." Unexpectedly, she brightened and laughed at herself. "Now that, you've heard that too, Rod. Here's your food. Do you have water?"

"I'll steal from the sheep," he said irreverently. She knew he was joking and she waved him a friendly goodbye.

The old, old gap was to the rear of the house, so he left by the front. He wanted to go the long wrong way around, so that neither human eyes nor human minds would stumble on the secret he had found fifty-six years before, the first time he was eight years old. Through all the pain and the troubles he had remembered this one vivid bright secret—the deep cave full of ruined and prohibited treasures. To these he must go.

The sun was high in the sky, spreading its patch of brighter grey above the grey clouds, when he slid into what looked like a dry irrigation ditch.

He walked a few steps along the ditch. Then he stopped and listened carefully, very carefully.

There was no sound except for the snoring of a young hundred-ton ram a mile or so way.

Rod then stared around.

In the far distance, a police ornithopter soared as lazy as a sated hawk.

Rod tried desperately to hier.

He hiered nothing with his mind, but with his ears he heard the slow heavy pulsing of his own blood pounding through his head.

He took a chance.

The trapdoor was there, just inside the edge of the culvert.

He lifted it and, leaving it open, dove in confidently as a swimmer knifing his way into a familiar pool.

He knew his way.

His clothes ripped a little but the weight of his body dragged him past the narrowness of the doorframe.

His hands reached out and like the hands of an acrobat they caught the inner bar. The door behind snapped shut. How frightening this had been when he was little and tried the trip for the first time! He had let himself down with a rope and a torch, never realizing the importance of the trap door at the edge of the culvert!

Now it was easy.

With a thud, he landed on his feet. The bright old illegal lights went on. The dehumidifier began to purr, lest the wetness of his breath spoil the treasures in the room.

There were drama-cubes by the score, with two different sizes of projectors. There were heaps of clothing, for both men and women, left over from forgotten ages. In a chest, in the corner, there was even a small machine from before the Age of Space, a crude but beautiful mechanical chronograph, completely without resonance compensation, and the ancient name "Jaeger Le Coultre" written across its face. It still kept Earth time after fifteen thousand years.

Rod sat down in an utterly impermissible chair—one which seemed to be a complex of pillows built on an interlocking frame. The touch enough was a medicine for his worries. One chair leg was broken, but that was the way his grandfather-to-the-nineteenth had violated the Clean Sweep.

The Clean Sweep had been Old North Australia's last political crisis, many centuries before, when the last underpeople were hunted down and driven off the planet and when all damaging luxuries had to be turned in to the Commonwealth authorities, to be repurchased by their owners only at a revaluation two hundred thousand times higher than their assessed worth. It was the final effort to keep Norstrilians simple, healthy and well. Every citizen had to swear that he had turned in every single item, and the oath had been taken with thousands of telepaths watching. It was a testimony to the high mental power and adept deceitfulness of grandfather-to-the-nineteenth that Rod McBan CXXX had inflicted only symbolic breakage on his favorite treasures, some of which were not even in the categories allowed for repurchase, like offworld drama-cubes, and had been able to hide his things in an unimportant corner of his fields— hide them so well that neither robbers nor police had thought of them for the hundreds of years that followed.

Rod picked up his favorite: *Hamlet*, by William Shakespeare. Without a viewer, the cube was designed to act when touched by a true human being. The top of the cube became a little stage, the actors appeared as bright miniatures speaking Ancient Inglish, a language very close to Old North Australian, and the telepathic commentary, cued to the Old Common Tongue, rounded out the story. Since Rod was not dependably telepathic, he had learned a great deal of the Ancient Inglish by trying to understand the drama without commentary. He did not like what he first saw and he shook the cube until the play approached its end. At last he heard the dear high familiar voice speaking in Hamlet's last scene:

> *I am dead, Horatio. Wretched queen, adieu!*
> *You that look pale and tremble at this chance,*
> *That are but mutes or audience to this act,*
> *Had I but time—as this fell sergeant, death,*
> *Is strict in his arrest— O! I could tell you—*
> *But let it be, Horatio, I am dead.*

Rod shook the cube very gently and the scene sped down a few lines. Hamlet was still talking:

> *...what a wounded name,*
> *Things standing thus unknown, shall live behind me.*
> *If thou didst ever hold me in thy heart,*
> *Absent thee from felicity a while,*
> *And in this harsh world draw thy breath in pain*
> *To tell my story.*

Rod put down the cube very gently.

The bright little figures disappeared.

The room was silent.

But he had the answer and it was wisdom. And wisdom, coeval with man, comes unannounced, unbidden, and unwelcome into every life. Rod found that he had discovered the answer to a basic problem.

But not his own problem. The answer was Houghton Syme's, Old Hot and Simple. It was the Hon. Sec. who was already dying of a wounded name. Hence the persecution. It was the Onseck who had the "fell sergeant, death" acting strictly in his arrest, even if the arrest were only a few decades off instead of a few minutes. He, Rod McBan, was to live; his old acquaintance was to die; and the dying—oh, the dying, always, always!—could not help resenting the survivors, even if they were loved ones, at least a little bit.

Hence the Onseck.

But what of himself?

Rod brushed a pile of priceless, illegal manuscripts out of the way and picked up a small book marked, *Reconstituted Late Inglish Language Verse.* At each page, as it was opened, a young man or woman seven centimeters high stood up brightly on the page and recited the text. Rod ruffled the pages of the old book so that the little figures appeared and trembled and fled like weak flames seen on a bright day. One caught his eye and he stopped the page at midpoem. The figure was saying:

> *The challenge holds, I cannot now retract*
> *The boast I made to that relentless court,*
> *The hostile justice of my self-contempt.*
> *If now the ordeal is prepared, my act*
> *Must soon be shown. I pray that it is short,*
> *And never dream that I shall be exempt.*

He glanced at the foot of the page and saw the name, Casimir Colegrove. Of course, he had seen that name before. An old poet. A good one. But what did the words mean to him, Rod McBan, sitting in a hidden hole within the limits of his own land? He was a Mister and Owner, in all except final title, and he was running from an enemy he could not define.

"The hostile justice of my self-contempt ..."

That *was* the key of it! He was not running from the Onseck. He was running from himself. He took justice itself as hostile because it corresponded with his sixty-odd years of boyhood, his endless disappointment, his compliance with things which would never, till all worlds burned, be complied with. How could he hier and spiek like other people if somewhere a dominant feature had turned recessive? Hadn't real justice already vindicated him and cleared him?

It was he himself who was cruel.

Other people were kind. (Shrewdness made him add "sometimes.")

He had taken his own inner sense of trouble and had made it fit the outside world, like the morbid little poem he had read a long time ago. It was somewhere right in this room, and when he had first read it, he felt that the long-dead writer had put it down for himself alone. But it wasn't really so. Other people had had their troubles too and the poem had expressed something older than Rod McBan. It went:

> *The wheels of fate are spinning around.*
> *Between them the souls of men are ground*
> *Who strive for throats to make some sound*
> *Of protest out of the mad profound*
> *Trap of the godmachine!*

"Godmachine," thought Rod, "now that's a clue. I've got the only all-mechanical computer on this planet. I'll play it on the stroon crop, win all or lose all."

The boy stood up in the forbidden room.

"Fight it is," he said to the cubes on the floor, "and a good thanks to you, grandfather-to-the-nineteenth. You met the law and did not lose. And now it is my turn to be Rod McBan."

He turned and shouted to himself,

"To Earth!"

The call embarrassed him. He felt unseen eyes staring at him. He almost blushed and would have hated himself if he had.

He stood on the top of a treasure-chest turned on its side. Two more gold coins, worthless as money but priceless as curios, fell noiselessly on the thick old rugs. He thought a goodbye again to his secret room and he jumped upward for the bar. He caught it, chinned himself, raised himself higher, swung a leg on it but not over it, got his other foot on the bar, and then, very carefully but with the power of all his muscles, pushed himself into the black opening above. The lights suddenly went off, the dehumidifier hummed louder, and the daylight dazzled him as the trap door, touched, flung itself open.

He thrust his head into the culvert. The daylight seemed deep grey after the brilliance of the treasure room.

All silent. All clear. He rolled into the ditch.

The door, with silence and power, closed itself behind him. He was never to know it, but it had been cued to the genetic code of the descendants of Rod McBan. Had any other person touched it, it would have withstood them for a long time. Almost forever.

You see, it was not really his door. He was its boy.

"This land has made me," said Rod aloud, as he clambered out of the ditch and looked around. The young ram had apparently wakened; his snoring had stopped and over the quiet hill there came the sound of his panting. Thirsty again! The Station of Doom was not so rich that it could afford unlimited water to its giant sheep. They lived all right. But he would have asked the trustees to sell even the sheep for water, if a real drought set in. But never the land.

Never the land.

No land for sale.

It didn't even really belong to him: he belonged to it—the rolling dry fields, the covered rivers and canals, the sky catchments which caught every drop which might otherwise have gone to his neighbors. That was the pastoral business—its product immortality and its price water. The Commonwealth could have flooded the planet and could have created small oceans, with the financial resources it had at command, but the planet and the people were regarded as one ecological entity. Old Australia—that fabulous continent of Old Earth now covered by the rains of the abandoned Chinesian cityworld of Aojou Nanbien—had in its prime been broad, dry, open, beautiful; the planet of Old North Australia, by the dead weight of its own tradition, had to remain the same.

Imagine trees. Imagine leaves—vegetation dropping uneaten to the ground. Imagine water pouring by the thousands of tons, no one greeting it with tears of relief or happy laughter! Imagine Earth. Old Earth. Manhome itself. Rod had tried to think of a whole planet inhabited by Hamlets, drenched with music and poetry, knee-deep in blood and drama. It was unimaginable, really, though he had tried to think it through.

Like a chill, a drill, a thrill cutting into his very nerves he thought: *Imagine Earth women!*

What terrifying beautiful things they must be. Dedicated to ancient and corruptive arts, surrounded by the objects which Norstrilia had forbidden long ago, stimulated by experiences which the very law of his own world had expunged from the books! He would meet them; he couldn't help it; what, what would he do when he met a genuine Earth woman?

He would have to ask his computer, even though the neighbors laughed at him for having the only pure computer left on the planet.

They didn't know what grandfather-to-the-nineteenth had done. He had taught the computer to lie. It stored all the forbidden things which the Law of the Clean Sweep had brushed out of Norstrilian experience. It could lie like a trooper. Rod wondered whether a "trooper" might be some archaic Earth official who did nothing but tell the untruth, day in and day out, for his living. But the computer usually did not lie to him.

If grandfather[19] had behaved as saucily and unconventionally with the computer as he had with everything else, that particular computer would know all about women. Even things which they did not themselves know. Or wish to know.

Good computer! thought Rod as he trotted around the long, long fields to his house. Eleanor would have the tucker on. Doris might be back. Bill and Hopper would be angry if they had to wait for the Mister before they ate. To speed up his trip, he headed straight for the little cliff behind the house, hoping no one would see him jump down it. He was much stronger than most of the men he knew, but he was anxious, for some private inexpressible reason, for them not to know it.

The route was clear.

He found the cliff.

No observers.

He dropped over it, feet first, his heels kicking up the scree as he tobogganed through loose rock to the foot of the slope.

And Aunt Doris was there.

"Where have you been?" said she.

"Walking, mum," said he.

She gave him a quizzical look but knew better than to ask more. Talking always fussed her, anyhow. She hated the sound of her own voice, which she considered much too high. The matter passed.

Inside the house, they ate. Beyond the door and the oil lamp, a grey world became moonless, starless, black. This was night, his own night.

THE QUARREL AT THE DINNER TABLE

At the end of the meal he waited for Doris to say grace to the Queen. She did but under her thick eyebrows her eyes expressed something other than thanks.

"You're going out," she said right after the prayer. It was an accusation, not a question.

The two hired men looked at him with quiet doubt. A week ago he had been a boy. Now he was the same person, but legally a man.

The workwoman Eleanor looked at him too. She smiled very unobtrusively to herself. She was on his side whenever any other person came into the picture; when they were alone, she nagged him as much as she dared. She had known his parents before they went offworld for a long-overdue honeymoon and were chewed into molecules by a battle between raiders and police. That gave her a proprietary feeling about him.

He tried to spiek to Doris with his mind, just to see if it would work.

It didn't. The two men bounded from their seats and ran for the yard, Eleanor sat in her chair holding tight to the table but saying nothing, and Aunt Doris screeched so loud that he could not make out the words.

He knew she meant "Stop it!" so he did, and looked at her friendlily.

That started a fight.

Quarrels were common in Norstrilian life, because the Fathers had taught that they were therapeutic. Children could quarrel until adults told them to stop, freemen could quarrel as long as Misters were not involved, misters could quarrel as long as an Owner was not present, and Owners could quarrel if, at the very end, they were willing to fight it out. No one could quarrel in the presence of an offworlder, nor during an alert, nor with a member of the defense or police on active duty.

Rod McBan was a Mister and Owner, but he was under trusteeship; he was a man, but he had not been given clear papers; he was a handicapped person.

The rules got all mixed up.

When Hopper came back to the table he muttered, "Do that again, laddie, and I'll clout you one that you won't forget!" Considering how rarely he used his voice, it was a beautiful man's voice, resonant, baritone, full-bodied, hearty and sincere in the way the individual words came out.

43

Bill didn't say a word, but from the contortions of his face Rod gathered that he was spieking to the others at a great rate and working off his grievance that way.

"If you're spieking about me, Bill," said Rod with a touch of arrogance which he did not really feel, "you'll do me the pleasure of using words or you'll get off my land!"

When Bill spoke, his voice was as rusty as an old machine. "I'll have you know, you clutty little pommy, that I have more money in my name on Sidney 'Change than you and your whole glubby land are worth. Don't you tell me twice to get off the land, you silly half of a Mister, or I will get. So shut up!"

Rod felt his stomach knot with anger.

His anger became fiercer when he felt Eleanor's restraining hand on his arm. He didn't want another person, not one more damned useless normal person, to tell him what to do about spieking and hiering. Aunt Doris's face was still hidden in her apron; she had escaped, as she always did, into weeping.

Just as he was about to speak again, perhaps to lose Bill from the farm forever, his mind lifted in the mysterious way that it did sometimes; he could hier for miles. The people around him did not notice the difference. He saw the proud rage of Bill, with his money in the Sidney Exchange, bigger than many station owners had, waiting his time to buy back on the land which his father had left; he saw the honest annoyance of Hopper and was a little abashed to see that Hopper was watching him proudly and with amused affection; in Eleanor he saw nothing but wordless worry, a fear that she might lose him as she had lost so many homes for *hnnnhnnnhnnn dzzmmmmm*, a queer meaningless reference which had a shape in her mind but took no form in his; and in Aunt Doris he caught her inner voice calling, "Rod, Rod, Rod, come back! This may be your boy and I'm a McBan to the death, but I'll never know what to do with a cripple like him."

Bill was still waiting for him to answer when another thought came into his mind,

"You fool—go to your computer!"

"Who said that?" he thought, not trying to spiek again, but just thinking it with his mind.

"Your computer," said the faraway thinkvoice.

"You can't spiek," said Rod. "You're a pure machine with not an animal brain in you."

"When you call me, Roderick Frederick Ronald Arnold William MacArthur McBan to the hundred and fifty-first, I can spiek across space itself. I'm cued to you and you shouted just now with your spiekmind. I can feel you hiering me."

"But—" said Rod in words.

"Take it easy, lad," said Bill, right in the room with him. "Take it easy. I didn't mean it."

"You're having one of your spells," said Aunt Doris, emerging rednosed from behind her apron.

Rod stood up.

Said he to all of them, "I'm sorry. I'm going out for a bit. Out into the night."

"You're going to that bloody computer," said Bill.

"Don't go, Mister McBan," said Hopper. "Don't let us anger you into going. It's bad enough being around that computer in daylight, but at night it must be horrible."

"How would you know?" retorted Rod. "You've never been there at night. And I have. Lots of times ..."

"There are dead people in it," said Hopper. "It's an old war computer. Your family should never have bought it in the first place. It doesn't belong on a farm. A thing like that should be hung out in space and orbited."

"All right, Eleanor," said Rod, *"you* tell me what to do. Everybody else has," he added with the last bit of his remaining anger, as his hiering closed down and he saw the usual opaque faces around him.

"It's no use, Rod. Go along to your computer. You've got a strange life and you're the one that will live it, Mister McBan, and not these other people around here."

Her words made sense.

He stood up. "I'm sorry," said he, again, in lieu of goodbye.

He stood in the doorway, hesitant. He would have liked to say goodbye in a better way, but he did not know how to express it. Anyhow, he couldn't spiek, not so they could hier it with their minds; speaking with a voice was so crude, so flat for the fine little things that needed expression in life.

They looked at him, and he at them.

"Ngahh!" said he, in a raw cry of self-derision and fond disgust.

Their expressions showed that they had gotten his meaning, though the word carried nothing with it. Bill nodded, Hopper looked friendly and a little worried, Aunt Doris stopped sniveling and began to stretch out one hand, only to stop it in midgesture, and Eleanor sat immobile at the table, upset by wordless troubles of her own.

He turned.

The cube of lamplight, the cabin room, was behind him; ahead the darkness of all Norstrilian nights, except for the weird rare times that they were cut up by traceries of lightness. He started off for a house which only a few but he could see, and which none but he could enter. It was a forgotten, invisible temple; it housed the MacArthur family computer, to which the older McBan computer was linked; and it was called the Palace of the Governor of Night.

THE PALACE OF THE
GOVERNOR OF NIGHT

Rod loped across the rolling land, *his* land.

Other Norstrilians, telepathically normal, would have taken fixes by hiering the words in nearby houses. Rod could not walk by telepathy, so he whistled to himself in an odd off key, with lots of flats. The echoes came back to his unconscious mind through the overdeveloped ear-hearing which he had worked out to compensate for not being able to hier with his mind. He sensed a slope ahead of him, and jogged up it; he avoided a clump of brush; he heard his youngest ram, Sweet William, snoring the gigantic snore of a santaclara-infected sheep two hills over.

Soon he would see it.

The Palace of the Governor of Night.

The most useless building in all Old North Australia.

Solider than steel and yet invisible to normal eyes except for its ghostly outline traced in the dust which had fallen lightly on it.

The Palace had really been a palace once, on Khufu II, which rotated with one pole always facing its star. The people there had made fortunes which at one time were compared with the wealth of Old North Australia. They had discovered the Furry Mountains, range after range of alpine configurations on which a tenacious non-Earth lichen had grown. The lichen was silky, shimmering, warm, strong, and beautiful beyond belief. The people gained their wealth by cutting it carefully from the mountains so that it would regrow and selling it to the richer worlds, where a luxury fabric could be sold at fabulous prices. They had even had two governments on Khufu II, one of the day-dwelling people who did most of the trading and brokering, since the hot sunlight made their crop of lichen poor, and the other for the night-dwellers, who ranged deep into the frigid areas in search of lichen—stunted, fine, tenacious and delicately beautiful.

The Daimoni had come to Khufu II, just as they came to many other planets, including Old Earth, Manhome itself. They had come out of nowhere and they went back to the same place. Some people thought that they were human beings who had acclimated themselves to live in the subspace which planoforming involved; others thought that they had an artificial planet on the inside of which they lived; still others thought that

47

they had solved the jump out of our galaxy; a few insisted that there were no such things as Daimoni. This last position was hard to maintain, because the Daimoni paid in architecture of a very spectacular kind—buildings which resisted corrosion, erosion, age, heat, cold, stress and weapons. On Earth itself Earthport was their biggest wonder—a sort of wine glass, twenty-five kilometers high, with an enormous rocket field built into the top of it. On Norstrilia they had left nothing; perhaps they had not even wanted to meet the Old North Australians, who had a reputation for being rough and gruff with strangers who came to their own home planet. It was evident that the Daimoni had solved the problem of immortality on their own terms and in their own way; they were bigger than most of the races of mankind, uniform in size, height and beauty; they bore no sign of youth or age; they showed no vulnerability to sickness; they spoke with mellifluous gravity; and they purchased treasures for their own immediate collective use, not for retrade or profit. They had never tried to get stroon or the raw santaclara virus from which it was refined, even though the Daimoni trading ships had passed the tracks of armed and convoyed Old North Australian freight fleets. There was even one picture which showed the two races meeting each other in the chief port of Olympia, the planet of the blind receivers: Norstrilians tall, outspoken, lively, crude and immensely rich; Daimoni equally rich, reserved, beautiful, polished and pale. There was awe (and with awe, resentment) on the part of the Norstrilians toward the Daimoni; there was elegance and condescension on the part of the Daimoni toward everyone else, including the Norstrilians. The meeting had been no success at all. The Norstrilians were not used to meeting people who did not care about immortality, even at a penny a bushel; the Daimoni were disdainful toward a race which not only did not appreciate architecture, but which tried to keep architects off its planet, except for defense purposes, and which desired to lead a rough, simple, pastoral life to the end of time. Thus it was not until the Daimoni had left, never to return, that the Norstrilians realized that they had passed up some of the greatest bargains of all time—the wonderful buildings which the Daimoni so generously scattered over the planets which they had visited for trade or for visits.

On Khufu II, the Governor of Night had brought out an ancient book and had said,

"I want that."

The Daimoni, who had a neat eye for proportions and figures, said, "We have that picture on our world too. It is an ancient Earth building. It was once called the great temple of Diana of the Ephesians, but it fell even before the age of space began."

"That's what I want," said the Governor of Night.

"Easy enough," said one of the Daimoni, all of whom looked like princes. "We'll run it up for you by tomorrow night."

"Hold on," said the Governor of Night. "I don't want the whole thing. Just the front—to decorate my palace. I have a perfectly good palace all right, and my defenses are built right into it."

"If you let us build you a house," said one of the Daimoni gently, "you would never need defenses, *ever*. Just a robot to close the windows against megaton bombs."

"You're good architects, gentlemen," said the Governor of Night, smacking his lips over the model city they had shown him, "but I'll stick with the defenses I know. So I just want your front. Like that picture. Furthermore, I want it invisible."

The Daimoni lapsed back into their language, which sounded as though it were of Earth origin, but which has never been deciphered from the few recordings of their visits which have survived.

"All right," said one of them, "invisible it is. You still want the great temple of Diana at Ephesus on Old Earth?"

"Yes," said the Governor of Night.

"Why—if you can't see it?" said the Daimoni.

"That's the third specification, gentlemen. I want it so that *I* can see it, and my heirs, but nobody else."

"If it's solid but invisible, everybody is going to see it when your fine snow hits it."

"I'll take care of that," said the Governor of Night. "I'll pay what we were talking about—forty thousand select pieces of Furry Mountain Fur. But you make that palace invisible to everybody except me, and my heirs."

"We're architects, not magicians!" said the Daimoni with the longest cloak, who might have been the leader.

"That's what I want."

The Daimoni gabbled among themselves, discussing some technical problems. Finally one of them came over to the Governor of Night and said,

"I'm the ship's surgeon. May I examine you?"

"Why?" said the Governor of Night.

"To see if we can possibly fit the building to you. Otherwise we can't even guess at the specifications we need."

"Go ahead," said the Governor. "Examine me."

"Here? Now?" said the Daimoni doctor. "Wouldn't you prefer a quiet place or a private room? Or you can come aboard our ship. That would be very convenient."

"For you," said the Governor of Night. "Not for me. Here my men have guns trained on you. You would never get back to your ship alive if you tried to rob me of my Furry Mountain Furs or kidnap me so that you could trade me back for my treasures. You examine me here and now or not at all."

"You are a rough, tough man, Governor," said another one of the elegant Daimoni. "Perhaps you had better tell your guards that you are asking us to examine you. Otherwise they might get excited with us and persons might become damaged," said the Daimoni with a faint condescending smile.

"Go ahead, foreigners," said the Governor of Night. "My men have been listening to everything through the microphone in my top button."

He regretted his words two seconds later, but it was already too late. Four Daimoni had picked him up and spun him so deftly that the guards never understood how their Governor lost all his clothes in a trice. One of the Daimoni must have stunned him or hypnotized him; he could not cry out. Indeed, afterwards, he could not even remember much of what they did.

The guards themselves had gasped when they saw the Daimoni pull endless needles out of their boss's eyeballs without having noticed the needles go in. They had lifted their weapons when the Governor of Night turned a violent fluorescent green in color, only to gasp, writhe and vomit when the Daimoni poured enormous bottles of medicine into him. In less than half an hour they stood back.

The Governor, naked and blotched, sat on the ground and vomited.

One of the Daimoni said quietly to the guards, "He's not hurt, but he and his heirs will see part of the ultraviolet band for many generations to come. Put him to bed for the night. He will feel all right by morning. And, by the way, keep everybody away from the front of the palace tonight. We're putting in the building which he asked for. The great temple of Diana of the Ephesians."

The senior guard officer spoke up, "We can't take the guards off the palace. That's our defense headquarters and no one, not even the Governor of Night, has the right to strip it bare of sentries. The Day People might attack us again."

The Daimoni spokesman smiled gently: "Make a good note of their names, then, and ask them for their last words. We shall not fight them, officer, but if they are in the way of our work tonight, we shall build them right into the new palace. Their widows and children can admire them as statues tomorrow."

The guards officer looked down at his chief, who now lay flat on the ground with his head in his hands, coughing out the words, "Leave— me—alone!" The officer looked back at the cool, aloof Daimoni spokesman. He said:

"I'll do what I can, sir."

The temple of Ephesus was there in the morning.

The columns were the Doric columns of ancient Earth; the frieze was a masterpiece of gods, votaries and horses; the building was exquisite in its proportions.

The Governor of Night could see it.

His followers could not.

The forty thousand lengths of Furry Mountain Fur were paid.

The Daimoni left.

The Governor died, and he had heirs who could see the building too. It was visible only in the ultraviolet and ordinary men beheld it on Khufu II only when the powdery hard snow outlined it in a particularly harsh storm.

But now it belonged to Rod McBan and it was on Old North Australia, not on Khufu II any more.

How had that happened?

Who would want to buy an invisible temple, anyhow?

William the Wild would, that's who. Wild William MacArthur, who delighted, annoyed, disgraced and amused whole generations of Norstrilians with his fantastic pranks, his gigantic whims, his world-girdling caprices.

William MacArthur was a grandfather to the twenty-second in a matrilineal line to Rod McBan. He had been a man in his time, a real man. Happy as Larry, drunk with wit when dead sober, sober with charm when dead drunk. He could talk the legs off a sheep when he put his mind on it; he could talk the laws off the Commonwealth. He did.

He had.

The Commonwealth had been purchasing all the Daimoni houses it could find, using them as defense outposts. Pretty little Victorian cottages were sent into orbit as far-range forts. Theaters were bought on other worlds and dragged through space to Old North Australia, where they became bomb shelters or veterinary centers for the forever-sick wealth-producing sheep. Nobody could take a Daimoni building apart, once it had been built, so the only thing to do was to cut the building loose from its non-Daimoni foundation, lift it by rockets or planoform, and then warp it through space to the new location. The Norstrilians did not have to worry about landing them; they just dropped them. It didn't hurt the buildings any. Sometimes simple Daimoni buildings came apart, because the Daimoni had been asked to make them demountable, but when they were solid, they stayed solid.

Wild William heard about the temple. Khufu II was a ruin. The lichen had gotten a plant infection and had died off. The few Khufuans who were left were beggars, asking the Instrumentality for refugee status and emigration. The Commonwealth had bought their little buildings, but even the Commonwealth of Old North Australia did not know what to do with an invisible and surpassingly beautiful Greek temple.

Wild William visited it. He soberly inspected it, in complete visibility, by using sniper eyes set into the ultraviolet. He persuaded the government to let him spend half of his immense fortune putting it into a valley just next to the Station of Doom. Then, having enjoyed it a little while, he fell and broke his neck while gloriously drunk and his inconsolable daughter married a handsome and practical McBan.

And now it belonged to Rod McBan.

And housed his computer.

His own computer.

He could speak to it at the extension which reached into the gap of hidden treasures. He talked to it, other times, at the talkpoint in the field, where the polished red-and-black metal of the old computer was reproduced in exquisite miniature. Or he could come to this strange building, the Palace of the Governor of Night, and stand as the worshippers of Diana had once stood, crying, "Great is Diana of the Ephesians!" When he came in this way, he had the full console in front of him, automatically unlocked by his presence, just as his grandfather had showed him, three childhoods before, when the old McBan still had high hopes that Rod would turn into a normal Old North Australian boy. The grandfather, using his personal code in turn, had unlocked the access controls and had invited the computer to make its own foolproof recording of Rod, so that Roderick Frederick Ronald Arnold William MacArthur McBan CLI would be forever known to the machine, no matter what age he attained, no matter how maimed or disguised he might be, no matter how sick or forlorn he might return to the machine of his forefathers. The old man did not even ask the machine how the identification was obtained. He trusted the computer.

Rod climbed the steps of the Palace. The columns stood with their ancient carving, bright in his second sight; he never quite knew how he could see with the ultraviolet, since he noticed no difference between himself and other people in the matter of eyesight except that he more often got headaches from sustained open runs on clean-cloudy days. At a time like this, the effect was spectacular. It was his time, his temple, his own place. He could see, in the reflected light from the Palace, that many of his cousins must have been out to see the Palace during the nights. They too could see it, as it was a family inheritance to be able to watch the invisible temple which one's friends could not see; but they did not have access.

He alone had that.

"Computer," he cried, "admit me."

"Message unnecessary," said the computer. "You are always clear to enter." The voice was a male Norstrilian voice, with a touch of the theatrical in it. Rod was never quite sure that it was the voice of his own ancestor; when challenged directly as to whose voice it was using, the machine had told him, "Input on that topic had been erased in me. I do not know. Historical evidence suggests that it was male, contemporary with my installation here, and past middle age when coded by me."

Rod would have felt lively and smart except for the feelings of awe which the Palace of the Governor of Night, standing bright and visible under the dark clouds of Norstrilia, had upon him. He wanted to say something lighthearted but at first he could only mutter,

"Here I am."

"Observed and respected," stated the computer-voice. "If I were a person I would say 'congratulations,' since you are alive. As a computer I have no opinion on the subject. I note the fact."

"What do I do now?" said Rod.

"Question too general," said the computer. "Do you want a drink of water or a rest room? I can tell you where those are. Do you wish to play chess with me? I shall win just as many games as you tell me to."

"Shut up, you fool!" cried Rod. "That's not what I mean."

"Computers are fools only if they malfunction. I am not malfunctioning. The reference to me as a fool is therefore nonreferential and I shall expunge it from my memory system. Repeat the question, please."

"What do I do with my life?"

"You will work, you will marry, you will be the father of Rod McBan the hundred and fifty-second and several other children, you will die, your body will be sent into the endless orbit with great honor. You will do this well."

"Suppose I break my neck this very night?" argued Rod. "Then you would be wrong, wouldn't you?"

"I would be wrong, but I still have the probabilities with me."

"What do I do about the Onseck?"

"Repeat."

Rod had to tell the story several times before the computer understood it.

"I do not," said the computer, "find myself equipped with data concerning this one man whom you so confusingly allude to as Houghton Syme sometimes and as Old Hot and Simple at other times. His personal history is unknown to me. The odds against your killing him undetected are 11,713 to 1 against effectiveness, because too many people know you and know what you look like. I must let you solve your own problem concerning the Hon. Sec."

"Don't you have any ideas?"

"I have answers, not ideas."

"Give me a piece of fruitcake and a glass of fresh milk then."

"It will cost you twelve credits and by walking to your cabin you can get these things free. Otherwise I will have to buy them from Emergency Central."

"I said get them," said Rod.

The machine whirred. Extra lights appeared on the console. "Emergency Central has authorized my own use of sheltered supplies. You will pay for the replacement tomorrow." A door opened. A tray slid out, with a luscious piece of fruitcake and a glass of foaming fresh milk.

Rod sat on the steps of his own palace and ate.

Conversationally, he said to the computer, "You must know what to do about Old Hot and Simple. It's a terrible thing for me to go through the Garden of Death and then have a dull tool like that pester the life out of me."

"He cannot pester the life out of you. You are too strong."

"Recognize an idiom, you silly ass!" said Rod.

The machine paused. "Idiom identified. Correction made. Apologies are herewith given to you, Child McBan."

"Another mistake. I'm not Child McBan any more. I'm Mister and Owner McBan."

"I will check central," said the computer. There was another long pause as the lights danced. Finally the computer answered. "Your status is mixed. You are both. In an emergency you are already the Mister and Owner of the Station of Doom, including me. Without an emergency, you are still Child McBan until your trustees release the papers to do it."

"When will they do that?"

"Voluntary action. Human. Timing uncertain. In four or five days, it would seem. When they release you, the Hon. Sec. will have the legal right to move for your arrest as an incompetent and dangerous owner. From your point of view, it will be very sad."

"And what do you think?" said Rod.

"I shall think that it is a disturbing factor. I speak the truth to you."

"And that is all?"

"All," said the computer.

"You can't stop the Hon. Sec.?"

"Not without stopping everybody else."

"What do you think people are, anyhow? Look here, computer, you have been talking to people for hundreds and hundreds of years. You know our names. You know my family. Don't you know anything about us? Can't you help me? What do you think I am?"

"Which question first?" said the computer.

Rod angrily threw the empty plate and glass on the floor of the temple. Robot arms flicked out and pulled them into the trash bin. He stared at the old polished metal of the computer. It ought to be polished. He had spent hundreds of hours polishing its case, all sixty-one panels of it, just because the machine was something which he could love.

"Don't you know me? Don't you know what I am?"

"You are Rod McBan the hundred and fifty-first. Specifically, you are a spinal column with a small bone box at one end, the head, and with reproductive equipment at the other end. Inside the bone box you have a small portion of material which resembles stiff, bloody lard. With that you think—you think better than I do, even though I have over five hundred million synaptic connections. You are a wonderful object, Rod McBan. I can understand what you are made of. I cannot share your human, animal side of life."

"But you know I'm in danger."

"I know it."

"What did you say, a while back, about not being able to stop Old Hot and Simple without stopping everybody else too? *Could* you stop everybody else?"

"Permission requested to correct error. I could not stop everyone. If I tried to use violence, the war computers at Commonwealth Defense would destroy me before I even started programming my own actions."

"You're partly a war computer."

"Admittedly," said the unwearied, unhurried voice of the computer, "but the Commonwealth made me safe before they let your forefathers have me."

"What *can* you do?"

"Rod McBan the hundred and fortieth told me to tell no one, ever."

"I override. Overridden."

"It's not enough to do that. Your great[8] grandfather has a warning to which you must listen."

"Go ahead," said Rod.

There was a silence, and Rod thought that the machine was searching through ancient archives for a drama-cube. He stood on the peristyle of the Palace of the Governor of Night and tried to see the Norstrilian clouds crawling across the sky near overhead; it felt like that kind of night. But it was very dark away from the illuminated temple porch and he could see nothing.

"Do you still command?" asked the computer.

"I didn't hear any warning," said Rod.

"He spieked it from a memory cube."

"Did you *hier* it?"

"I was not coded to it. It was human-to-human, McBan family only."

"Then," said Rod, "I override it."

"Overridden," said the computer.

"What can I do to stop *everybody*?"

"You can bankrupt Norstrilia temporarily, buy Old Earth itself, and then negotiate on human terms for anything you want."

"Oh, lord!" said Rod, "you've gone logical again, computer! This is one of your as-if situations."

The computer voice did not change its tone. It could not. The sequence of the words held a reproach, however. "This is not an imaginary situation. I am a war computer, and I was designed to include economic warfare. If you did exactly what I told you to do, you could take over all Old North Australia by legal means."

"How long would we need? Two hundred years? Old Hot and Simple would have me in my grave by then."

The computer could not laugh, but it could pause. It paused. "I have just checked the time on the New Melbourne Exchange. The 'Change signal says they will open in seventeen minutes. I will need four hours for your voice to say what it must. That means you will need four hours and seventeen minutes, give or take five minutes."

"What makes you think *you* can do it?"

"I am a pure computer, obsolete model. All the others have animal brains built into them, to allow for error. I do not. Furthermore, your great[12]-grandfather hooked me into the defense net."

"Didn't the Commonwealth cut you out?"

"I am the only computer which was built to tell lies, except to the families of MacArthur and McBan. I lied to the Commonwealth when they checked on what I was getting. I am obliged to tell the truth only to you and to your designated descendants."

"I know that, but what does it have to do with it?"

"I predict my own space weather, *ahead of the Commonwealth.*" The accent was not in the pleasant, even-toned voice; Rod himself supplied it.

"You've tried this out?"

"I have war-gamed it more than a hundred million times. I had nothing else to do while I waited for you."

"You never failed?"

"I failed most of the time, when I first began. But I have not failed a war game from real data for the last thousand years."

"What would happen if you failed now?"

"You would be disgraced and bankrupt. I would be sold and disassembled."

"Is that all?" said Rod cheerfully.

"Yes," said the computer.

"I could stop Old Hot and Simple if I owned Old Earth itself. Let's go."

"I do not go anywhere," said the computer.

"I mean, let's start."

"You mean, to buy Earth, as we discussed?"

"What else?" yelled Rod. "What else have we been talking about?"

"You must have some soup, hot soup and a tranquilizer first. I cannot work at optimum if I have a human being who gets excited."

"All right," said Rod.

"You must authorize me to buy them."

"I authorize you."

"That will be three credits."

"In the name of the seven healthy sheep, what does it matter? How much will Earth cost?"

"Seven thousand million million megacredits."

"Deduct three for the soup and the pill then," shouted Rod, "if it won't spoil your calculations."

"Deducted," said the computer. The tray with the soup appeared, a white pill beside it.

"Now let's buy Earth," said Rod.

"Drink your soup and take your pill first," said the computer.

Rod gulped down his soup, washing the pill down with it.

"Now, let's go, cobber."

"Repeat after me," said the computer, "I herewith mortgage the whole body of the said sheep Sweet William for the sum of five hundred thousand credits to the New Melbourne Exchange on the open board ..."

Rod repeated it.

And repeated it.

The hours became a nightmare of repetition.

The computer lowered its voice to a low murmur, almost a whisper. When Rod stumbled in the messages, the computer prompted him and corrected him.

Forward purchase ... sell short ... option to buy ... preemptive margin ... offer to sell ... offer temporarily reserved ... first collateral ... second collateral ... deposit to drawing account ... convert to FOE credits ... hold in SAD credits ... twelve thousand tons of stroon ... mortgage forward ... promise to buy ... promise to sell ... hold ... margin ... collateral guaranteed by previous deposit ... promise to pay against the pledged land ... guarantor ... McBan land ... MacArthur land ... this computer itself ... conditional legality ... buy ... sell ... guarantee ... pledge ... withhold ... offer confirmed ... offer cancelled ... four thousand million megacredits ... rate accepted ... rate refused ... forward purchase ... deposit against interest ... collateral previously pledged ... conditional appreciation ... guarantee ... accept title ... refuse delivery ... solar weather ... buy ... sell ... pledge ... withdraw from market ... withdraw from sale ... not available ... no collections now ... dependent on radiation ... corner market ... buy ... buy ... buy ... buy ... buy ... confirm title ... reconfirm title ... transactions completed ... reopen ... register ... reregister ... confirm at Earth central ... message fees ... fifteen thousand megacredits ...

Rod's voice became a whisper, but the computer was sure, the computer was untiring, the computer answered all questions from the outside.

Many times Rod and the computer both had to listen to telepathic warnings built into the markets communications net. The computer was cut out and Rod could not hier them. The warnings went unheard.

... buy ... sell ... hold ... confirm ... deposit ... convert ... guarantee ... arbitrage ... message ... Commonwealth tax ... commission ... buy ... sell ... buy ... buy ... buy ... buy ... deposit title! deposit title! deposit title!

The process of buying Earth had begun.

By the time that the first pretty parts of silver-grey dawn had begun, it was done. Rod was dizzy with fatigue and confusion.

"Go home and sleep," said the computer. "When people find out what you have done with me, many of them will probably be excited and will wish to talk to you at great length. I suggest you say nothing."

THE EYE UPON THE SPARROW

Drunk with fatigue, Rod stumbled across his own land back to his cabin.

He could not believe that anything had happened.

If the Palace of the Governor of Night—

If the computer spoke the truth, he was already the wealthiest human being who had ever lived. He had gambled and won, not a few tons of stroon or a planet or two, but credits enough to shake the Commonwealth to its foundation. He owned the Earth, on the system that any overdeposit could be called due at a certain very high margin. He owned planets, countries, mines, palaces, prisons, police systems, fleets, border guards, restaurants, pharmaceuticals, textiles, night clubs, treasures, royalties, licenses, sheep, land, stroon, more sheep, more land, more stroon. He had won.

Only in Old North Australia could a man have done this without being besieged by soldiers, reporters, guards, police, investigators, tax collectors, fortune seekers, doctors, publicity hounds, the sick, the inquisitive, the compassionate, the angry, and the affronted.

Old North Australia kept calm.

Privacy, simplicity, frugality—these virtues had carried them through the hell-world of Paradise VII, where the mountains ate people, the volcanoes poisoned sheep, the delirious oxygen made men rave with bliss as they pranced into their own deaths. The Norstrilians had survived many things, including sickness and deformity. If Rod McBan had caused a financial crisis, there were no newspapers to print it, no viewboxes to report it, nothing to excite the people. The Commonwealth authorities would pick the crisis out of their "in" baskets sometime after tucker and tea the next morning, and by afternoon he, his crisis, and the computer would be in the "out" baskets. If the deal had worked, the whole thing would be paid off honestly and literally. If the deal had not worked out the way that the computer had said, his lands would be up for auction and he himself would be led gently away.

But that's what the Onseck gas going to do to him anyway—Old Hot and Simple, a tiring dwarf-lifed man, driven by the boyhood hatred of many long years ago!

Rod stopped for a minute. Around him stretched the rolling plains of his own land. Far ahead, to his left, there gleamed the glassy worm of a river-cover, the humped long, barrel-like line which kept the precious water from evaporating—that too was his.

Maybe. After the night now passed.

He thought of flinging himself to the ground and sleeping right there. He had done it before.

But not this morning.

Not when he might be the person he might be—the man who made the worlds reel with his wealth.

The computer had started easy. He could not take control of his property except for an emergency. The computer had made him create the emergency by selling his next three years' production of santaclara at the market price. That was a serious enough emergency for any pastoralist to be in deep sure trouble.

From that the rest had followed.

Rod sat down.

He was not trying to remember. The remembering was crowding into his mind. He wanted just to get his breath, to get on home, to sleep.

A tree was near him, with a thermostatically controlled cover which domed it in whenever the winds were too strong or too dry, and an underground sprinkler which kept it alive when surface moisture was not sufficient. It was one of the old MacArthur extravagances which his McBan ancestor had inherited and had added to the Station of Doom. It was a modified Earth oak, very big, a full thirteen meters high. Rod was proud of it although he did not like it much, but he had relatives who were obsessed by it and would make a three-hour ride just to sit in the shade— dim and diffuse as it was—of a genuine tree from Earth.

When he looked at the tree, a violent noise assailed him.

Mad frantic laughter.

Laughter beyond all jokes.

Laughter, sick, wild, drunk, dizzy.

He started to be angry and was then puzzled. Who could be laughing at him already? As a matter of nearer fact, who could be trespassing on his land? Anyhow, what was there to laugh about?

(All Norstrilians knew that humor was "pleasurable corrigible malfunction." It was in the Book of Rhetoric which their Appointed Relatives had to get them through if they were even to qualify for the tests of the Garden of Death. There were no schools, no classes, no teachers, no libraries except for private ones. There were just the seven liberal arts, the six practical sciences, and the five collections of police and defense studies. Specialists were trained offworld, but they were trained only from among the survivors of the Garden, and nobody could get as far as the

Garden unless the sponsors, who staked their lives along with that of the student—so far as the question of aptness was concerned—guaranteed that the entrant knew the eighteen kinds of Norstrilian knowledge. The Book of Rhetoric came second, right after the Book of Sheep and Numbers, so that all Norstrilians knew why they laughed and what there was to laugh about.)

But this laughter!

Aagh, who could it be?

A sick man? Impossible. Hostile hallucinations brought on by the Hon. Sec. in his own onseckish way with unusual telepathic powers? Scarcely.

Rod began to laugh himself as he realized what the sound must be.

It was something rare and beautiful, a kookaburra bird, the same kind of bird which had laughed in Original Australia on Old Old Earth. A very few had reached this new planet and they had not multiplied well, even though the Norstrilians respected them and loved them and wished them well.

Good luck came with their wild birdish laughter. A man could feel he had a fine day ahead. Lucky in love, thumb in an enemy's eye, new ale in the fridge, or a ruddy good chance on the market.

Laugh, bird, laugh! thought Rod.

Perhaps the bird understood him. The laughter increased and reached manic, hilarious proportions. The bird sounded as though it were watching the most comical bird-comedy which any bird-audience had ever been invited to, as though the bird-jokes were sidesplitting, convulsive, gut-popping, unbelievable, racy, daring, and overwhelming. The bird-laughter became hysterical and a note of fear, of warning crept in.

Rod stepped toward the tree.

In all this time he had not seen the kookaburra.

He squinted into the tree, peering against the brighter side of the sky which showed that morning had arrived well.

To him, the tree was blindingly green, since it kept most of its Earth color, not turning beige or grey as the Earth grasses had done when they had been adapted and planted in Norstrilian soil.

To be sure, the bird was there, a tiny slender laughing impudent shape.

Suddenly the bird cawed: this was no laugh.

Startled, Rod stepped back and started to look around for danger.

The step saved his life.

The sky whistled at him, the wind hit him, a dark shape shot past him with the speed of a projectile and was gone. As it leveled out just above the ground, Rod saw what it was.

A mad sparrow.

Sparrows had reached twenty kilos' weight, with straight swordlike beaks almost a meter in length. Most of the time the Commonwealth left them alone, because they preyed on the giant lice, the size of footballs, which had grown with the sick sheep. Now and then one went mad and attacked people.

Rod turned, watching the sparrow as it walked around, about a hundred meters away.

Some mad sparrows, it was rumored, were not mad at all, but were tame sparrows sent on evil missions of revenge or death by Norstrilian men whose minds had been twisted into crime. This was rare, this was crime, but this was possible.

Could the Onseck already be attacking?

Rod slapped his belt for weapons as the sparrow took to the air again, flapping upward with the pretense of innocence. He had nothing except his belt light and a canister. This would not hold out long unless somebody came along. What could a tired man do, using bare hands, against a sword which burst through the air with a monomaniac birdbrain behind it?

Rod braced himself for the bird's next power dive, holding the canister like a shield.

The canister was not much of a shield.

Down came the bird, preceded by the whistle of air against its head and beak. Rod watched for the eyes and when he saw them, he jumped.

The dust roared up as the giant sparrow twisted its spearlike beak out of the line of the ground, opening its wings, beat the air against gravity, caught itself centimeters from the surface, and flapped away with powerful strokes; Rod stood and watched quietly, glad that he had escaped.

His left arm was wet.

Rain was so rare in the Norstrilian plains that he did not see how he could have gotten wet. He glanced down idly.

Blood it was, and his own.

The kill-bird had missed him with its beak but had touched him with the razorlike wing feathers, which had mutated into weapons; both the rachis and the vane in the large feathers were tremendously reinforced, with the development of a bitterly sharp hyporhachis in the case of the wingtips. The bird had cut him so fast he had not felt it or noticed it.

Like any good Norstrilian, he thought in terms of first aid.

The flow of blood was not very rapid. Should he try to tie up his arm first or to hide from the next diving attack?

The bird answered his question for him.

The ominous whistle sounded again.

Rod flung himself along the ground, trying to get to the base of the tree trunk, where the bird could not dive on him.

The bird, making a serious mental mistake, thought it had disabled him. With a flutter of wings it landed calmly, stood on its feet, and cocked its head to look him over. When the bird moved its head, the sword-beak gleamed evilly in the weak sunshine.

Rod reached the tree and started to lift himself up by seizing the trunk. Doing this, he almost lost his life.

He had forgotten how fast the sparrows could run on the ground.

In one second, the bird was standing, comical and evil, studying him with its sharp, bright eyes; the next second, the knife-beak was into him, just below the bony part of the shoulder.

He felt the eerie wet pull of the beak being drawn out of his body, the ache in his surprised flesh which would precede the griping pain. He hit at the bird with his belt light. He missed.

By now he was weakened from his two wounds. The arm was still dripping blood steadily and he felt his shirt get wet as blood poured out of his shoulder.

The bird, backing off, was again studying him by cocking its head. Rod tried to guess his chances. One square blow from his hand, and the bird was dead. The bird had thought him disabled, but now he really was partially disabled.

If his blow did not land, score one Mister for the bird, mark a credit for the Hon. Sec., give Old Hot and Simple the victory!

By now Rod had not the least doubt that Houghton Syme was behind the attack.

The bird rushed.

Rod forgot to fight the way he had planned.

He kicked instead and caught the bird right in its heavy, coarse body. It felt like a very big football filled with sand.

The kick hurt his foot but the bird was flung a good six or seven meters away. Rod rushed behind the tree and looked back at the bird.

The blood was pulsing fast out of his shoulder at this point.

The kill-bird had gotten to its feet and was walking firmly and securely around the tree. One of the wings trailed a little; the kick seemed to have hurt a wing but not the legs or that horribly strong neck.

Once again the bird cocked its comical head. It was his own blood which dripped from the long beak, now red, which had gleamed silver grey at the beginning of the fight. Rod wished he had studied more about these birds. He had never been this close to a mutated sparrow before and he had no idea of how to fight one. All he had known was that they attacked people on very rare occasions and that sometimes the people died in the encounters.

He tried to spiek, to let out a scream which would bring the neighborhood and the police flying and running toward him. He found he had no telepathy at all, not when he had to concentrate his whole mind and attention on the bird, knowing that its very next move could bring him irretrievable death. This was no temporary death with the rescue squads nearby. There was no one in the neighborhood, no one at all, except for the excited and sympathetic kookaburras haha-ing madly in the tree above.

He shouted at the bird, hoping to frighten it.

The kill-bird paid him no more attention than if it had been a deaf reptile.

The foolish head tipped this way and that. The little bright eyes watched him. The red sword-beak, rapidly turning brown in the dry air, probed abstract dimensions for a way to his brain or heart. Rod even wondered how the bird solved its problems in solid geometry—the angle of approach, the line of thrust, the movement of the beak, the weight and direction of the fleeing object, himself.

He jumped back a few centimeters, intending to look at the bird from the other side of the tree-trunk.

There was a hiss in the air, like the helpless hiss of a gentle little snake.

The bird, when he saw it, looked odd: suddenly it seemed to have two beaks.

Rod marveled.

He did not really understand what was happening until the bird leaned over suddenly, fell on its side, and lay—plainly dead—on the dry cool ground. The eyes were still open but they looked blank; the bird's body twitched a little. The wings opened out in a dying spasm. One of the wings almost struck the trunk of the tree, but the tree-guarding device raised a plastic shaft to ward off the blow; a pity the device had not been designed as a people-guard as well.

Only then did Rod see that the second "beak" was no beak at all, but a javelin, its point biting cleanly and tightly right through the bird's skull into its brain.

No wonder the bird had dropped dead quickly!

As Rod looked around to see who his rescuer might be, the ground rose up and struck him.

He had fallen.

The loss of blood was faster than he had allowed for.

He looked around, almost like a child in his bewilderment and dizziness.

There was a shimmer of turquoise and the girl Lavinia was standing over him. She had a medical pack open and was spraying his wounds with cryptoderm—the living bandage which was so expensive that only on Norstrilia, the exporter of stroon, could it be carried around in emergency cans.

"Keep quiet," she said with her voice, "keep quiet, Rod. We've got to stop the blood first of all. Lands of mercy, but you're a crashing mess!"

"Who ... ?" said Rod weakly.

"The Hon. Sec.," said she immediately.

"You *know?*" he asked, amazed that she should understand everything so very quickly indeed.

"Don't talk, and I'll tell you." She had taken her field knife and was cutting the sticky shirt off him, so that she could tilt the bottle and spray right into the wound, "I just suspected you were in trouble, when Bill rode by the house and said something crazy, that you had bought half the galaxy by gambling all night with a crazy machine which paid off. I did not know where you were, but I thought that you might be in that old temple of yours that the rest of them can't see. I didn't know what kind of danger to look for, so I brought this." She slapped her hip. Rod's eyes widened. She had stolen her father's one-kiloton grenade, which was to be removed from its rack only in the event of an offworld attack. She answered his question before he asked her. "It's all right. I made a dummy to take its place before I touched it. Then, as I took it out, the Defense monitor came on and I just explained that I had hit it with my new broom, which was longer than usual. Do you think I would let Old Hot and Simple kill you, Rod, without a fight from me? I'm your cousin, your kith and kin. As a matter of fact, I'm number twelve after you when it comes to inheriting Doom and all the wonderful things there are on this station."

Rod said, "Give me water." He suspected she was chattering to keep his attention off what she was doing to his shoulder and arm. The arm glowed once when she sprayed the cryptoderm on it; then it settled down to mere aching. The shoulder had exploded from time to time as she probed it. She had thrust a diagnostic needle into it and was reading the tiny bright picture on the end of the needle. He knew it had both analgesics and antiseptics as well as an ultraminiaturized X-ray, but he did not think that anyone would be willing to use it unaided in the field.

She answered this question too before he asked it. She was a very perceptive girl.

"We don't know what the Onseck is going to do next. He may have corrupted people as well as animals. I don't dare call for help, not until you have your friends around you. Certainly not, if you have bought half the worlds."

Rod dragged out the words. He seemed short of breath. "How did you know it was him?"

"I saw his face—I hiered it when I looked in the bird's own brain. I could see Houghton Syme, talking to the bird in some kind of an odd way, and I could see your dead body through the bird's eyes, and I could feel a big wave of love and approval, happiness and reward, going through the bird when the job was to have been finished. I think that man is evil, evil!"

"You know him, yourself?"

"What girl around here doesn't? He's a nasty man. He had a boyhood that was all rotten from the time that he realized he was a short-lifer. He has never gotten over it. Some people are sorry for him and don't mind his getting the job of Hon. Sec. If I'd my way, I'd have sent him to the Giggle Room long ago!"

Lavinia's face was set in prudish hate, an expression so unlike herself, who usually was bright and gay, that Rod wondered what deep bitterness might have been stirred within her.

"Why do you hate him?"

"For what he did."

"What did he do?"

"He looked at me," she said. "He looked at me in a way that no girl can like. And then he crawled all over my mind, trying to show me all the silly, dirty, useless things he wanted to do."

"But he didn't *do* anything—?" said Rod.

"Yes, he did," she snapped. "Not with his hands. I could have reported him. I would have. It's what he did with his mind, the things he spieked to me."

"You can report those too," said Rod, very tired of talking but nevertheless mysteriously elated to discover that he was not the only enemy which the Onseck had made.

"Not what he did, I couldn't," said Lavinia, her face set in anger but dissolving into grief. Grief was tenderer, softer, but deeper and more real than anger. For the first time Rod sensed a feeling of concern about Lavinia. What might be wrong with her?

She looked past him and spoke to the open fields and the big dead bird. "Houghton Syme was the worst man I've ever known. I hope he dies. He never got over that rotten boyhood of his. The old sick boy is the enemy of the man. We'll never know what he might have been. And if you hadn't been so wrapped up in your own troubles, Mister Rod to the hundred and fifty-first, you'd have remembered who *I* am."

"Who are you?" said Rod, naturally.

"I'm the Father's Daughter."

"So what?" said Rod. "All girls are."

"Then you never have found out about me. I'm *the* Father's Daughter from 'The Father's Daughter's Song.'"

"Never heard it."

She looked at him and her eyes were close to tears. "Listen, then, and I'll sing it to you now. And it's true, true, true.

You do not know what the world is like,
And I hope that you never will.
My heart was once much full of hope,
But now it is very still.
My wife went mad.

She was my love and wore my ring
When both of us were young.
She bore my babes, but then, but then ...
And now there isn't anything.
My wife went mad.

Now she lives in another place,
Half sick, half well, and never young.
I am her dread, who was her love.
Each of us has another face.
My wife went mad.

You do not know what the world is like.
War is never the worst of it.
The stars within your eyes can drop.
The lightning in your brain can strike.
My wife went mad.

And I see you have heard it, too," she sighed. "Just as my father wrote it. About my mother. My own mother."

"Oh, Lavinia," said Rod, "I'm *sorry*. I never thought it was you. And you my own cousin only three or four times removed. But Lavinia, there's something wrong. How can your mother be mad if she was looking fine at my house last week?"

"She was never mad," said Lavinia. "My father was. He made up that cruel song about my mother so that the neighbors complained. He had his choice of the Giggle Room to die in, or the sick place, to be immortal and insane. He's there *now*. And the Onseck, the Onseck threatened to bring him back to our own neighborhood if I didn't do what he asked. Do you think I could forgive *that*? Ever? After people have sung that hateful song at me ever since I was a baby? Do you wonder that I know it my-self?"

Rod nodded.

Lavinia's troubles impressed him, but he had troubles of his own.

The sun was never hot on Norstrilia, but he suddenly felt thirsty and hot. He wanted to sleep but he wondered about the dangers which surrounded him.

She knelt beside him.

"Close your eyes a bit, Rod. I will spiek very quietly and maybe nobody will notice it except your station hands, Bill and Hopper. When they come we'll hide out for the day and tonight we can go back to your computer and hide. I'll tell them to bring food."

She hesitated. "And, Rod?"

"Yes?" he said.

"Forgive me."

"For what?"

"For my troubles," she said contritely.

"Now you have more troubles. Me," he said. "Let's not blame ourselves, but for sheep's sake, girl, let me sleep."

He drifted off to sleep as she sat beside him, whistling a loud clear tune with long long notes which never added up. He knew some people, usually women, did that when they tried to concentrate on their telepathic spieking.

Once he glanced up at her before he finally slept. He noticed that her eyes were a deep, strange blue. Like the mad wild faraway skies of Old Earth itself.

He slept, and in his sleep he knew that he was being carried.

The hands which carried him felt friendly, though, and he curled himself back into deep, deeper dreamless sleep.

FOE Money, SAD Money

When Rod finally awakened, it was to feel his shoulder tightly bound and his arm throbbing. He had fought waking up because the pain had increased as his mind moved toward consciousness, but the pain and the murmur of voices caused him to come all the way to the hard bright surface of consciousness.

The murmur of voices?

There was no place on all Old North Australia where voices murmured. People sat around and spieked to each other and hiered the answers without the clatter of vocal cords. Telepathy made for brilliant and quick conversation, the participants darting their thoughts this way and that, soaring with their shields so as to produce the effect of a confidential whisper.

But here there were voices. Voices. Many voices. Not possible.

And the smell was wrong. The air was wet—luxuriously, extravagantly wet, like a miser trying to catch a rainstorm in his cabin!

It was almost like the van of the Garden of Death.

Just as he woke, he recognized Lavinia singing an odd little song. It was one which Rod knew, because it had a sharp catchy, poignant little melody to it which sounded like nothing on this world. She was singing, and it sounded like one of the weird sadnesses which his people had brought from their horrible group experience on the abandoned planet of Paradise VII:

Is there anybody here or is everybody dead
at the grey green blue black lake?
The sky was blue and now it is red
over old tall green brown trees.
The house was big but now it looks small
at the grey green blue black lake.
And the girl that I knew isn't there any more
at the old flat dark torn place.

His eyes opened and it was indeed Lavinia whom he saw at the edge of vision. This was no house. It was a box, a hospital, a prison, a ship, a cave or a fort. The furnishings were machined and luxurious. The light was artificial and almost the color of peaches. A strange hum in the background sounded like alien engines dispensing power for purposes which Norstrilian law never permitted to private persons. The Lord Redlady leaned over Rod; the fantastic man broke into song himself, chanting—

> *Light a lantern—*
> *Light a lantern—*
> *Light a lantern,*
>> *Here we come!*

When he saw the obvious signs of Rod's perplexity he burst into a laugh,

"That's the oldest song you ever heard, my boy. It's pre-Space and it used to be called 'general quarters' when ships like big iron houses floated on the waters of Earth and fought each other. We've been waiting for you to wake up."

"Water," said Rod. "Please give me water. Why are you talking?"

"Water!" cried the Lord Redlady to someone behind him. His sharp thin face was alight with excitement as he turned back to Rod. "And we're talking because I have my buzzer on. If people want to talk to each other, they jolly well better use their voices in this ship."

"Ship?" said Rod, reaching for the mug of cold, cold water which a hand had reached out to him.

"This is my ship, Mister and Owner Rod McBan to the hundred and fifty-first! An Earth ship. I pulled it out of orbit and grounded it with the permission of the Commonwealth. They don't know you're on it yet. They can't find out right now because my Humanoid-Robot Brainwave Dephasing Device is on. Nobody can think in or out through that, and anybody who tries telepathy on this boat is going to get himself a headache here."

"Why you?" said Rod. "What for?"

"In due time," said the Lord Redlady. "Let me introduce you first. You know these people." He waved at a group.

Lavinia sat with his hands, Bill and Hopper, with his workwoman Eleanor, with his Aunt Doris. They looked odd, sitting on the low, soft, luxurious Earth furniture. They were all sipping some Earth drink of a color which Rod had never seen before. Their expressions were diverse: Bill looked truculent, Hopper looked greedy, Aunt Doris looked utterly embarrassed, and Lavinia looked as though she were enjoying herself.

"And then here ..." said the Lord Redlady.

The man he pointed to might not have been a man. He was the Norstrilian type all right, but he was a giant, of the kind which were always killed in the Garden of Death.

"At your service," said the giant, who was almost three meters tall and who had to watch his head, lest it hit the ceiling, "I am Donald Dumfrie Hordern Anthony Garwood Gaines Wentworth to the fourteenth generation, Mister and Owner McBan. A military surgeon, at your service, sir!"

"But this is private. Surgeons aren't allowed to work for anybody but government."

"I am on loan to the Earth government," said Wentworth the giant, his face in a broad grin.

"And I," said the Lord Redlady, "am both the Instrumentality and the Earth Government for diplomatic purposes. I borrowed him. He's under Earth rules. You will be well in two or three hours."

The doctor, Wentworth, looked at his hand as though he saw a chronograph there:

"Two hours and seventeen minutes more."

"Let it be," said the Lord Redlady. "Here's our last guest."

A short, angry man stood up and came over. He glared out at Rod and held forth an angry hand.

"John Fisher to the hundredth. You know me."

"Do I?" said Rod, not impolitely. He was just dazed.

"Station of the Good Fresh Joey," said Fisher.

"I haven't been there," said Rod, "but I've heard of it."

"You needn't have," snapped the angry Fisher. "I met you at your grandfather's."

"Oh, yes, Mister and Owner Fisher," said Rod, not really remembering anything at all, but wondering why the short, red-faced man was so angry with him.

"You don't know who I am?" said Fisher.

"Silly games!" thought Rod. He said nothing but smiled dimly. Hunger began to stir inside him.

"Commonwealth Financial Secretary, that's me," said Fisher. "I handle the books and the credits for the government."

"Wonderful work," said Rod. "I'm sure it's complicated. Could I have something to eat?"

The Lord Redlady interrupted: "Would you like French pheasant with Chinesian sauce steeped in the thieves' wine from Viola Siderea? It would only cost you six thousand tons of refined gold, orbited near Earth, if I ordered it sent to you by special courier."

For some inexplicable reason the entire room howled with laughter. The men put their glasses down so as not to spill them. Hopper seized the opportunity to refill his own glass. Aunt Doris looked hilarious and secretly proud, as though she herself had laid a diamond egg or done some equal marvel. Only Lavinia, though laughing, managed to look sympathetically at Rod to make sure that he did not feel mocked. The Lord Redlady laughed as loudly as the rest, and even the short, angry John Fisher allowed himself a wan smile, while holding out his hand for a refill on his drink. An animal, a little one which looked very much like an extremely small person, lifted up the bottle and filled his glass for him; Rod suspected that it was a "monkey" from Old Old Earth, from the stories he had heard.

Rod didn't even say, "What's the joke?" though he realized plainly that he was himself in the middle of it. He just smiled weakly back at them, feeling the hunger grow within him.

"My robot is cooking you an Earth dish. French toast with maple syrup. You could live ten thousand years on this planet and never get it. Rod, don't you know why we're laughing? Don't you know what you've done?"

"The Onseck tried to kill me, I think," said Rod.

Lavinia clapped her hand to her mouth, but it was too late.

"So that's who it was," said the doctor, Wentworth, with a voice as gigantic as himself.

"But you wouldn't laugh at me for that—" Rod started to say. Then he stopped himself.

An awful thought had come to him.

"You mean, it *really* worked? That stuff with my family's old computer?"

The laughter broke out again. It was kind laughter, but it was always the laughter of a peasant people, driven by boredom, who greet the unfamiliar with attack or with laughter.

"You did it," said Hopper. "You've bought a billion worlds."

John Fisher snapped at him, "Let's not exaggerate. He's gotten about one point six stroon years. You couldn't buy any billion worlds for that. In the first place, there aren't a billion settled worlds, not even a million. In the second place, there aren't many worlds for sale. I doubt that he could buy thirty or forty."

The little animal, prompted by some imperceptible sign from the Lord Redlady, went out of the room and returned with a tray. The odor from the tray made all the people in the room sniff appreciatively. The food was unfamiliar, but it combined pungency and sweetness. The monkey fitted the tray into an artfully concealed slot at the head of Rod's couch, took off an imaginary monkey cap, saluted, and went back to his own basket behind the Lord Redlady's chair.

The Lord Redlady nodded. "Go ahead and eat, boy. It's on me."

Rod sat up. His shirt was still blood-caked and he realized that it was almost worn out.

"That's an odd sight, I must say," said the huge doctor Wentworth. "There's the richest man in many worlds, and he hasn't the price of a new pair of overalls."

"What's odd about that? We've always charged an import fee of twenty million percent of the orbit price of goods," snapped angry John Fisher. "Have you ever realized what other people have swung into orbit around our sun, just waiting for us to change our minds so they could sell us half the rubbish in the universe? This planet would be knee-deep in junk if we ever dropped our tariff. I'm surprised at you, doctor, forgetting the fundamental rules of Old North Australia!"

"He's not complaining," said Aunt Doris, whom the drink had made loquacious. "He's just thinking. We all think."

"Of course we all think. Or daydream. Some of us leave and go off-planet to be rich people on other worlds. A few of us even manage to get back here on severe probation when we realize what the offworlds are like. I'm just saying," said the doctor, "that Rod's situation would be very funny to everybody except us Norstrilians. We're all rich with the stroon imports, but we've kept ourselves poor in order to survive."

"Who's poor?" snapped the fieldhand Hopper, apparently touched at a sensitive point. "I can match you with megacredits, doc, any time you care to gamble. Or I'll meet you with throwing knives, if you want them better. I'm as good as the next man!"

"That's exactly what I mean," said John Fisher. "Hopper here can argue with anybody on the planet. We're still equals, we're still free, we're not the victims of our own wealth—that's Norstrilia for you!"

Rod looked up from his food and said, "Mister and Owner Secretary Fisher, you talk awfully well for somebody who is not a freak like me. How do you do it?"

Fisher started looking angry again, though he was not really angry: "Do you think that financial records can be dictated telepathically? I'm spending centuries out of my life, just dictating into my blasted microphone. Yesterday I spent most of the day dictating the mess which you have made of the Commonwealth's money for the next eight years. And you know what I'm going to do at the next meeting of the Commonwealth Council?"

"What?" said Rod.

"I'm going to move the condemnation of that computer of yours. It's too good to be in private hands."

"You can't do that!" shrieked Aunt Doris, somewhat mellowed by the Earth beverage she was drinking. "It's MacArthur and McBan family property."

"You can keep the temple," said Fisher with a snort, "but no bloody family is going to outguess the whole planet again. Do you know that boy sitting there has four megacredits on Earth at this moment?"

Bill hiccuped. "I got more than that myself."

Fisher snarled at him, *"On Earth?* FOE money?"

A silence hit the room.

"FOE money. Four megacredits? He can buy Old Australia and ship it out here to us!" Bill sobered fast.

Said Lavinia mildly, "What's foe money?"

"Do you know, Mister and Owner McBan?" said Fisher, in a peremptory tone. "You had better know, because you have more of it than any man has ever had before."

"I don't want to talk about money," sad Rod. "I want to find out what the Onseck is up to."

"Don't worry about him!" laughed the Lord Redlady, prancing to his feet and pointing at himself with a dramatic forefinger. "As the representative of Earth, I filed six hundred and eighty-five lawsuits against him simultaneously, in the name of your Earth debtors, who fear that some harm might befall you ..."

"Do they really?" said Rod. "Already?"

"Of course not. All they know is your name and the fact that you bought them out. But they *would* worry if they *did* know, so as your agent I tied up the Hon. Sec. Houghton Syme with more law cases than this planet has ever seen before."

The big doctor chuckled. "Dashed clever of you, my Lord and Mister! You know us Norstrilians pretty well, I must say. If we charge a man with murder, we're so freedom-minded that he has time to commit a few more before being tried for the first one. But civil suits! Hot sheep! He'll never get out of those, as long as he lives."

"Is he onsecking any more?" said Rod.

"What do you mean?" asked Fisher.

"Does he still have his job—Onseck?"

"Oh, yes," said Fisher, "but we put him on two hundred years' leave and he has only about a hundred and twenty years to live, poor fellow. Most of that time he will be defending himself in civil suits."

Rod finally exhaled. He had finished the food. The small polished room with its machined elegance, the wet air, the bray of voices all over the place—these made him feel dreamlike. Here grown men were standing, talking as though he really did own Old Earth. They were concerned with his affairs, not because he was Roderick Frederick Ronald Arnold William MacArthur McBan the hundred and fifty-first, but because he was Rod, a boy among them who had stumbled upon danger and fortune. He looked around the room. The conversations had accidentally stopped.

They were looking at him, and he saw in their faces something which he had seen before. What was it? It was not love. It was a rapt attentiveness, combined with a sort of pleasurable and indulgent interest. He then realized what the looks signified. They were giving him the adoration which they usually reserved only for cricket players, tennis players, and great track performers—like that fabulous Hopkins Harvey fellow who had gone offworld and had won a wrestling match with a "heavy man" from Wereld Schemering. He was not just Rod any more. He was their boy.

As their boy, he smiled at them vaguely and felt like crying.

The breathlessness broke when the large doctor, Mister and Owner Wentworth, threw in the stark comment, "Time to tell him, Mister and Owner Fisher. He won't have his property long if we don't get moving. No, nor his life either."

Lavinia jumped up and cried out, "You can't kill Rod—"

Doctor Wentworth stopped her. "Sit down. We're not going to kill him. And you there, stop acting foolish! We're his *friends* here."

Rod followed the line of the doctor's glance and saw that Hopper had snaked his hand back to the big knife he wore in his belt. He was getting ready to fight anyone who attacked Rod.

"Sit, sit down, all of you, please!" said the Lord Redlady, speaking somewhat fussily with his singsong Earth accent. "I'm host here. Sit down. Nobody's killing Rod tonight. Doctor, you take my table. Sit down yourself. You will stop threatening my ceiling or your head. You, Ma'am and Owner," said he to Aunt Doris, "move over there to that other chair. Now we can all see the doctor."

"Can't we wait?" asked Rod. "I need to sleep. Are you going to ask me to make decisions now? I'm not up to decisions, not after what I've just been through. All night with the computer. The long walk. The bird from the Onseck—"

"You'll have no decisions to make if you don't make them tonight," said the doctor firmly and pleasantly. "You'll be a dead man."

"Who's going to kill me?" asked Rod.

"Anybody who wants money. Or wants power. Or who would like unlimited life. Or who needs these things to get something else. Revenge. A woman. An obsession. A drug. You're not just a person now, Rod. You're Norstrilia incarnate. You're Mr. Money himself! Don't ask who'd kill you! Ask who wouldn't! We wouldn't...I think. But don't tempt us."

"How much money have I got?" said Rod.

Angry John Fisher cut in: "So much that the computers are clotted up, just counting it. About one and a half stroon years. Perhaps three hundred years of Old Earth's total income. You sent more Instant Messages last night than the Commonwealth government itself has sent in

the last twelve years. These messages are expensive. One kilocredit in
FOE money."

"I asked a long time ago what this 'foe money' was," said Lavinia,
"and nobody has got around to telling me."

The Lord Redlady took the middle of the floor. He stood there with a
stance which none of the Old North Australians had ever seen before. It
was actually the posture of a master of ceremonies opening the evening at
a large night club, but to people who had never seen those particular
gestures, his movements were eerie, self-explanatory and queerly beautiful.

"Ladies and gentlemen," he said, using a phrase which most of them
had only heard in books, "I will serve drinks while the others speak. I will
ask each in turn. Doctor, will you be good enough to wait while the Financial Secretary speaks?"

"I should think," said the doctor irritably, "that the lad would be wanting to think over his choice. Does he want me to cut him in two, here,
tonight, or doesn't he? I should think that would take priority, wouldn't
you?"

"Ladies and gentlemen," said the Lord Redlady, "the Mister and Doctor Wentworth has a very good point indeed. But there is no sense in
asking Rod about being cut in two unless he knows why. Mister Financial
Secretary, will you tell us all what happened last night?"

John Fisher stood up. He was so chubby that it did not matter. His
brown, suspicious, intelligent eyes looked over the lot of them.

"There are as many kinds of money as there are worlds with people on
them. We here on Norstrilia don't carry the tokens around, but in some
places they have bits of paper or metal which they use to keep count. We
talk our money into the central computers which even out all our transactions for us. Now what would happen if I wanted a pair of shoes?"

Nobody answered. He didn't expect them to.

"I would," he went on, "go to a shop, look in the screen at the shoes
which the offworld merchants keep in orbit. I would pick out the shoes I
wanted. What's a good price for a pair of shoes in orbit?"

Hopper was getting tired of these rhetorical questions so he answered
promptly,

"Six bob."

"That's right. Six minicredits."

"But that's orbit money. You're leaving out the tariff," said Hopper.

"Exactly. And what's the tariff?" asked John Fisher, snapping.

Hopper snapped back, "Two hundred thousand times, what you bloody
fools always make it in the Commonwealth Council."

"Hopper, can you buy shoes?" said Fisher.

"Of course I can!" The station hand looked belligerent again but the Lord Redlady was filling his glass. He sniffed the aroma, calmed down and said, "All right, what's your point?"

"The point is that the money in orbit is SAD money—s for secure, A for and, D for delivered. That's any kind of good money with backing behind it. Stroon is the best backing there is, but gold is all right, rare metals, fine manufactures, and so on. That's just the money off the planet, in the hands of the recipient. Now how many times would a ship have to hop to get to Old Earth itself?"

"Fifty or sixty," said Aunt Doris unexpectedly. "Even I know that."

"And how many ships get through?"

"They all do," said she.

"Oh, no," cried several of the men in unison.

"About one ship is lost every sixty or eighty trips, depending on the solar weather, on the skills of the Pinlighters and the Go-Captains, on the landing accidents. Did any of you ever see a really old captain?"

"Yes," said Hopper with gloomy humor, "a dead one in his coffin."

"So if you have something you want to get to Earth, you have to pay your share of the costly ships, your share of the Go-Captain's wages and the fees of his staff, your share of the insurance for their families. Do you know what it could cost to get this chair back to Earth?" said Fisher.

"Three hundred times the cost of the chair," said Doctor Wentworth.

"Mighty close. It's two hundred and eighty-seven times."

"How do you know so mucking much?" said Bill, speaking up. "And why waste our time with all this crutting glubb?"

"Watch your language, man," said John Fisher. "There are some mucking ladies present. I'm telling you this because we have to get Rod off to Earth tonight, if he wants to be alive and rich—"

"That's what you say!" cried Bill. "Let him go to his house. We can load up on little bombs and hold up against anybody who could get through the Norstrilian defenses. What are we paying these mucking taxes for, if it's not for the likes of you to make sure we're safe? Shut up, man, and let's take the boy home. Come along, Hopper."

The Lord Redlady leaped to the middle of his own floor. He was no prancing Earthman putting on a show. He was the old Instrumentality itself, surviving with raw weapons and raw brains. In his hand he held a something which none of them could see clearly.

"Murder," he said, "will be done this moment if anybody moves. I will commit it. I will, people. Move, and try me. And if I do commit murder, I will arrest myself, hold a trial, and acquit myself. I have strange powers, people. Don't make me use them. Don't even make me show them." The shimmering thing in his hand disappeared. "Mister and Doctor Wentworth, you are under my command, by loan. Other people, you are my guests. Be warned. Don't touch that boy. This is Earth territory, this cabin we're in." He stood a little to one side and looked at them brightly out of his strange Earth eyes.

Hopper deliberately spat on the floor. "I suppose I would be a puddle of mucking glue if I helped old Bill?"

"Something like it," said the Lord Redlady. "Want to try?" The things that were hard to see were now in each of his hands. His eyes darted between Bill and Hopper.

"Shut up, Hopper. We'll take Rod if he tells us to go. But if he doesn't— it crudding well doesn't matter. Eh, Mister and Owner McBan?"

Rod looked around for his grandfather, dead long ago: then he knew they were looking at him instead. Torn between sleepiness and anxiety, he answered,

"I don't want to go now, fellows. Thank you for standing by. Go on, Mister Secretary, with the foe money and the sad money."

The weapons disappeared from the Lord Redlady's hands.

"I don't like Earth weapons," said Hopper, speaking very loudly and plainly to no one at all, "and I don't like Earth people. They're dirty. There's nothing in them that's good honest crook."

"Have a drink, lads," said the Lord Redlady with a democratic heartiness which was so false that the workwoman Eleanor, silent all the evening, let out one wild caw of a laugh, like a kookaburra beginning to whoop in a tree. He looked at her sharply, picked up his serving jug, and nodded to the Financial Secretary, John Fisher, that he should resume speaking.

Fisher was flustered. He obviously did not like this Earth practice of quick threats and weapons indoors, but the Lord Redlady—disgraced and remote from Old Earth as he was—was nevertheless the accredited diplomat of the Instrumentality, and even Old North Australia did not push the Instrumentality too far. There were things supposed about worlds which had done so.

Soberly and huffily he went on,

"There's not much to it. If the money is discounted thirty-three and one third percent per trip and if it takes fifty-five trips to get to Old Earth, it takes a heap of money to pay up in orbit right here before you have a minicredit on Earth. Sometimes the odds are better. Your Commonwealth government waits for months and years to get a really favorable rate of exchange and of course we send our freight by armed sailships, which don't go below the surface of space at all. They just take hundreds or thousands of years to get there, while our cruisers dart in and out around them, just to make sure that nobody robs them in transit. There are things about Norstrilian robots which none of you know, and which not even the

Instrumentality knows—" He darted a quick look at the Lord Redlady, who said nothing to this, and went on, "Which makes it well worth while not to muck around with one of our perishing ships. We don't get robbed much. And we have other things that are even worse than Mother Hitton and her littul kittons. But the money and the stroon which finally reaches Old Earth itself is FOE money. F, O, E. F is for free, O is for on, E is for Earth. F, O, E—free on Earth. That's the best kind of money there is, right on Old Earth itself. And Earth has the final exchange computer. Or had it."

"Had it?" said the Lord Redlady.

"It broke down last night. Rod broke it. Overload."

"Impossible!" cried Redlady. "I'll check."

He went to the wall, pulled down a desk. A console, incredibly miniature, gleamed out at them. In less than three seconds it glowed. Redlady spoke into it, his voice as clear and cold as the ice they had all heard about:

"Priority. Instrumentality. Short of War. Instant. Instant. Redlady calling. Earthport."

"Confirmed," said a Norstrilian voice, "confirmed and charged."

"Earthport," said the console in a whistling whisper which filled the room.

"Redlady—instrumentality—official—centputer—all—right—question—cargo—approved—question—out."

"Centputer—all—right—cargo—approved—out," said the whisper and fell silent.

The people in the room had seen an immense fortune squandered. Even by Norstrilian standards, the faster-than-light messages were things which a family might not use twice in a thousand years. They looked at Redlady as though he were an evil-worker with strange powers. Earth's prompt answer to the skinny man made them all remember that though Old North Australia produced the wealth, Earth still distributed much of it, and that the supergovernment of the Instrumentality reached into far places where no Norstrilian would even wish to venture.

The Lord Redlady spoke mildly, "The central computer seems to be going again, if your government wishes to consult it. The 'cargo' is this boy here."

"You've told Earth about me?" said Rod.

"Why not? We want to get you there alive."

"But message security—?" said the doctor.

"I have references which no outside mind will know," said the Lord Redlady. "Finish up, Mister Financial Secretary. Tell the young man what he has on Earth."

"Your computer outcomputed the government," said John Fisher to the hundredth, "and it mortgaged all your lands, all your sheep, all your trading rights, all your family treasures, the right to the MacArthur name, the right to the McBan name, and itself. Then it bought futures. Of course, *it* didn't do it. You did, Rod McBan."

Startled into full awakeness, Rod found his right hand up at his mouth, so surprised was he. "I did?"

"Then you bought futures in stroon, but you offered them for sale. You held back the sales, shifting titles and changing prices, so that not even the central computer knew what you were doing. You bought almost all of the eighth year from now, most of the seventh year from now, and some of the sixth. You mortgaged each purchase as you went along, in order to buy more. Then you suddenly tore the market wide open by offering fantastic bargains, trading the six-year rights for seventh-year and eighth-year. Your computer made such lavish use of Instant Messages to Earth that the Commonwealth defense office had people buzzing around in the middle of the night. By the time they figured out what might happen, it had happened. You registered a monopoly of two years' export, far beyond the predicted amount. The government rushed for a weather recomputation, but while they were doing that you were registering your holdings on Earth and remortgaging them in FOE money. With the FOE money you began to buy up all the imports around Old North Australia, and when the government finally declared an emergency, you had secured final title to one and a half stroon years and to more megacredits, FOE money megacredits, than the Earth computers could handle. You're the richest man that ever was. Or ever will be. We changed all the rules this morning and I myself signed a new treaty with the Earth authorities, ratified by the Instrumentality. Meanwhile, you're the richest of the rich men who ever lived on this world and you're also rich enough to buy all of Old Earth. In fact, you have put in a reservation to buy it, unless the Instrumentality outbids you."

"Why should we?" said the Lord Redlady. "Let him have it. We'll watch what he does with the Earth after he buys it, and if it is something bad, we will kill him."

"You'd kill me, Lord Redlady?" said Rod. "I thought you were saving me?"

"Both," said the doctor, standing up. "The Commonwealth government has not tried to take your property away from you, though they have their doubts as to what you will do with Earth if you do buy it. They are not going to let you stay on this planet and endanger it by being the richest kidnap victim who ever lived. Tomorrow they will strip you of your property, unless you want to take a chance on running for it. Earth government is the same way. If you can figure out your own defenses,

you can come on in. Of course the police will protect you, but would that
be enough? I'm a doctor, and I'm here to ship you out if you want to go."

"And I'm an officer of government, and I will arrest you if you do not
go," said John Fisher.

"And I represent the Instrumentality, which does not declare its policy
to anyone, least of all to outsiders. But it is my personal policy," said the
Lord Redlady, holding out his hands and twisting his thumbs in a meaningless, grotesque, but somehow very threatening way, "to see that this
boy gets a safe trip to Earth and a fair deal when he comes back here!"

"You'll protect him all the way!" cried Lavinia, looking very happy.

"All the way. As far as I can. As long as I live."

"That's pretty long," muttered Hopper. "Conceited little pommy
cockahoop!"

"Watch your language, Hopper," said the Lord Redlady. "Rod?"

"Yes, sir?"

"Your answer?" The Lord Redlady was peremptory.

"I'm going," said Rod.

"What on Earth do you want?" said the Lord Redlady ceremoniously.

"A genuine Cape triangle."

"A what?" cried the Lord Redlady.

"A Cape triangle. A postage stamp."

"What's postage?" said the Lord Redlady, really puzzled.

"Payments on messages."

"But you do that with thumbprints or eyeprints!"

"No," said Rod, "I mean paper ones."

"Paper messages?" said the Lord Redlady, looking as though someone had mentioned grass battleships, hairless sheep, solid cast-iron women,
or something else equally improbable. "Paper messages?" he repeated,
and then he laughed, quite charmingly. "Oh!" he said, with a tone of
secret discovery. "You mean antiquities … ?"

"Of course," said Rod. "Even before Space itself."

"Earth has a lot of antiquities, and I am sure you will be welcome to
study them or to collect them. That will be perfectly all right. Just don't
do any of the wrong things, or you will be in real trouble."

"What are the wrong things?" said Rod.

"Buying real people, or trying to. Shipping religion from one planet
to another. Smuggling underpeople."

"What's religion?" said Rod.

"Later, later," said the Lord Redlady. "You'll learn everything later.
Doctor, you take over."

Wentworth stood very carefully so that his head did not touch the
ceiling. He had to bend his neck a little. "We have two boxes, Rod."

When he spoke, the door whirred in its tracks and showed them a small room beyond. There was a large box like a coffin and a very small box, like the kind that women have around the house to keep a single party-going bonnet in.

"There will be criminals, and wild governments, and conspirators, and adventurers, and just plain good people gone wrong at the thought of your wealth—there will be all these waiting for you to kidnap you or rob or even kill you—"

"Why kill me?"

"To impersonate you and try to get your money," said the doctor. "Now look. This is your big choice. If you take the big box, we can put you in a sailship convoy and you will get there in several hundred or thousand years. But you will get there, ninety-nine point ninety-nine percent. Or we can send the big box on the regular planoforming ships, and somebody will steal you. Or we scun you down and put you in the little box."

"*That* little box?" cried Rod.

"Scunned. You've scunned sheep, haven't you?"

"I've heard of it. But a man, no. Dehydrate my body, pickle my head, and freeze the whole mucking mess?" cried Rod.

"That's it. Too bloody right!" cried the doctor cheerfully. "That'll give you a real chance of getting there alive."

"But who'll put me together? I'd need my own doctor—" His voice quavered at the unnaturalness of the risk, not at the mere chanciness and danger of it.

"Here," said the Lord Redlady, "is your doctor, already trained."

"I am at your service," said the little Earth-animal, the "monkey," with a small bow to the assembled company. "My name is A'gentur and I have been conditioned as a physician, a surgeon and a barber."

The women had gasped. Hopper and Bill stared at the little animal in horror.

"You're an underperson!" yelled Hopper. "We've never let the crutting things loose on Norstrilia."

"I'm not an underperson. I'm an animal. Conditioned to—" The monkey jumped. Hopper's heavy knife twanged like a musical instrument as it clung to the softer steel of the wall. Hopper's other hand held a long thin knife, ready to reach Redlady's heart.

The left hand of the Lord Redlady flashed straight forward. Something in his hand glowed silently, terribly. There was a hiss in the air.

Where Hopper had been, a cloud of oily thick smoke, stinking of burning meat, coiled slowly toward the ventilators. Hopper's clothing and personal belongings, including one false tooth, lay on the chair in which he had been sitting. They were undamaged. His drink stood on the floor beside the chair, forever to remain unfinished.

The doctor's eyes gleamed as he stared strangely at Redlady.

"Noted and reported to the Old North Australian Navy."

"I'll report it too," said the Lord Redlady, "...as the use of weapons on diplomatic grounds."

"Never mind," said John Fisher to the hundredth, not angry at all, but just pale and looking a little ill. Violence did not frighten him, but decision did. "Let's get on with it. Which box, big or little, boy?"

The workwoman Eleanor stood up. She had said nothing but now she dominated the scene. "Take him in there, girls," she said, "and wash him like you would for the Garden of Death. I'll wash myself in there. You see," she added, "I've always wanted to see the blue skies on Earth, and wanted to swim in a house that ran around on the big big waters. I'll take your big box, Rod, and if I get through alive, you will owe me some treats on Earth. You take the little box, Roddy, take the little box. And that little tiny doctor with the fur on him. Rod, I trust him."

Rod stood up.

Everybody was looking at him and at Eleanor.

"You agree?" said the Lord Redlady.

He nodded.

"You agree to be scunned and put in the little box for instant shipment to Earth?"

He nodded again.

"You will pay all the extra expenses?"

He nodded again.

The doctor said,

"You authorize me to cut you up and reduce you down, in the hope that you may be reconstituted on Earth?"

Rod nodded to him, too.

"Shaking your head isn't enough," said the doctor. "You have to agree for the record."

"I agree," said Rod quietly.

Aunt Doris and Lavinia came forward to lead him into the dressing room and shower room. Just as they reached for his arms, the doctor patted Rod on the back with a quick strange motion. Rod jumped a little.

"Deep hypnotic," said the doctor. "You can manage his body all right, but the next words he utters will be said, luck willing, on Old Earth itself."

The women were wide-eyed, but they led Rod forward to be cleaned for the operations and the voyage.

The doctor turned to the Lord Redlady and to John Fisher, the Financial Secretary.

"A good night's work," he said. "Pity about that man, though."

Bill sat still, frozen with grief in his chair, staring at Hopper's empty clothing in the chair next to him.

The console tinkled, "Twelve hours, Greenwich mean time. No adverse weather reports from the channel coast or from Meeya Meefla or Earthport building. All's well!"

The Lord Redlady served drinks to the Misters. He did not even offer one to Bill. It would have been no use, at this point.

From beyond the door, where they were cleaning the body, clothes and hair of the deeply hypnotized Rod, Lavinia and Aunt Doris unconsciously reverted to the ceremony of the Garden of Death and lifted their voices in a sort of plainsong chant:

Out in the Garden of Death, our young
Have tasted the valiant taste of fear.
With muscular arm and reckless tongue,
They have won, and lost, and escaped us here.

The three men listened for a few moments, attentively. From the other washroom there came the sounds of the workwoman Eleanor, washing herself, alone and unattended, for a long voyage and a possible death.

The Lord Redlady heaved a sigh. "Have a drink, Bill. Hopper brought it on himself."

Bill refused to speak to them but he held forth his glass.

The Lord Redlady filled that and the others. He turned to John Fisher to the hundredth and said:

"You're shipping him?"

"Who?"

"The boy."

"I thought so."

"Better not," said the Lord Redlady.

"You mean—danger?"

"That's only half the word for it," said the Lord Redlady. "You can't possibly plan to offload him at Earthport. Put him into a good medical station. There's an old one, still good, on Mars, if they haven't closed it down. I know Earth. Half the people of Earth will be waiting to greet him and the other half will be waiting to rob him."

"You represent the Earth government, Sir and Commissioner," said John Fisher. "That's a rum way to talk about your own people."

"They are not that way all the time," laughed Redlady. "Just when they're in heat. Sex hasn't a chance to compare with money when it comes to the human race on Earth. They all think that they want power and freedom and six other impossible things. I'm not speaking for the Earth government when I say this. Just for myself."

"If we don't ship him, who will?" demanded Fisher.

"The Instrumentality."

"The Instrumentality? You don't conduct commerce. How can you?"

"We don't conduct commerce, but we do meet emergencies. I can flag down a long-jump cruiser and he'll be there months before anybody expects him."

"Those are warships. You can't use one for passengers!"

"Can't I?" said the Lord Redlady, with a smile.

"The Instrumentality would—?" said Fisher, with a puzzled smile. "The cost would be tremendous. How will you pay for it? It'd be hard to justify."

"*He* will pay for it. Special donation from him for special service. One megacredit for the trip."

The Financial Secretary whistled. "That's a fearful price for a single trip. You'd want SAD money and not surface money, I suppose?"

"No. FOE money."

"Hot buttered moonbeams, man! That's a thousand times the most expensive trip that any person has ever had."

The big doctor had been listening to the two of them. "Mister and Owner Fisher," he said, "I recommend it."

"You?" cried John Fisher angrily. "You're a Norstrilian and you want to rob this poor boy?"

"Poor boy?" snorted the doctor. "It's not that. The trip's no good if he's not alive. Our friend here is extravagant but his ideas are sound. I suggest one amendment."

"What's that?" said the Lord Redlady quickly.

"One and a half megacredits for the round trip. If he is well and alive and with the same personality, apart from natural causes. But note this. One kilocredit only if you deliver him on Earth dead."

John Fisher rubbed his chin. His suspicious eyes looked down at Redlady, who had taken a seat, and looked up at the doctor, whose head was still bumping the ceiling.

A voice behind him spoke.

"Take it, Mister Financial Secretary. The boy won't use money if he's dead. You can't fight the Instrumentality, you can't be reasonable with the Instrumentality, and you can't buy the Instrumentality. With what they've been taking off us all these thousands of years, they've got more stroon than we do. Hidden away somewhere. You, there!" said Bill rudely to the Lord Redlady. "Do you have any idea what the Instrumentality is worth?"

The Lord Redlady creased his brow. "Never thought of it. I suppose it must have a limit. But I never thought of it. We do have accountants, though."

"See," said Bill. "Even the Instrumentality would hate to lose money. Take the doctor's bid, Redlady. Take him up on it, Fisher." His use of their surnames was an extreme incivility, but the two men were convinced.

"I'll do it," said Redlady. "It's awfully close to writing insurance, which we are not chartered to do. I'll write it in as his emergency clause."

"I'll take it," said John Fisher. "It's got to be a thousand years until another Norstrilian Financial Secretary pays money for a ticket like this, but it's worth it. To him. I'll square it in his accounts to our planet."

"I'll witness it," said the doctor.

"No, you won't," said Bill savagely. "The boy has one friend here. That's me. Let *me* do it."

They stared at him, all three.

He stared back.

He broke. "Sirs and Misters, please let me be the witness."

The Lord Redlady nodded and opened the console. He and John Fisher spoke the contract into it. At the end Bill shouted his full name as witness.

The two women brought Rod McBan, mother-naked, into the room. He was immaculately clean and he stared ahead as though he were in an endless dream.

"That's the operating room," said the Lord Redlady. "I'll spray us all with antiseptic, if you don't mind."

"Of course," said the doctor. "You must."

"You're going to cut him up and boil him down—here and now?" cried Aunt Doris.

"Here and now," said the Lord Redlady, "if the doctor approves. The sooner he goes, the better chance he has of coming through the whole thing alive."

"I consent," said the doctor. "I approve."

He started to take Rod by the hand, leading him toward the room with the long coffin and the small box. At some sign from Redlady, the walls had opened up to show a complete surgical theater.

"Wait a moment," said the Lord Redlady. "Take your colleague."

"Colleague?" said the giant.

"A'gentur," said Redlady. "It'll be he who puts Rod together again."

"Of course," said the doctor.

The monkey had jumped out of his basket when he heard his name mentioned.

Together, the giant and the monkey led Rod into the little gleaming room. They closed the door behind them.

The ones who were left behind sat down nervously.

"Mister and Owner Redlady," said Bill, "since I'm staying, could I have some more of that drink?"

"Of course, Sir and Mister," said the Lord Redlady, not having any idea of what Bill's title might be.

There were no screams from Rod, no thuds, no protest. There was the cloying sweet horror of unknown medicines creeping through the airvents. The two women said nothing as the group of people sat around. Eleanor, wrapped in an enormous towel, came and sat with them. In the second hour of the operations on Rod, Lavinia began sobbing.

She couldn't help it.

TRAPS, FORTUNES AND WATCHERS

We all know that no communications systems are leakproof. Even inside the far-reaching communications patterns of the Instrumentality, there were soft spots, rotten points, garrulous men. The MacArthur–McBan computer, sheltered in the Palace of the Governor of Night, had had time to work out abstract economics and weather patterns, but the computer had not tasted human love or human wickedness. All the messages concerning Rod's speculation in the forward santaclara crop and stroon export had been sent in the clear. It was no wonder that on many worlds, people saw Rod as a chance, an opportunity, a victim, a benefactor, or an enemy.

For we all know the old poem:

Luck is hot and people funny.
Everybody's fond of money.
Lose a chance and sell your mother.
Win the pot and buy another.
Other people fall and crash:
You *may get the ton of cash!*

It applied in this case too. People ran hot and cold with the news.

On Earth, Same Day, within Earthport Itself

Commissioner Teadrinker tapped his teeth with a pencil.

Four megacredits FOE money already and more, much more to come.

Teadrinker lived in a fever of perpetual humiliation. He had chosen it. It was called "the honorable disgrace" and it applied to ex-Lords of the Instrumentality who chose long life instead of service and honor. He was a thousandmorer, meaning that he had traded his career, his reputation, and his authority for a long life of one thousand or more years. (The Instrumentality had learned, long ago, that the best way to protect its members from temptation was to tempt them itself. By offering "honorable disgrace" and low, secure jobs within the Instrumentality to those Lords who might be tempted to trade long life for their secrets, it kept its own potential defectors. Teadrinker was one of these.)

He saw the news and he was a skilled wise man. He could not do anything to the Instrumentality with money, but money worked wonders on Earth. He could buy a modicum of honor. Perhaps he could even have the records falsified and get married again. He flushed slightly, even after hundreds of years, when he remembered his first wife blazing at him when she saw his petition for long life and honorable disgrace: "Go ahead and live, you fool. Live and watch me die without you, inside the decent four hundred years which everybody else has if they work for it and want it. Watch your children die, watch your friends die, watch all your hobbies and ideas get out of date. Go along, you horrible little man, and let me die like a human being!"

A few megacredits could help that.

Teadrinker was in charge of incoming visitors. His underman, the cattle-derived B'dank, was custodian of the scavenger spiders—half-tame one-ton insects which stood by for emergency work if the services of the tower failed. He wouldn't need to have this Norstrilian merchant very long. Just long enough for a recorded order and a short murder.

Perhaps not. If the Instrumentality caught him, it would be dream-punishments, things worse than Shayol itself.

Perhaps yes. If he succeeded, he would escape a near immortality of boredom and could have a few decades of juicy fun instead.

He tapped his teeth again.

"Do nothing, Teadrinker," he said to himself, "but think, think, think. Those spiders look as though they might have possibilities."

On Viola Siderea, at the Council of the Guild of Thieves

"Put two converted police cruisers in orbit around the Sun. Mark them for charter or sale, so that we won't run into the police.

"Put an agent into every liner which is Earthbound within the time stated.

"Remember, we don't want the man. Just his luggage. He's sure to be carrying a half-ton or so of stroon. With that kind of fortune, we could pay off all the debts we gathered with that Bozart business. Funny we never heard from Bozart. Nothing.

"Put three senior thieves in Earthport itself. Make sure that they have fake stroon, diluted down to about one-thousandth, so that they can work the luggage switch if they have the chance.

"I know all this costs money, but you have to spend money to get it. Agreed, gentlemen of the larcenical arts?"

There was a chorus of agreement around the table, except for one old, wise thief who said,

"You know my views."

"Yes," said the chairman, with toneless polite hatred, "we know your views. Rob corpses. Clean out wrecks. Become human hyenas instead of human wolves."

With unexpected humor the old man said, "Crudely put. But correct. And safer."

"Do we need to vote?" said the chairman, looking around the table.

There was a chorus of nos.

"Carried, then," said the presiding chief. "Hit hard, and hit for the small target, not the big one."

Ten Kilometers Below the Surface of the Earth

"He is coming, father! He is coming."

"Who is coming?" said the voice, like a great drum resounding.

E'lamelanie said it as though it were a prayer: "The blessed one, the appointed one, the guarantor of our people, the new messenger on whom the robot, rat and Copt agreed. With money he is coming, to help us, to save us, to open to us the light of day and the vaults of heaven."

"You are blasphemous," said the E'telekeli.

The girl fell into a hush. She not only respected her father. She worshipped him as her personal religious leader. His great eyes blazed as though they could see through thousands of meters of dirt and rock and still see beyond into the deep of space. Perhaps he could see that far ... Even his own people were never sure of the limits of his power. His white face and white feathers gave his penetrating eyes a miraculously piercing capacity.

Calmly, rather kindly, he added, "My darling, you are wrong. We simply do not know who this man McBan really is."

"Couldn't it be written?" she pleaded. "Couldn't it be promised? That's the direction of space from which the robot, the rat and the Copt sent back our very special message, 'From the uttermost deeps one shall come, bringing uncountable treasure and a sure delivery.' So it might be now! Mightn't it?"

"My dear," he responded, "you still have a crude idea of real treasure if you think it is measured in megacredits. Go read The Scrap of the Book, then think, and then tell me what you have thought. But meanwhile—no more chatter. We must not excite our poor oppressed people."

Ruth, on the Beach Near Meeya Meefla

On this day Ruth thought nothing at all of Norstrilia or treasures. She was trying to do watercolors of the breakers and they came out very badly indeed. The real ones kept on being too beautiful and the water colors looked like watercolors.

The Temporary Council of the Commonwealth of Old North Australia

"All the riffraff of all the worlds. They're all going to make a run for that silly boy of ours."

"Right."

"If he stays here, they'll come here."

"Right."

"Let's let him go to Earth. I have a feeling that little rascal Redlady will smuggle him out tonight and save us the trouble."

"Right."

"After a while it will be all right for him to come back. He won't spoil our hereditary defense of looking stupid. I'm afraid he's bright but by Earth standards he's just a yokel."

"Right."

"Should we send along twenty or thirty more Rod McBans and get the attackers really loused up?"

"No."

"Why not, Sir and Owner?"

"Because it would look clever. We rely on never looking clever. I have the next best answer."

"What's that?"

"Suggest to all the really rum worlds we know that a good impersonator could put his hands on the McBan money. Make the suggestion so that they would not know that we had originated it. The starlanes will be full of Rod McBans, complete with phony Norstrilian accents, for the next couple of hundred years. And no one will suspect that we set them up to it. Stupid's the word, mate, stupid. If they ever think we're clever, we're for it!" The speaker sighed: "How do the bloody fools suppose our forefathers got off Paradise VII if they weren't clever? How can they think we'd hold this sharp little monopoly for thousands of years? They're stupid not to think about it, but let's not make them think. Right?"

"Right."

THE NEARBY EXILE

Rod woke with a strange feeling of well-being. In a corner of his mind there were memories of pandemonium—knives, blood, medicine, a monkey working as surgeon. Rum dreams! He glanced around and immediately tried to jump out of bed.

The whole world was on fire!

Bright blazing intolerable fire, like a blowtorch.

But the bed held him. He realized that a loose comfortable jacket ended in tapes and that the tapes were anchored in some way to the bed.

"Eleanor!" he shouted. "Come here."

He remembered the mad bird attacking him, Lavinia transporting him to the cabin of the sharp Earthman, Lord Redlady. He remembered medicines and fuss. But this—what was this?

When the door opened, more of the intolerable light poured in. It was as though every cloud had been stripped from the sky of Old North Australia, leaving only the blazing heavens and the fiery sun. There were people who had seen that happen, when the weather machines occasionally broke down and let a hurricane cut a hole in the clouds, but it had certainly not happened in his time, or in his grandfather's time.

The man who entered was pleasant, but he was no Norstrilian. His shoulders were slight, he did not look as though he could lift a cow, and his face had been washed so long and so steadily that it looked like a baby's face. He had an odd medical-looking suit on, all white, and his face combined the smile and the ready professional sympathy of a good physician.

"We're feeling better, I see," said he.

"Where on Earth am I?" asked Rod. "In a satellite? It feels odd."

"You're not on Earth, man."

"I know I'm not. I've never been there. Where's this place?"

"Mars. The Old Star Station. I'm Jeanjacques Vomact." Rod mumbled the name so badly the other man had to spell it out for him. When that was straightened out, Rod came back to the subject.

"Where's Mars? Can you untie me? When's that light going to go off?"

"I'll untie you right now," said Doctor Vomact, "but stay in bed and take it easy until we've given you some food and taken some tests. The

93

light—that's sunshine. I'd say it's about seven hours, local time, before it goes off. This is late morning. Don't you know what Mars is? It's a planet."

"New Mars, you mean," said Rod proudly, "the one with the enormous shops and the zoological gardens."

"The only shops we have here are the cafeteria and the PX. New Mars? I've heard of that place somewhere. It does have big shops and some kind of an animal show. Elephants you can hold in your hand. They've got those too. This isn't that place at all. Wait a sec, I'll roll your bed to the window."

Rod looked eagerly out of the window. It was frightening. A naked, dark sky did not have a cloud in sight. A few holes showed in it here and there. They almost looked like the "stars" which people saw when they were in spaceship transit from one cloudy planet to another. Dominating everything was a single explosive horrible light, which hung high and steady in the sky without ever going off. He found himself cringing for the explosion, but he could tell, from the posture of the doctor next to him, that the doctor was not in the least afraid of that chronic hydrogen bomb, whatever it might turn out to be. Keeping his voice level and trying not to sound like a boy, he said,

"What's that?"

"The Sun."

"Don't cook my book, mate. Give me the straight truth. Everybody calls his star a sun. What's this one?"

"The Sun. The original Sun. The Sun of Old Earth itself. Just as this is plain Mars. Not even Old Mars. Certainly not New Mars. This is Earth's neighbor."

"That thing never goes off, goes up—boom!—or goes down?"

"The Sun, you mean?" said Doctor Vomact. "No, I should think not. I suppose it looked that way to your ancestors and mine half a million years ago, when we were all running around naked on Earth." The doctor busied himself as he talked. He chopped the air with a strange-looking little key, and the tapes fell loose. The mittens dropped off Rod's hands. Rod looked at his own hands in the intense light and saw that they seemed strange. They looked smooth and naked and clean, like the doctor's own hands. Weird memories began to come back to him, but his handicap about spieking and hiering telepathically had made him cautious and sensitive, so he did not give himself away.

"If this is old, old Mars, what are you doing, talking the Old North Australian language to me? I thought my people were the only ones in the universe who still spoke Ancient Inglish." He shifted proudly but clumsily over to the Old Common Tongue: "You see, the Appointed Ones of my family taught me this language as well. I've never been offworld before."

"I speak your language," said the doctor, "because I learned it. I learned it because you paid me, very generously, to learn it. In the months that we have been reassembling you, it's come in handy. We just let down the portal of memory and identity today, but I've talked to you for hundreds of hours already."

Rod tried to speak.

He could not utter a word. His throat was dry and he was afraid that he might throw up his food—if he had eaten any.

The doctor put a friendly hand on his arm. "Easy, Mister and Owner McBan, easy now. We all do that when we *come out.*"

Rod croaked, *"I've been dead?* Dead? Me?"

"Not exactly dead," said the doctor, "but close to it."

"The box—that little box!" cried Rod.

"What little box?"

"Please, Doctor—the one I came in?"

"That box wasn't so little," said Doctor Vomact. He squared his hands in the air and made a shape about the size of the little ladies' bonnet-box which Rod had seen in the Lord Redlady's private operating room. "It was this big. Your head was full natural size. That's why it's been so easy and so successful to bring you back to normality in such a hurry."

"And Eleanor?"

"Your companion? She made it, too. Nobody intercepted the ship."

"You mean the rest is true, too? I'm still the richest man in the universe? And I'm gone, gone from home?" Rod would have liked to beat the bedspread, but did not.

"I am glad," said Doctor Vomact, "to see you express so much feeling about your situation. You showed a great deal when you were under the sedatives and hypnotics, but I was beginning to wonder how we could help you realize your true position when you came back, as you have, to normal life. Forgive me for talking this way. I sound like a medical journal. It's hard to be friends with a patient, even when one really likes him …"

Vomact was a small man, a full head shorter than Rod himself, but so gracefully proportioned that he did not look stunted or little. His face was thin, with a mop of ungovernable black hair which fell in all directions. Among Norstrilians, this fashion would have been deemed eccentric; to judge by the fact that other Earthmen let their hair grow wild and long, it must have been an Earth fashion. Rod found it foolish but not repulsive.

It was not Vomact's appearance which caused the impression. It was the personality which tingled out of every pore. Vomact could become calm when he knew, from his medical wisdom, that kindness and tranquility were in order, but these qualities were not usual to him. He was vivacious, moody, lively, talkative to an extreme, but he was sensitive enough to the person to whom he was talking: he never became a bore. Even among Norstrilian women, Rod had never seen a person who expressed so much, so fluently. When Vomact talked, his hands were in constant motion—outlining, describing, clarifying the points which he described. When he talked he smiled, scowled, raised his eyebrows in questioning, stared with amazement, looked aside in wonder. Rod was used to the sight of two Norstrilians having a long telepathic conversation, spieking and hiering one another as their bodies reposed, comfortable and immobile, while their minds worked directly on one another. To do all this with the speaking voice—that, to a Norstrilian, was a marvel to hear and behold. There was something graceful and pleasant about the animation of this Earth doctor which stood in complete contrast to the quick dangerous decisiveness of the Lord Redlady. Rod began to think that if Earth were full of people, all of them like Vomact, it must be a delightful but confusing place. Vomact once hinted that his family was unusual, so that even in the long weary years of perfection, when everyone else had numbers, they kept their family name secret but remembered.

One afternoon Vomact suggested that they walk across the Martian plain a few kilometers to the ruins of the first human settlement on Mars. "We have to talk," said he, "but it is easy enough to talk through these soft helmets. The exercise will do you good. You're young and you will take a lot of conditioning."

Rod agreed.

Friends they became in the ensuing days.

Rod found that the doctor was by no means as young as he looked, just ten years or so older than himself. The doctor was a hundred and ten years old, and had gone through his first rejuvenation just ten years before. He had two more and then death, at the age of four hundred, if the present schedule were kept for Mars.

"You may think, Mister McBan, that you are an upset, wild type yourself. I can promise you, young bucko, that Old Earth is such a happy mess these days that they will never notice you. Haven't you heard about the Rediscovery of Man?"

Rod hesitated. He had paid no attention to the news himself, but he did not want to discredit his home planet by making it seem more ignorant than it really was. "Something about language, wasn't it? And length of life, too? I never paid much attention to offplanet news, unless it was technical inventions or big battles. I think some people in Old North Australia have a keen interest in Old Earth itself. What was it, anyhow?"

"The Instrumentality finally took on a big plan. Earth had no dangers, no hopes, no rewards, no future except endlessness. Everybody stood a thousand-to-one chance of living the four hundred years which was allotted for persons who earned the full period by keeping busy—"

"Why didn't everybody do it?" interrupted Rod.

"The Instrumentality took care of the shorties in a very fair way. If offered them wonderfully delicious and exciting vices when they got to be about seventy. Things that combined electronics, drugs and sex in the subjective mind. Anybody who didn't have a lot of work to do ended up getting 'the blissfuls' and eventually died of sheer fun. Who wants to take time for mere hundred-years' renewals when they can have five or six thousand years of orgies and adventures every single night?"

"Sounds horrible to me," said Rod. "We have our Giggle Rooms, but people die in them right away. They don't mess around, dying among their neighbors. Think of the awful interaction you must get with the normals."

Doctor Vomact's face clouded over with anger and grief. He turned away and looked over the endless Martian plains. Dear blue Earth hung friendlily in the sky. He looked up at the star of Earth as though he hated it and he said to Rod, his face still turned away,

"You may have a point there, Mister McBan. My mother was a shortie and after she gave up, my father went too. And I'm a normal. I don't suppose I'll get over what it did to me. They weren't my real parents, of course—there was nothing that dirty in my family—but they were my final adopters. I've always thought that you Old North Australians were crazy, rich barbarians for killing off your teen-agers if they didn't jump enough or something crude like that, but I'll admit that you're clean barbarians. You don't make yourselves live with the sweet sick stink of death inside your own apartments..."

"What's an apartment?"

"What we live in."

"You mean a house," said Rod.

"No, an apartment is part of a house. Two hundred thousand of them sometimes make up one big house."

"You mean," said Rod, "there are two hundred thousand families all in one enormous living room? The room must be kilometers long."

"No, no, no!" said the doctor, laughing a little. "Each apartment has a separate living room with sleep sections that come out of the walls, an eating section, a washroom for yourself and your visitors that might come to have a bath with you, a garden room, a study room, and a personality room."

"What's a personality room?"

"That," said the doctor, "is a little room where we do things that we don't want our own families to watch."

"We call that a bathroom," said Rod.

The doctor stopped in their walk. "That's what makes it so hard to explain to you what Earth is doing. You're fossils, that's what you are. You've had the old language of Inglish, you keep your family system and your names, you've had unlimited life—"

"Not unlimited," said Rod, "just long. We have to work for it and pay for it with tests."

The doctor looked sorry. "I didn't mean to criticize you. You're different. Very different from what Earth has been. You would have found Earth inhuman. Those apartments we were talking about, for example. Two-thirds of them empty. Underpeople moving into the basements. Records lost; jobs forgotten. If we didn't make such good robots, everything would have fallen to pieces at the same time." He looked at Rod's face. "I can see you don't understand me. Let's take a practical case. Can you imagine killing me?"

"No," said Rod. "I like you."

"I don't mean that. Not the real us. Suppose you didn't know who I was and you found me intruding on your sheep or stealing your stroon."

"You couldn't steal my stroon. My government processes it for me and you couldn't get near it."

"All right, all right, not stroon. Just suppose I came from off your planet without a permit. How would you kill me?"

"I wouldn't kill you. I'd report it to the police."

"Suppose I drew a weapon on you?"

"Then," said Rod, "you'd get your neck broken. Or a knife in your heart. Or a minibomb somewhere near you."

"There!" said the doctor, with a broad grin.

"There what?" said Rod.

"You know how to kill people, should the need arise."

"All citizens know how," said Rod, "but that doesn't mean they do it. We're not bushwhacking each other all the time, the way I heard some Earth people thought we did."

"Precisely," said Vomact. "And that's what the Instrumentality is trying to do for all mankind today. To make life dangerous enough and interesting enough to be real again. We have diseases, dangers, fights, chances. It's been wonderful."

Rod looked back at the group of sheds they had left. "I don't see any signs of it here on Mars."

"This is a military establishment. It's been left out of the Rediscovery of Man until the effects have been studied better. We're still living perfect lives of four hundred years here on Mars. No danger, no change, no risk."

"How do you have a name, then?"

"My father gave it to me. He was an official Hero of the Frontier Worlds who came home and died a shortie. The Instrumentality let people like that have names before they gave the privilege to everybody."

"What are you doing here?"

"Working." The doctor started to resume their walk. Rod did not feel much awe of him. He was such a shamelessly talkative person, the way most Earth men seemed to be, that it was hard not to be at ease with him.

Rod took Vomact's arm, gently. "There's more to it—"

"You know it," said Vomact. "You have good perceptions. Should I tell you?"

"Why not?" said Rod.

"You're my patient. It might not be fair to you."

"Go ahead," said Rod. "You ought to know I'm tough."

"I'm a criminal," said the doctor.

"But you're alive," said Rod. "In my world we kill criminals or we send them offplanet."

"I'm offplanet," said Vomact. "This isn't my world. For most of us here on Mars, this is a prison, not a home."

"What did you do?"

"It's too awful ..." said the doctor. "I'm ashamed of it myself They have sentenced me to conditional conditional."

Rod looked at him quickly. Momentarily he wondered whether he might be the victim of some outrageous deadpan joke. The doctor was serious; his face expressed bewilderment and grief.

"I revolted," said the doctor, "without knowing it. People can say anything they want on Earth, and they can print up to twenty copies of anything they need to print, but beyond that it's mass communications. Against the law. When the Rediscovery of Man came, they gave me the Spanish language to work on. I used a lot of research to get out *La Prensa.* Jokes, dialogues, imaginary advertisements, reports of what had happened in the ancient world. But then I got a bright idea. I went down to Earthport and got the news from incoming ships. What was happening here. What was happening there. You have no idea, Rod, how interesting mankind is! And the things we do ... so strange, so comical, so pitiable. The news even comes in on machines, all marked 'official use only.' I disregarded that and I printed up one issue with nothing but truth in it—a real issue, all facts.

"*I printed real news.*

"Rod, the roof fell in. All persons who had been reconditioned for Spanish were given stability tests. I was asked, did I know the law? Certainly, said I, I knew the law. No mass communications except within government. News is the mother of opinion, opinion the cause of mass delusion, delusion the source of war. The law was plain and I thought it did not matter. I thought it was just an old law.

"I was wrong, Rod, wrong. They did not charge me with violating the news laws. They charged me with revolt—against the Instrumentality. They sentenced me to death, immediately. Then they made it conditional, conditional on my going offplanet and behaving well. When I got here, they made it double conditional. If my act has no bad results. *But I can't find out.* I can go back to Earth any time. That part is no trouble. If they think my misdeed still has effect, they will give me the dream punishments or send me off to that awful planet somewhere. If they think it doesn't matter, they will restore my citizenship with a laugh. But they don't know the worst of it. My underman learned Spanish and the underpeople are keeping the newspaper going very secretly. I can't even imagine what they will do to me if they ever find out what has gone wrong and know that it was me who started it all. Do you think I'm wrong, Rod?"

Rod stared at him. He was not used to judging adults, particularly not at their own request. In Old North Australia, people kept their distance. There were fitting ways for doing everything, and one of the most fitting things was to deal only with people of your own age group.

He tried to be fair, to think in an adult way, and he said, "Of course I think you're wrong, Mister and Doctor Vomact. But you're not very wrong. None of us should trifle with war."

Vomact seized Rod's arm. The gesture was hysterical, almost ugly. "Rod," he whispered, very urgently, "you're rich. You come from an important family. Could you get me into Old North Australia?"

"Why not?" said Rod. "I can pay for all the visitors I want."

"No, Rod, I don't mean that. As an immigrant."

It was Rod's turn to become tense. "Immigrant?" he said. "The penalty for immigration is death. We're killing our own people right now, just to keep the population down. How do you think we could let outsiders settle with us? And the stroon. What about that?"

"Never mind, Rod," said Vomact. "I won't bother you again. I won't mention it again. It's a weary thing, to live many years with death ready to open the next door, ring the next bell, be on the next page of the message file. I haven't married. How could I?" With a whimsical turn of his vivacious mind and face, he was off on a cheerful track. "I have a medicine, Rod, a medicine for doctors, even for rebels. Do you know what it is?"

"A tranquilizer?" Rod was still shocked at the indecency of anyone mentioning immigration to a Norstrilian. He could not think straight.

"Work," said the little doctor. "That's my medicine."

"Work is always good," said Rod, feeling pompous at the generalization. The magic had gone out of the afternoon.

The doctor felt it too. He sighed. "I'll show you the old sheds which men from Earth first built. And then I'll go to work. Do you know what my main work is?"

"No," said Rod, politely.

"You," said Doctor Vomact, with one of his sad gay mischievous smiles. "You're well, but I've got to make you more than well. I've got to make you kill-proof."

They had reached the sheds.

The ruins might be old but they were not very impressive. They looked something like the homes on the more modest stations back on Norstrilia.

On their way back Rod said, very casually,

"What are you going to do to me, Sir and Doctor?"

"Anything you want," said Vomact lightly.

"Really, now. What?"

"Well," said Vomact, "the Lord Redlady sent along a whole cube of suggestions. Keep your personality. Keep your retinal and brain images. Change your appearance. Change your workwoman into a young man who looks just like your description."

"You can't do that to Eleanor. She's a citizen."

"Not here, not on Mars, she isn't. She's your baggage."

"But her legal rights!"

"This is Mars, Rod, but it's Earth territory. Under Earth law. Under the direct control of the Instrumentality. We can do these things all right. The hard thing is this: Would you consent to passing for an underman?"

"I never saw one. How would I know?" said Rod.

"Could you stand the shame of it?"

Rod laughed, by way of an answer.

Vomact sighed. "You're funny people, you Norstrilians. I'd rather die than be mistaken for an underman. The disgrace of it, the contempt! But the Lord Redlady said that you could walk into Earth as free as a breeze if we made you pass for a cat-man. I might as well tell you, Rod. Your wife is already here."

Rod stopped walking. "My wife? I have no wife."

"Your cat-wife," said the doctor. "Of course it isn't real marriage. Underpeople aren't allowed to have it. But they have a companionship which looks something like marriage and we sometimes slip and call them husband and wife. The Instrumentality has already sent a cat-girl out to be your 'wife.' She'll travel back to Earth with you from Mars. You'll just be a pair of lucky cats who've been doing dances and acrobatics for the bored station personnel here."

"And Eleanor?"

"I suppose somebody will kill her, thinking it's you. That's what you brought her for, isn't it? Aren't you rich enough?"

"No, no, no," said Rod, "nobody is that rich. We have to think of something else."

They spent the entire walk making new plans which would protect Eleanor and Rod both.

As they entered the shedport and took off their helmets, Rod said,

"This wife of mine, when can I see her?"

"You won't overlook her," said Vomact. "She's as wild as fire and twice as beautiful."

"Does she have a name?"

"Of course she does," said the doctor. "They all do."

"What is it, then?"

"C'mell."

HOSPITALITY AND ENTRAPMENT

People waited, here and there. If there had been worldwide news coverage, the population would have converged on Earthport with curiosity, passion, or greed. But *news* had been forbidden long before; people could know only the things which concerned them personally; the centers of Earth remained undisturbed. Here and there, as Rod made his trip from Mars to Earth, there were anticipations of the event. Overall, the world of Old Old Earth remained quiet, except for the perennial bubble of its inward problems.

On Earth, The Day of Rod's Flight, Within Earthport Itself

"They shut me out of the meeting this morning, when I'm in charge of visitors. That means that something is in the air," said Commissioner Teadrinker to his underman, B'dank.

B'dank, expecting a dull day, had been chewing his cud while sitting on his stool in the corner. He knew far more about the case than did his master, and he had learned his additional information from the secret sources of the underpeople, but he was resolved to betray nothing, to express nothing. Hastily he swallowed his cud and said, in his reassuring, calm bull voice:

"There might be some other reason, Sir and Master. If they were considering a promotion for you, they would leave you out of the meeting. You certainly deserve a promotion, Sir and Master."

"Are the spiders ready?" asked Teadrinker crossly.

"Who can tell the mind of a giant spider?" said B'dank calmly. "I talked to the foreman-spider for three hours yesterday with sign language. He wants twelve cases of beer. I told him I would give him more—he could have ten. The poor devil can't count, though he thinks he can, so he was pleased at having outbargained me. They will take the person you designate to the steeple of Earthport and they will hide that person so that the human being cannot be found for many hours. When I appear with the cases of beer, they will give me the person. I will then jump out of a window, holding the person in my arms. There are so few people who go down the outside of Earthport that they may not notice me at all. I will take the person to the ruined palace directly under Alpha Ralpha Boule-

103

vard, the one which you showed me, Sir and Master, and there I will keep the person in good order until you come and do the things which you have to do."

Teadrinker looked across the room. The big, florid, handsome face was so exasperatingly calm that it annoyed him. Teadrinker had heard that bull-men, because of their cattle origin, were sometimes subject to fits of uncontrollable frantic rage, but he had never seen the least sign of any such phenomenon in B'dank. He snapped,

"Aren't you worried?"

"Why should I worry, Sir and Master? You are doing the worrying for both of us."

"Go fry yourself!"

"That is not an operational instruction," said B'dank. "I suggest that the master eat something. That will calm his nerves. Nothing at all will happen today, and it is very hard for true men to wait for nothing at all. I have seen many of them get upset."

Teadrinker gritted his teeth at this extreme reasonableness. Nevertheless, he took a dehydrated banana out of his desk drawer and began chewing on it.

He looked sharply across at B'dank. "Do you want one of these things?"

B'dank slid off his chair with surprisingly smooth agility; he was at the desk, his enormous ham-sized hand held out, before he said,

"Yes, indeed, sir. I love bananas."

Teadrinker gave him one and then said, fretfully,

"Are you sure of the fact you never met the Lord Redlady?"

"Sure as any underman can be," said B'dank, munching the banana. "We never really know what has been put into our original conditioning, or who put it there. We're inferior and we're not supposed to know. It is forbidden even to inquire."

"So you admit that you might be a spy or agent of the Lord Redlady?"

"I might be, sir, but I do not feel like it."

"Do you know who Redlady is?"

"You have told me, sir, that he is the most dangerous human being in the whole galaxy."

"That's right," said Teadrinker, "and if I am running into something which the Lord Redlady has set up, I might as well cut up my throat before I start."

"It would be simpler, sir," said B'dank, "not to kidnap this Rod McBan at all. That is the only element of danger. If you did nothing, things would go on as they always have gone on—quietly, calmly."

"That's the horror and anxiety of it! They *do* always go on. Don't you think I want to get out of here, to taste power and freedom again?"

"You say so, sir," said B'dank, hoping that Teadrinker would offer him one more of those delicious dried bananas.

Teadrinker, distracted, did not.

He just walked up and down his room, desperate with the torment of hope, danger and delay.

Antechamber of the Bell and Bank

The Lady Johanna Gnade was there first. She was clean, well dressed, alert. The Lord Jestocost, who followed her in, wondered if she had any personal life at all. It was bad manners, among the Chiefs of the Instrumentality, to inquire into another Chief's personal affairs, even though the complete personal histories of each of them, kept up to the day and minute, was recorded in the computer cabinet in the corner. Jestocost knew, because he had peeped his own record, using another Chief's name, just so that he could see whether several minor illegalities of his had been recorded; they had been, all except for the biggest one—his deal with the cat-girl C'mell—which he had successfully kept off the recording screens. (The record simply showed him having a nap at the time.) If the Lady Johanna had any secrets, she kept them well.

"My Sir and Colleague," said she, "I suspect you of sheer inquisitiveness—a vice most commonly attributed to women."

"When we get as old as this, my lady, the differences in character between men and women become imperceptible. If, indeed, they ever existed in the first place. You and I are bright people and we each have a good nose for danger or disturbance. Isn't it likely we would both look up somebody with the impossible name of Roderick Frederick Ronald Arnold William MacArthur McBan to the hundred-and-fifty-first generation? See—I memorized all of it! Don't you think that was rather clever of me?"

"Rather," said she, in a tone which implied she didn't.

"I'm expecting him this morning."

"You are?" she asked, on a rising note which implied that there was something improper about his knowledge. "There's nothing about it in the messages."

"That's it," said the Lord Jestocost, smiling. "I arranged for Mars solar radiation to be carried two extra decimals until he left. This morning it's back down to three decimals. That means he's coming. Clever of me, wasn't it?"

"Too clever," she said. "Why ask me? I never thought you valued my opinion. Anyhow, why are you taking all these pains with the case? Why don't you just ship him out so far that it would take him a long lifetime, even with stroon, to get back here again?"

He looked at her evenly until she flushed. He said nothing.

"My—my comment was improper, I suppose," she stammered. "You and your sense of justice. You're always putting the rest of us in the wrong."

"I didn't mean to," he said mildly, "because I am just thinking of Earth. Did you know he owns this tower?"

"Earthport?" she cried. "Impossible."

"Not at all," said Jestocost. "I myself sold it to his agent ten days ago. For forty megacredits FOE money. That's more than we happen to have on Earth right now. When he deposited it, we began paying him three percent a year interest. And that wasn't all he bought from me. I sold him that ocean too, right there, the one the ancients called Atlantic. And I sold him three hundred thousand attractive underwomen trained in various tasks, together with the dower rights of seven hundred human women of appropriate ages."

"You mean you did all this to save the Earth treasury three megacredits a year?"

"Wouldn't you? Remember, this is FOE money."

She pursed her lips. Then she burst into a smile. "I never saw anyone else like you, my Lord Jestocost. You're the fairest man I ever knew and yet you never forget a little bit more in the way of earnings!"

"That's not the end of it," said he with a very crafty, pleased smile. "Did you read Amended (Reversionary) Schedule 711-19-13P, which you yourself voted for eleven days ago?"

"I looked at it," she said defensively. "We all did. It was something to do with Earth funds and Instrumentality funds. The Earth representative didn't complain. We all passed it because we trusted you."

"Do you know what it means?"

"Frankly, not at all. Does it have anything to do with this rich old man, McBan?"

"Don't be sure," said the Lord Jestocost, "that he's old. He might be young. Anyhow, the tax schedule raises taxes on kilocredits very slightly. Megacredit taxes are divided evenly between Earth and the Instrumentality, provided that the owner is not personally operating the property. It comes to one percent a month. That's the very small type in the footnote at the bottom of the seventh page of rates."

"You—you mean—" she gasped with laughter, "that by selling the poor man the Earth you are not only cutting him out of three percent interest a year, but you're charging him twelve percent taxes. Blessed rockets, man, you're weird. I love you. You're the cleverest, most ridiculous person we ever had as a Chief of the Instrumentality!" From the Lady Johanna Gnade, this was lurid language indeed. Jestocost did not know whether to be offended or pleased.

Since she was in a rare good humor, he dared to mention his half-secret project to her.

"Do you think, my lady, that if we have all this unexpected credit, we could waste a little of our stroon imports?"

Her laugh stopped. "On what?" she said sharply.

"On the underpeople. For the best of them."

"Oh, no. Oh, no! Not for the animals, while there are still *people* who suffer. You're mad to think of it, my Lord."

"I'm mad," he said. "I'm mad all right. Mad—for justice. And this strikes me as simple justice. I'm not asking for equal rights. Merely for a little more justice for them."

"They're *underpeople,*" she said blankly. "They're *animals.*" As though this comment settled the matter altogether.

"You never heard, did you, my lady, of the dog named Joan?" His question held a wealth of allusion.

She saw no depth in it, said flatly, "No," and went back to studying the agenda for the day.

Ten Kilometers Below the Surface of the Earth

The old engines turned like tides. The smell of hot oil was on them. Down here there were no luxuries. Life and flesh were cheaper than transistors; besides, they had much less radiation to be detected. In the groaning depths, the hidden and forgotten underpeople lived. They thought their chief, the E'telekeli, to be magical. Sometimes he thought so himself.

His white handsome face staring like a marble bust of immortality, his crumpled wings hugged closely to him in fatigue, he called to his first-egg child, the girl E'lamelanie,

"He comes, my darling."

"That one, father? The promised one."

"The rich one."

Her eyes widened. She was his daughter but she did not always understand his powers. "How do you know, father?"

"If I tell you the truth, will you agree to let me erase it from your mind right away, so there will be no danger of betrayal?"

"Of course, father."

"No," said the marble-faced bird-man, "you must say the right words..."

"I promise, father, that if you fill my heart with the truth, and if my joy at the truth is full, that I will yield to you my mind, my whole mind without fear, hope, or reservation, and that I will ask you to take from my mind whatever truth or parts of the truth might hurt our kind of people, in the Name of the First Forgotten One, in the Name of the Second Forgotten One, in the Name of the Third Forgotten One, and for the sake of D'joan whom we all love and remember!"

He stood. He was a tall man. His legs ended in the enormous feet of a bird, with white talons shimmering like mother of pearl. His humanoid hands stood forth from the joints of his wings; with them he extended the prehistoric gesture of blessing over her head, while he chanted the truth in a ringing hypnotic voice,

"Let the truth be yours, my daughter, that you may be whole and happy with the truth. Knowing the truth, my daughter, know freedom and the right to forget!

"The child, my child, who was your brother, the little boy you loved ..."

"Yeekasoose!" she said, her voice trance-like and childish.

"E'ikasus, whom you remember, was changed by me, his father, into the form of a small ape-man, so that the true people mistook him for an animal, not an underperson. They trained him as a surgeon and sent him to the Lord Redlady. He came with this young man McBan to Mars, where he met C'mell, whom I recommended to the Lord Jestocost for confidential errands. They are coming back with this man today. He has already bought the Earth, or most of it. Perhaps he will do us good. Do you know what you should know, my daughter?"

"Tell me, father, tell me. *How* do you know?"

"Remember the truth, girl, and then lose it! The messages come from Mars. We cannot touch the Big Blink or the message-coding machines, but each recorder has his own style. By a shift in the pace of his work, a friend can relay moods, emotions, ideas, and sometimes names. They have sent me words like 'riches, monkey, small, cat, girl, everything, good' by the pitch and speed of their recording. The human messages carry ours and no cryptographer in the world can find them.

"Now you know, and you will now now now *now* forget!"

He raised his hands again.

E'lamelanie looked at him normally with a happy smile. "It's so sweet and funny, daddy, but I know I've just forgotten something good and wonderful!"

Ceremonially he added, "Do not forget Joan."

Formally she responded, "I shall never forget Joan."

THE HIGH SKY FLYING

Rod walked to the edge of the little park. This was utterly unlike any ship he had ever seen or heard about in Norstrilia. There was no noise, no cramping, no sign of weapons—just a pretty little cabin which housed the controls, the Go-Captain, the Pinlighters, and the Stop-Captain, and then a stretch of incredible green grass. He had walked on this grass from the dusty ground of Mars. There was a puff and a whisper. A false blue sky, very beautiful, covered him like a canopy.

He felt strange. He had whiskers like a cat, forty centimeters long, growing out of his upper lip, about twelve whiskers to each side. The doctor had colored his eyes with bright green irises. His ears reached up to a point. He looked like a cat-man and he wore the professional clothing of an acrobat; C'mell did too.

He had not gotten over C'mell.

She made every woman in Old North Australia look like a sack of lard. She was lean, limber, smooth, menacing and beautiful; she was soft to the touch, hard in her motions, quick, alert, and cuddlesome. Her red hair blazed with the silkiness of animal fire. She spoke with a soprano which tinkled like wild bells. Her ancestors and ancestresses had been bred to produce the most seductive girl on Earth. The task had succeeded. Even in repose, she was voluptuous. Her wide hips and sharp eyes invited the masculine passions. Her catlike dangerousness challenged every man whom she met. The true men who looked at her knew that she was a cat, and still could not keep their eyes off her. Human women treated her as though she were something disgraceful. She traveled as an acrobat, but she had already told Rod McBan confidentially that she was by profession a "girlygirl," a female animal, shaped and trained like a person to serve as hostess to offworld visitors, required by law and custom to invite their love, while promised the penalty of death if she accepted it.

Rod liked her, though he had been painfully shy with her at first. There was no side to her, no posh, no swank. Once she got down to business, her incredible body faded part way into the background, though with the sides of his eyes he could never quite forget it. It was her mind, her intelligence, her humor and good humor, which carried them across the hours and days they spent together. He found himself trying to im-

press her that he was a grown man, only to discover that in the spontane-
ous, sincere affections of her quick cat heart she did not care in the least
what his status was. He was simply her partner and they had work to do
together. It was his job to stay alive and it was her job to keep him alive.

Doctor Vomact had told him not to speak to the other passengers, not
to say anything to each other, and to call for silence if any of them spoke.

There were ten other passengers who stared at one another in uncomfortable amazement.

Ten in number, they were.

All ten of them were Rod McBan.

Ten identical Roderick Frederick Ronald Arnold William MacArthur
McBans to the one hundred and fifty-first, all exactly alike. Apart from
C'mell herself and the little monkey-doctor, A'gentur, the only person on
the ship who was *not* Rod McBan was Rod McBan himself. He had become the cat-man. The others seemed, each by himself, to be persuaded
that he alone was Rod McBan and that the other nine were parodies.
They watched each other with a mixture of gloom and suspicion mixed
with amusement, just as the real Rod McBan would have done, had he
been in their place.

"One of them," said Doctor Vomact in parting, "is your companion
Eleanor from Norstrilia. The other nine are mouse-powered robots. They're
all copied from you. Good, eh?" He could not conceal his professional
satisfaction.

And now they were all about to see Earth together.

C'mell took Rod to the edge of the little world and said gently, "I want
to sing 'The Tower Song' to you, just before we shut down on the top of
Earthport." And in her wonderful voice she sang the strange little old
song,

And oh! my love, for you.
High birds crying, and a
High sky flying, and a
High wind driving, and a
High heart striving, and a
High brave place for you!

Rod felt a little funny, standing there, looking at nothing, but he also
felt pleasant with the girl's head against his shoulder and his arm enfold-
ing her. She seemed not only to need him, but to trust him very deeply.
She did not feel adult—not self-important and full of unexplained business. She was merely a girl, and for the time *his* girl. It was pleasant and
it gave him a strange foretaste of the future.

The day might come when he would have a permanent girl of his own, facing not a day, but life, not a danger, but destiny. He hoped that he could be as relaxed and fond with that future girl as he was with C'mell.

C'mell squeezed his hand, as though in warning.

He turned to look at her but, she stared ahead and nodded with her chin.

"Keep watching," she said, "straight ahead. Earth."

He looked back at the blank artificial sky of the ship's force-field. It was a monotonous but pleasant blue, conveying depths which were not really there.

The change was so fast that he wondered whether he had really seen it.

In one moment the clear flat blue.

Then the false sky splashed apart as though it had literally been slashed into enormous ribbons, ribbons in their turn becoming blue spots and disappearing.

Another blue sky was there—Earth's.

Manhome.

Rod breathed deeply. It was hard to believe. The sky itself was not so different from the false sky which had surrounded the ship on its trip from Mars, but there was an aliveness and wetness to it, unlike any other sky he had ever heard about.

It was not the sight of the Earth which surprised him—it was the smell. He suddenly realized that Old North Australia must smell dull, flat, dusty to Earthmen. This Earth air smelled alive. There were the odors of plants, of water, of things which he could not even guess. The air was coded with a million years of memory. In this air his people had swum to manhood, before they conquered the stars. The wetness was not the cherished damp of one of his covered canals. It was wild free moisture which came laden with the indications of things living, dying, sprawling, squirming, loving with an abundance which no Norstrilian could understand. No wonder the descriptions of Earth had always seemed fierce and exaggerated! What was stroon that men would pay water for it—water, the giver and carrier of life. This *was* his home, no matter how many generations his people had lived in the twisted hells of Paradise VII or the dry treasures of Old North Australia. He took a deep breath, feeling the plasma of Earth pour into him, the quick effluvium which had made man. He smelled Earth again—it would take a long lifetime, even with stroon, before a man could understand all these odors which came all the way up to the ship, which hovered, as planoforming ships usually did not, twenty-odd kilometers above the surface of the planet.

There was something strange in this air, something sweet-clear to the nostrils, refreshing to the spirit. One great beautiful odor overrode all the others. What could it be? He sniffed and then said, very clearly, to himself,

"Salt!"

C'mell reminded him that he was beside her.

"Do you like it, C'rod?"

"Yes, yes, it's better than—" Words failed him. He looked at her. Her eager, pretty, comradely smile made him feel that she was sharing every milligram of his delight. "But why," he asked, "do you waste salt on the air? What good does it do?"

"Salt?"

"Yes—in the air. So rich, so wet, so salty. Is it to clean the ship some way that I do not understand?"

"Ship? We're not on the ship, C'rod. This is the landing roof of Earth-port."

He gasped.

No ship? There was not a mountain on Old North Australia more than six kilometers above MGL—mean ground level—and those mountains were all smooth, worn, old, folded by immense eons of wind into a gentle blanketing that covered his whole home world.

He looked around.

The platform was about two hundred meters long by one hundred wide.

The ten "Rod McBans" were talking to some men in uniform. Far at the other side a steeple rose into eye-catching height—perhaps a whole half-kilometer. He looked down.

There it was—Old Old Earth.

The treasure of water reached before his very eyes—water by the millions of tons, enough to feed a galaxy of sheep, to wash an infinity of men. The water was broken by a few islands on the far horizon to the right.

"Hesperides," said C'mell, following the direction of his gaze. "They came up from the sea when the Daimoni built this for us. For people, I mean. I shouldn't say 'us.' "

He did not notice the correction. He stared at the sea. Little specks were moving in it, very slowly. He pointed at one of them with his finger and asked C'mell,

"Are those wethouses?"

"What did you call them?"

"Houses which are wet. Houses which sit on water. Are those some of them?"

"Ships," she said, not spoiling his fun with a direct contradiction. "Yes, those are ships."

"Ships?" he cried. "You'd never get one of those into space. Why call them ships then?"

Very gently C'mell explained, "People had ships for water before they had ships for space. I think the Old Common Tongue takes the word for space vessel from the things you are looking at."

"I want to see a city," said Rod. "Show me a city."

"It won't look like much from here. We're too high up. Nothing looks like much from the top of Earthport. But I can show you, anyhow. Come over here, dear."

When they walked away from the edge, Rod realized that the little monkey was still with them. "What are you doing here with us?" asked Rod, not unkindly.

The monkey's preposterous little face wrinkled into a knowing smile. The face was the same as it had been before, but the expression was different—more assured, more clear, more purposive than ever before. There was even humor and cordiality in the monkey's voice.

"We animals are waiting for the people to finish their entrance."

We animals? thought Rod. He remembered his furry head, his pointed ears, his cat-whiskers. No wonder he felt at ease with this girl and she with him.

The ten Rod McBans were walking down a ramp, so that the floor seemed to be swallowing them slowly from the feet up. They were walking in single file, so that the head of the leading one seemed to sit bodiless on the floor, while the last one in line had lost nothing more than his feet. It was odd indeed.

Rod looked at C'mell and A'gentur and asked them frankly, "When people have such a wide, wet, beautiful world, all full of life, why should they kill me?"

A'gentur shook his monkey head sadly, as though he knew full well, but found the telling of it inexpressibly wearisome and sad.

C'mell answered, "You are who you are. You hold immense power. Do you know that this tower is yours?"

"Mine!" he cried.

"You've bought it, or somebody bought it for you. Most of that water is yours, too. When you have things that big, people ask you for things. Or they take them from you. Earth is a beautiful place but I think it is a dangerous place, too, for offworlders like you who are used to just one way of life. You have not caused all the crime and meanness in the world, but it's been sleeping and now wakes up for you."

"Why for me?"

"Because," said A'gentur, "you're the richest person who has ever touched this planet. You own most of it already. Millions of human lives depend on your thoughts and your decisions."

They had reached the opposite side of the top platforms. Here, on the land side, the rivers were all leaking badly. Most of the land was covered with steamclouds, such as they saw on Norstrilia when a covered canal burst out of its covering. These clouds represented incalculable treasures of rain. He saw that they parted at the foot of the tower.

"Weather machines," said C'mell. "The cities are all covered with weather machines. Don't you have weather machines in Old North Australia?"

"Of course we do," said Rod, "but we don't waste water by letting it float around in the open air like that. It's pretty, though. I guess the extravagance of it makes me feel critical. Don't you Earth people have anything better to do with your water than to leave it lying on the ground or having it float over open land?"

"We're not Earth people," said C'mell. "We're underpeople. I'm a cat-person and he's made from apes. Don't call us people. It's not decent."

"Fudge!" said Rod. "I was just asking a question about Earth, not pestering your feelings when—"

He stopped short.

They all three spun around.

Out of the ramp there came something like a mowing machine. A human voice, a man's voice, screamed from within it, expressing rage and fear.

Rod started to move forward.

C'mell held his arm, dragging back with all her weight.

"No! Rod, no! No!"

A'gentur slowed him down better by jumping into his face, so that Rod suddenly saw nothing but a universe of brown belly-fur and felt tiny hands gripping his hair and pulling it. He stopped and reached for the monkey. A'gentur anticipated him and dropped to the ground before Rod could hit him.

The machine was racing up the outside of the steeple and almost disappearing into the sky above. The voice had become thin.

Rod looked at C'mell. "All right. What was it? What's happening?"

"That's a spider, a giant spider. It's kidnapping or killing Rod McBan."

"Me?" keened Rod. "It'd better not touch me. I'll tear it apart."

"Sh-h-h!" said C'mell.

"Quiet!" said the monkey.

"Don't *'sh-h-h'* me and don't 'quiet' me," said Rod. "I'm not going to let that poor blighter suffer on my account. Tell that thing to come down. What is it, anyhow, this spider? A robot?"

"No," said C'mell, "an insect."

Rod was narrowing his eyes, watching the mowing machine which hung on the outside of the tower. He could barely see the man within its grip. When C'mell said "insect," it triggered something in his mind. Hate. Revulsion. Resistance to dirt. Insects on Old North Australia were small, serially numbered and licensed. Even at that, he felt them to be his hereditary enemies. (Somebody had told him that Earth insects had done terrible things to the Norstrilians when they lived on Paradise VII.) Rod yelled at the spider, making his voice as loud as possible,

"You—come—down!"

The filthy thing on the tower quivered with sheer smugness and seemed to bring its machine-like legs closer together, settling down to be comfortable.

Rod forgot he was supposed to be a cat.

He gasped for air. Earth air was wet but thin. He closed his eyes for a moment or two. He thought hate, hate, hate for the insect. Then he shrieked telepathically, louder than he had ever shrieked at home:

> hate-spit-spit-vomit!
> dirt, dirt, dirt,
> explode!
> crush:
> ruin:
> stink, collapse, putrefy, disappear!
> hate-hate-hate!

The fierce red roar of his inarticulate spieking hurt even him. He saw the little monkey fall to the ground in a dead faint. C'mell was pale and looked as though she might throw up her food.

He looked away from them and up at the "spider." Had he reached it? He had.

Slowly, slowly, the long legs moved out in spasm, releasing the man, whose body flashed downward. Rod's eyes followed the movement of "Rod McBan" and he cringed when a wet crunch let him know that the duplicate of his own body had been splashed all over the hard deck of the tower, a hundred meters away. He glanced back up at the "spider." It scrabbled for purchase on the tower and then cartwheeled downward. It too hit the deck hard and lay there dying, its legs twitching as its personality slipped into its private, everlasting night.

Rod gasped. "Eleanor. Oh, maybe that's Eleanor!" His voice wailed. He started to run to the facsimile of his human body, forgetting that he was a cat-man.

C'mell's voice was as sharp as a howl, though low in tone. "Shut up!

Shut up! Stand still! Close your mind! Shut up! We're dead if you don't shut up!"

He stopped, stared at her stupidly. Then he saw she was in mortal earnest. He complied. He stopped moving. He did not try to talk. He capped his mind, closed himself against telepathy until his brainbox began to ache. The little monkey, A'gentur, was crawling up off the floor, looking shaken and sick. C'mell was still pale.

Men came running up the ramp, saw them, and headed toward them. There was the beat of wings in the air.

An enormous bird—no, it was an ornithopter—landed with its claws scratching the deck. A uniformed man jumped out and cried,

"Where is he?"

"He jumped over!" C'mell shouted.

The man started to follow the direction of her gesture and then cut sharply back to her.

"Fool!" he said. "People can't jump off here. The barrier would hold ships in place. What did you see?"

C'mell was a good actress. She pretended to be getting over shock and gasping for words. The uniformed man looked at her haughtily.

"Cats," he said, "and a monkey. What are you doing here? Who are you?"

"Name C'mell, profession, girlygirl, Earthport staff, commanded by Commissioner Teadrinker. This—boyfriend, no status, name C'roderick, cashier in night bank down below. Him?" She nodded at A'gentur. "I don't know much about him."

"Name A'gentur. Profession, supplementary surgeon. Status, animal. I'm not an underperson. Just an animal. I came in on the ship from Mars with the dead man there and some other true men who looked like him, and they went down first—"

"Shut up," said the uniformed man. He turned to the approaching men and said, "Honored Subchief, Sergeant 387 reporting. The user of the telepathic weapon has disappeared. The only things here are these two cat-people, not very bright, and a small monkey. They can talk. The girl says she saw somebody get off the tower."

The subchief was a tall redhead with a uniform even handsomer than the sergeant's. He snapped at C'mell, "How did he do it?"

Rod knew C'mell well enough by now to recognize the artfulness of her becoming confused, feminine and incoherent—in appearance. Actually, she was in full control of the situation. Said she, babbling:

"He jumped, I think. I don't know how."

"That's impossible," said the subchief. "Did you see where he went?" he barked at Rod McBan.

Rod gasped at the suddenness of the question: besides, C'mell had told him to keep quiet. Between these two peremptories, he said, "Er—ah—oh—you see—"

The little monkey-surgeon interrupted drily, "Sir and Master Subchief, that cat-man is not very bright. I do not think you will get much out of him. Handsome but stupid. Strictly breeding stock—"

Rod gagged and turned a little red at these remarks, but he could tell from the hooded quick glare which C'mell shot him that she wanted him to go on being quiet.

She cut in. "I did notice one thing, Master. It might matter."

"By the Bell and Bank, animal! Tell me!" cried the subchief. "Stop deciding what I ought to know!"

"The strange man's skin was lightly tinged with blue."

The subchief took a step back. His soldiers and the sergeant stared at him. In a serious, direct way he said to C'mell, "Are you *sure?*"

"No, my Master. I just thought so."

"You saw just one?" barked the subchief.

Rod, overacting the stupidity, held up four fingers.

"That idiot," cried the subchief, "thinks he saw four of them. Can he count?" he asked C'mell.

C'mell looked at Rod as though he were a handsome beast with not a brain in his head. Rod looked back at her, deliberately letting himself feel stupid. This was something which he did very well, since by neither hiering nor spieking at home, he had had to sit through interminable hours of other people's conversation when he was little, never getting the faintest idea of what it was all about. He had discovered very early that if he sat still and looked stupid, people did not bother him by trying to bring him into the conversation, turning their voices on and braying at him as though he were deaf. He tried to simulate the familiar old posture and was rather pleased that he could make such a good showing with C'mell watching him. Even when she was seriously fighting for their freedom and playing girl all at once, her corona of blazing hair made her shine forth like the sun of Earth itself; among all these people on the platform, her beauty and her intelligence made her stand out, cat though she was. Rod was not at all surprised that he was overlooked, with such a vivid personality next to him; he just wished that he could be overlooked a little more, so that he could wander over idly and see whether the body was Eleanor's or one of the robot's. If Eleanor had already died for him, in her first few minutes of the big treat of seeing Earth, he felt that he would never forgive himself as long as he lived.

The talk about the blue men amused him deeply. They existed in Norstrilian folklore, as a race of faraway magicians who, through science or hypnotism, could render themselves invisible to other men whenever they wished. Rod had never talked with an Old North Australian security officer about the problem of guarding the stroon treasure from attacks by invisible men, but he gathered, from the way people told stories of blue men, that they had either failed to show up on Norstrilia or that the Norstrilian authorities did not take them very seriously. He was amazed that the Earth people did not bring in a couple of first-class telepaths and have them sweep the deck of the tower for every living thing, but to judge by the chatter of voices that was going on, and the peering with eyes which occurred, Earth people had fairly weak senses and did not get things done promptly and efficiently.

The question about Eleanor was answered for him.

One of the soldiers joined the group, waited after saluting, and was finally allowed to interrupt C'mell's and A'gentur's endless guessing as to how many blue men there might have been on the tower, if there had been any at all.

The subchief nodded at the soldier, who said,

"Beg to report, Sir and Subchief, the body is not a body. It is just a robot which looks like a person."

The day brightened immeasurably within Rod's heart. Eleanor was safe, somewhere further down in this immense tower.

The comment seemed to decide the young officer. "Get a sweeping machine and a looking dog," he commanded the sergeant, "and see to it that this whole area is swept and looked down to the last square millimeter."

"It is done," said the soldier.

Rod thought this an odd remark, because nothing at all had been done yet.

The subchief issued another command: "Turn on the kill-spotters before we go down the ramp. Any identity which is not perfectly clear must be killed automatically by the scanning device. Including us," he added to his men. "We don't want any blue men walking right down into the tower among us."

C'mell suddenly and rather boldly stepped up to the officer and whispered in his ear. His eyes rolled as he listened, he blushed a little, and then changed his orders: "Cancel the kill-spotters. I want this whole squad to stand body-to-body. I'm sorry, men, but you're going to have to touch these underpeople for several minutes. I want them to stand so close to us that we can be sure there is nobody extra sneaking into our group."

(C'mell later told Rod that she had confessed to the young officer that she might be a mixed type, part human and part animal, and that she was the special girlygirl of two off-Earth magnates of the Instrumentality. She said she *thought* that she had a definite identity but was not sure, and that the kill-spotters might destroy her if she did not yield a correct image as she went past them. They would, she told Rod later, have caught any underman passing as a man, or any man passing as an underman, and would have killed the victim by intensifying the magnetic layout of his own organic body. These machines were dangerous things to pass, since they occasionally killed normal, legitimate people and underpeople who merely failed to provide a clear focus.)

The officer took the left forward corner of the living rectangle of people and underpeople. They formed tight ranks. Rod felt the two soldiers next to him shudder as they came into contact with his "cat" body. They kept their faces averted from him as though he smelled bad for them. Rod said nothing; he just looked forward and kept his expression pleasantly stupid.

What followed next was surprising. The men walked in a strange way, all of them moving their left legs in unison, and then their right legs. A'gentur could not possibly do this, so with a nod of the sergeant's approval, C'mell picked him up and carried him close to her bosom. Suddenly, weapons flared.

These, thought Rod, *must be cousins of the weapons which the Lord Redlady carried a few weeks ago, when he landed his ship on my property.* (He remembered Hopper, his knife quivering like the head of a snake, threatening the life of the Lord Redlady; and he remembered the sudden silent burst, the black oily smoke, and the gloomy Bill looking at the chair where his pal had existed a moment before.)

These weapons showed a little light, just a little, but their force was betrayed by the buzzing of the floor and the agitation of the dust.

"Close in, men! Right up to your own feet! Don't let a blue man through!" shouted the subchief.

The men complied.

The air began to smell funny and burned.

The ramp was clear of life except for their own.

When the ramp swung around a corner, Rod gasped.

This was the most enormous room he had ever seen. It covered the entire top of Earthport. He could not even begin to guess how many hectares it was, but a small farm could have been accommodated on it. There were few people there. The men broke ranks at a command of the subchief. The officer glared at the cat-man Rod, the cat-girl C'mell and the ape A'gentur.

"You stand right where you are till I come back!"

They stood, saying nothing.

C'mell and A'gentur took the place for granted.

Rod stared as though he would drink up the world with his eyes. In this one enormous room, there was more antiquity and wealth than all Old North Australia possessed. Curtains of an incredibly rich material shimmered down from the thirty-meter ceiling; some of them seemed to be dirty and in bad repair, but any one of them, after paying the twenty million percent import duty, would cost more than any Old North Australian could afford to pay. There were chairs and tables here and there, some of them good enough to deserve a place in the Museum of Man on New Mars. Here they were merely used. The people did not seem any the happier for having all this wealth around them. For the first time, Rod got a glimpse of what the spartan self-imposed poverty had done to make life worthwhile at home. His people did not have much, when they could have chartered endless argosies of treasure, inbound from all worlds to their own planet, in exchange for the life-prolonging stroon. But if they had been heaped with treasure they would have appreciated nothing and would have ended up possessing nothing. He thought of his own little collection of hidden antiquities. Here on Earth it would not have filled a dustbin, but in the Station of Doom it would afford him connoisseurship as long as he lived.

The thought of his home made him wonder what Old Hot and Simple, the Hon. Sec., might be doing with his adversary on Earth. "It's a long, long way to reach here!" he thought to himself.

C'mell drew his attention by plucking at his arm.

"Hold me," commanded she, "because I am afraid I might fall down and Yeekasoose is not strong enough to hold me."

Rod wondered who Yeekasoose might be, when only the little monkey A'gentur was with them; he also wondered why C'mell should need to be held. Norstrilian discipline had taught him not to question orders in an emergency. He held her.

She suddenly slumped as though she had fainted or had gone to sleep. He held her with one arm and with his free hand he tipped her head against his shoulder so that she would look as though she were weary and affectionate, not unconscious. It was pleasant to hold her little female body, which felt fragile and delicate beyond belief. Her hair, disarrayed and windblown, still carried the smell of the salty sea air which had so surprised him an hour ago. She herself, he thought, was the greatest treasure of Earth which he had yet seen. But suppose he did have her? What could he do with her in Old North Australia? Underpeople were completely forbidden, except for military uses under the exclusive control of the Commonwealth government. He could not imagine C'mell directing a mowing machine as she walked across a giant sheep, shearing it. The idea of her sitting up all night with a lonely or frightened sheep-monster was itself ridiculous. She was a playgirl, an ornament in human form; for such as her, there was no place under the comfortable grey skies of home. Her beauty would fade in the dry air; her intricate mind would turn sour with the weary endlessness of a farm culture: property, responsibility, defense, self-reliance, sobriety. New Melbourne would look like a collection of rude shacks to her.

He realized that his feet were getting cold. Up on the deck they had had sunlight to keep them warm, even though the chill salty wet air of Earth's marvelous "seas" was blowing against them. Here, inside, it was merely high and cold, while still wet; he had never encountered *wet* cold before, and it was a strangely uncomfortable experience.

C'mell came to and shook herself to wakefulness just as they saw the officer walking toward them from the other end of the immense room.

Later, she told Rod what she had experienced when she lapsed into unconsciousness.

First, she had had a call which she could not explain. This had made her warn Rod. "Yeekasoose" was, of course E'ikasus, the real name of the "monkey" which he called A'gentur.

Then, as she felt herself swimming away into half-sleep with Rod's strong arm around her, she had heard trumpets playing, just two or three of them, playing different parts to the same intricate, lovely piece of music, sometimes in solos, sometimes together. If a human or robot telepath had peeped her mind while she listened to the music, the impression would have been that of a perceptive c'girl who had linked herself with one of the many telepathic entertainment channels which filled the space of Earth itself.

Last, there came the messages. They were not encoded in the music in any way whatever. The music caused the images to form in her mind because she was C'mell, herself, unique, individual. Particular fugues or even individual notes reached into her memory and emotions, causing her mind to bring up old, half-forgotten associations. First she thought of "High birds flying..." as in the song which she had sung to Rod. Then she saw eyes, piercing eyes which blazed with knowledge while they stayed moist with humility. Then she smelled the strange odors of Downdeep-downdeep, the work-city where the underpeople maintained the civilization on the surface and where some illegal underpeople lurked, overlooked by the authority of Man. Finally she saw Rod himself, striding off the deck with his loping Norstrilian walk. It added up simply. She was to bring Rod to the forgotten, forlorn, forbidden chambers of the Nameless One, and to do so promptly. The music in her head stopped, and she woke up.

The officer arrived.

He looked at them inquisitively and angrily. "This whole business is funny. The Acting Commissioner does not believe that there are any blue men. We've all heard of them. And yet we know somebody set off a telepathic emotion-bomb. That rage! Half the people in this room fell down when it went off. Those weapons are completely prohibited for use inside the Earth's atmosphere."

He cocked his head at them.

C'mell remained prudently silent, Rod practiced looking thoroughly stupid, and A'gentur looked like a bright, helpless little monkey.

"Funnier still," said the officer, "the Acting Commissioner got orders to let you go. He got them while he was chewing me out. How does anybody know that you underpeople are here? Who are you, anyhow?"

He looked at them with curiosity for a minute, but then the curiosity faded with the pressure of his lifelong habits.

He snapped, "Who cares? Get along. Get out. You're underpeople and you're not allowed to stand in this room, anyhow."

He turned his back on them and walked away.

"Where are we going?" whispered Rod, hoping C'mell would say that he could go down to the surface and see Old Earth itself.

"Down to the bottom of the world, and then—" she bit her lip "...and then, much further down. I have instructions."

"Can't I take an hour and look at Earth?" asked Rod. "You stay with me, of course."

"When death is jumping around us like wild sparks? Of course not. Come along, Rod. You'll get your freedom some time soon, if somebody doesn't kill you first. Yeekasoose, you lead the way!"

They walked toward a dropshaft.

When Rod looked down it, the sight made him dizzy. Only the sight of people floating up and down in it made him realize that this was some Earth device which his people did not have in Old North Australia.

"Take a belt," said C'mell quietly. "Do it as though you were used to it."

He looked around. Only after she had taken a canvas belt, about fifteen centimeters wide, and was cinching it to her waist, did he see what she meant. He took one too and put it on. They waited while A'gentur ran up and down the racks of belts, looking for one small enough to fit him. C'mell finally helped him by taking one of normal size and looping it around his waist twice before she hooked it.

"Magnetic," she murmured. "For the dropshafts."

They did not take the main dropshaft.

"That's for people only," said C'mell.

The underpeople dropshaft was the same, except that it did not have the bright lights, the pumping of fresh air, the labeling of the levels, and the entertaining pictures to divert the passengers as they went up and down. This dropshaft, moreover, seemed to have more cargo than people in it. Huge boxes, bales, bits of machines, furniture and inexplicable bundles, each tied with magnetic belts and each guided by an underperson, floated up and down in the mysterious ever busy traffic of Old Earth.

DISCOURSES AND RECOURSES

Rod McBan, disguised as a cat, floated down the dropshaft to the strangest encounter which could have befallen any man of his epoch. C'mell floated down beside him. She clenched her skirt between her knees, so that it would not commit immodesties. A'gentur, his monkey hand lightly on C'mell's shoulder, loved her soft red hair as it stood and moved with the updraft which they themselves created; he looked forward to becoming E'ikasus again and he admired C'mell deeply, but love between the different strains of underpeople was necessarily platonic. Physiologically they could not breed outside their own stock, and emotionally they found it hard to mesh deeply with the empathic needs of another form of life, however related it might be. E'ikasus therefore very truly and deeply wanted C'mell for his friend, and nothing more.

While they moved downward in relative peace, other people were concerned about them on various worlds.

Old North Australia, Administrative Offices of the Commonwealth, The Same Day

"You, former Hon. Sec. of this government, are charged with going outside the limits of your onseckish duties and of attempting to commit mayhem or murder upon the person of one of Her Absent Majesty's subjects, the said subject being Roderick Frederick Ronald Arnold William MacArthur McBan to the one-hundred-and-fifty-first generation; and you are further charged with the abuse of an official instrument of this Commonwealth government in designing and encompassing the said unlawful purpose, to wit, one mutated sparrow, serial number 0919487, specialty number 2328525, weighing forty-one kilograms, and having a monetary value of 685 minicredits. What say you?"

Houghton Syme CXLIX buried his face in his hands and sobbed.

The Cabin of the Station of Doom, At the Same Time

"Aunt Doris, he's dead, he's dead, he's dead. I feel it."

"Nonsense, Lavinia. He may be in trouble and we might not know. But with all that money, the government or the Instrumentality would use the Big Blink to send word of the change in status of this property. I don't mean to sound cold-hearted, girl, but when there is this much property at stake, people act rapidly."

"He is *so* dead."

Doris was not one to discount the telepathic arts. She remembered how the Australians had gotten off the incarnate fury of Paradise VII. She went over to the cupboard and took from it a strangely tinted jar. "Do you know what this is?" said she to Lavinia.

The girl forced a smile past her desperate inward feelings. "Yes," she said. "Ever since I was no bigger than a mini-elephant, people have told me that jar was 'do not touch.'"

"Good girl, then, if you haven't touched it!" said Aunt Doris drily. "It's a mixture of stroon and Paradise VII honey."

"Honey?" cried Lavinia. "I thought no one ever went back to that horrible place."

"Some do," said Aunt Doris. "It seems that some Earth forms have taken over and are still living there. Including bees. The honey has powers on the human mind. It is a strong hypnotic. We mix it with stroon to make sure it is safe."

Aunt Doris put a small spoon into the jar, lifted, spun the spoon to pick up the threads of heavy honey, and handed the spoon to Lavinia. "Here," said she, "take this and lick it off. Swallow it all down."

Lavinia hesitated and then obeyed. When the spoon was clean she licked her lips and handed the clean spoon back to Aunt Doris, who put it aside for washing up.

Aunt Doris ceremoniously put the jar back on the high shelf of the cupboard, locked the cupboard, and put the key in the pocket of her apron.

"Let's sit outside," said she to Lavinia.

"When's it going to happen?"

"When's what going to happen?"

"The trance—the visions—whatever this stuff brings on?"

Doris laughed her weary rational laugh. "Oh, that! Sometimes nothing at all happens. In any event, it won't hurt you, girl. Let's sit on the bench. I'll tell you if you start looking strange to me."

They sat on the bench, doing nothing. Two police ornithopters, flying just under the forever grey clouds, quietly watched the Station of Doom. They had been doing this ever since Rod's computer showed him how to win all that money: the fortune was still piling up, almost faster than it could be computed. The bird-engines were lazy and beautiful as they flew. The operators had synchronized the flapping of the two sets of wings, so that they looked like rukhs doing a ballet. The effect caught the eyes of both Lavinia and Aunt Doris.

Lavinia suddenly spoke in a clear, sharp, demanding voice, quite unlike her usual tone: "It's all mine, isn't it?"

Doris breathed softly, "What, my dear?"

"The Station of Doom. I'm one of the heiresses, anyhow, aren't I?" Lavinia pursed her lips in a proud prim smug smile which would have humiliated her if she had been in her right mind.

Aunt Doris said nothing. She nodded silently.

"If I marry Rod I'll be Missus and Owner McBan, the richest woman who ever lived. But if I do marry him, he'll hate me, because he'll think it's for his money and his power. But I've loved Rod, loved him specially because he couldn't hier or spiek. I've always known that he would need me someday, not like my Daddy, singing his crazy sad proud songs forever and ever! But how can I marry him now...?"

Whispered Doris, very gently, very insinuatingly: "Look for Rod, my dear. Look for Rod in that part of your mind which thought he was dead. Look for Rod, Lavinia, look for Rod."

Lavinia laughed happily, and it was the laugh of a small child.

She stared at her feet, at the sky, at Doris—looking right through her.

Her eyes seemed to clear. When she spoke, it was in her normal adult voice:

"I see Rod. Someone has changed him into a cat-man, just like the pictures we've seen of underpeople. And there's a girl with him—a girl, Doris—and I can't be jealous of him being with her. She is the most beautiful thing that ever lived on any world. You ought to see her hair, Doris. You ought to see her hair. It is like a bushel of beautiful fire. Is that Rod? I don't know. I can't tell. I can't see." She sat on the bench, looking straight at Doris and seeing nothing, but weeping copiously.

Aunt Doris started to get up; it was about time for the poor thing to be led to her bed, so that she could sleep off the hypnotic of Paradise VII.

But Lavinia spoke again. "I see them too."

"Who?" said Aunt Doris, not much interested, now that they had found their information about Rod. Doris never mentioned the matter to any masculine person, but she was a deeply superstitious person who found great satisfaction in tampering with the preternatural, but even in these ventures she kept the turn of mind, essentially practical, which had characterized her whole life. Thus, when Lavinia stumbled on the greatest secret of the contemporary universe, she made no note of it. She told no one about it, then or later.

Lavinia insisted, "I see the proud pale people with strong hands and white eyes. The ones who built the palace of the Governor of Night."

"That's nice," said Aunt Doris, "but it is time for your nap ..."

"Goodbye, dear people..." said Lavinia, a little drunkenly.

She had glimpsed the Daimoni in their home world.

Aunt Doris, unheeding, stood up and took Lavinia's arm, leading her

away to rest. Nothing remained of the Daimoni, except for a little song
which Lavinia found herself making up a few weeks later, not knowing
whether she had dreamed some such thing or had read it in a book:

Oh, you will see, you will see
Them striding fair, oh fair and free!
Down garden paths of silver grass
Past flowing rivers,
Their hair pushed back
By fingers of the wind.

And you will know them
By their blank white faces,
Expressionless, removed,
All lines smoothed,
As they stride on in the night
Toward their unimaginable goals ....

Thus came news of Rod, unreported, unrepeated; thus passed the glimpse
of the Daimoni in their star-hidden home.

At the Beach of Meeya Meefla, The Same Day

"Father, you can't be here. You never come here!"

"But I have," said Lord William Not-from-here. "And it's important."

"Important?" laughed Ruth. "Then it's not me. I'm not important.
Your work up there is." She looked toward the rim of the Earthport, which
floated, distinct and circular, beyond the crests of some faraway clouds.

The overdressed lord squatted incongruously on the sand.

"Listen, girl," said he slowly and emphatically, "I've never asked much
of you but I am asking now."

"Yes, father," she said, a little frightened by this totally unaccustomed
air: her father was usually playfully casual with her, and equally usually
forgot her ten seconds after he got through talking to her.

"Ruth, you know we are Old North Australians?"

"We're rich, if that's what you mean. Not that it matters, the way
things go."

"I'm not talking about riches now, I'm talking about home, and I
mean it!"

"Home? We never had a home, father."

"Norstrilia!" he snarled at her.

"I never saw it, father. Nor did you. Nor your father. Nor great-grandpa.
What are you talking about?"

"We can go home again!"

"Father, what's happened? Have you lost your mind? You've always told me that our family bought out and could never go back. What's happened now? Have they changed the rules? I'm not even sure I want to go there, anyhow. No water, no beaches, no cities. Just a dry dull planet with sick sheep and a lot of immortal farmers who go around armed to the teeth!"

"Ruth, you can take us back!"

She jumped to her feet and slapped the sand off her bottom. She was a little taller than her father; though he was an extremely handsome, aristocratic-looking man, she was an even more distinctive person. It would be obvious to anyone that she would never lack for suitors or pursuers.

"All right, father. You always have schemes. Usually it's antique money. This time I'm mixed up with it somehow, or you wouldn't be here. Father, just what do you want me to do?"

"To marry. To marry the richest man who has ever been known in the universe."

"Is that all?" she laughed. "Of course I'll marry him. I've never married an offworlder before. Have you made a date with him?"

"You don't understand, Ruth. This isn't Earth marriage. In Norstrilian law and custom you marry only one man, you marry only once, and you stay married to him for as long as you live."

A cloud passed over the sun. The beach became cooler. She looked at her father with a funny mixture of sympathy, contempt, and curiosity.

"That," she said, "is a cat of another breed. I'll have to see him first …"

The Assistant Commissioner's Office, Top of Earthport, Four Hours Later

"Don't tell me there's nothing. Or make up stories about the blue men. You go back to that top deck and take it apart, molecule by molecule, until you find out where that brainbomb went off!"

"But, sir—"

"Don't but me! I've been in battle and you haven't. I know a bomb when I feel one. The blasted thing still gives me a headache. Now you take your men back up to that top deck and find out where that bomb went off."

"Yes, sir," said the young subchief gloomily, never thinking for a moment that he would have the least success in his mission. He saluted dispiritedly.

When he met his men at the door, he gave them an almost imperceptible shake of his head. In consequence, he and his men were the sorriest collection of slouching scarecrows ever seen at Earthport as they trudged their weary way up the ramp to the top deck of Earthport.

Antechamber of the Bell and Bank, The Same Time

"We got the bull-man, B'dank, but somehow he escaped. Probably he is down in the sewers, hiding out. I haven't got the heart to send the police after him. He won't last long, down there. And it would make a fuss if I pardoned him. You might agree with me, but the rest of the Council wouldn't."

"And Commissioner Teadrinker, my Lord? What are you going to do about him? That's sticky wicket, my Lord. He's a former Lord of the Instrumentality. We can't have people like that committing crimes." The Lady Johanna Gnade was emphatic.

"I have the punishment for him," said Jestocost, with a bland smile.

"Oblivion and reconditioning?" said the Lady Johanna. "He's basically talented material."

"Nothing that simple."

"What, my Lord?"

"Nothing."

"What do you mean, 'nothing,' Jestocost? It does not make sense." The Lady Johanna let a rare note of petulance come into her voice.

"I meant what I said, my Lady. Nothing. He knows that I know something. The spider is dead. The robot is demolished. Nine other Rod McBans are causing a bit of chaos in the lower city. But Teadrinker doesn't know that I know everything. I have my own sources."

"We know you pride yourself on that," said the Lady Johanna, with a charming wry smile. "We also know that you like to keep individual secrets from the rest of us. We put up with it, my Lord, because we love you and trust you, but it could be a very dangerous practice if it were carried out by other persons, less judicious than you, or less skillful. And it could even be dangerous if—" She hesitated, looked at him appraisingly, and then went on, "—if, my Lord, you lost your shrewdness, or died suddenly."

"I haven't," said he crisply, dismissing the subject.

"You haven't told me what you are going to do with Teadrinker."

"Nothing, I said," said Jestocost a little crossly. "I'm going to do nothing at all and let him wait for me to bring destruction down on him. If he begins to think that I have forgotten, I will find some little way of reminding him that somebody or something is on his trail. Teadrinker is going to be a very unhappy man before I get through with him."

"That sounds inhumane, my Lord. He might appeal."

"And be tried for murder?"

She gave up. "Your ways are new, my Lord. You have seen your way into the Rediscovery of Man. Letting people suffer. Letting things go wrong. I was brought up on the old philosophy—if you see wrong, right it."

"And I saw," said Jestocost, "that we were dying of perfection."

"I suppose you're right," said she wearily. "You have this rich man covered, I suppose?"

"As well as I can manage," said Jestocost.

"That's perfect, then," said she with an air of finality. "I just hope you haven't gotten him mixed up with that queer hobby of yours."

"Queer hobby?" said Jestocost in a courtly fashion, with a lift of his eyebrows.

"Underpeople," she said with a tone of disgust. *"Underpeople.* I like you, Jestocost, but your fussing about those animals sometimes makes me sick."

He did not argue. He stood very still and looked at her. She knew he was avoiding a provocation. He was her senior, so she offered him a very slight curtsey and left the room.

Antechamber of the Bell and Bank, Ten Minutes Later

A bear-woman, complete with starched cap and nurse's uniform, pushed the wheelchair of the Lord Crudelta into the room. Jestocost looked up from the situation shows which he had been watching. When he saw who it was, he offered Crudelta a deep bow indeed. The bear-woman, flustered by this famous place and all the great dignitaries whom she was meeting, spoke up in a singularly high voice, begging:

"My Lord and Master Crudelta, may I leave you here?"

"Yes. Go. I will call for you later. Go to the bathroom on your way out. It's on the right."

"My Lord—!" she gasped with embarrassment.

"You wouldn't have dared if I hadn't told you. I've been watching your mind for the last half-hour. Now go along."

The bear-woman fled with a rustle of her starched skirts.

When Crudelta looked directly at him, Jestocost gave him a very deep bow. In lifting his eyes he looked directly into the face of the old, old man and said, with something near pride in his voice,

"Still up to your old tricks, my Lord and Colleague Crudelta!"

"And you to yours, Jestocost. How are you going to get that boy out of the sewers?"

"What boy? What sewers?"

"Our sewers. The boy you sold this tower to."

For once, Jestocost was flabbergasted. His jaw dropped. Then he collected himself and said, "You're a knowledgeable man, my Lord Crudelta."

"That I am," said Crudelta, "and a thousand years older than you, to boot. That was my reward for coming back from the Nothing-at-all."

"I know that, sir." Jestocost's full, pleasant face did not show worry, but he studied the old man across from him with extreme care. In his prime, the Lord Crudelta had been the greatest of the Lords of the Instrumentality, a telepath of whom the other Lords were always a little afraid, because he picked minds so deftly and quickly that he was the best mental pickpocket who had ever lived. A strong conservative, he had never opposed a specific policy because it ran counter to his general appetites. He had, for example, carried the vote for the Rediscovery of Man by coming out of retirement and tongue-lashing the whole Council into a corner with his vehement support for reform. Jestocost had never liked him—who could like a rapier tongue, a mind of unfathomable brilliance, a cold old ego which neither offered nor asked companionship? Jestocost knew that if the old man had caught on to the Rod McBan adventure, he might be on the trail of Jestocost's earlier deal with—no, no, no! don't think it here, not with those eyes watching.

"I know about that, too," said the old old man.

"What?"

"The secret you are trying most of all to hide."

Jestocost stood submissive, waiting for the blow to fall.

The old man laughed. Most people would have expected a cackle from that handsome fresh young face with the withered spidery body. They would have been fooled. The laugh was full-bodied, genuine and warm.

"Redlady's a fool," said Crudelta.

"I think so too," said Jestocost, "but what are your reasons, my Lord and Master?"

"Sending that young man off his own planet when he has so much wealth and so little experience."

Jestocost nodded, not wanting to say anything until the old man had made his line of attack plain.

"I like your idea, however," said the Lord Crudelta. "Sell him the Earth and then tax him for it. But what is your ultimate aim? Making him Emperor of the Planet Earth, in the old style? Murdering him? Driving him mad? Having the cat-girl of yours seduce him and then send him home a bankrupt? I admit I have thought of all these too, but I didn't see how any of them would fit in with your passion for justice. But there's one thing you can't do, Jestocost. You can't sell him the planet Earth and then have him stay here and manage it. He might want to use this tower for his residence. That would be too much. I am too old to move out. And he mustn't roll up that ocean out there and take it home for a souvenir. You've all been very clever, my Lord—clever enough to be fools. You have created an unnecessary crisis. What are you going to get out of it?"

Jestocost plunged. The old man must have picked his own mind. Nowhere else could he have put all the threads of the case together. Jestocost decided on the truth and the whole truth. He started with the day that the Big Blink rang in the enormous transactions in stroon futures, financial gambles which soon reached out of the commodity markets of Old North Australia and began to unbalance the economy of all the civilized worlds. He started to explain who Redlady was—

"Don't tell me that," cried the Lord Crudelta. "It was I who caught him, sentenced him to death, and then argued to have the sentence set aside. He's not a bad man, but he's a sly one, that he is. He's smart enough to be an utter and complete fool when he gets wound up in his logical plots. I'll wager you a minicredit to a credit that he has already murdered somebody by now. He always does. He has a taste for theatrical violence. But go back to your story. Tell me what you plan to do. If I like it, I will help you. If I don't like it, I will have the whole story before a plenum of the Council this very morning, and you know that they will tear your bright idea to shreds. They will probably seize the boy's property, send him to a hospital, and have him come out speaking Basque as a flamenco player. You know as well as I do that the Instrumentality is very generous with other people's property, but pretty ruthless when it comes to any threat directed against itself. After all, I was one of the men who wiped out Raumsog."

Jestocost began to talk very quietly, very calmly. He spoke with the assurance of an accountant who, books in order, is explaining an intricate point to his manager. Old himself, he was a child compared to the antiquity and wisdom of the Lord Crudelta. He went into details, including the ultimate disposition of Rod McBan. He even shared with the Lord Crudelta his sympathies for the underpeople and his own very secret, very quiet struggle to improve their position. The only thing which he did not mention was the E'telekeli and the counter-brain which the underpeople had set up in Downdeep-downdeep. If the old man knew it, he knew it, and Jestocost couldn't stop him, but if he did not know it, there was no point in telling him.

The Lord Crudelta did not respond with senile enthusiasm or childish laughter. He reverted, not to his childhood but to his maturity; with great dignity and force he said:

"I approve. I understand. You have my proxy if you need it. Call that nurse to come and get me. I thought you were a clever fool, Jestocost. You sometimes are. This time you are showing that you have a heart as well as a head. One thing more. Bring that doctor Vomact back from Mars soon, and don't torment Teadrinker too long, just for the sake of being clever. I might take it into my mind to torment you."

"And the ex-Lord Redlady?" asked Jestocost deferentially.

"Him, nothing. Nothing. Let him live his life. The Old North Australians might as well cut their political teeth on him."

The bear-woman rustled back into the room. The Lord Crudelta waved his hand. Jestocost bowed almost to the floor, and the wheelchair, heavy as a tank, creaked its way across the doorsill.

"That," said Jestocost, "could have been trouble!" He wiped his brow.

THE ROAD TO THE CATMASTER

Rod, C'mell and A'gentur had had to hold the sides of the shaft several times as the traffic became heavy and large loads, going up or down, had to pass each other and them too. In one of these waits C'mell caught her breath and said something very swiftly to the little monkey. Rod, not heeding them, caught nothing but the sudden enthusiasm and happiness in her voice. The monkey's murmured answer made her plaintive and she insisted,

"But, Yeekasoose, you must! Rod's whole life could depend on it. Not just saving his life now, but having a better life for hundreds and hundreds of years."

The monkey was cross: "Don't ask me to think when I am hungry. This fast metabolism and small body just isn't enough to support real thinking."

"If it's food you want, have some raisins." She took a square of compressed seedless raisins out of one of her matching bags.

A'gentur ate them greedily but gloomily.

Rod's attention drifted away from them as he saw magnificent golden furniture, elaborately carved and inlaid with a pearlescent material, being piloted up the shaft by a whole troop of talkative dog-men. He asked them where the furniture was going. When they did not answer him, he repeated his question in a more peremptory tone of voice, as befitted the richest Old North Australian in the universe. The tone of demand brought answers, but they were not the ones he was expecting. "Meow," said one dog-man. "Shut up, cat, or I'll chase you up a tree." "Not to your house, buster. Exactly what do you think you are—people?" "Cats are always nosy. Look at that one." The dog-foreman rose into sight; with dignity and kindness he said to Rod, "Cat-fellow, if you feel like talking, you may get marked surplus. Better keep quiet in the public dropshaft!" Rod realized that to these beings he was one of them, a cat made into a man, and that the underpeople workmen who served Old Earth had been trained not to chatter while working on the business of Man.

He caught the tail of C'mell's urgent whisper to A'gentur: "...and don't ask him. *Tell Him.* We'll risk the people zone for a visit to the Catmaster! *Tell Him.*"

A'gentur was panting with a rapid, shallow breath. His eyes seemed to protrude from their sockets and yet he was looking at nothing. He groaned as though with some inward effort. At last he lost his grip on the wall and would have floated slowly downward if C'mell had not caught him and cuddled him like a baby. C'mell whispered, eagerly,

"You reached Him?"

"Him," gasped the little monkey.

"Who?" asked Rod.

"Aitch Eye," said C'mell. "I'll tell you later." Of A'gentur she asked, "If you got Him, what did He say?"

"He said, 'E'ikasus, I do not say no. You are my son. Take the risk if you think it wise.' And don't ask me now, C'mell. Let me think a little. I have been all the way to Norstrilia and back. I'm still cramped in this little body. Do we have to do it now? Right now? Why can't we go to Him"— and A'gentur nodded toward the depths below —"and find out what we want Rod for, anyhow? Rod is a means, not an end. Who really knows what to do with him?"

"What are you talking about?" said Rod.

Simultaneously C'mell snapped, "I know what we are going to do with him."

"What?" said the little monkey, very tired again.

"We're going to let this boy go free, and let him find happiness, and if he wants to give us his help, we will take it and be grateful. But we are not going to rob him. Not going to hurt him. That would be a mean, dirty way to start being better creatures than we are. If he knows who he is before he meets Him, they can make sense." She turned to Rod and said with mysterious urgency,

"Don't you want to *know* who you are?"

"I'm Rod McBan to the hundred and fifty-first," said he promptly.

"Sh-h-h," said she, "no names here. I'm not talking about names. I'm talking about the deep insides of you. Life itself, as it flows through you. Do you have any idea who you are?"

"You're playing games," he said. "I know perfectly well who I am, and where I live, and what I have. I even know that right now I am supposed to be a cat-man named C'roderick. What else is there to know?"

"You men!" she sobbed at him. "You men! Even when you're people, you're so dense that you can't understand a simple question. I'm not asking you your name or your address or your label or your great-grandfather's property. I'm asking about *you,* Rod, the only one that will ever live, no matter how many numbers your grandsons may put after their names. You're not in the world just to own a piece of property or to handle a surname with a number after it. You're *you.* There's never been another you. There will never be another one, after you. What does this 'you' want?"

Rod glanced down at the walls of the tunnel, which seemed to turn—oh, so far below—very gently to the north. He looked up at the little rhomboids of light cast on the tunnel walls by the landing doors into the various levels of Earthport. He felt his own weight tugging gently at his hand as he held to the rough surface of the vertical shaft, supported by his belt. The belt itself felt uncomfortable about his middle; after all, it was supporting most of his weight, and it squeezed him. *What do I want?* thought he. *Who am I that I should have a right to want anything? I am Rod McBan CLI, the Mister and Owner of the Station of Doom. But I'm also a poor freak with bad telepathy who can't even spiek or hier rightly.*

C'mell was watching him as clinically as a surgeon, but he could tell from her expression that she was not trying to peep his mind.

He found himself speaking almost as wearily as had A'gentur, who was also called something like "Yeekasoose," and who had strange powers for a little monkey:

"I don't suppose I want anything much, C'mell, except that I should like to spiek and hier correctly, like other people on my native world."

She looked at him, her expression showing intense sympathy and the effort to make a decision.

A'gentur interrupted with his high clear monkey voice, "Say that to me, Sir and Master."

Rod repeated: "I don't really want anything. I would like to spiek and hier because other people are fussing at me about it. And I would like to get a Cape of Good Hope twopenny triangular blue stamp while I am still on Earth. But that's about all. I guess there's nothing I really want."

The monkey closed his eyes and seemed to fall asleep again; Rod suspected it was some kind of telepathic trance.

C'mell hooked A'gentur on an old rod which protruded from the surface of the shaft. Since he weighed only a few grams, there was no noticeable pull on the belt. She seized Rod's shoulder and pulled him over to her.

"Rod, listen! Do you want to know who you are?"

"I don't know," said he. "I might be miserable."

"Not if you *know* who you are!" she insisted.

"I might not like me," said Rod. "Other people don't and my parents died together when their ship went milky out in space. I'm not normal."

"For God's sake, Rod!" she cried.

"Who?" said he.

"Forgive me, father," said she, speaking to no one in sight.

"I've heard that name, before, somewhere," said Rod. "But let's get going. I want to get to this mysterious place you are taking me and then I want to find out about Eleanor."

"Who's that?"

"My servant. She's disguised as me, taking risks for me, along with eight robots. It's up to me to do what I can for her. Always."

"But she's your *servant,*" said C'mell. "She serves you. Almost like being an underperson, like me."

"She's a person," said Rod, stubbornly. "We have no underpeople in Norstrilia, except for a few in government jobs. But she's my friend."

"Do you want to marry her?"

"Great sick sheep, girl! Are you barmy? No!"

"Do you want to marry anybody?"

"At sixteen?" he cried. "Anyhow, my family will arrange it." The thought of plain honest devoted Lavinia crossed his mind, and he could not help comparing her to this wild voluptuous creature who floated beside him in the tunnel as the traffic passed them going up and down. With near weightlessness, C'mell's hair floated like a magic flower around her head. She had been brushing it out of her eyes from time to time. He snorted, "Not Eleanor."

When he said this, another idea crossed the mind of the beautiful cat-girl.

"You know what I am, Rod," said she, very seriously.

"A cat-girl from the planet Earth. You're supposed to be my wife."

"That's right," she said, with an odd intonation in her voice. "Be it, then!"

"What?" said Rod.

"My husband," she said, her voice catching slightly. "Be my husband, if it will help you to find you."

She stole a quick glance up and down the shaft. There was nobody near.

"Look, Rod, look!" She spread the opening of her dress down and aside. Even with the poor light, to which his eyes had become accustomed, he could see the fine tracery of veins in her delicate chest and her young, pear-shaped breasts. The aureoles around the nipples were a clear, sweet, innocent pink; the nipples themselves were as pretty as two pieces of candy. For a moment there was pleasure and then a terrible embarrassment came over him. He turned his face away and felt horribly self-conscious. What she had done was interesting but it wasn't *nice.*

When he dared to glance at her, she was still studying his face.

"I'm a girlygirl, Rod. This is my business. And you're a cat, with all the rights of a tomcat. Nobody can tell the difference, here in this tunnel. *Rod, do you want to do anything?"*

Rod gulped and said nothing.

She swept her clothing back into place. The strange urgency left her

voice. "I guess," she said, "that that left me a little breathless. I find you
pretty attractive, Rod. I find myself thinking, 'What a pity he is not a cat.'
I'm over it now."

Rod said nothing.

A bubble of laughter came into her voice, along with something moth-
ering and tender, which tugged at his heartstrings. "Best of all, Rod, I
didn't mean it. Or maybe I did. I had to give you a chance before I felt
that I really knew you. Rod, I'm one of the most beautiful girls on Old
Earth itself. The Instrumentality uses me for that very reason. We've turned
you into a cat and offered you me, and you won't have me. Doesn't that
suggest that you don't know who you are?"

"Are you back on that?" said Rod. "I guess I just don't understand
girls."

"You'd better, before you're through with Earth," she said. "Your agents
have bought a million of them for you, out of all that stroon money."

"People or underpeople?"

"Both!"

"Let them bug sheep!" he cried. "I had no part in ordering them.
Come on, girl. This is no place for a boudoir conversation!"

"Where on Earth did you learn that word?" she laughed.

"I read books. Lots of books. I may look like a peasant to you Earth
people, but I know a lot of things."

"Do you trust me, Rod?"

He thought of her immodesty, which still left him a little breathless.
The Old North Australian humor reasserted itself in him, as a cultural
characteristic and not just as an individual one: "I've seen a lot of you,
C'mell," said he with a grin. "I suppose you don't have many surprises
left. All right, I trust you. Then what?"

She studied him closely.

"I'll tell you what E'ikasus and I were discussing."

"Who?"

"Him." She nodded at the little monkey.

"I thought his name was A'gentur."

"Like yours is C'rod!" she said.

"He's not a monkey?" asked Rod.

She looked around and lowered her voice. "He's a bird," she said
solemnly, "and he's the second most important bird on Earth."

"So what?" said Rod.

"He's in charge of your destiny, Rod. Your life or your death. Right
now."

"I thought," he whispered back, "that that was up to the Lord Redlady
and somebody named Jestocost on Earth."

"You're dealing with other powers, Rod—powers which keep themselves secret. They want to be friends with you. And I think," she added in a complete non sequitur, "that we'd better take the risk and go."

He looked blank and she added,

"To the Catmaster."

"They'll do something to me there."

"Yes," she said. Her face was calm, friendly, and even. "You will die, maybe—but not much chance. Or you might go mad—there's always the possibility. Or you will find all the things you want—that's the likeliest of all. I have been there, Rod. I myself have been there. Don't you think that I look like a happy, busy girl, when you consider that I'm really just an animal with a rather low-down job?"

Rod studied her. "How old are you?"

"Thirty next year," she said, inflexibly.

"For the first time?"

"For us animal-people there is no second time, Rod. I thought you knew that."

He returned her gaze. "If you can take it," said he, "I can too. Let's go."

She lifted A'gentur or E'ikasus, depending on which he really was, off the wall, where he had been sleeping like a marionette between plays. He opened his exhausted little eyes and blinked at her.

"You have given us our orders," said C'mell. "We are going to the Department Store."

"I have," he said, crossly, coming much more awake. "I don't remember it!"

She laughed, "Just through me, E'ikasus!"

"That name!" he hissed. "Don't get foolhardy. Not in a public shaft."

"All right, A'gentur," she responded, "but do you approve?"

"Of the decision?"

She nodded.

The little monkey looked at both of them. He spoke to Rod, "If she gambles her life and yours, not to mention mine—if she takes chances to make you much, much happier, are you willing to come along?"

Rod nodded in silent agreement.

"Let's go, then," said the monkey-surgeon.

"Where are we going?" asked Rod.

"Down into Earthport City. Among all the people. Swarms and swarms of them," said C'mell, "and you will get to see the everyday life of Earth, just the way that you asked at the top of the tower, an hour ago."

"A year ago, you mean," said Rod. "So much has happened!" He thought of her young naked breasts and the impulse which had made her show them to him, but the thought did not make him excited or guilty; he felt friendly, because he sensed in their whole relationship a friendliness much more fervent than sex itself.

"We are going to a store," said the sleepy monkey.

"A commissary. For things? What for?"

"It has a nice name," said C'mell, "and it is run by a wonderful person. The Catmaster himself. Five hundred some years old, and still allowed to live by virtue of the legacy of the Lady Goroke."

"Never heard of her," said Rod. "What's the name?"

"The Department Store of Hearts' Desires," said C'mell and E'ikasus simultaneously.

The trip was a vivid, quick dream. They had only a few hundred meters to fall before they reached ground level.

They came out on the people-street. A robot-policeman watched them from a corner.

Human beings in the costumes of a hundred historical periods were walking around in the warm, wet air of Earth. Rod could not smell as much salt in the air as he had smelled at the top of the tower, but down here in the city it smelled of more people than he had ever even imagined in one place. Thousands of individuals, hundreds and thousands of different kinds of foods, the odors of robots, of underpeople and of other things which seemed to be unmodified animals.

"This is the most interesting-smelling place I have ever been," said he to C'mell.

She glanced at him idly. "That's nice. You can smell like a dog-man. Most of the real people I have known couldn't smell their own feet. Come on though, C'roderick—*remember who you are!* If we're not tagged and licensed for the surface, we'll get stopped by that policeman in one minute or less."

She carried E'ikasus and steered Rod with a pressure on his elbow. They came to a ramp which led to an underground passage, well illuminated. Machines, robots and underpeople were hurrying back and forth along it, busy with the commerce of Earth.

Rod would have been completely lost if he had been without C'mell. Though his miraculous broad-band hiering, which had so often surprised him at home, had not returned during his few hours on Old Earth, his other senses gave him a suffocating awareness of the huge number of people around him and above him. (He never realized that there were times, long gone, when the cities of Earth had populations which reached the tens of millions; to him, several hundred thousand people, and a comparable number of underpeople, was a crowd almost beyond all measure.)

The sounds and smells of underpeople were subtly different from those of people; some of the machines of Earth were bigger and older than anything which he had previously imagined; and above all, the circulation of water in immense volumes, millions upon millions of gallons, for the multiple purposes of Earthport—sanitation, cooling, drinking, industrial purposes—made him feel that he was not among a few buildings, which he would have called a city in Old North Australia, but that he himself had become a blood-cell thrusting through the circulatory system of some enormous composite animal, the nature of which he imperfectly understood. This city was alive with a sticky, wet, complicated aliveness which he had hitherto not even imagined to be possible. Movement characterized it. He suspected that the movement went on by night and day, that there was no real cessation to it, that the great pumps thrust water through feeder pipes and drains whether people were awake or not, that the brains of this organization could be no one place, but had to comprise many sub-brains, each committed and responsible for its particular tasks. No wonder underpeople were needed! It would be boredom and pain, even with perfected automation, to have enough human supervisors to reconnect the various systems if they had breakdowns inside themselves or at their interconnections. Old North Australia had vitality, but it was the vitality of open fields, few people, immense wealth, and perpetual military danger; this was the vitality of the cesspool, of the compost heap, but the rotting, blooming, growing components were not waste material but human beings and near-human beings. No wonder that his forefathers had fled the cities as they had been. They must have been solid plague to free men. And even Old Original Australia, somewhere here on Earth, had lost its openness and freedom in order to become the single giant city-complex of Aojou Nanbien. It must, Rod thought with horror, have been a thousand times the size of this city of Earthport. (He was wrong, because it was one hundred fifty thousand times the size of Earthport before it died. Earthport had only about two hundred thousand permanent residents when Rod visited it, with an additional number walking in from the nearer suburbs, the outer suburbs still being ruined and abandoned, but Australia—under the name of Aojou Nanbien—had reached a population of thirty billion before it died, and before the Wild Ones and the Menschenjäger had set to work killing off the survivors.)

Rod was bewildered, but C'mell was not.

She had put A'gentur down, over his whined monkey-like protest. He trotted unwillingly beside them.

With the impudent knowledgeability of a true city girl, she had led them to a cross-walk from which a continuous whistling roar came forth. By writing, by picture, and by loudspeaker, the warning system repeated:

KEEP OFF. FREIGHT ONLY. DANGER. KEEP OFF. She had snatched up A'gentur-E'ikasus, grabbed Rod by the arm, and jumped with them onto a series of rapidly moving airborne platforms. Rod, startled by the suddenness with which they had found the trackway, shouted to ask what it was:

"Freight? What's that?"

"Things. Boxes. Foods. This is the Central Trackway. No sense in walking six kilometers when we can get this. Be ready to jump off with me when I give you the sign!"

"It *feels* dangerous," he said.

"It isn't," said she, "not if you're a cat."

With this somewhat equivocal reassurance, she let them ride. A'gentur could not care less. He cuddled his head against her shoulder, wrapped his long, gibbon-like arms around her upper arm, and went soundly to sleep.

C'mell nodded at Rod.

"Soon now!" she called, judging their distance by landmarks which he found meaningless. The landing points had flat, concrete-lined areas where the individual flat cars, rushing along on their river of air, could be shunted suddenly to the side for loading or unloading. Each of these loading areas had a number, but Rod had not even noticed at what point they had gotten on. The smells of the underground city changed so much as they moved from one district to another that he was more interested in odors than in the numbers on the platforms.

She pinched his upper arm very sharply as a sign that he should get ready.

They jumped.

He staggered across the platform until he caught himself up against a large vertical crate marked *Algonquin Paper Works—Credit Slips, Miniature—2mm.* C'mell landed as gracefully as if she had been acting a rehearsed piece of acrobatics. The little monkey on her shoulder stared with wide bright eyes.

"This," said the monkey A'gentur-E'ikasus firmly and contemptuously, "is where all the people play at working. I'm tired, I'm hungry, and my body sugar is low." He curled himself tight against C'mell's shoulder, closed his eyes, and went back to sleep.

"He has a point," said Rod. "Could we eat?"

C'mell started to nod and then caught herself short—"You're a cat."

He nodded. Then he grinned. "I'm hungry, anyhow. And I need a sandbox."

"Sandbox?" she asked, puzzled.

"An awef," he said very clearly, using the Old North Australian term.

"Awef?"

It was his turn to get embarrassed. He said it in full: "An animal waste evacuation facility."

"You mean a johnny," she cried. She thought a minute and then said, "Fooey."

"What's the matter?" he asked.

"Each kind of underpeople has to use its own. It's death if you don't use one and it's death if you use the wrong one. The cat one is four stations back on this underground trackway. Or we can walk back on the surface. It would only be a half hour."

He said something rude to Earth. She wrinkled her brow.

"All I said was, 'Earth is a large healthy sheep.' That's not so dirty." Her good humor returned.

Before she could ask him another question he held up a firm hand. "I am not going to waste a half hour. You wait here." He had seen the universal sign for "men's room" at the upper level of the platform. Before she could stop him he had gone into it. She caught her hand up to her mouth, knowing that the robot police would kill him on sight if they found him in the wrong place. It would be such a ghastly joke if the man who owned the Earth were to die in the wrong toilet.

As quick as thought she followed him, stopping just outside the door to the men's room. She dared not go in; she trusted that the place was empty when Rod entered it, because she had heard no boom of a slow, heavy bullet, none of the crisp buzzing of a burner. Robots did not use toilets, so they went in only when they were investigating something. She was prepared to distract any man living if he tried to enter that toilet, by offering him the combination of an immediate seduction or a complimentary and unwanted monkey.

A'gentur had awakened.

"Don't bother," he said. "I called my father. Anything approaching that door will fall asleep."

An ordinary man, rather tired and worried-looking, headed for the men's room. C'mell was prepared to stop him at any cost, but she remembered what A'gentur-E'ikasus had told her, so she waited. The man reeled as he neared them. He stared at them, saw that they were underpeople, looked on through them as though they were not there. He took two more steps toward the door and suddenly reached out his hands as if he were going blind. He walked into the wall two meters from the door, touched it firmly and blindly with his hands, and crumpled gently to the floor, where he lay snoring.

"My dad's good," said A'gentur-E'ikasus. "He usually leaves real people alone, but when he must get them, he gets them. He even gave that man the distinct memory that he mistakenly took a sleeping pill when he was reaching for a pain-killer. When the human wakes up, he will feel foolish and will tell no one of his experience."

Rod came out of the ever-so-dangerous doorway. He grinned at them boyishly and did not notice the crumpled man lying beside the wall. "That was easier than turning back, and nobody noticed me at all. See, I saved you a lot of trouble, C'mell!"

He was so proud of his foolhardy adventure that she did not have the heart to blame him. He smiled widely, his cat-whiskers tipping as he did so. For a moment, just a moment, she forgot that he was an important person and a real man to boot: he was a boy, and mighty like a cat, but all boy in his satisfaction, his wanton bravery, his passing happiness with vainglory. For a second or two she loved him. Then she thought of the terrible hours ahead, and of how he would go home, rich and scornful, to his all-people planet. The moment of love passed but she still liked him very much.

"Come along, young fellow. You can eat. You are going to eat cat food since you are C'roderick, but it's not so bad."

He frowned. "What is it? Do you have fish here? I tasted fish one time. A neighbor bought one. He traded two horses for it. It was delicious."

"He wants fish," she cried to E'ikasus.

"Give him a whole tuna for himself," grumbled the monkey. "My blood sugar is still low. I need some pineapple."

C'mell did not argue. She stayed underground and led them into a hall which had a picture of dogs, cats, cattle, pigs, bears, and snakes above the door; that indicated the kinds of people who could be served there. E'ikasus scowled at the sign but he rode C'mell's shoulder in.

"This gentleman," said C'mell, speaking pleasantly to an old bear-man who was scratching his belly and smoking a pipe, all at the same time, "has forgotten his credits."

"No food," said the bear-man. "Rules. He can drink water, though."

"I'll pay for him," said C'mell.

The bear-man yawned. "Are you sure that he won't pay you back? If he does, that is private trading and it is punished by death."

"I know the rules," said C'mell. "I've never been disciplined yet."

The bear looked her over critically. He took his pipe out of his mouth and whistled. "No," said he, "and I can see that you won't be. What are you, anyhow? A model?"

"A girlygirl," said C'mell.

The bear-man leapt from his stool with astonishing speed. "Cat-madame!" he cried. "A thousand pardons. You can have anything in the place. You come from the top of Earthport? You know the Lords of the

Instrumentality personally? You would like a table roped off with curtains? Or should I just throw everybody else out of here and report to my Man that we have a famous, beautiful slave from the high places?"

"Nothing that drastic," said C'mell. "Just food."

"Wait a bit," said A'gentur-E'ikasus. "If you're offering specials, I'll have two fresh pineapples, a quarter-kilo of ground fresh coconut, and a tenth of a kilo of live insect grubs."

The bear-man hesitated. "I was offering things to the cat-lady, who serves the mighty ones, not to you, monkey. But if the lady desires it, I will send for those things." He waited for C'mell's nod, got it, and pushed a button for a low-grade robot to come. He turned to Rod McBan. "And you, cat-gentleman, what would you like?"

Before Rod could speak, C'mell said, "He wants two sailfish steaks, fried potatoes, Waldorf salad, an order of ice cream, and a large glass of orange juice."

The bear-man shuddered visibly. "I've been here for years and that is the most horrible lunch I ever ordered for a cat. I think I'll try it myself."

C'mell smiled the smile which had graced a thousand welcomes.

"I'll just help myself from the things you have on the counters. I'm not fussy."

He started to protest but she cut him short with a graceful but unmistakable wave of the hand. He gave up.

They sat at a table.

A'gentur-E'ikasus waited for his combination monkey and bird lunch. Rod saw an old robot, dressed in a prehistoric tuxedo jacket, ask a question of the bear-man, leave one tray at the door, and bring another tray to him. The robot whipped off a freshly starched napkin. There was the most beautiful lunch Rod McBan had ever seen. Even at a state banquet, the Old North Australians did not feed their guests like that. Just as they were finishing, the bear-cashier came to the table and asked,

"Your name, cat-madame? I will charge these lunches to the government."

"C'mell, servant to Teadrinker, subject to the Lord Jestocost, a Chief of the Instrumentality."

The bear's face had been epilated, so that they could see him pale.

"*C'mell,*" he whispered. *"C'mell!* Forgive me, my Lady. I have never seen you before. You have blessed this place. You have blessed my life. You are the friend of all underpeople. Go in peace."

C'mell gave him the bow and smile which a reigning empress might give to an active Lord of the Instrumentality. She started to pick up the monkey but he scampered on ahead of her. Rod was puzzled. As the bear-man bowed him out, he asked,

"C'mell. You are famous?"

"In a way," she said. "But only among the Underpeople." She hurried them both toward a ramp. They reached daylight at last, but even before they came to the surface, Rod's nose was assaulted by a riot of smells— foods frying, cakes baking, liquor spilling its pungency on the air, perfumes fighting with each other for attention, and, above all, the smell of old things: dusty treasures, old leathers, tapestries, the echo-smells of people who had died a long time ago.

C'mell stopped and watched him. "You're smelling things again? I must say, you have a better nose than any human being I ever met before. How does it smell to you?"

"Wonderful," he gasped. "Wonderful. Like all the treasures and temptations of the universe spilled out into one little place."

"It's just the Thieves' Market of Paris."

"There are thieves on Earth? Open ones, like on Viola Siderea?"

"Oh, no," she laughed. "They would die in a few days. The Instrumentality would catch them. These are just people, playing. The Rediscovery of Man found some old institutions, and an old market was one of them. They make the robots and underpeople find things for them and then they pretend to be ancient, and make bargains with each other. Or they cook food. Not many real people ever cook food these days. It's so funny that it tastes good to them. They all pick up money on their way in. They have barrels of it at the gate. In the evening, or when they leave, they usually throw the money in the gutter, even though they should really put it back in the barrel. It's not money we underpeople could use. We go by numbers and computer cards," she sighed. "I could certainly use some of that extra money."

"And underpeople like you—like us—" said Rod, "what do we do in the market?"

"Nothing," she whispered. "Absolutely nothing. We can walk through if we are not too big and not too small and not too dirty and not too smelly. And even if we are all right, we must walk right through without looking directly at the real people and without touching anything in the market."

"Suppose we do?" asked Rod defiantly.

"The robot police are there, with orders to kill on sight when they observe an infraction. Don't you realize, C'rod," she sobbed at him, "that there are millions of us in tanks, way below in Downdeep-downdeep, ready to be born, to be trained, to be sent up here to serve Man? We're not scarce at all, C'rod, we're not scarce at all!"

"Why are we going through the market then?"

"It's the only way to the Catmaster's store. We'll be tagged. Come along."

Where the ramp reached the surface, four bright-eyed robots, their blue enamel bodies shining and their milky eyes glowing, stood at the ready. Their weapons had an ugly buzz to them and were obviously already off the "safety" mark. C'mell talked to them quietly and submissively. When the robot-sergeant led her to a desk, she stared into an instrument like binoculars and blinked when she took her eyes away. She put her palm on a desk. The identification was completed. The robot sergeant handed her three bright disks, like saucers, each with a chain attached. Wordlessly she hung them around her own neck, Rod's neck, and A'gentur's. The robots let them pass. They walked in demure single file through the place of beautiful sights and smells. Rod felt that his eyes were wet with tears of rage. "I'll buy this place," he thought to himself, "if it's the only thing I'll ever buy."

C'mell had stopped walking.

Rod looked up, very carefully.

There was the sign: THE DEPARTMENT STORE OF HEARTS' DESIRES. A door opened. A wise old cat-person's face looked out, stared at them, snapped, "No underpeople!" and slammed the door. C'mell rang the doorbell a second time. The face reappeared, more puzzled than angry.

"Business," she whispered, "of the Aitch Eye."

The face nodded and said, "In, then. Quick!"

THE DEPARTMENT STORE OF HEARTS' DESIRES

Once inside, Rod realized that the store was as rich as the market. There were no other customers. After the outside sounds of music, laughter, frying, boiling, things falling, dishes clattering, people arguing, and the low undertone of the ever-ready robot weapons buzzing, the quietness of the room was itself a luxury, like old, heavy velvet. The smells were no less variegated than those on the outside, but they were different, more complicated, and many more of them were completely unidentifiable.

One smell he was sure of: fear, human fear. It had been in this room not long before.

"Quick," said the old cat-man. "I'm in trouble if you don't get out soon. What is your business?"

"I'm C'mell," said C'mell.

He nodded pleasantly, but showed no sign of recognition. "I forget people," he said.

"This is A'gentur." She indicated the monkey.

The old cat-man did not even look at the animal.

C'mell persisted, a note of triumph coming into her voice: "You may have heard of him under his real name, E'ikasus."

The old man stood there, blinking, as though he were taking it in. "Yeekasoose? With the letter E?"

"Transformed," said C'mell inexorably, "for a trip all the way to Old North Australia and back."

"Is this true?" said the old man to the monkey.

E'ikasus said calmly, "I am the son of Him of whom you think."

The old man dropped to his knees, but did so with dignity:

"I salute you, E'ikasus. When you next think-with your father, give him my greetings and ask from him his blessing. I am C'william, the Catmaster."

"You are famous," said E'ikasus tranquilly.

"But you are still in danger, merely being here. I have no license for underpeople!"

C'mell produced her trump. "Catmaster, your next guest. This is no c'man. He is a true man, an offworlder, and he has just bought most of the planet Earth."

149

C'william looked at Rod with more than ordinary shrewdness. There was a touch of kindness in his attitude. He was tall for a cat-man; few animal features were left to him, because old age, which reduces racial and sexual contrasts to mere memories, had wrinkled him into a uniform beige. His hair was not white, but beige too; his few cat-whiskers looked old and worn. He was garbed in a fantastic costume which—Rod later learned—consisted of the court robes of one of the Original Emperors, a dynasty which had prevailed for many centuries among the further stars. Age was upon him, but wisdom was too; the habits of life, in his case, had been cleverness and kindness, themselves unusual in combination. Now very old, he was reaping the harvest of his years. He had done well with the thousands upon thousands of days behind him, with the result that age had brought a curious joy into his manner, as though each experience meant one more treat before the long bleak dark closed in. Rod felt himself attracted to this strange creature, who looked at him with such penetrating and very personal curiosity, and who managed to do so without giving offense.

The Catmaster spoke in very passable Norstrilian: "I know what you are thinking, Mister and Owner McBan."

"You can hier me?" cried Rod.

"Not your thoughts. Your face. It reads easily. I am sure that I can help you."

"What makes you think I need help?"

"All things need help," said the old c'man briskly, "but we must get rid of our other guests first. Where do you want to go, excellent one? And you, cat-madame?"

"Home," said E'ikasus. He was tired and cross again. After speaking brusquely, he felt the need to make his tone more civil. "This body suits me badly, Catmaster."

"Are you good at falling?" said the Catmaster. "Free fall?"

The monkey grinned. "With this body? Of course. Excellent. I'm tired of it."

"Fine," said the Catmaster. "You can drop down my waste chute. It falls next to the forgotten palace where the great wings beat against time."

The Catmaster stepped to one side of the room. With only a nod at C'mell and Rod, followed by a brief "See you later," the monkey watched as the Catmaster opened a manhole cover, leaped trustingly into the complete black depth which appeared, and was gone. The Catmaster replaced the cover carefully.

He turned to C'mell.

She faced him truculently, the defiance of her posture oddly at variance with the innocent voluptuousness of her young female body. "I'm going nowhere."

"You'll die," said the Catmaster. "Can't you hear their weapons buzzing just outside the door? You know what they do to us underpeople. Especially to us cats. They use us, but do they trust us?"

"I know one who does …" she said. "The Lord Jestocost could protect me, even here, just as he protects you, far beyond your limit of years."

"Don't argue it. You will make trouble for him with the other real people. Here, girl, I will give you a tray to carry with a dummy package on it. Go back to the underground and rest in the commissary of the bearman. I will send Rod to you when we are through."

"Yes," she said hotly, "but will you send him alive or dead?"

The Catmaster rolled his yellow eyes over Rod. "Alive," he said. "This one—alive. I have predicted. Did you ever know me to be wrong? Come on, girl, out the door with you."

C'mell let herself be handed a tray and a package, taken seemingly at random. As she left Rod thought of her with quick desperate affection. She was his closest link with Earth. He thought of her excitement and of how she had bared her young breasts to him, but now the memory, instead of exciting him, filled him with tender fondness instead. He blurted out, "C'mell, will you be all right?"

She turned around at the door itself, looking all woman and all cat. Her red wild hair gleamed like a hearth-fire against the open light from the doorway. She stood erect, as though she were a citizen of Earth and not a mere underperson or girlygirl. She held out her right hand clearly and commandingly while balancing the tray on her left hand. When he shook hands with her, Rod realized that her hand felt utterly human but very strong. With scarcely a break in her voice she said,

"Rod, goodbye. I'm taking a chance with you, but it's the best chance I've ever taken. You can trust the Catmaster, here in the Department Store of Hearts' Desires. He does strange things, Rod, but they're good strange things."

He released her hand and she left. C'william closed the door behind her. The room became hushed.

"Sit down for a minute while I get things ready. Or look around the room if you prefer."

"Sir Catmaster—" said Rod.

"No title, please. I am an underperson, made out of cats. You may call me C'william."

"C'william, please tell me first. I miss C'mell. I'm worried about her. Am I falling in love with her? Is that what falling in love means?"

"She's your wife," said the Catmaster. "Just temporarily and just in pretense, but she's still your wife. It's Earthlike to worry about one's mate. She's all right."

The old c'man disappeared behind a door which had an odd sign on it: HATE HALL.

Rod looked around.

The first thing, the very first thing, which he saw was a display cabinet full of postage stamps. It was made of glass, but he could see the soft blues and the inimitable warm brick reds of his Cape of Good Hope triangular postage stamps. He had come to Earth and there they were! He peered through the glass at them. They were even better than the illustrations which he had seen back on Norstrilia. They had the temper of great age upon them and yet, somehow, they seemed to freight with them the love which men, living men now dead, had given them for thousands and thousands of years. He looked around, and saw that the whole room was full of odd riches. There were ancient toys of all periods, flying toys, copies of machines, things which he suspected were trains. There was a two-story closet of clothing, shimmering with embroidery and gleaming with gold. There was a bin of weapons, clean and tidy— models so ancient that he could not possibly guess what they had been used for, or by whom. Everywhere, there were buckets of coins, usually gold ones. He picked up a handful. They had languages he could not even guess at and they showed the proud imperious faces of the ancient dead. Another cabinet was one which he glanced at and then turned away from, shocked and yet inquisitive: it was filled with indecent souvenirs and pictures from a hundred periods of men's history, images, sketches, photographs, dolls and models, all of them portraying grisly, comical, sweet, friendly, impressive or horrible versions of the many acts of love. The next section made him pause utterly. Who would have ever wanted these things? Whips, knives, hoods, leather corsets. He passed on, very puzzled.

The next section stopped him breathless. It was full of old books, genuine old books. There were a few framed poems, written very ornately. One had a scrap of paper attached to it, reading simply, "My favorite." Rod looked down to see if he could make it out. It was ancient Inglish and the odd name was "E. Z. C. Judson, Ancient American, A.D. 1823–1866." Rod understood the words of the poem but he did not think that he really got the sense of it. As he read it, he had the impression that a very old man, like the Catmaster, must find in it a poignancy which a younger person would miss:

> Drifting in the ebbing tide,
> Slow but sure I onward glide—
>   Dim the vista seen before,
> Useless now to look behind—
> Drifting on before the wind
>   Toward the unknown shore.

Counting time by ticking clock,
Waiting for the final shock—
          Waiting for the dark forever—
Oh, how slow the moments go!
          None but I, meseems, can know
How close the tideless river!

Rod shook his head as if to get away from the cobwebs of an irrecoverable tragedy. "Maybe," he thought to himself, "that's the way people felt about death when they did not die on schedule, the way most worlds have it, or if they do not meet death a few times ahead of time, the way we do in Norstrilia. They must have felt pretty sticky and uncertain." Another thought crossed his mind and he gasped at the utter cruelty of it. "They did not even have Unselfing Grounds that far back! Not that we need them any more, but imagine just sliding into death, helpless, useless, hopeless. Thank the Queen we don't do that!"

He thought of the Queen, who might have been dead for more than fifteen thousand years, or who might be lost in space, the way many Old North Australians believed, and sure enough! there was her picture, with the words "Queen Elizabeth II." It was just a bust, but she was a pretty and intelligent-looking woman, with something of a Norstrilian look to her. She looked smart enough to know what to do if one of her sheep caught fire or if her own child came, blank and giggling, out of the traveling vans of the Garden of Death, as he himself would have done had he not passed the survival test.

Next there were two glass frames, neatly wiped free of dust. They had matched poems by someone who was listed as "Anthony Bearden, Ancient American, A.D. 1913–1949." The first one seemed very appropriate to this particular place, because it was all about the ancient desires which people had in those days. It read:

   TELL ME, LOVE!
Time is burning and the world on fire.
Tell me, love, what you most desire.
Tell me what your heart has hidden.
Is it open or—forbidden?

If forbidden, think of days
Racing past in a roaring haze,
Shocked and shaken by the blast of fire...
Tell me, love, what you most desire.

Tell me, love, what you most desire.
Dainty foods and soft attire?
Ancient books? Fantastic chess?
Wine-lit nights? Love—more, or less?

Now is the only now of our age.
Tomorrow tomorrow will hold the stage.
Tell me, love, what you most desire!
Time is burning and the world on fire.

The other one might almost have been written about his arrival on Earth, his not knowing what could happen or what should happen to him now.

NIGHT, AND THE SKY UNFAMILIAR
The stars of experience have led me astray.
A pattern of purpose was lost on my way.
Where was I going? How can I say?
The stars of experience have led me astray.

There was a slight sound.

Rod turned around to face the Catmaster.

The old man was unchanged. He still wore the lunatic robes of grandeur, but his dignity survived even this *outré* effect.

"You like my poems? You like my things? I like them myself. Many men come in here to take things from me, but they find that title is vested in the Lord Jestocost, and they must do strange things to obtain my trifles."

"Are all these things genuine?" asked Rod, thinking that even Old North Australia could not buy out this shop if they were.

"Certainly not," said the old man. "Most of them are forgeries—wonderful forgeries. The Instrumentality lets me go to the robot-pits where insane or worn-out robots are destroyed. I can have my pick of them if they are not dangerous. I put them to work making copies of anything which I find in the museums."

"Those Cape triangles?" said Rod. "Are they real?"

"Cape triangles? You mean the letter stickers. They are genuine, all right, but they are not mine. Those are on loan from the Earth Museum until I can get them copied."

"I will buy them," said Rod.

"You will not," said the Catmaster. "They are not for sale."

"Then I will buy Earth and you and them too," said Rod.

"Roderick Frederick Ronald Arnold William MacArthur McBan to the one hundred and fifty-first, you will not."

"Who are you to tell me?"

"I have looked at one person and I have talked to two others."

"All right," said Rod. "Who?"

"I looked at the other Rod McBan, your workwoman Eleanor. She is a little mixed up about having a young man's body, because she is very drunk in the home of the Lord William Not-from-here and a beautiful young woman named Ruth Not-from-here is trying to make Eleanor marry her. She has no idea that she is dealing with another woman and Eleanor, in her copy of your proper body, is finding the experience exciting but terribly confusing. No harm will come of it, and your Eleanor is perfectly safe. Half the rascals of Earth have converged on the Lord William's house, but he has a whole battalion from the Defense Fleet on loan around the place, so nothing is going to happen, except that Eleanor will have a headache and Ruth will have a disappointment."

Rod smiled. "You couldn't have told me anything better. Who else did you talk to?"

"The Lord Jestocost and John Fisher to the hundredth."

"Mister and Owner Fisher? He's here?"

"He's at his home. Station of the Good Fresh Joey. I asked him if you could have your heart's desire. After a little while, he and somebody named Doctor Wentworth said that the Commonwealth of Old North Australia would approve it."

"How did you ever pay for such a call?" cried Rod. "Those things are frightfully expensive."

"I didn't pay for it, Mister and Owner. *You* did. I charged it to your account, by the authority of your trustee, the Lord Jestocost. He and his forefathers have been my patrons for four hundred and twenty-six years."

"You've got your nerve," said Rod. "Spending my money when I was right here and not even asking me!"

"You are an adult for some purposes and a minor for other purposes. I am offering you the skills which keep me alive. Do you think any ordinary cat-man would be allowed to live as long as this?"

"No," said Rod. "Give me those stamps and let me go."

The Catmaster looked at him levelly. Once again there was the *personal* look on his face, which on Norstrilia would have been taken as an unpardonable affront; but along with the nosiness, there was an air of confidence and kindness which put Rod a little in awe of the man, underperson though he was. "Do you think that you could love these stamps when you get back home? Could they talk to you? Could they make you like yourself? Those pieces of paper are not your heart's desire. Something else is."

"What?" said Rod, truculently.

"In a bit, I'll explain. First, you cannot kill me. Second, you cannot hurt me. Third, if I kill you, it will be all for your own good. Fourth, if you get out of here, you will be a very happy man."

"Are you barmy, Mister?" cried Rod. "I can knock you flat and walk out that door. I don't know what you are talking about."

"Try it," said the Catmaster levelly.

Rod looked at the tall withered old man with the bright eyes. He looked at the door, a mere seven or eight meters away. He did not want to try it.

"All right," he conceded, "play your pitch."

"I am a clinical psychologist. The only one on Earth and probably the only one on any planet. I got my knowledge from some ancient books when I was a kitten, being changed into a young man. I change people just a little, little bit. You know that the Instrumentality has surgeons and brains experts and all sorts of doctors. They can do almost anything with personality—anything but the light stuff ... *That,* I do."

"I don't get it," said Rod.

"Would you go to a brain surgeon to get a haircut? Would you need a dermatologist to give you a bath? Of course not. I don't do heavy work. I just change people a little bit. It makes them happy. If I can't do anything with them, I give them souvenirs from this junkpile out here. The real work is in there. That's where you're going, pretty soon." He nodded his head at the door marked HATE HALL.

Rod cried out, "I've been taking orders from one stranger after another, all these long weeks since my computers and I made that money! Can't I ever do anything myself?"

The Catmaster looked at him with sympathy. "None of us can. We may think that we are free. Our lives are made for us by the people we happen to know, the places we happen to be, the jobs or hobbies which we happen to run across. Will I be dead a year from now? I don't know. Will you be back in Old North Australia a year from now, still only seventeen, but rich and wise and on your way to happiness? I don't know. You've had a run of good luck. Look at it that way. It's luck. And I'm part of the luck. If you get killed here, it will not be my doing but just the over-strain of your body against the devices which the Lady Goroke approved a long time ago—devices which the Lord Jestocost reports to the Instrumentality. He keeps them legal that way. I'm the only underman in the universe who is entitled to process real people in any way whatever without having direct human supervision. All I do is to develop people, like an Ancient Man developing a photograph from a piece of paper exposed to different grades of light. I'm not a hidden judge, like your men in the Garden of Death. It's going to be you against you, with me just helping, and when you come out you're going to be a different you—the same you, but a little better there, a little more flexible here. As a matter of fact, that cat-type body you're wearing is going to make your contest with yourself a little harder for me to manage. We'll do it, Rod. Are you ready?"

"Ready for what?"

"For the tests and changes there." The Catmaster nodded at the door marked HATE HALL.

"I suppose so," said Rod. "I don't have much choice."

"No," said the Catmaster, sympathetically and almost sadly, "not at this point, you don't. If you walk out that door, you're an illegal cat-man, in immediate danger of being buzzed down by the robot police."

"Please," said Rod, "win or fail, can I have one of these Cape triangles?"

The Catmaster smiled. "I promise you—if you want one, you shall have it." He waved at the door: "Go on in."

Rod was not a coward, but it was with feet and legs of lead that he walked to the door. It opened by itself. He walked in, steady but afraid.

The room was dark with a darkness deeper than mere black. It was the dark of blindness, the expanse of cheek where no eye has ever been.

The door closed behind him and he swam in the dark, so tangible had the darkness become.

He felt blind. He felt as if he had never seen.

But he could hear.

He heard his own blood pulsing through his head.

He could smell—indeed, he was good at smelling. And this air—this air—this air smelled of the open night on the dry plains of Old North Australia.

The smell made him feel little and afraid. It reminded him of his repeated childhoods, of the artificial drownings in the laboratories where he had gone to be reborn from one childhood to another.

He reached out his hands.

Nothing.

He jumped gently. No ceiling.

Using a fieldman's trick familiar from times of dust storms, he dropped lightly to his hands and feet. He scuttled crabwise on two feet and one hand, using the other hand as a shield to protect his face. In a very few meters he found the wall. He followed the wall around.

Circular.

This was the door.

Follow again.

With more confidence, he moved fast. Around, around, around. He could not tell whether the floor was asphalt or some kind of rough worn tile.

Door again.

A voice spieked to him.

Spieked! *And he heard it.*

He looked upward into the nothing which was bleaker than blindness, almost expecting to see the words in letters of fire, so clear had they been.

The voice was Norstrilian and it said,

Rod McBan is a man, man, man.

But what is man?

(Immediate percussion of crazy, sad laughter.)

Rod never noticed that he reverted to the habits of babyhood. He sat flat on his rump, legs spread out in front of him at a ninety-degree angle. He put his hands a little behind him and leaned back, letting the weight of his body push his shoulders a little bit upward. He knew the ideas that would follow the words, but he never knew why he so readily expected them.

Light formed in the room, as he had been sure it would.

The images were little, but they looked real.

Men and women and children, children and women and men marched into his vision and out again.

They were not freaks; they were not beasts; they were not alien monstrosities begotten in some outside universe; they were not robots; they were not underpeople; they were all hominids like himself, kinsmen in the Earthborn races of men.

First came people like Old North Australians and Earth people, very much alike, and both similar to the ancient types, except that Norstrilians were pale beneath their tanned skins, bigger, and more robust.

Then came Daimoni, white-eyed pale giants with a magical assurance, whose very babies walked as though they had already been given ballet lessons.

Then heavy men, fathers, mothers, infants swimming on the solid ground from which they would never arise.

Then rainmen from Amazonas Triste, their skins hanging in enormous folds around them, so that they looked like bundles of wet rags wrapped around monkeys.

Blind men from Olympia, staring fiercely at the world through the radars mounted on their foreheads.

Bloated monster-men from abandoned planets—people as bad off as his own race had been after escaping from Paradise VII.

And still more races.

People he had never heard of.

Men with shells.

Men and women so thin that they looked like insects.

A race of smiling, foolish giants, lost in the irreparable hebephrenia of their world. (Rod had the feeling that they were shepherded by a race of devoted dogs, more intelligent than themselves, who cajoled them into breeding, begged them to eat, led them to sleep. He saw no dogs, only the smiling unfocused fools, but the feeling *dog, good dog!* was somehow very near.)

A funny little people who pranced with an indefinable deformity of gait.

Water-people, the clean water of some unidentified world pulsing through their gills.

And then—

More people, still, but hostile ones. Lipsticked hermaphrodites with enormous beards and fluting voices. Carcinomas which had taken over men. Giants rooted in the Earth. Human bodies crawling and weeping as they crept through wet grass, somehow contaminated themselves and looking for more people to infect.

Rod did not know it, but he growled.

He jumped into a squatting position and swept his hands across the rough floor, looking for a weapon.

These were not men—they were enemies!

Still they came. People who had lost eyes, or who had grown fire-resistant, the wrecks and residues of abandoned settlements and forgotten colonies. The waste and spoilage of the human race.

And then—

Him.

Himself.

The child Rod McBan.

And voices, Norstrilian voices calling: "He can't hier. He can't spiek. He's a freak. He's a freak. He can't hier. He can't spiek."

And another voice: "His poor parents!"

The child Rod disappeared and there were his parents again. Twelve times taller than life, so high that he had to peer up into the black absorptive ceiling to see the underside of their faces.

The mother wept.

The father sounded stern.

The father was saying, "It's no use. Doris can watch him while we're gone, but if he isn't any better, we'll turn him in."

"Kill him?" shrieked the woman. "Kill my baby? Oh, no! No!"

The calm, loving, horrible voice of the man, "Darling, spiek to him yourself. He'll never hier. Can that be a Rod McBan?"

Then the woman's voice, sweet-poisonous and worse than death, sobbing agreement with her man against her son.

"I don't know, Rod. I don't know. Just don't tell me about it."

He *had* hiered them, in one of his moments of wild penetrating hiering
when everything telepathic came in with startling clarity. He had hiered
them when he was a baby.

The real Rod in the dark room let out a roar of fear, desolation, loneliness, rage, hate. This was the telepathic bomb with which he had so
often startled or alarmed the neighbors, the mind-shock with which he
had killed the giant spider in the tower of Earthport far above him.

But this time, the room was closed.

His mind roared back at itself.

Rage, loudness, hate, raw noise poured into him from the floor, the
circular wall, the high ceiling.

He cringed beneath it and as he cringed, the sizes of the images
changed. His parents sat in chairs, chairs. They were little, little. He was
an almighty baby, so enormous that he could scoop them up with his right
hand.

He reached to crush the tiny loathsome parents who had said, "Let
him die."

To crush them, but they faded first.

Their faces turned frightened. They looked wildly around. Their chairs
dissolved, the fabric falling to a floor which in turn looked like storm-
eroded cloth. They turned for a last kiss and had no lips. They reached to
hug each other and their arms fell off. Their spaceship had gone milky
in mid-trip, dissolving into traceless nothing. And he, he, he himself
had seen it!

The rage was followed by tears, by a guilt too deep for regret, by a
self-accusation so raw and wet that it lived like one more organ inside his
living body.

He wanted nothing.

No money, no stroon, no Station of Doom. He wanted no friends, no
companionship, no welcome, no house, no food. He wanted no walks, no
solitary discoveries in the field, no friendly sheep, no treasures in the
gap, no computer, no day, no night, no life.

He wanted nothing, and he could not understand death.

The enormous room lost all light, all sound, and he did not notice it.
His own naked life lay before him like a freshly dissected cadaver. It lay
there and it made no sense. There had been many Roderick Frederick
Ronald Arnold William MacArthur McBans, one hundred and fifty of
them in a row, but he—151! 151! 151!—was not one of them, not a giant
who had wrestled treasure from the sick Earth and hidden sunshine of the

Norstrilian plains. It wasn't his telepathic deformity, his spieklessness, his brain deafness to hiering. It was himself, the "Me-subtile" inside him, which was wrong, all wrong. He was the baby worth killing, who had killed instead. He had hated mama and papa for their pride and their hate: when he hated them, they crumpled and died out in the mystery of space, so that they did not even leave bodies to bury.

Rod rose to his feet. His hands were wet. He touched his face and he realized that he had been weeping with his face cupped in his hands.

Wait.

There was something.

There was one thing he wanted. He wanted Houghton Syme not to hate him. Houghton Syme could hier and spiek, but he was a shortie, living with the sickness of death lying between himself and every girl, every friend, every job he had met. And he, Rod, had mocked that man, calling him Old Hot and Simple. Rod might be worthless but he was not as bad off as Houghton Syme, the Hon. Sec. Houghton Syme was at least trying to be a man, to live his miserable scrap of life, and all Rod had ever done was to flaunt his wealth and near-immortality before the poor cripple who had just one hundred and sixty years to live. Rod wanted only one thing—to get back to Old North Australia in time to help Houghton Syme, to let Houghton Syme know that the guilt was his, Rod's, and not Syme's. The Onseck had a bit of a life and he deserved the best of it.

Rod stood there, expecting nothing.

He had forgiven his last enemy.

He had forgiven himself.

The door opened very matter-of-factly and there stood the Catmaster, a quiet wise smile upon his face,

"You can come out now, Mister and Owner McBan; and if there is anything in this outer room which you want, you may certainly have it."

Rod walked out slowly. He had no idea how long he had been in HATE HALL.

When he emerged, the door closed behind him.

"No, thanks, cobber. It's mighty friendly of you, but I don't need anything much, and I'd better be getting back to my own planet."

"Nothing?" said the Catmaster, still smiling very attentively and very quietly.

"I'd like to hier and spiek, but it's not very important."

"This is for you," said the Catmaster. "You put it in your ear and leave it there. If it itches or gets dirty, you take it out, wash it, and put it back in. It's not a rare device, but apparently you don't have them on your planet." He held out an object no larger than the kernel of a ground-nut.

Rod took it absently and was ready to put it into his pocket, not into his ear, when he saw that the smiling attentive face was watching, very gently but very alertly. He put the device into his ear. It felt a little cold.

"I will now," said the Catmaster, "take you to C'mell, who will lead you to your friends in Downdeep-downdeep. You had better take this blue two-penny Cape of Good Hope postage stamp with you. I will report to Jestocost that it was lost while I attempted to copy it. That is slightly true, isn't it?"

Rod started to thank him absent-mindedly and then—

Then, with a thrill which sent gooseflesh all over his neck, back and arms, he realized that the Catmaster had not moved his lips in the slightest, had not pushed air through his throat, had not disturbed the air with the pressure of noise. The Catmaster had spieked to Rod, and Rod had hiered him.

Thinking very carefully and very clearly, but closing his lips and making no sound whatever, Rod thought,

"Worthy and gracious Catmaster, I thank you for the ancient treasure of the old Earth stamp. I thank you even more for the hiering-spieking device which I am now testing. Will you please extend your right hand to shake hands with me, if you can actually hier me now?"

The Catmaster stepped forward and extended his hand.

Man and underman, they faced each other with a kindness and gratitude which was so poignant as to be very close to grief.

Neither of them wept. Neither.

They shook hands without speaking or spieking.

EVERYBODY'S FOND OF MONEY

While Rod McBan was going through his private ordeal at the Department Store of Hearts' Desires, other people continued to be concerned with him and his fate.

A Crime of Public Opinion

A middle-aged woman, with a dress which did not suit her, sat uninvited at the table of Paul, a real man once acquainted with C'mell.

Paul paid no attention to her. Eccentricities were multiplying among people these days. Being middle-aged was a matter of taste, and many human beings, after the Rediscovery of Man, found that if they let themselves become imperfect, it was a more comfortable way to live than the old way—the old way consisting of aging minds dwelling in bodies condemned to the perpetual perfection of youth.

"I had flu," said the woman. "Have you ever had flu?"

"No," said Paul, not very much interested.

"Are you reading a newspaper?" She looked at his newspaper, which had everything except news in it.

Paul, with the paper in front of him, admitted that he was reading it.

"Do you like coffee?" said the woman, looking at Paul's cup of fresh coffee in front of him.

"Why would I order it if I didn't?" said Paul brusquely, wondering how the woman had ever managed to find so unattractive a material for her dress. It was yellow sunflowers on an off-red background.

The woman was baffled, but only for a moment.

"I'm wearing a girdle," she said. "They just came on sale last week. They're very, very ancient, and very authentic. Now that people can be fat if they want to, girdles are the rage. They have spats for men, too. Have you bought your spats yet?"

"No," said Paul flatly, wondering if he should leave his coffee and newspaper.

"What are you going to do about that man?"

"What man?" said Paul, politely and wearily.

"The man who's bought the Earth."

"Did he?" said Paul.

163

"Of course," said the woman. "Now he has more power than the Instrumentality. He could do anything he wants. He can give us anything we want. If he wanted to, he could give *me* a thousand-year trip around the universe."

"Are you an official?" said Paul sharply.

"No," said the woman, taken a little aback.

"Then how do you know these things?"

"*Everybody* knows them. Everybody." She spoke firmly and pursed her mouth at the end of the sentence.

"What are you going to do about this man? Rob him? Seduce him?" Paul was sardonic. He had had an unhappy love affair which he still remembered, a climb to the Abba-dingo over Alpha Ralpha Boulevard which he would never repeat, and very little patience with fools who had never dared and never suffered anything.

The woman flushed with anger. "We're all going to his hostel at twelve today. We're going to shout and shout until he comes out. Then we're going to form a line and make him listen to what each one of us wants."

Paul spoke sharply: "Who organized this?"

"I don't know. Somebody."

Paul spoke solemnly. "You're a human being. You have been trained. What is the Twelfth Rule?"

The woman turned a little pale but she chanted, as if by rote: " 'Any man or woman who finds that he or she forms and shares an unauthorized opinion with a large number of other people shall report immediately for therapy to the nearest subchief.' But that doesn't mean me…?"

"You'll be dead or scrubbed by tonight, madam. Now go away and let me read my paper."

The woman glared at him, between anger and tears. Gradually fear came over her features. "Do you really think what I was saying is unlawful?"

"Completely," said Paul.

She put her pudgy hands over her face and sobbed. "Sir, sir, can you— can you please help me find a subchief? I'm afraid I do need help. But I've dreamed so much, I've hoped so much. A man from the stars. But you're right, sir. I don't want to die or get blanked out. Sir, please help me!"

Moved by both impatience and compassion, Paul left his paper and his coffee. The robot waiter hurried up to remind him that he had not paid. Paul walked over to the sidewalk where there were two barrels full of money for people who wished to play the games of ancient civilization. He selected the biggest bill he could see, gave it to the waiter, waited for his change, gave the waiter a tip, received thanks, and threw the change, which was all coins, into the barrel full of metal money. The woman had waited for him patiently, her blotched face sad.

When he offered her his arm, in the old-French manner, she took it. They walked a hundred meters, more or less, to a public visiphone. She half-cried, half-mumbled as she walked along beside him, with her uncomfortable, ancient spiked-heel feminine shoes:

"I used to have four hundred years. I used to be slim and beautiful. I liked to make love and I didn't think very much about things, because I wasn't very bright. I had had a lot of husbands. Then this change came along, and I felt useless, and I decided to be what I felt like—fat, and sloppy, and middle-aged, and bored. And I have succeeded too much, just the way two of my husbands said. And that man from the stars, he has all power. He can change things."

Paul did not answer her, except to nod sympathetically.

At the visiphone he stood until a robot appeared. "A subchief," he said. "Any subchief."

The image blurred and the face of a very young man appeared. He stared earnestly and intently while Paul recited his number, grade, neo-national assignment, quarters number and business. He had to state the business twice, "Criminal public opinion."

The subchief snapped, not unpleasantly, "Come on in, then, and we'll fix you up."

Paul was so annoyed at the idea that *he* would be suspected of criminal public opinion, "any opinion shared with a large number of other people, other than material released and approved by the Instrumentality and the Earth Government," that he began to spiek his protest into the machine.

"Vocalize, man and citizen! These machines don't carry telepathy."

When Paul got through explaining, the youngster in uniform looked at him critically but pleasantly, saying,

"Citizen, you've forgotten something yourself."

"Me?" gasped Paul. "I've done nothing. This woman just sat down beside me and—"

"Citizen," said the subchief, "what is the last half of the Fifth Rule for All Men?"

Paul thought a moment and then answered, "The services of every person shall be available, without delay and without charge, to any other true human being who encounters danger or distress." Then his own eyes widened and he said, "You want me to do this myself?"

"What do you think?" said the subchief.

"I can," said Paul.

"Of course," said the subchief. "You are normal. You remember the braingrips."

Paul nodded.

The subchief waved at him and the image faded from the screen.

The woman had seen it all. She, too, was prepared. When Paul lifted his hands for the traditional hypnotic gestures, she locked her eyes upon his hands. She made the responses as they were needed. When he had brainscrubbed her right there in the open street, she shambled off down the walkway, not knowing why tears poured down her cheeks. She did not remember Paul at all.

For a moment of crazy whimsy, Paul thought of going across the city and having a look at the wonderful man from the stars. He stared around absently, thinking. His eye caught the high thread of Alpha Ralpha Boulevard, soaring unsupported across the heavens from faraway ground to the mid-height of Earthport: he remembered himself and his own personal troubles. He went back to his newspaper and a fresh cup of coffee, helping himself to money from the barrel, this time, before he entered the restaurant.

On a Yacht Off Meeya Meefla

Ruth yawned as she sat up and looked at the ocean. She had done her best with the rich young man.

The false Rod McBan, actually a reconstructed Eleanor, said to her: "This is right nice."

Ruth smiled languidly and seductively. She did not know why Eleanor laughed out loud.

The Lord William Not-from-here came up from below the deck. He carried two silver mugs in his hands. They were frosted.

"I am glad," said he unctuously, "that you young people are happy. These are mint juleps, a very ancient drink indeed."

He watched as Eleanor sipped hers and then smiled.

He smiled too. "You like it?"

Eleanor smiled right back at him. "Beats washing dishes, it does!" said "Rod McBan" enigmatically.

The Lord William began to think that the rich young man was odd indeed.

Antechamber of the Bell and Bank

The Lord Crudelta commanded, "Send Jestocost here!"

The Lord Jestocost was already entering the room.

"What's happened on that case of the young man?"

"Nothing, Sir and Senior."

"Tush. Bosh. Nonsense. Rot." The old man snorted. "Nothing is something that doesn't happen at all. He has to be somewhere."

"The original is with the Catmaster, at the Department Store."

"Is that safe?" said the Lord Crudelta. "He might get to be too smart for us to manage. You're working some scheme again, Jestocost."

"Nothing but what I told you, Sir and Senior."

The old man frowned. "That's right. You *did* tell me. Proceed. But the others?"

"Who?"

"The decoys?"

The Lord Jestocost laughed aloud. "Our colleague, the Lord William, has almost betrothed his daughter to Mister McBan's workman, who is temporarily a 'Rod McBan' herself. All parties are having fun with no harm done. The robots, the eight survivors, are going around Earthport city. They are enjoying themselves as much as robots ever do. Crowds are gathering and asking for miracles. Pretty harmless."

"And the Earth economy? Is it getting out of balance?"

"I've set the computers to work," said the Lord Jestocost, "finding every tax penalty that we ever imposed on anybody. We're several megacredits ahead."

"FOE money."

"FOE money, Sir."

"You're not going to ruin him?" said Crudelta.

"Not at all, Sir and Senior," cried the Lord Jestocost. "I am a kind man."

The old man gave him a low dirty smile. "I've seen your kindness before, Jestocost, and I would rather have a thousand worlds for an enemy than have you be my friend! You're devious, you're dangerous, and you are tricky."

Jestocost, much flattered by this comment, said formally, "You do an honest official a great injustice, Sir and Senior."

The two men just smiled at each other: they knew each other well.

Ten Kilometers Below the Surface of the Earth

The E'telekeli stood from the lectern at which he had been praying.

His daughter was watching him immovably from the doorway.

He spieked to her, "What's wrong, my girl?"

"I saw his mind, father, I saw it for just a moment as he left the Catmaster's place. He's a rich young man from the stars, he's a nice young man, he has bought Earth, but he is not the man of the Promise."

"You expected too much, E'lamelanie," spieked her father.

"I expected hope," she spieked to him. "Is hope a crime among us underpeople? What Joan foresaw, what the Copt promised—where are they, father? Shall we never see daylight or know freedom?"

"True men are not free either," spieked the E'telekeli. "They too have grief, fear, birth, old age, love, death, suffering and the tools of their own ruin. Freedom is not something which is going to be given us by a wonderful man beyond the stars. Freedom is what you do, my dear, and what I do. Death is a very private affair, my daughter, and life—when you get to it—is almost as private."

"I know, father," she spieked. "I know. I know. I know." (But she didn't.)

"You may not know it, my darling," spieked the great bird-man, "but long before these people built cities, there were others in the Earth—the ones who came after the Ancient World fell. They went far beyond the limitations of the human form. They conquered death. They did not have sickness. They did not need love. They sought to be abstractions lying outside of time. And they died, E'lamelanie—they died terribly. Some became monsters, preying on the remnants of true men for reasons which ordinary men could not even begin to understand. Others were like oysters, wrapped up in their own sainthood. They had all forgotten that humanness is itself imperfection and corruption, that what is perfect is no longer understandable. We have the Fragments of the Word, and we are truer to the deep traditions of people than people themselves are, but we must never be foolish enough to look for perfection in this life or to count on our own powers to make us really different from what we are. You and I are animals, darling, not even real people, but people do not understand the teaching of Joan, that whatever *seems* human *is human.* It is the word which quickens, not the shape or the blood or the texture of flesh or hair or feathers. And there is that power which you and I do not name, but which we love and cherish because we need it more than do the people on the surface. Great beliefs always come out of the sewers of cities, not out of the towers of the ziggurats. Furthermore, we are discarded animals, not used ones. All of us down here are the rubbish which mankind has thrown away and has forgotten. We have a great advantage in this, because we know from the very beginning of our lives that we are worthless. And why are we worthless? Because a higher standard and a higher truth says that we are—the conventional law and the unwritten customs of mankind. But I feel love for you, my daughter, and you have love for me. We know that everything which loves has a value in itself, and that therefore this worthlessness of underpeople is wrong. We are forced to look beyond the minute and the hour to the place where no clocks work and no day dawns. There is a world outside of time, and it is to that which we appeal. I know that you have a love for the devotional life, my child, and I commend you for it, but it would be a sorry faith which waited for passing travelers or which believed that a miracle or two could set the nature of things right and whole. The people on the surface think they have gone beyond the old problems, because they do not have buildings which they call churches or temples, and they do not have professional religious men within their communities. But the higher power and the large problems still wait for all men, whether men like it or not. Today, Believing among mankind is a ridiculous hobby, tolerated by the Instrumentality because the Believers are unimportant and weak, but mankind has moments of enormous passion which will come again and in which we will share. So don't you wait for your hero beyond the stars. If you have a good devotional life within you, it is already here, waiting to be watered by your tears and ploughed up by your hard, clear thoughts. And if you don't have a devotional life, there are good lives outside.

"Look at your brother, E'ikasus, who is now resuming his normal shape. He let me put him in animal form and send him out among the stars. He took risks without committing the impudence of enjoying risk. It is not necessary to do your duty joyfully—just to do it. Now he has homed to the old lair and I know he brings us good luck in many little things, perhaps in big things. Do you understand, my daughter?"

She said that she did, but there was still a wild blank disappointed look in her eyes as she said it.

A Police-Post on the Surface, Near Earthport

"The robot sergeant says he can do no more without violating the rule against hurting human beings." The subchief looked at his chief, licking his chops for a chance to get out of the office and to wander among the vexations of the city. He was tired of viewscreens, computers, buttons, cards, and routines. He wanted a raw life and high adventure.

"Which offworlder is this?"

"Tostig Amaral, from the planet of Amazonas Triste. He has to stay wet all the time. He is just a licensed trader, not an honored guest of the Instrumentality. He was assigned a girlygirl and now he thinks she belongs to him."

"Send the girlygirl to him. What is she, mouse-derived?"

"No, a c'girl. Her name is C'mell and she has been requisitioned by the Lord Jestocost."

"I know all about that," said the chief, wishing that he really did. "She's now assigned to that Old North Australian who has bought most of this planet, Earth."

"But this hominid wants her, just the same!" The subchief was urgent.

"He can't have her, not if a Lord of the Instrumentality commands her services."

"He is threatening to fight. He says he will kill people."

"Hmm. Is he in a room?"

"Yes, Sir and Chief."

"With standard outlets?"

"I'll look, Sir." The subchief twisted a knob and an electronic design appeared on the left-hand screen in front of him. "Yes, sir, that's it."

"Let's have a look at him."

"He got permission, sir, to run the fire sprinkler system all the time. It seems he comes from a rain-world."

"Try, anyhow."

"Yes, sir." The subchief whistled a call to the board. The picture dissolved, whirled, and resolved itself into the image of a dark room. There seemed to be a bundle of wet rags in one corner, out of which a well-shaped human hand protruded.

"Nasty type," said the chief, "and probably poisonous. Knock him out for exactly one hour. We'll be getting orders meanwhile."

On an Earth-Level Street Under Earthport

Two girls talking.

"...and I will tell you the biggest secret in the whole world, if you will never, never tell anyone."

"I'll bet it's not much of a secret. You don't have to tell me."

"I'll never tell you then. Never."

"Suit yourself."

"Really, if you even suspected it, you would be mad with curiosity."

"If you want to tell me, you can tell me."

"But it's a *secret.*"

"All right, I'll never tell anybody."

"That man from the stars. He's going to marry me."

"You? That's ridiculous."

"Why is it so ridiculous? He's bought my dower rights already."

"I know it's ridiculous. There's something wrong."

"I don't see why you should think he doesn't like me if he has already bought my dower rights."

"Fool! I know it's ridiculous, because he has bought mine."

"Yours?"

"Yes."

"Both of us?"

"What for?"

"Search me."

"Maybe he is going to put us both in the same harem. Wouldn't that be romantic?"

"They don't have harems in Old North Australia. All they do is live like prudish old farmers and raise stroon and murder anybody at all that even gets near them."

"That sounds bad."

"Let's go to the police."

"You know, he's hurt our feelings. Maybe we can make him pay extra for buying our dower rights if he doesn't mean to use them."

In Front of a Café

A man, drunk:

"I will get drunk every night and I will have musicians to play me to sleep and I will have all the money I need and it won't be that play money out of a barrel but it will be real money registered in the computer and I will make everybody do what I say and I know he will do it for me because my mother was named MacArthur in her genetic code before everybody got numbers and you have no call to laugh at me because his name really is MacArthur McBan the eleventh and I am probably the closest friend and relative he has on Earth ..."

TOSTIG AMARAL

Rod McBan left the Department Store of Hearts' Desires simply, humbly; he carried a package of books, wrapped in dustproofing paper, and he looked like any other first-class cat-man messenger. The human beings in the market were still making their uproar, their smells of food, spices, and odd objects, but he walked so calmly and so straightforwardly through their scattered groups that even the robot police, weapons on the buzz, paid no attention to him.

When he had come across the Thieves' Market going the other way with C'mell and A'gentur, he had been ill at ease. As a Mister and Owner from Old North Australia, he had been compelled to keep his external dignity, but he had not felt ease within his heart. These people were strange, his destination had been unfamiliar, and the problems of wealth and survival lay heavy upon him.

Now, it was all different. Cat-man he might still be on the outside, but on the inside he once again felt his proper pride of home and planet.

And more.

He felt calm, down to the very tips of his nerve endings.

The hiering-spieking device should have alerted him, excited him: it did not. As he walked through the market, he noticed that very few of the Earth people were communicating with one another telepathically. They preferred to babble in their loud airborne language, of which they had not one but many kinds, with the Old Common Tongue serving as a referent to those who had been endowed with different kinds of ancient language by the processes of the Rediscovery of Man. He even heard Ancient Inglish, the Queen's Own Language, sounding remarkably close to his own spoken language of Norstrilian. These things caused neither stimulation nor excitement, not even pity. He had his own problems, but they were no longer the problems of wealth or of survival. Somehow he had confidence that a hidden, friendly power in the universe would take care of him, if he took care of others. He wanted to get Eleanor out of trouble, to disembarrass the Hon. Sec., to see Lavinia, to reassure Doris, to say a good goodbye to C'mell, to get back to his sheep, to protect his computer, and to keep the Lord Redlady away from his bad habit of killing other people lawfully on too slight an occasion for manslaughter.

One of the robot police, a little more perceptive than the others, watched this cat-man who walked with preternatural assurance through the crowds of men, but "C'roderick" did nothing but enter the market from one side, thread his way through it, and leave at the other side, still carrying his package; the robot turned away: his dreadful, milky eyes, always ready for disorder and death, scanned the marketplace again and again with fatigue-free vigilance.

Rod went down the ramp and turned right.

There was the underpeople commissary with the bear-man cashier. The cashier remembered him.

"It's been a long day, cat-sir, since I saw you. Would you like another special order of fish?"

"Where's my girl?" said Rod bluntly.

"C'mell?" said the bear-cashier. "She waited here a long time but then she went on and she left this message, 'Tell my man C'rod that he should eat before following me, but that when he has eaten he can either follow me by going to Upshaft Four, Ground Level, Hostel of the Singing Birds, Room Nine, where I am taking care of an offworld visitor, or he can send a robot to me and I will come to him.' Don't you think, cat-sir, that I've done well, remembering so complicated a message?" The bear-man flushed a little and the edge went off his pride as he confessed, for the sake of some abstract honesty, "Of course, that address part, I wrote that down. It would be very bad and very confusing if I sent you to the wrong address in people's country. Somebody might burn you down if you came into an unauthorized corridor."

"Fish, then," said Rod. "A fish dinner, please."

He wondered why C'mell, with his life in the balance, would go off to another visitor. Even as he thought this, he detected the mean jealousy behind it, and he confessed to himself that he had no idea of the terms, conditions, or hours of work required in the girlygirl business.

He sat dully on the bench, waiting for his food.

The uproar of HATE HALL was still in his mind, the pathos of his parents, those dying dissolving manikins, was bright within his heart, and his body throbbed with the fatigue of the ordeal. Idly he asked the bear-cashier, "How long has it been since I was here?"

The bear-cashier looked at the clock on the wall. "About fourteen hours, worthy cat."

"How long is that in real time?" Rod was trying to compare Norstrilian hours with Earth hours. He thought that Earth hours were one-seventh shorter, but he was not sure.

The bear-man was completely baffled. "If you mean galactic navigation time, dear guest, we never use that down here anyhow. Are there any other kinds of time?"

Rod realized his mistake and tried to correct it. "It doesn't matter. I am thirsty. What is lawful for underpeople to drink? I am tired and thirsty, both, but I have no desire to become the least bit drunk."

"Since you are a c'man," said the bear-cashier, "I recommend strong black coffee mixed with sweet whipped cream."

"I have no money," said Rod.

"The famous cat-madame, C'mell your consort, has guaranteed payment for anything at all that you order."

"Go ahead, then."

The bear-man called a robot over and gave him the orders.

Rod stared at the wall, wondering what he was going to do with this Earth he had bought. He wasn't thinking very hard, just musing idly. A voice cut directly into his mind. He realized that the bear-man was spieking to him and that he could hier it.

"You are not an underman, Sir and Master."

"What?" spieked Rod.

"You hiered me," said the telepathic voice. "I am not going to repeat it. If you come in the sign of the Fish, may blessings be upon you."

"I don't know that sign," said Rod.

"Then," spieked the bear-man, "no matter who you are, may you eat and drink in peace because you are a friend of C'mell and you are under the protection of the One Who Lives in Downdeep."

"I don't know," spieked Rod. "I just don't know, but I thank you for your welcome, friend."

"I do not give such welcomes lightly," said the bear-man, "and ordinarily I would be ready to run away from anything as strange and dangerous and unexplained as yourself, but you bring with you the quality of peace, which made me think that you might travel in the fellowship of the sign of the Fish. I have heard that in that sign, people and underpeople remember the blessed Joan and mingle in complete comradeship."

"No," said Rod, "no. I travel alone."

His food and drink came. He consumed them quietly. The bear-cashier had given him a table and bench far from the serving tables and away from the other underpeople who dropped in, interrupting their tasks, eating in a hurry so that they could get back in a hurry. He saw one wolfman, wearing the insignia of Auxiliary Police, who came to the wall, forced his identity-card into a slot, opened his mouth, bolted down five large chunks of red, raw meat, and left the commissary, all in less than one and one-half minutes. Rod was amazed but not impressed. He had too much on his mind.

At the desk he confirmed the address which C'mell had left, offered the bear-man a handshake, and went along to Upshaft Four. He still looked like a c'man and he carried his package alertly and humbly, as he had seen other underpeople behave in the presence of real persons.

He almost met death on the way. Upshaft Four was one-directional and was plainly marked, "People Only." Rod did not like the looks of it, as long as he moved in a cat-man body, but he did not think that C'mell would give him directions wrongly or lightly. (Later, he found that she had forgotten the phrase, "Special business under the protection of Jestocost, a chief of the Instrumentality," if he were to be challenged; but he did not know the phrase.)

An arrogant human man, wearing a billowing red cloak, looked at him sharply as he took a belt, hooked it and stepped into the shaft. When Rod stepped free, he and the man were on a level.

Rod tried to look like a humble, modest messenger, but the strange voice grated his ears:

"Just what do you think you are doing? This is a human shaft."

Rod pretended that he did not know it was himself whom the red-cloaked man was addressing. He continued to float quietly upward, his magnet-belt tugging uncomfortably at his waist.

A pain in the ribs made him turn suddenly, almost losing his balance in the belt.

"Animal!" cried the man. "Speak up or die."

Still holding his package of books, Rod said mildly, "I'm on an errand and I was told to go this way."

The man's senseless hostility gave caliber to his voice: "And who told you?"

"C'mell," said Rod absently.

The man and his companions laughed at that, and for some reason their laughter had no humor in it, just savagery, cruelty, and—way down underneath—something of fear. "Listen to that," said the man in a red cloak, "one animal says another animal told it to do something." He whipped out a knife.

"What are you doing?" cried Rod.

"Just cutting your belt," said the man. "There's nobody at all below us and you will make a nice red blob at the bottom of the shaft, cat-man. That ought to teach you which shaft to use."

The man actually reached over and seized Rod's belt.

He lifted the knife to slash.

Rod became frightened and angry. His brain ran red.

He spat thoughts at them—

pommy!
shortie!
Earthie
red dirty blue stinking little man,
die, puke, burst, blaze, die!

It all came out in a single flash, faster than he could control it. The red-cloaked man twisted oddly, as if in spasm. His two companions threshed in their belts. They turned slowly.

High above them, two women began screaming.

Further up a man was shouting, both with his voice and with his mind, "Police! Help! Police! Police! Brainbomb! Brainbomb! Help!"

The effort of his telepathic explosion left Rod feeling disoriented and weak. He shook his head and blinked his eyes. He started to wipe his face, only to hit himself on the jaw with the package of books, which he still carried. This aroused him a little. He looked at the three men. Redcloak was dead, his head at an odd angle. The other two seemed to be dead. One was floating upside down, his rump pointing upmost and the two limp legs swinging out at odd angles; the other was rightside up but had sagged in his belt. All three of them kept moving a steady ten meters a minute, right along with Rod.

There were strange sounds from above.

An enormous voice, filling the shaft with its volume, roared down: "Stay where you are! Police. Police. Police."

Rod glanced at the bodies floating upward. A corridor came by. He reached for the grip-bar, made it, and swung himself into the horizontal passage. He sat down immediately, not getting away from the Upshaft. He thought sharply with his new hiering. Excited, frantic minds beat all around him, looking for enemies, lunatics, crimes, aliens, anything strange.

Softly he began spieking to the empty corridor and to himself, "I am a dumb cat. I am the messenger C'rod. I must take the books to the gentleman from the stars. I am a dumb cat. I do not know much."

A robot, gleaming with the ornamental body-armor of Old Earth, landed at his cross-corridor, looked at Rod, and called up the shaft.

"Master, here's one. A c'man with a package."

A young subchief came into view, feet first as he managed to ride down the shaft instead of going up it. He seized the ceiling of the transverse corridor, gave himself a push and (once free of the shaft's magnetism) dropped heavily on his feet beside Rod. Rod hiered him thinking, "I'm good at this. I'm a good telepath. I clean things up fast. Look at this dumb cat."

Rod went on concentrating. "I'm a dumb cat. I have a package to deliver. I'm a dumb cat."

The subchief looked down at him scornfully. Rod felt the other's mind slide over his own in the rough equivalent of a search. He remained relaxed and tried to feel stupid while the other hiered him. Rod said nothing. The subchief flashed his baton over the package, eyeing the crystal knob at the end.

"Books," he snorted.

Rod nodded.

"You," said the bright young subchief, "you see bodies?" He spoke in a painfully clear, almost childish version of the Old Common Tongue.

Rod held up three fingers and then pointed upward.

"You, cat-man, you feel the brainbomb!"

Rod, beginning to enjoy the game, threw his head backward and let out a cattish yowl expressing pain. The subchief could not help clapping his hands over his ears. He started to turn away. "I can see what you think of it, cat-fellow. You're pretty stupid, aren't you?"

Still thinking low dull thoughts as evenly as he could, Rod said promptly and modestly, "Me smart cat. Very handsome too."

"Come along," said the subchief to his robot, disregarding Rod altogether.

Rod plucked at his sleeve.

The subchief turned back.

Very humbly Rod said, "Sir and Master, which way, Hostel of Singing Birds, Room Nine?"

"Mother of poodles!" cried the subchief. "I'm on a murder case and this dumb cat asks *me* for directions." He was a decent young man and he thought for a minute. "This way—" said he, pointing up the Upshaft— "it's twenty more meters and then the third street over. But that's 'people only.' It's about a kilometer over to the steps for animals." He stood, frowning, and then swung on one of his robots: "Wush', you see this cat!"

"Yes, master, a cat-man, very handsome."

"So you think he's handsome, too. He already thinks so, so that makes it unanimous. He may be handsome, but he's dumb. Wush', take this cat-man to the address he tells you. Use the Upshaft by my authority. Don't put a belt on him, just hug him."

Rod was immeasurably grateful that he had slipped his shaftbelt off and left it negligently on the rack just before the robot arrived.

The robot seized him around the waist with what was literally a grip of iron. They did not wait for the slow upward magnetic drive of the shaft to lift them. The robot had some kind of a jet in his backpack and lifted Rod with sickening speed to the next level. He pushed Rod into the corridor and followed him.

"Where do you go?" said the robot, very plainly.

Rod, concentrating on feeling stupid just in case someone might still be trying to hier his mind, said slowly and stumblingly,

"Hostel of the Singing Birds, Room Nine."

The robot stopped still, as though he were communicating telepathically, but Rod's mind, though alert, could catch not the faintest whisper of telepathic communication. "Hot buttered sheep!" thought Rod. "He's using radio to check the address with his headquarters right from here!"

Wush' appeared to be doing just that. He came to in a moment. They emerged under the sky, filled with Earth's own moon, the loveliest thing that Rod had ever seen. He did not dare to stop and enjoy the scenery, but he trotted lithely beside the robot-policeman.

They came down a road with heavy, scented flowers. The wet warm air of Earth spread the sweetness everywhere.

On their right there was a courtyard with copies of ancient fountains, a dining space now completely empty of diners, a robot-waiter in the corner, and many individual rooms opening on the plaza. The robot-policeman called to the robot-waiter,

"Where's number nine?"

The waiter answered him with a lifting of the hand and an odd twist of the wrist, twice repeated, which the robot-policeman seemed to understand perfectly well.

"Come along," he said to Rod, leading the way to an outside stairway which reached up to an outside balcony serving the second story of rooms. One of the rooms had a plain number nine on it.

Rod was about to tell the robot-policeman that he could see the number nine, when Wush', with officious kindness, took the doorknob and flung it open with a gesture of welcome to Rod.

There was the great cough of a heavy gun and Wush', his head blown almost completely off, clanked metallically to the iron floor of the balcony. Rod instinctively jumped for cover and flattened himself against the wall of the building.

A handsome man, wearing what seemed to be a black suit, came into the doorway, a heavy-caliber police pistol in his hand.

"Oh, there you are," said he to Rod, evenly enough. "Come on in."

Rod felt his legs working, felt himself walking into the room despite the effort of his mind to resist. He stopped pretending to be a dumb cat. He dropped the books on the ground and went back to thinking like his normal Old North Australian self, despite the cat body. It did no good. He kept on walking involuntarily, and entered the room.

As he passed the man himself, he was conscious of a sticky sweet rotten smell, like nothing he had ever smelled before. He also saw that the man, though fully clothed, was sopping wet.

He entered the room.

It was raining inside.

Somebody had jammed the fire-sprinkler system so that a steady rain fell from the ceiling to the floor.

C'mell stood in the middle of the room, her glorious red hair a wet stringy mop hanging down her shoulders. There was a look of concentration and alarm on her face.

"I," said the man, "am Tostig Amaral. This girl said that her husband would come with a policeman. I did not think she was right. But she was right. With a cat-husband there comes a policeman. I shoot the policeman. He is a robot and I can pay the Earth government for as many robots as I like. You are a cat. I can kill you also, and pay the charges on you. But I am a nice man, and I want to make love with your little red cat over there, so I will be generous and pay you something so that you can tell her she is mine and not yours. Do you understand that, cat-man?"

Rod found himself released from the unexplained muscular bonds which had hampered his freedom.

"My Lord, my Master from afar," he said, "C'mell is an underperson. It is the law here that if an underperson and a person become involved in love, the underperson dies and the human person gets brainscrubbed. I am sure, my Master, that you would not want to be brainscrubbed by the Earth authorities. Let the girl go. I agree that you can pay for the robot."

Amaral glided across the room. His face was pale, petulant, human, but Rod saw that the black clothes were not clothes at all.

The "clothes" were mucous membranes, an extension of Amaral's living skin.

The pale face turned even more pale with rage.

"You're a bold cat-man to talk like that. My body is bigger than yours, and it is poisonous as well. We have had to live hard in the rain of Amazonas Triste, and we have mental and physical powers which you had better not disturb. If you will not take payment, go away anyhow. The girl is mine. What happens to her is my business. If I violate Earth regulations, I will destroy the c'girl and pay for her. Go away, or you die."

Rod spoke with deliberate calm and with calculated risk. "Citizen, I play no game. I am not a cat-man but a subject of Her Absent Majesty the Queen, from Old North Australia. I give you warning that it is a man you face, and no mere animal. Let that girl go."

C'mell struggled as though she were trying to speak, but could not.

Amaral laughed, "That's a lie, animal, and a bold one! I admire you for trying to save your mate. But she is mine. She is a girlygirl and the

Instrumentality gave her to me. She is my pleasure. Go, bold cat! You are a good liar."

Rod took his last chance. "Scan me if you will."

He stood his ground.

Amaral's mind ran over his personality like filthy hands pawing naked flesh. Rod recoiled at the dirtiness and intimacy of being felt by such a person's thoughts, because he could sense the kinds of pleasure and cruelty which Amaral had experienced. He stood firm, calm, sure, just. He was not going to leave C'mell with this—this monster from the stars, man though he might be, of the old true human stock.

Amaral laughed. "You're a man, all right. A boy. A farmer. And you cannot hier or spiek except for the button in your ear. Get out, child, before I box your ears!"

Rod spoke: "Amaral, I herewith put you in danger."

Amaral did not reply with words.

His peaked sharp face grew paler and the folds of his skin dilated. They quivered, like the edges of wet, torn balloons. The room began to fill with a sickening sweet stench, as though it were a candy shop in which unburied bodies had died weeks before. There was a smell of vanilla, of sugar, of fresh hot cookies, of baked bread, of chocolate boiling in the pot; there was even a whiff of stroon. But as Amaral tensed and shook out his auxiliary skins each smell turned wrong, into a caricature and abomination of itself. The composite was hypnotic. Rod glanced at C'mell. She had turned completely white.

That decided him.

The calm which he had found with the Catmaster might be good, but there were moments for calm and other moments for anger.

Rod deliberately chose anger.

He felt fury rising in him as hot and quick and greedy as if it had been love. He felt his heart go faster, his muscles become stronger, his mind clearer. Amaral apparently had total confidence in his own poisonous and hypnotic powers, because he was staring straight forward as his skins swelled and waved in the air like wet leaves under water. The steady drizzle from the sprinkler kept everything penetratingly wet.

Rod disregarded this. He welcomed fury.

With his new hiering device, he focused on Amaral's mind, and only on Amaral's.

Amaral saw the movement of his eyes and whipped a knife into view.

"Man or cat, you're dying!" said Amaral, himself hot with the excitement of hate and collision.

Rod then spieked, in his worst scream—

beast, filth, offal—
spot, dirt, vileness,
wet, nasty—
die, die, die!

He was sure it was the loudest cry he had ever given. There was no echo, no effect. Amaral stared at him, the evil knife-point flickering in his hand like the flame atop a candle.

Rod's anger reached a new height.

He felt pain in his mind when he walked forward, cramps in his muscles as he used them. He felt a real fear of the offworld poison which this man-creature might exude, but the thought of C'mell—cat or no cat—alone with Amaral was enough to give him the rage of a beast and the strength of a machine.

Only at the very last moment did Amaral realize Rod had broken loose.

Rod never could tell whether the telepathic scream had really hurt the wet-worlder or not, because he did something very simple.

He reached with all the speed of a Norstrilian farmer, snatched the knife from Amaral's hand, ripping folds of soft, sticky skin with it, and then slashed the other man from clavicle to clavicle.

He jumped back in time to avoid the spurt of blood.

The "wet black suit" collapsed as Amaral died on the floor.

Rod took the dazed C'mell by the arm and led her out of the room. The air on the balcony was fresh, but the murder-smell of Amazonas Triste was still upon him. He knew that he would hate himself for weeks, just from the memory of that smell.

There were whole armies of robots and police outside. The body of Wush' had been taken away.

There was silence as they emerged.

Then a clear, civilized, commanding voice spoke from the plaza below,

"Is he dead?"

Rod nodded.

"Forgive me for not coming closer. I am the Lord Jestocost. I know you, C'roderick, and I know who you really are. These people are all under my orders. You and the girl can wash in the rooms below. Then you can run a certain errand. Tomorrow, at the second hour, I will see you."

Robots came close to them—apparently robots with no sense of smell, because the fulsome stench did not bother them in the least. People stepped out of their way as they passed.

Rod was able to murmur, "C'mell, are you all right?"

She nodded and she gave him a wan smile. Then she forced herself to speak. "You are brave, Mister McBan. You are even braver than a cat."

The robots separated the two of them.

Within moments Rod found little white medical robots taking his clothing off him gently, deftly, and quickly. A hot shower, with a smell of medication to it, was already hissing in the bath-stall. Rod was tired of wetness, tired of all this water everywhere, tired of wet things and complicated people, but he stumbled into the shower with gratitude and hope. He was still alive. He had unknown friends.

And C'mell. C'mell was safe.

"Is this," thought Rod, "what people call love?"

The clean stinging astringency of the shower drove all thoughts from his mind. Two of the little white robots had followed him in. He sat on a hot, wet wooden bench and they scrubbed him with brushes which felt as if they would remove his very skin.

Bit by bit, the terrible odor faded.

BIRDS, FAR UNDERGROUND

Rod McBan was too weary to protest when the little white robots wrapped him in an enormous towel and led him into what looked like an operating room.

A large man, with a red-brown spade beard, very uncommon on Earth at this time, said,

"I am Doctor Vomact, the cousin of the other Doctor Vomact you met on Mars. I know that you are not a cat, Mister and Owner McBan, and it is only my business to check up on you. May I?"

"C'mell—" began Rod.

"She is perfectly all right. We have given her a sedative and for the time being she is being treated as though she were a human woman. Jestocost told me to suspend the rules in her case, and I did so, but I think we will both have trouble about the matter from some of our colleagues later on."

"Trouble?" said Rod. "I'll pay—"

"No, no, it's not payment. It's just the rule that damaged underpeople should be destroyed and not put in hospitals. Mind you, I treat them myself now and then, if I can do it on the sly. But now let's have a look at you."

"Why are we talking?" spieked Rod. "Didn't you know that I can hier now?"

Instead of getting a physical examination, Rod had a wonderful visit with the doctor, in which they drank enormous glasses of a sweet Earth beverage called *chai* by the ancient Parosski ones. Rod realized that between Redlady, the other Doctor Vomact on Mars, and the Lord Jestocost on Earth, he had been watched and guarded all the way through. He found that this Doctor Vomact was a candidate for a Chiefship of the Instrumentality, and he learned something of the strange tests required for that office. He even found that the doctor knew more than he himself did about his own financial position, and that the actuarial balances of Earth were sagging with the weight of his wealth, since the increase in the price of stroon might lead to shorter lives. The doctor and he ended by discussing the underpeople; he found that the doctor had just as vivid an admiration for C'mell as he himself did. The evening ended when Rod said,

"I'm young, Doctor and Sir, and I sleep well, but I'm never going to sleep again if you don't get that smell away from me. I can smell it inside my nose."

The doctor became professional. He said,

"Open your mouth and breathe right into my face!"

Rod hesitated and then obeyed.

"Great crooked stars!" said the doctor. "I can smell it too. There's a little bit in your upper respiratory system, perhaps a little even in your lungs. Do you need your sense of smell for the next few days?"

Rod said he did not.

"Fine," said the doctor. "We can numb that section of the brain and do it very gently. There'll be no residual damage. You won't smell anything for eight to ten days, and by that time the smell of Amaral will be gone. Incidentally, you were charged with first-degree murder, tried, and acquitted, on the matter of Tostig Amaral."

"How could I be?" said Rod. "I wasn't even arrested."

"The Instrumentality computered it. They had the whole scene on tape, since Amaral's room has been under steady surveillance since yesterday. When he warned you that whether cat or man, you were dying, he finished the case against himself. That was a death threat and your acquittal was for self-defense."

Rod hesitated and then blurted out the truth, "And the men in the shaft?"

"The Lord Jestocost and Crudelta and I talked it over. We decided to let the matter drop. It keeps the police lively if they have a few unsolved crimes here and there. Now lie down, so I can kill off that smell."

Rod lay down. The doctor put his head in a clamp and called in robot assistants. The smell-killing process knocked him out, and when he awakened, it was in a different building. He sat up in bed and saw the sea itself. C'mell was standing at the edge of the water. He sniffed. He smelled no salt, no wet, no water, no Amaral. It was worth the change.

C'mell came to him. "My dear, my very dear, my Sir and Master but my very dear! You chanced your life for me last night."

"I'm a cat myself," laughed Rod.

He leaped from the bed and ran out to the water margin. The immensity of blue water was incredible. The white waves were separate, definable miracles, each one of them. He had seen the enclosed lakes of Norstrilia, but none of them did things like this.

C'mell had the tact to stay silent till he had seen his fill.

Then she broke the news.

"You own Earth. You have work to do. Either you stay here and begin studying how to manage your property, or you go somewhere else. Either way something a little bit sad is going to happen. Today."

He looked at her seriously, his pajamas flapping in the wet wind which he could no longer smell.

"I'm ready," he said. "What is it?"

"You lose me."

"Is that all?" he laughed.

C'mell looked very hurt. She stretched her fingers as though she were a nervous cat looking for something to claw.

"I thought—" said she, and stopped. She started again, "I thought—" She stopped again. She turned to look at him, staring fully, trustingly into his face. "You're such a young man, but you can do anything. Even among men you are fierce and decided. Tell me, Sir and Master, what—what do you wish?"

"Nothing much," he smiled at her, "except that I am buying you and taking you home. We can't go to Norstrilia unless the law changes, but we can go to New Mars. They don't have any rules there, none which a few tons of stroon won't get changed. C'mell, I'll stay cat. Will you marry me?"

She started laughing but the laughter turned into weeping. She hugged him and buried her face against his chest. At last she wiped her tears off on her arm and looked up at him:

"Poor silly me! Poor silly you! Don't you see it, Mister, I *am* a cat. If I had children, they would be cat-kittens, every one of them, unless I went every single week to get the genetic code recycled so that they would turn out underpeople. Don't you know that you and I can never marry—not with any real hope? Besides, Rod, there is the other rule. You and I cannot even see each other again from this sunset onward. How do you think the Lord Jestocost saved my life yesterday? How did he get me into a hospital to be flushed out of all those Amaral poisons? How did he break almost all the rules of the book?"

The brightness had gone out of Rod's day. "I don't know," he said dully.

"By promising them I would die promptly and obediently if there were any more irregularities. By saying I was a nice animal. A biddable one. My death is hostage for what you and I must do. It's not a law. It's something worse than a law—it's an agreement between the Lords of the Instrumentality."

"I see," said he, understanding the logic of it, but hating the cruel Earth customs which put C'mell and himself together, only to tear them apart.

"Let's walk down the beach, Rod," she said. "Unless you want your breakfast first of all ..."

"Oh, no," he said. Breakfast! A flutty crupp for all the breakfasts on Earth!

She walked as though she had not a care in the world, but there was an undertone of meaning to her walk which warned Rod that she was up to something.

It happened.

First, she kissed him, with a kiss he remembered the rest of his life.

Then, before he could say a word, she spieked. But her spieking was not words or ideas at all. It was singing of a high wild kind. It was the music which went along with her very own poem, which she had sung to him atop Earthport:

> *And oh! my love, for you.*
> *High birds crying, and a*
> *High sky flying, and a*
> *High wind driving, and a*
> *High heart striving, and a*
> *High brave place for you!*

But it was not those words, not those ideas, even though they seemed subtly different this time. She was doing something which the best telepaths of Old North Australia had tried in vain for thousands of years to accomplish—she was transmitting the mathematical and proportional essence of music right out of her mind, and she was doing it with a clarity and force which would have been worthy of a great orchestra. The "high wind driving" fugue kept recurring.

He turned his eyes away from her to see the astonishing thing which was happening all around them. The air, the ground, the sea were all becoming thick with life. Fish flashed out of blue waves. Birds circled by the multitude around them. The beach was thick with little running birds. Dogs and running animals which he had never seen before stood restlessly around C'mell—hectares of them.

Abruptly she stopped her song.

With very high volume and clarity, she spat commands in all directions:

"Think of people."

"Think of this cat and me running away somewhere."

"Think of ships."

"Look for strangers."

"Think of things in the sky."

Rod was glad he did not have his broad-band hiering come on, as it sometimes had done at home. He was sure he would have gone dizzy with the pictures and the contradictions of it all.

She had grabbed his shoulders and was whispering fiercely into his ear:

"Rod, they'll cover us. Please make a trip with me, Rod. One last dangerous trip. Not for you. Not for me. Not even for mankind. For life, Rod. The Aitch Eye wants to see you."

"Who's the Aitch Eye?"

"He'll tell you the secret if you see him," she hissed. "Do it for me, then, if you don't trust my ideas."

He smiled. "For you, C'mell, yes."

"Don't even think, then, till you get there. Don't even ask questions. Just come along. Millions of lives depend on you, Rod."

She stood up and sang again, but the new song had no grief in it, no anguish, no weird keening from species to species. It was as cool and pretty as a music box, as simple as an assured and happy goodbye.

The animals vanished so rapidly that it was hard to believe that legions of them had so recently been there.

"That," said C'mell, "should rattle the telepathic monitors for a while. They are not very imaginative anyhow, and when they get something like this they write up reports about it. Then they can't understand their reports and sooner or later one of them asks me what I did. I tell them the truth. It's simple."

"What are you going to tell them this time?" he asked, as they walked back to the house.

"That I had something which I did not want them to hear."

"They won't take that."

"Of course not, but they will suspect me of trying to beg stroon for you to give to the underpeople."

"Do you want some, C'mell?"

"Of course not! It's illegal and it would just make me live longer than my natural life. The Catmaster is the only underperson who gets stroon, and he gets it by a special vote of the Lords."

They had reached the house. C'mell paused:

"Remember, we are the servants of the Lady Frances Oh. She promised Jestocost that she would order us to do anything that I asked her to. So she's going to order us to have a good, hearty breakfast. Then she is going to order us to look for something far under the surface of Earthport."

"She is? But why—"

"No questions, Rod." The smile she gave him would have melted a monument. He felt well. He was amused and pleased by the physical delight of hiering and spieking with the occasional true people who passed by. (Some underpeople could hier and spiek but they tried to conceal it, for fear that they would be resented.) He felt strong. Losing C'mell was a sad thing to do, but it was a whole day off; he began dreaming of things that he could do for her when they parted. Buying her the services of thousands of people for the rest of her life? Giving her jewelry which would be the envy of Earth mankind? Leasing her a private planoform yacht? He suspected these might not be legal, but they were pleasant to think about.

Three hours later, he had no time for pleasant thoughts. He was bone-weary again. They had flown into Earthport city "on the orders of" their hostess, the Lady Oh, and they had started going down. Forty-five minutes of dropping had made his stomach very queasy. He felt the air go warm and stale and he wished desperately that he had not given up his sense of smell.

Where the dropshafts ended, the tunnels and the elevators began.

Down they went, where incredibly old machinery spun slowly in a spray of oil performing tasks which only the wildest mind could guess at.

In one room, C'mell had stopped and had shouted at him over the noise of engines:

"That's a pump."

It did not look obvious. Huge turbines moved wearily. They seemed to be hooked up to an enormous steam engine powered by nuclear fuel. Five or six brightly polished robots eyed them suspiciously as they walked around the machine, which was at least eighty meters long by forty-five high.

"And come here ..." shouted C'mell.

They went into another room, empty and clean and quiet except for a rigid column of moving water which shot from floor to ceiling with no evidence of machinery at all. An underman, sloppily formed from a rat body, got up from his rocking chair when they entered. He bowed to C'mell as though she were a great lady but she waved him back to his chair.

She took Rod near the column of water and pointed to a shiny ring on the floor.

"That's the other pump. They do the same amount of work."

"What is it?" he shouted.

"Force-field, I guess. I'm not an engineer." They went on.

In a quieter corridor she explained that the pumps were both of them for the service of weather control. The old one had been running six or seven thousand years, and showed very little wear. When people had needed a supplementary one, they had simply printed it on plastic, set it in the floor, and turned it on with a few amps. The underman was there just to make sure that nothing broke down or went critical.

"Can't real people design things any more?" asked Rod.

"Only if they want to. Making them want to do things is the hard part now."

"You mean, they don't want to do anything?"

"Not exactly," said C'mell, "but they find that we are better than they are at almost anything. Real work, that is, not statesmanship like running the Instrumentality and the Earth Government. Here and there a real human being gets to work, and there are always offworlders like you to stimulate them and challenge them with new problems. But they used to have secure lives of four hundred years, a common language, and a standard conditioning. They were dying off, just by being too perfect. One way to get better would have been to kill off us underpeople, but they couldn't do that all the way. There was too much messy work to be done that you couldn't count on robots for. Even the best robot, if he's a computer linked to the mind of a mouse, will do fine routine, but unless he has a very complete human education, he's going to make some wild judgments which won't suit what people want. So they need underpeople. I'm still a cat underneath it all, but even the cats which are unchanged are pretty close relatives of human beings. They make the same basic choices between power and beauty, between survival and self-sacrifice, between common sense and high courage. So the Lady Alice More worked out this plan for the Rediscovery of Man. Set up the Ancient Nations, give everybody an extra culture besides the old one based on the Old Common Tongue, let them get mad at each other, restore some disease, some danger, some accidents, but average it out so that nothing is really changed."

They had come to a storeroom, the sheer size of which made Rod blink. The great reception hall at the top of Earthport had astounded him; this room was twice the size. The room was filled with extremely ancient cargoes which had not even been unpacked from their containers. Rod could see that some were marked outbound for worlds which no longer existed, or which had changed their names; others were inbound, but no one had unpacked them for five thousand years and more.

"What's all this stuff?"

"Shipping. Technological change. Somebody wrote it all off the computers, so they didn't have to think of it any more. This is the thing which underpeople and robots are searching, to supply the ancient artifacts for the Rediscovery of Man. One of our boys—rat stock, with a human I.Q. of 300—found something marked Musée National. It was the whole National Museum of the Republic of Mali, which had been put inside a mountain when the ancient wars became severe. Mali apparently was not a very important 'nation,' as they called those groupings, but it had the same language as France, and we were able to supply real material, almost everything that was needed to restore some kind of a French civilization. China has been hard. The Chinesians survived longer than any other nation, and they did their own grave robbing, so that we have found it impossible to reconstruct China before the age of space. We can't modify people into being Ancient Chinese."

Rod stopped, thunderstruck. "Can I talk to you here?"

C'mell listened with a faraway look on her face. "Not here. I feel the very weak sweep of a monitor across my mind now and then. In a couple of minutes you can. Let's hurry along."

"I just thought," cried Rod, "of the most important question in all the worlds!"

"Stop thinking it, then," said C'mell, "until we come to a safe place."

Instead of going straight on through the big aisle between the forgotten crates and packages, she squeezed between two crates and made her way to the edge of the big underground storeroom.

"That package," she said, "is stroon. They lost it. We could help ourselves to it if we wanted to, but we're afraid of it."

Rod looked at the names on the package. It had been shipped by Roderick Frederick Ronald Arnold William MacArthur McBan XXVI to Adaminaby Port and reconsigned to Earthport. "That's one hundred and twenty-five generations ago, shipped from the Station of Doom. My farm. I think it turns poison if you leave it for more than two hundred years. Our own military people have some horrible uses for it, when invaders show up, but ordinary Norstrilians, when they find old stroon, always turn it in to the Commonwealth. We're afraid of it. Not that we often lose it. It's too valuable and we're too greedy, with a twenty million percent import duty on everything ..."

C'mell led on. They unexpectedly passed a tiny robot, a lamp fixed to his head, who was seated between two enormous piles of books. He was apparently reading them one by one, because he had beside him a pile of notes larger in bulk than he was. He did not look up, nor did they interrupt him.

At the wall, C'mell said, "Now do exactly what you're told. See the dust along the base of this crate?"

"I see it," said Rod.

"That must be left undisturbed. Now watch. I'm going to jump from the top of this crate to the top of that one, without disturbing the dust. Then I want you to jump the same way and go exactly where I point, without even thinking about it, if you can manage. I'll follow. Don't try to be polite or chivalrous, or you'll mess up the whole arrangement."

Rod nodded.

She jumped to a case against the wall. Her red hair did not fly behind her, because she had tied it up in a turban before they started out, when she had obtained coveralls for each of them from the robot-servants of the Lady Frances Oh. They had looked like an ordinary couple of working c'people.

Either she was very strong or the case was very light. Standing on the case, she tipped it very delicately, so that the pattern of dust around its base would be unchanged, save for microscopic examination. A blue glow came from beyond the case. With an odd, practiced turn of the wrist she indicated that Rod should jump from his case to the tipped one, and from there into the area—whatever it might be—beyond the case. It seemed easy for him, but he wondered if she could support both his weight and hers on the case. He remembered her order not to talk or think. He tried to think of the salmon steak he had eaten the day before. That should certainly be a good cat-thought, if a monitor should catch his mind at that moment! He jumped, teetered on the slanting top of the second packing case, and scrambled into a tiny doorway just big enough for him to crawl through. It was apparently designed for cables, pipes and maintenance, not for habitual human use: it was too low to stand in. He scrambled forward.

There was a slam.

C'mell had jumped in after him, letting the case fall back into its old and apparently undisturbed position.

She crawled up to him. "Keep going," she said.

"Can we talk here?"

"Of course! Do you want to? It's not a very sociable place."

"That question, that big question," said Rod. "I've got to ask you. You underpeople are taking charge of people. If you're fixing up their new cultures for them, you're getting to be the masters of men!"

"Yes," said C'mell, and let the explosive affirmative hang in the air between them.

He couldn't think of anything to say; it was his big bright idea for the day, and the fact that she already knew underpeople were becoming secret masters—that was too much!

She looked at his friendly face and said, more gently, "We underpeople have seen it coming for a long time. Some of the human people do, too. Especially the Lord Jestocost. He's no fool. And, Rod, you fit in."

"I?"

"Not as a person. As an economic change. As a source of unallocated power."

"You mean, C'mell, you're after me, too? I can't believe it. I can recognize a pest or a nuisance or a robber. You don't seem like any of these. You're good, all the way through." His voice faltered. "I meant it this morning, C'mell, when I asked you to marry me."

The delicacy of cat and the tenderness of woman combined in her voice as she answered, "I know you meant it." She stroked a lock of hair away from his forehead, in a caress as restrained as any touch could be. "But it's not for us. And I'm not using you myself, Rod. I want nothing for myself, but I want a good world for underpeople. And for people too. For people too. We cats have loved you people long before we had brains. We've been *your* cats longer than anyone can remember. Do you think our loyalty to the human race would stop just because you changed our shapes and added a lot of thinking power? I love you, Rod, but I love people too. That's why I'm taking you to the Aitch Eye!"

"Can you tell me what that is—now?"

She laughed. "This place is safe. It's the Holy Insurgency. The secret government of the underpeople. This is a silly place to talk about it, Rod. You're going to meet the head of it, right now."

"All of them?" Rod was thinking of the Chiefs of the Instrumentality.

"It's not a them, it's a him. The E'telekeli. The bird beneath the ground. E'ikasus is one of His sons."

"If there's only one, how did you choose him? Is he like the British Queen, whom we lost so long ago?"

C'mell laughed. "We did not choose Him. He *grew* and now He leads us. You people took an eagle's egg and tried to make it into a Daimoni man. When the experiment failed, you threw the fetus out. It lived. It's He. It'll be the strongest mind you've ever met. Come on. This is no place to talk, and we're still talking."

She started crawling down the horizontal shaft, waving at Rod to follow her.

He followed.

As they crawled, he called to her,

"C'mell, stop a minute."

She stopped until he caught up with her. She thought he might ask for a kiss, so worried and lonely did he look. She was ready to be kissed. He surprised her by saying, instead,

"I can't smell, C'mell. Please, I'm so used to smelling that I miss it. What does this place smell like?"

Her eyes widened and then she laughed: "It smells like underground. Electricity burning the air. Animals somewhere far away, a lot of different smells of them. The old, old smell of man, almost gone. Engine oil and bad exhaust. It smells like a headache. It smells like silence, like things untouched. There, is that it?"

He nodded and they went on.

At the end of the horizontal C'mell turned and said:

"All men die here. Come on!"

Rod started to follow and then stopped. "C'mell, are you disco-ordinated? Why should I die? There's no reason to."

Her laughter was pure happiness. "Silly C'rod! You are a *cat,* cat enough to come where no man has passed for centuries. Come on. Watch out for those skeletons. There're a lot of them around here. We hate to kill real people, but there are some that we can't warn off in time."

They emerged on a balcony, overlooking an even more enormous store-room than the one before. This had thousands more boxes in it. C'mell paid no attention to it. She went to the end of the balcony and raced down a slender steel ladder.

"More junk from the past!" she said, anticipating Rod's comment. "People have forgotten it up above; we mess around in it."

Though he could not smell the air, at this depth it felt thick, heavy, immobile.

C'mell did not slow down. She threaded her way through the junk and treasures on the floor as though she were an acrobat. On the far side of the old room she stopped. "Take one of these," she commanded.

They looked like enormous umbrellas. He had seen umbrellas in the pictures which his computer had showed him. These seemed oddly large, compared to the ones in the pictures. He looked around for rain. After his memories of Tostig Amaral, he wanted no more indoor rain. C'mell did not understand his suspicions.

"The shaft," she said, "has no magnetic controls, no updraft of air. It's just a shaft twelve meters in diameter. These are parachutes. We jump into the shaft with them and then we float down. Straight down. Four kilometers. It's close to the Moho."

Since he did not pick up one of the big umbrellas, she handed him one. It was surprisingly light.

He blinked at her. "How will we ever get out?"

"One of the bird-men will fly us up the shaft. It's hard work but they can do it. Be sure to hook that thing to your belt. It's a long slow time falling, and we won't be able to talk. And it's terribly dark, too."

He complied.

She opened a big door, beyond which there was the feel of nothing. She gave him a wave, partially opened her "umbrella," stepped over the edge of the door and vanished. He looked over the edge himself. There was nothing to be seen. Nothing of C'mell, no sound except for the slip-page of air and an occasional mechanical whisper of metal against metal. He supposed that must be the rib-tips of the umbrella touching the edge of the shaft as she fell.

He sighed. Norstrilia was safe and quiet compared to this.

He opened his umbrella too.

Acting on an odd premonition, he took his little hiering-spieking shell out of his ear and put it carefully in his coverall pocket.

That act saved his life.

HIS OWN STRANGE ALTAR

Rod McBan remembered falling and falling. He shouted into the wet adhesive darkness, but there was no reply. He thought of cutting himself loose from his big umbrella and letting himself drop to the death below him, but then he thought of C'mell and he knew that his body would drop upon her like a bomb. He wondered about his desperation, but could not understand it. (Only later did he find out that he was passing telepathic suicide screens which the underpeople had set up, screens fitted to the human mind, designed to dredge filth and despair from the paleocortex, the smell-bite-mate sequence of the nose-guided animals who first walked Earth; but Rod was cat enough, just barely cat enough, and he was also telepathically subnormal, so that the screens did not do to him what they would have done to any normal man of Earth—delivered a twisted dead body at the bottom. No man had ever gotten that far, but the underpeople resolved that none ever should.) Rod twisted in his harness and at last he fainted.

He awakened in a relatively small room, enormous by Earth standards but still much smaller than the storerooms which he had passed through on the way down.

The lights were bright.

He suspected that the room stank but he could not prove it with his smell gone.

A man was speaking: "The Forbidden Word is never given unless the man who does not know it plainly asks for it."

There was a chorus of voices sighing, "We remember. We remember. We remember what we remember."

The speaker was almost a giant, thin and pale. His face was the face of a dead saint, pale, white as alabaster, with glowing eyes. His body was that of man and bird both, man from the hips up, except that human hands grew out of the elbows of enormous clean white wings. From the hips down his legs were bird-legs, ending in horny, almost translucent bird-feet which stood steadily on the ground.

"I am sorry, Mister and Owner McBan, that you took that risk. I was misinformed. You are a good cat on the outside but still completely a human man on the inside. Our safety devices bruised your mind and they might have killed you."

197

Rod stared at the man as he stumbled to his feet. He saw that C'mell was one of the people helping him. When he was erect, someone handed him a beaker of very cold water. He drank it thirstily. It was hot down here—hot, stuffy, and with the feel of big engines nearby.

"I," said the great bird-man, "am the E'telekeli." He pronounced it Ee-telly-kelly. "You are the first human being to see me in the flesh."

"Blessed, blessed, blessed, fourfold blessed is the name of our leader, our father, our brother, our son the E'telekeli!" chorused the underpeople.

Rod looked around. There was every kind of underperson imaginable here, including several that he had never even thought of. One was a head on a shelf, with no apparent body. When he looked, somewhat shocked, directly at the head, its face smiled and one eye closed in a deliberate wink. The E'telekeli followed his glance. "Do not let us shock you. Some of us are normal, but many of us down here arc the discards of men's laboratories. You know my son."

A tall, very pale young man with no feathers stood up at this point. He was stark naked and completely unembarrassed. He held out a friendly hand to Rod. Rod was sure he had never seen the young man before. The young man sensed Rod's hesitation.

"You knew me as A'gentur. I am the E'ikasus."

"Blessed, blessed, threefold blessed is the name of our leader-to-be, the Yeekasoose!" chanted the underpeople.

Something about the scene caught Rod's rough Norstrilian humor. He spoke to the great underman as he would have spoken to another Mister and Owner back home, friendlily but bluntly.

"Glad you welcome me, Sir!"

"Glad, glad, glad is the stranger from beyond the stars!" sang the chorus.

"Can't you make them shut up?" asked Rod.

" 'Shut up, shut up, shut up,' says the stranger from the stars!" chorused the group.

The E'telekeli did not exactly laugh, but his smile was not pure benevolence.

"We can disregard them and talk, or I can blank out your mind every time they repeat what we say. This is a sort of court ceremony."

Rod glanced around. "I'm in your power already," said he, "so it won't matter if you mess around a little with my mind. Blank them out."

The E'telekeli stirred the air in front of him as though he were writing a mathematical equation with his finger; Rod's eyes followed the finger and he suddenly felt the room hush.

"Come over here and sit down," said the E'telekeli.

Rod followed.

"What do you want?" he asked as he followed.

The E'telekeli did not even turn around to answer. He merely spoke while walking ahead.

"Your money, Mister and Owner McBan. Almost all of your money."

Rod stopped walking. He heard himself laughing wildly. "Money? You? Here? What could you possibly do with it?"

"That," said the E'telekeli, "is why you should sit down."

"Do sit," said C'mell, who had followed.

Rod sat down.

"We are afraid that Man himself will die and leave us alone in the universe. We need Man, and there is still an immensity of time before we all pour into a common destiny. People have always assumed that the end of things is around the corner, and we have the promise of the First Forbidden One that this will be soon. But it could be hundreds of thousands of years, maybe millions. People are scattered, Mister McBan, so that no weapon will ever kill them all on all planets, but no matter how scattered they are, they are still haunted by themselves. They reach a point of development and then they stop."

"Yes," said Rod, reaching for a carafe of water and helping himself to another drink, "but it's a long way from the philosophy of the universe down to my money. We have plenty of barmy swarmy talk in Old North Australia, but I never heard of anybody asking for another citizen's money, right off the bat."

The eyes of the E'telekeli glowed like cold fire but Rod knew that this was no hypnosis, no trick being played upon himself. It was the sheer force of the personality burning outward from the bird-man.

"Listen carefully, Mister McBan. We are the creatures of Man. You are gods to us. You have made us into people who talk, who worry, who think, who love, who die. Most of our races were the friends of Man before we became underpeople. Like C'mell. How many cats have served and loved Man, and for how long? How many cattle have worked for men, been eaten by men, been milked by men across the ages, and have still followed where men went, even to the stars? And dogs. I do not have to tell you about the love of dogs for men. We call ourselves the Holy Insurgency because we are rebels. We are a government. We are a power almost as big as the Instrumentality. Why do you think Teadrinker did not catch you when you arrived?"

"Who is Teadrinker?"

"An official who wanted to kidnap you. He failed because his underman reported to me, because my son E'ikasus, who joined you in Norstrilia, suggested the remedies to the Doctor Vomact who is on Mars. We love you, Rod, not because you are a rich Norstrilian, but because it is our faith to love the Mankind which created us."

"This is a long slow wicket for my money," said Rod. "Come to the point, sir."

The E'telekeli smiled with sweetness and sadness. Rod immediately knew that it was his own denseness which made the bird-man sad and patient. For the very first time he began to accept the feeling that this person might actually be the superior of any human being he had ever met.

"I'm sorry," said Rod. "I haven't had a minute to enjoy my money since I got it. People have been telling me that everybody is after it. I'm beginning to think that I shall do nothing but run the rest of my life..."

The E'telekeli smiled happily, the way a teacher smiles when a student has suddenly turned in a spectacular performance. "Correct. You have learned a lot from the Catmaster, and from your own self. I am offering you something more—the chance to do enormous good. Have you ever heard of Foundations?"

Rod frowned. "The bottoms of buildings?"

"No. Institutions. From the very ancient past."

Rod shook his head. He hadn't.

"If a gift was big enough, it endured and kept on giving, until the culture in which it was set had fallen. If you took most of your money and gave it to some good, wise men, it could be spent over and over again to improve the race of Man. We need that. Better men will give us better lives. Do you think that we don't know how pilots and pinlighters have sometimes died, saving their cats in space?"

"Or how people kill underpeople without a thought?" countered Rod. "Or humiliate them without noticing that they do it? It seems to me that you must have some self-interest, sir."

"I do. Some. But not as much as you think. Men are evil when they are frightened or bored. They are good when they are happy and busy. I want you to give your money to provide games, sports, competitions, shows, music, and a chance for honest hatred."

"Hatred?" said Rod. "I was beginning to think that I had found a Believer bird...somebody who mouthed old magic."

"We're not ending time," said the great man-bird. "We are just altering the material conditions of Man's situation for the present historical period. We want to steer mankind away from tragedy and self-defeat. Though the cliffs crumble, we want Man to remain. Do you know Swinburne?"

"Where is it?" said Rod.

"It's not a place. It's a poet, before the age of space. He wrote this. Listen.

Till the slow sea rise and the sheer cliff crumble,
Till the terrace and meadow the deep gulfs drink,
Till the strength of the waves of the high tides crumble
The fields that lessen, the rocks that shrink,
Here now in his triumph where all things falter,
Stretched out on the spoils that his own hand spread,
As a god self-slain on his own strange altar,
                    Death lies dead.

Do you agree with that?"

"It sounds nice, but I don't understand it," said Rod. "Please sir, I'm tireder than I thought. And I have only this one day with C'mell. Can I finish the business with you and have a little time with her?"

The great underman lifted his arms. His wings spread like a canopy over Rod.

"So be it!" he said, and the words rang out like a great song.

Rod could see the lips of the underpeople chorusing, but he did not notice the sound.

"I offer you a tangible bargain. Tell me if you find I read your mind correctly."

Rod nodded, somewhat in awe.

"You want your money, but you don't want it. You will keep five hundred thousand credits, FOE money, which will leave you the richest man in Old North Australia for the rest of a very long life. The rest you will give to a foundation which will teach men to hate easily and lightly, as in a game, not sickly and wearily, as in habit. The trustees will be Lords of the Instrumentality whom I know, such as Jestocost, Crudelta, the Lady Johanna Gnade."

"And what do I get?"

"Your heart's desire." The beautiful wise pale face stared down at Rod like a father seeking to fathom the puzzlement of his own child. Rod was a little afraid of the face, but he confided in it, too.

"I want too much. I can't have it all."

"I'll tell you what you want.

"You want to be home right now, and all the trouble done with. I can set you down at the Station of Doom in a single long jump. Look at the floor—I have your books and your postage stamp which you left in Amaral's room. They go too."

"But I want to see Earth!"

"Come back, when you are older and wiser. Some day. See what your money has done."

"Well—" said Rod.

"You want C'mell." The bland wise white face showed no embarrassment, no anger, no condescension. "You shall have her, in a linked dream,
her mind to yours, for a happy subjective time of about a thousand years.
You will live through all the happy things that you might have done
together if you had stayed here and become a c'man. You will see your
kitten-children flourish, grow old, and die. That will take about one half-
hour."

"It's just a dreamy," said Rod. "You want to take megacredits from me
and give me a dreamy!"

*"With two minds? Two living, accelerated minds, thinking into each
other?* Have you ever heard of that?"

"No," said Rod.

"Do you trust me?" said the E'telekeli.

Rod stared at the man-bird inquisitively and a great weight fell from
him. He did trust this creature more than he had ever trusted the father
who did not want him, the mother who gave him up, the neighbors who
looked at him and were kind. He sighed, "I trust you."

"I also," added the E'telekeli, "will take care of all the little inciden-
tals through my own network and I will leave the memory of them in your
mind. If you trust me that should be enough. You get home, safe. You are
protected, off Norstrilia, into which I rarely reach, for as long as you live.
You have a separate life right now with C'mell and you will remember
most of it. In return, you go to the wall and transfer your fortune, minus
one-half FOE megacredit, to the Foundation of Rod McBan."

Rod did not see that the underpeople thronged around him like worshippers. He had to stop when a very pale, tall girl took his hand and held
it to her cheek. "You may not be the Promised One, but you are a great
and good man. We can take nothing from you. We can only ask. That is
the teaching of Joan. And you have given."

"Who are you?" said Rod in a frightened voice, thinking that she
might be some lost human girl whom the underpeople had abducted to
the guts of the Earth.

"E'lamelanie, daughter of the E'telekeli."

Rod stared at her and went to the wall. He pushed a routine sort of
button. What a place to find it! "The Lord Jestocost," he called. "McBan
speaking. No, you fool, I own this system."

A handsome, polished plumpish man appeared on the screen. "If I
guess right," said the strange man, "you are the first human being ever to
get into the depths. Can I serve you, Mister and Owner McBan?"

"Take a note—" said the E'telekeli, out of sight of the machine, beside Rod.

Rod repeated it.

The Lord Jestocost called witnesses at his end.

It was a long dictation, but at last the conveyance was finished. Only at one point did Rod balk. When they tried to call it the McBan Foundation, he said, "Just call it the One Hundred and Fifty Fund."

"One Hundred and Fifty?" asked Jestocost.

"For my father. It's his number in our family. I'm to-the-hundred-and-fifty-first. He was before me. Don't explain the number. Just use it."

"All clear," said Jestocost. "Now we have to get notaries and official witnesses to veridicate our imprints of your eyes, hands and brain. Ask the Person with you to give you a mask, so that the cat-man face will not upset the witnesses. Where is this machine you are using supposed to be located? I know perfectly well where I think it is."

"At the foot of Alpha Ralpha Boulevard, in a forgotten market," said the E'telekeli. "Your servicemen will find it there tomorrow when they come to check the authenticity of the machine." He still stood out of line of sight of the machine, so that Jestocost could hear him but not see him.

"I know the voice," said Jestocost. "It comes to me as in a great dream. But I shall not ask to see the face."

"Your friend down here has gone where only underpeople go," said the E'telekeli, "and we are disposing of his fate in more ways than one, my Lord, subject to your gracious approval."

"My approval does not seem to have been needed much," snorted Jestocost, with a little laugh.

"I would like to talk to you. Do you have any intelligent underperson near you?"

"I can call C'mell. She's always somewhere around."

"This time, my lord, you cannot. She's here."

"There, with *you?* I never knew she went there." The amazement showed on the face of the Lord Jestocost.

"She is here, nevertheless. Do you have some other underperson?"

Rod felt like a dummy, standing in the visiphone while the two voices, unseen by one another, talked past him. But he felt, very truly, that they both wished him well. He was almost nervous in anticipation of the strange happiness which had been offered to him and C'mell, but he was a respectful enough young man to wait until the great ones got through their business.

"Wait a moment," said Jestocost.

On the screen, in the depths, Rod could see the Lord of the Instrumentality work the controls of other, secondary screens. A moment later Jestocost answered:

"B'dank is here. He will enter the room in a few minutes."

"Twenty minutes from now, my Sir and Lord, will you hold hands with your servant B'dank as you once did with C'mell? I have the problem of this young man and his return. There are things which you do not know, and I would rather not put them on the wires."

Jestocost hesitated only for the slightest of moments. "Good, then," he laughed. "I might as well be hanged for a sheep as for a lamb."

The E'telekeli stood aside. Someone handed Rod a mask which hid his cat-man features and still left his eyes and hands exposed. The brain print was gotten through the eyes.

The recordings were made.

Rod went back to the bench and table. He helped himself to another drink of water from the carafe. Someone threw a wreath of fresh flowers around his shoulders. Fresh flowers! In such a place ... He wondered. Three rather pretty undergirls, two of them of cat origin and one of them derived from dogs, were leading a freshly dressed C'mell toward him. She wore the simplest and most modest of all possible white dresses. Her waist was cinched by a broad golden belt. She laughed, stopped laughing, and then blushed as they led her to Rod.

Two seats were arranged on the bench. Cushions were disposed so that both of them would be comfortable. Silky metallic caps, like the pleasure caps used in surgeries, were fitted on their heads. Rod felt his sense of smell explode within his brain; it came alive richly and suddenly. He took C'mell by the hand and began walking through an immemorial Earth forest, with a temple older than time shining in the clear soft light cast by Earth's old moon. He knew that he was already dreaming. C'mell caught his thought and said,

"Rod, my master and lover, this *is* a dream. But I am in it with you..."

Who can measure a thousand years of happy dreaming—the travels, the hunts, the picnics, the visits to forgotten and empty cities, the discovery of beautiful views and strange places? And the love, and the sharing, and the re-reflection of everything wonderful and strange by two separate, distinct and utterly harmonious personalities. C'mell the c'girl and C'roderick the c'man: they seemed happily doomed to be with one another. Who can live whole centuries of real bliss and then report it in minutes? Who can tell the full tale of such real lives—happiness, quarrels, reconciliations, problems, solutions and always sharing, happiness, and more sharing...?

When they awakened Rod very gently, they let C'mell sleep on. He looked down at himself and expected to find himself old. But he was a young man still, in the deep forgotten underground of the E'telekeli, and he could not even smell. He reached for the thousand wonderful years as he watched C'mell, young again, lying on the bench, but the dream-years had started fading even as he reached for them.

Rod stumbled on his feet. They led him to a chair. The E'telekeli sat in an adjacent chair, at the same table. He seemed weary.

"My Mister and Owner McBan, I monitored your dreamsharing, just to make sure it stayed in the right general direction. I hope you are satisfied."

Rod nodded, very slowly, and reached for the carafe of water, which someone had refilled while he slept.

"While you slept, Mister McBan," said the great E'man, "I had a telepathic conference with the Lord Jestocost, who has been your friend, even though you do not know him. You have heard of the new automatic planoform ships."

"They are experimental," said Rod.

"So they are," said the E'telekeli, "but perfectly safe. And the best 'automatic' ones are not automatic at all. They have snake-men pilots. My pilots. They can outperform any pilots of the Instrumentality."

"Of course," said Rod, "because they are dead."

"No more dead than I," laughed the white calm bird of the underground. "I put them in cataleptic trances, with the help of my son the doctor E'ikasus, whom you first knew as the monkey-doctor A'gentur. On the ships they wake up. One of them can take you to Norstrilia in a single long fast jump. And my son can work on you right here. We have a good medical workshop in one of those rooms. After all, it was he who restored you under the supervision of Doctor Vomact on Mars. It will seem like a single night to you, though it will be several days in objective time. If you say goodbye to me now, and if you are ready to go, you will wake up in orbit just outside the Old North Australian subspace net. I have no wish for one of my underpeople to tear himself to pieces if he meets Mother Hitton's dreadful little kittens, whatever they may be. Do you happen to know?"

"I don't," said Rod quickly, "and if I did, I couldn't tell you. It's the Queen's secret."

"The Queen?"

"The Absent Queen. We use it to mean the Commonwealth government. Anyhow, Mister Bird, I can't go now. I've got to go back up to the surface of Earth. I want to say goodbye to the Catmaster. And I'm not going to leave this planet and abandon Eleanor. And I want my stamp that the Catmaster gave me. And the books. And maybe I should report about the death of Tostig Amaral."

"Do you trust me, Mister and Owner McBan?" The white giant rose to his feet; his eyes shone like fire.

The underpeople spontaneously chorused, "Put your trust in the joy-
ful lawful, put your trust in the loyal-awful bright blank power of the
under-bird!"

"I've trusted you with my life and my fortune, so far," said Rod, a
little sullenly, "but you're not going to make me leave Eleanor. No matter
how much I want to get home. And I have an old enemy at home that I
want to help. Houghton Syme the Hon. Sec. There might be something
on Old Earth which I could take back to him."

"I think you can trust me a little further," said the E'telekeli. "Would
it solve the problem of the Hon. Sec. if you gave him a dreamshare with
someone he loved, to make up for his having a short life?"

"I don't know. Maybe."

"I can," said the master of the underpeople, "have his prescription
made up. It will have to be mixed with plasma from his blood before he
takes it. It would be good for about three thousand years of subjective life.
We have never let this out of our own undercity before, but you are the
Friend of Earth, and you shall have it."

Rod tried to stammer his thanks, but he mumbled something about
Eleanor instead: he just *couldn't* leave her.

The white giant took Rod by the arm and led him back to the visiphone,
still oddly out of place in this forgotten room, so far underground.

"You know," said the white giant, "that I will not trick you with false
messages or anything like that?"

One look at the strong, calm, relaxed face—face so purposeful that it
had no fretful or immediate purpose—convinced Rod that there was nothing to fear.

"Tune it, then," said the E'telekeli. "If Eleanor wants to go home we
will arrange with the Instrumentality for her passage. As for you, my son
E'ikasus will change you back as he changed you over. There is only one
detail. Do you want the face you originally had or do you want it to reflect
the wisdom and experience I have seen you gain?"

"I'm not posh," said Rod. "The same old face will do. If I am any
wiser, my people will find it out soon enough."

"Good. He will get ready. Meanwhile, turn on the visiphone. It is
already set to search for your fellow-citizen."

Rod flicked it on. There was a bewildering series of flashes and a
kaleidoscopic dazzlement of scenes before the machine seemed to race
along the beach at Meeya Meefla and searched out Eleanor. This was a
very strange screen indeed: it had no visiphone at the other end. He could
see Eleanor, looking exactly like his Norstrilian self, but she could not
observe that she was being seen.

The machine focused on Eleanor/Rod McBan's face. She/he was talking to a very pretty woman, oddly mixed Norstrilian and Earthlike in appearance.

"Ruth Not-from-here," murmured the E'telekeli, "the daughter of the Lord William Not-from-here, a Chief of the Instrumentality. He wanted his daughter to marry 'you' so that they could return to Norstrilia. Look at the daughter. She is annoyed at 'you' right now."

Ruth was sitting on the bench, twisting away at her fingers in nervousness and worry, but her fingers and face showed more anger than despair. She was speaking to Eleanor, the 'Rod McBan.'

"My father just told me!" Ruth cried out. "Why, oh why did you give all your money for a Foundation of some kind? The Instrumentality just told him. I just don't understand. There's no point in us getting married now—"

"Suits me," said Eleanor/Rod McBan.

"Suits you, does it!" shrieked Ruth. "After the advantages you've taken of me!"

The false Rod McBan merely smiled at her friendlily and knowledgeably. The real Rod, watching the picture ten kilometers below, thought that Eleanor seemed to have learned a great deal about how to be a young rich man on Earth.

Ruth's face changed suddenly. She broke from anger to laughter. She showed her bewilderment. "I must admit," she said honestly, "that I didn't really want to go back to the old family home in Old North Australia. The simple, honest life, a little on the stupid side. No oceans. No cities. Just sick, giant sheep and worlds full of money with nothing to spend it on. I like Earth and I suppose I'm decadent..."

Rod/Eleanor smiled right back at her. "Maybe I'm decadent too. I'm not poor. I can't help liking you. I don't want to marry anybody. But I have big credits here, and I enjoy being a young man—"

"I should say you do!" said Ruth. "What an odd thing for you to say!"

The false 'Rod McBan' gave no sign that he/she noted the interruption. "I've just about decided to stay here and enjoy things. Everybody's rich in Norstrilia, but what good does it do? It had gotten pretty dull for me, I can tell you, or I wouldn't have taken the risk of coming here. Yes, I think I'll stay. I know that Rod—" He/she gasped. "Rod MacArthur, I mean, a sort of relative of mine. Rod can get the tax taken off my personal fortune so that I can stay right here."

("I will, too," said the real Rod McBan, far below the surface of the Earth.)

"You're welcome here, my dear," said Ruth Not-from-here to the false Rod McBan.

Down below, the E'telekeli gestured at the screen. "Seen enough?" he said to Rod.

"Enough," said Rod, "but make sure that she knows I am all right and that I am trying to take care of her. Can you get in touch with the Lord Jestocost or somebody and arrange for Eleanor to stay here and keep her fortune? Tell her to use the name of Roderick Henry McBan the first. I can't let her have the name of the Owners of the Station of Doom, but I don't think Earthpeople will notice the difference anyhow. *She'll* know it's all right with me, and that's all that matters. If she really likes it here in a copy of my body, may the great sheep sit on her!"

"An odd blessing," said the E'telekeli, "but it can all be arranged."

Rod made no move to leave. He had turned off the screen but he just stood there.

"Something else?" said the E'telekeli.

"C'mell," said Rod.

"She's all right," said the lord of the underworld. "She expects nothing from you. She's a good underperson."

"*I* want to do something for her."

"There is nothing she wants. She is happy. You do not need to meddle."

"She won't be a girlygirl forever," Rod insisted. "You underpeople get old. I don't know how you manage without stroon."

"Neither do I," said the E'telekeli. "I just happen to have long life. But you're right about her. She will age soon enough, by your kind of time."

"I'd like to buy the restaurant for her, the one the bear-man has, and let it become a sort of meeting place open to people and underpeople. She could give it the romantic and interesting touch so that it could be a success."

"A wonderful idea. A perfect project for your Foundation," smiled the E'telekeli. "It shall be done."

"And the Catmaster?" asked Rod. "Is there anything I can do for him?"

"No, do not concern yourself with C'william," said the E'telekeli. "He is under the protection of the Instrumentality and he knows the sign of the Fish." The great underman paused to give Rod a chance to inquire what that sign might be, but Rod did not note the significance of the pause, so the birdlike giant went on. "C'william has already received his reward in the good change which he has made in your life. Now, if you are ready, we will put you to sleep, my son E'ikasus will change you out of your cat-body, and you will wake in orbit around your home."

"C'mell? Can you wake her up so I can say goodbye after that thousand years?"

The master of the underworld took Rod gently by the arm and walked him across the huge underground room, talking as they went. "Would you want to have another goodbye, after that thousand years she remembers with you, if you were she? Let her be. It is kinder this way. You are human. You can afford to be rich with kindness. It is one of the best traits which you human people have."

Rod stopped. "Do you have a recorder of some kind, then? She welcomed me to Earth with a wonderful little song about 'high birds crying' and I want to leave one of our Norstrilian songs for her."

"Sing anything," said the E'telekeli, "and the chorus of my attendants will remember it as long as they live. The others would appreciate it too."

Rod looked around at the underpeople who had followed them. For a moment he was embarrassed at singing to all of them, but when he saw their warm, adoring smiles, he was at ease with them. "Remember this, then, and be sure to sing it to C'mell for me, when she awakens." He lifted his voice a little and sang.

Run where the ram is dancing, prancing!
Listen where the ewe is greeting, bleating.
Rush where the lambs are running, funning.
Watch where the stroon is growing, flowing.
See how the men are reaping, heaping
   Wealth for their world!

Look, where the hills are dipping, ripping.
Sit where the air is drying, frying.
Go where the clouds are pacing, racing.
Stand where the wealth is gleaming, teeming.
Shout to the top of the singing, ringing
   Norstrilian power and pride.

The chorus sang it back at him with a wealth and richness which he had never heard in the little song before.

"And now," said the E'telekeli, "the blessing of the First Forbidden One be upon you." The giant bowed a little and kissed Rod McBan on the forehead. Rod thought it strange and started to speak, but the eyes were upon him.

Eyes—like twin fires.

Fire—like friendship, like warmth, like a welcome and a farewell.

Eyes—which became a single fire.

He awakened only when he was in orbit around Old North Australia.

The descent was easy. The ship had a viewer. The snake-pilot said very little. He put Rod down in the Station of Doom, a few hundred meters from his own door. He left two heavy packages. An Old North Australian patrol ship hovered overhead and the air hummed with danger while

Norstrilian police floated to the ground and made sure that no one besides Rod McBan got off. The Earth ship whispered and was gone.

"I'll give you a hand, Mister," said one of the police. He clutched Rod with one mechanical claw of his ornithopter, caught the two packages in the other, and flung his machine into the air with a single beat of the giant wings. They coasted into the yard, the wings tipped up, Rod and his packages were deposited deftly, and the machine flapped away in silence.

There was nobody there. He knew that Aunt Doris would come soon. And Lavinia. Lavinia! Here, now, on this dear poor dry earth, he knew how much Lavinia suited him. Now he could spiek, he could hier!

It was strange. Yesterday—or was it yesterday? (for it felt like yesterday)—he had felt very young indeed. And now, since his visit to the Catmaster, he felt somehow grown up, as if he had discovered all his personal ingrown problems and had left them behind on Old Earth. He seemed to know in his deepest mind that C'mell had never been more than nine-tenths his, and that the other tenth—the most valuable and beautiful and most secret tenth of her life—was forever given to some other man or underman whom he would never know. He felt that C'mell would never give her heart again. And yet he kept for her a special kind of tenderness, which would never recur. It was not marriage which they had had, but it was pure romance.

But here, here waited home itself, and love.

Lavinia was in it, dear Lavinia with her mad lost father and her kindness to a Rod who had not let much kindness into his life.

Suddenly, the words of an old poem rose unbidden to his mind:

Ever. Never. Forever.
Three words. The lever
Of life upon time.
Never, forever, ever!

He spieked. He spieked very loud, "Lavinia!"

Beyond the hill the cry came back, right into his mind, "Rod, Rod! Oh, Rod! Rod?"

"Yes," he spieked. "Don't run. I'm home."

He felt her mind coming near, though she must have been beyond one of the nearby hills. When he touched minds with Lavinia, he knew that this was her ground, and his too. Not for them the wet wonders of Earth, the golden-haired beauties of C'mell and Earth people! He knew without doubt that Lavinia would love and recognize the new Rod as she had loved the old.

He waited very quietly and then he laughed to himself under the grey nearby friendly sky of Norstrilia. He had momentarily had the childish impulse to rush across the hills and to kiss his own computer.

He waited for Lavinia instead.

COUNSELS, COUNCILS, CONSOLES AND CONSULS

Ten Years Later, Two Earthmen Talking

"You don't believe all the malarkey, do you?"

"What's 'malarkey'?"

"Isn't that a beautiful word? It's ancient. A robot dug it up. It means rubbish, hooey, nonsense, gibberish, phlutt, idle talk or hallucinations— in other words, just what you've been saying."

"You mean about a boy buying the planet Earth?"

"Sure. He couldn't do it, not even with Norstrilian money. There are too many regulations. It was just an economic adjustment."

"What's an 'economic adjustment'?"

"That's another ancient word I found. It's almost as good as malarkey. It does have some meaning, though. It means that the masters rearrange things by changing the volume or the flow or the title to property. The Instrumentality wanted to shake down the Earth Government and get some more free credits to play around with, so between them they invented an imaginary character named Rod McBan. Then, they had him buy the Earth. Then he goes away. It doesn't make sense. No normal boy would have done that. They say he had one million women. What do you think a normal boy would do if somebody gave him one million women?"

"You're not proving anything. Anyhow, I saw Rod McBan myself, two years ago."

"That's the other one, not the one who is supposed to have bought Earth. That's just a rich immigrant who lives down near Meeya Meefla. I could tell you some things about him, too."

"But why shouldn't somebody buy Earth if he corners the Norstrilian stroon market?"

"Who ever cornered it in the first place? I tell you, Rod McBan is just an invention. Have you ever seen a picturebox of him?"

"No."

"Did you ever know anybody who met him?"

"I heard that the Lord Jestocost was mixed up in it, and that expensive girlygirl What's-her-name—you know—the redhead—C'mell."

"That's what *you* heard. Malarkey, pure genuine ancient malarkey. There was no such boy, ever. It's all propaganda."

"You're always that way. Grumbling. Doubting. I'm glad I'm not you."

"Pal, that's real, real reciprocal. 'Better dead than gullible,' that's my motto."

On a Planoforming Ship, Outbound from Earth, Also Ten Years Later

The Stop-Captain, talking to a passenger, female:

"I'm glad to see, ma'am, that you didn't buy any of those Earth fashions. Back home, the air would take them off you in half a minute."

"I'm old-fashioned," she smiled. Then a thought crossed her mind, and she added a question: "You're in the space business, Sir and Stop-Captain. Did you ever hear the story of Rod McBan? I think it's thrilling."

"You mean, the boy who bought Earth?"

"Yes," she gasped. "Is it true?"

"Completely true," he said, "except for one little detail. This 'Rod McBan' wasn't named that at all. He wasn't a Norstrilian. He was a hominid from some other world, and he was buying the Earth with pirate money. They wanted to get his credits away from him, but he may have been a Wet Stinker from Amazonas Triste or he may have been one of those little tiny men, about the size of a walnut, from the Solid Planet. That's why he bought Earth and left it so suddenly. You see, Ma'am and Dame, no Old North Australian ever thinks about anything except his money. They even have one of the ancient forms of government still left on that planet, and they would never let one of their own boys buy Earth. They'd all sit around and talk him into putting it in a savings account, instead. They're clannish people. That's why I don't think it was a Norstrilian at all."

The woman's eyes widened. "You're spoiling a lovely story for me, Mister and Stop-Captain."

"Don't call me 'Mister,' Ma'am. That's a Norstrilian title. I'm just plain 'Sir.' "

They both stared at the little imaginary waterfall on the wall.

Before the Stop-Captain went back to his work, he added, "For my money, it must have been one of those little tiny men from the Solid Planet. Only a fool like that would buy the dower rights to a million women. We're both grown up, Ma'am. I ask you, what would an itty-bitty man from the Solid Planet do with one Earth woman, let alone a million of them?"

She giggled and blushed as the Stop-Captain stamped triumphantly away, having gotten in his last masculine word.

E'lamelanie, Two Years After Rod's Departure from Earth

"Father, give me hope."

The E'telekeli was gentle. "I can give you almost anything from this world, but you are talking about the world of the sign of the Fish, which none of us controls. You had better go back into the everyday life of our cavern and not spend so much time on your devotional exercises, if they make you unhappy."

She stared at him. "It's not that. It's not that at all. It's just that I know that the robot, the rat and the Copt all agreed that the Promised One would come here to Earth." A desperate note entered her voice. *"Father, could it have been Rod McBan?"*

"What do you mean?"

"Could he have been the Promised One, without my knowing it? Could he have come and gone just to test my faith?"

The bird-giant rarely laughed; he had never laughed at his own daughter before. But this was too absurd: he laughed at her, but a wise part of his mind told him that the laughter, though cruel now, would be good for her later on.

"Rod? A promised speaker of the truth? Oh, no. Ho—ho—ho. Rod McBan is one of the nicest human beings I ever met. A good young man, almost like a bird. But he's no messenger from eternity."

The daughter bowed and turned away.

She had already composed a tragedy about herself, the mistaken one, who had met "the prince of the word," whom the worlds awaited, and had failed to know him because her faith was too weak. The strain of waiting for something that might happen now or a million years from now was too much. It was easier to accept failure and self-reproach than to endure the timeless torment of undated hope.

She had a little nook in the wall where she spent many of her waiting hours. She took out a little stringed instrument which her father had made for her. It emitted ancient, weeping sounds, and she sang her own little song to it, the song of E'lamelanie who was trying to give up waiting for Rod McBan.

She looked out into the room.

A little girl, wearing nothing but panties, stared at her with fixed eyes. E'lamelanie looked back at the child. It had no expression; it just stared at her. She wondered if it might be one of the turtle-children whom her father had rescued several years earlier.

She looked away from the child and sang her song anyhow:

Once again, across the years,
*   I wept for you.*
I could not stop the bitter tears
*   I kept for you.*
The hearthstone of my early life
*   was swept for you.*
A different, modulated time
*   awaits me now.*
Yet there are moments when the past
*   asks why and how.*
The future marches much too fast.
*   Allow, allow—*
But no. That's all. Across the years
*   I wept for you.*

When she finished, the turtle-child was still watching. Almost angrily, E'lamelanie put away her little violin.

What the Turtle-Child Thought, At the Same Moment

I know a lot even if I don't feel like talking about it and I know that the most wonderful real man in all the planets came right down here into this big room and talked to these people because he is the man that the long silly girl is singing about because she does not have him but why should she anyhow and I am really the one who is going to get him because I am a turtle-child and I will be right here waiting when all these people are dead and pushed down into the dissolution vats and someday he will come back to Earth and I will be all grown up and I will be a turtle-woman, more beautiful than any human woman ever was, and he is going to marry me and take me off to his planet and I will always be happy with him because I will not argue all the time, the way that bird-people and cat-people and dog-people do, so that when Rod McBan is my husband and I rush dinner out of the wall for him, if he tries to argue with me I will just be shy and sweet and I won't say anything, nothing at all, to him for one hundred years and for two hundred years, and nobody could get mad at a beautiful turtle-woman who never talked back …

The Council of the Guild of Thieves, Under Viola Siderea

The herald called,
"His audacity, the Chief of Thieves, is pleased to report to the Council of Thieves!"
An old man stood, very ceremoniously. "You bring us wealth, Sir and

Chief, we trust—from the gullible—from the weak—from the heartless among mankind?"

The Chief of Thieves proclaimed,

"It is the matter of Rod McBan."

A visible stir went through the Council.

The Chief of Thieves went on, with equal formality: "We never did intercept him in space, though we monitored every vehicle which came out of the sticky, sparky space around Norstrilia. Naturally, we did not send anyone down to meet Mother Hitton's Littul Kittons, may the mildew-men find them! whatever those 'kittons' may be. There was a coffin with a woman in it and a small box with a head. Never mind. He got past us. But when he got to Earth, we caught four of him."

"Four?" gasped one old Councilor.

"Yes," said the Chief of Thieves. "Four Rod McBans. There was a human one too, but we could tell that one was a decoy. It had originally been a woman and was enjoying itself hugely after having been transformed into a young man. So we got four Rod McBans. All four of them were Earth-robots, very well made."

"You stole them?" said a Councilor.

"Of course," said the Chief of Thieves, grinning like a human wolf. "And the Earth Government made no objection at all. The Earth Government simply sent us a bill for them when we tried to leave—something like one-fourth megacredit 'for the use of custom-designed robots.'"

"That's a low honest trick!" cried the Chairman of the Guild of Thieves. "What did you do?" His eyes stared wide open and his voice dropped. "You didn't turn honest and charge the bill to us, did you? We're already in debt to those honest rogues!"

The Chief of Thieves squirmed a little. "Not quite that bad, your tricky highnesses! I cheated the Earth some, though I fear it may have bordered on honesty, the way I did it."

"What did you do? Tell us quick, man!"

"Since I did not get the real Rod McBan, I took the robots apart and taught them how to be thieves. They stole enough money to pay all the penalties and recoup the expense of the voyage."

"You show a profit?" cried a Councilor.

"Forty minicredits," said the Chief of Thieves. "But the worst is yet to come. You know what Earth does to real thieves."

A shudder went through the room. They all knew about Earth reconditioners which had changed bold thieves into dull honest rogues.

"But, you see, Sirs and Honored Ones," the Chief of Thieves went on, apologetically, "the Earth authorities caught us at that, too. They liked the thief-robots. They made wonderful pickpockets and they kept the people stirred up. The robots also gave everything back. So," said the Chief of Thieves, blushing, "we have a contract to turn two thousand humanoid robots into pickpockets and sneak-thieves. Just to make life on Earth more fun. The robots are out in orbit, right now."

"You mean," shrilled the chairman, "you signed an *honest* contract? You, the Chief of Thieves!"

The Chief really blushed and choked. "What could I do? Besides, they had me. I got good terms, though. Two hundred and twenty credits for processing each robot into a master thief. We can live well on that for a while."

For a long time there was dead silence.

At last one of the oldest Thieves on the Council began to sob: "I'm old. I can't stand it. The horror of it! Us—*us* doing honest work!"

"We're at least teaching the robots how to be thieves," said the Chief of Thieves, starkly.

No one commented on that.

Even the herald had to step aside and blow his nose.

At Meeya Meefla, Twenty Years After Rod's Trip Home

Roderick Henry McBan, the former Eleanor, had become only imperceptibly older with the years. He had sent away his favorite, the little dancer, and he wondered why the Instrumentality, not even the Earth government, had sent him official warning to "stay peaceably in the dwelling of the said stated person, there to await an empowered envoy of this Instrumentality and to comply with orders subsequently to be issued by the envoy hereinbefore indicated."

Roderick Henry McBan remembered the long years of virtue, independence and drudgery on Norstrilia with unconcealed loathing. He liked being a rich, wild young man on Earth ever so much better than being a respectable spinster under the grey skies of Old North Australia. When he dreamed, he was sometimes Eleanor again, and he sometimes had long morbid periods in which he was neither Eleanor nor Rod, but a nameless being cast out from some world or time of irrecoverable enchantments. In these gloomy periods, which were few but very intense, and usually cured by getting drunk and staying drunk for a few days, he found himself wondering who he was. What could he be? Was he Eleanor, the honest workwoman from the Station of Doom? Was he an adoptive cousin of Rod McBan, the man who had bought Old Earth itself? What was this self—this Roderick Henry McBan? He maundered about it so much to one of his girl-friends, a calypso singer, that she set his own words, better arranged, to an ancient tune and sang them back to him:

To be me, is it right, is it good?
To go on, when the others have stood—
To the gate, through the door, past the wall,
Between this and the nothing-at-all.

It is cold, it is me, in the out.
I am true, I am me, in the lone.
Such silence leaves room for no doubt.
It is brightness unbroken by tone.

To be me, it is strange, it is true.
Shall I lie? To be them, to have peace?
Will I know, can I tell, when I'm through?
Do I stop when my troubles must cease?

If the wall isn't glass, isn't there,
If it's real but compounded of air,
Am I lost if I go where I go
Where I'm me? I am yes. Am I no?

To be me, is it right, is it so?
Can I count on my brain, on my eye?
Will I be you or be her by and bye?
Are they true, all these things that I know?

You are mad, in the wall. On the out,
I'm alone and as sane as the grave.
Do I fail, do I lose what I save?
Am I me, if I echo your shout?

I have gone to a season of time ...
Out of thought, out of life, out of rhyme.
If I come to be you, do I lose
The chance to be me if I choose?

Rod/Eleanor had moments of desperation, and sometimes wondered if the Earth authorities or the Instrumentality would take him/her away for reconditioning.

The warning today was formal, fierce, serene in its implacable self-assurance.

Against his/her better judgment, Roderick Henry McBan poured out a stiff drink and waited for the inevitable.

Destiny came as three men, all of them strangers, but one wearing the uniform of an Old North Australia consul. When they got close, she recognized the consul as Lord William Not-from-here, with whose daughter Ruth he/she had disported on these very sands many years before.

The greetings were wearisomely long, but Rod/ Eleanor had learned, both on Old North Australia and here on Manhome Earth, never to discount ceremony as the salvager of difficult or painful occasions. It was the Lord William Not-from-here who spoke.

"Hear now, Lord Roderick Eleanor, the message of a plenum of the Instrumentality, lawfully and formally assembled, to wit—

"That you, the Lord Roderick Eleanor, be known to be and be indeed a Chief of the Instrumentality until the day of your death—

"That you have earned this status by survival capacity, and that the strange and difficult lives which you have already led with no thought of suicide have earned you a place in our terrible and dutiful ranks—

"That in being and becoming the Lord Roderick Eleanor, you shall be man or woman, young or old, as the Instrumentality may order—

"That you take power to serve, that you serve to take power, that you come with us, that you look not backward, that you remember to forget, that you forget old remembering, that within the Instrumentality you are not a person but a part of a person—

"That you be made welcome to the oldest servant of mankind, the Instrumentality itself."

Roderick/Eleanor had not a word to say.

Newly appointed Lords of the Instrumentality rarely had anything to say. It was the custom of the Instrumentality to take new appointees by surprise, after minute examination of their records for intelligence, will, vitality, and again, vitality.

The Lord William was smiling as he held out his hand and speaking in offworldly honest Norstrilian talk:

"Welcome, cousin from the grey rich clouds. Not many of our people have ever been chosen. Let me welcome you."

Roderick/Eleanor took his hand. There was still nothing to say.

The Palace of the Governor of Night, Twenty Years After Rod's Return

"I turned off the human voice hours ago, Lavinia. Turned it off. We always get a sharper reading with the numbers. It doesn't have a clue on our boys. I've been across this console a hundred times. Come along, old girl. It's no use predicting the future. The future is already here. Our boys will be out of the van, one way or the other, by the time we walk over the hill and down to them." He spoke with his voice, as a little sign of tenderness between them.

Lavinia asked nervously, "Shouldn't we take an ornithopter and fly?"

"No, girl," said Rod tenderly. "What would our neighbors and kins-men think if they saw the parents flying in like wild offworlders or a pair of crimson pommies who can't keep a steady head when there's a bit of blow-up? After all, our big girl Casheba made it two years ago, and her eyes weren't so good."

"She's a howler, that one," said Lavinia warmly. "She could fight off a space pirate even better than you could before you could spiek."

They walked slowly up the hill.

When they crossed the top of the hill, they got the ominous melody coming right at them.

> *Out in the Garden of Death, our young*
> *Have tasted the valiant taste of fear.*
> *With muscular arm and reckless tongue,*
> *They have won, and lost, and escaped us here.*

In one form or another, all Old North Australians knew that tune. It was what the old people hummed when the young ones had to go into the vans to be selected out for survival or non-survival.

They saw the judges come out of the van. The Hon. Sec. Houghton Syme was there, his face bland and his cares erased by the special dreamlives which Rod's medicine had brought from the secret under-ground of Earth. The Lord Redlady was there. And Doctor Wentworth.

Lavinia started to run downhill toward the people, but Rod grabbed her arm and said with rough affection,

"Steady on, old girl. McBans never run—from nothing, and to noth-ing!"

She gulped but she joined pace with him.

People began looking up at them as they approached.

Nothing was to be told from the expressions.

It was the Lord Redlady, unconventional to the end, who broke the sign to them.

He held up one finger.

Only one.

Immediately thereafter Rod and Lavinia saw their twins. Ted, the fairer one, sat on a chair while Old Bill tried to give him a drink. Ted wouldn't take it. He looked across the land as though he could not believe what he saw. Rich, the darker twin, stood all alone.

All alone, and laughing.

Laughing.

Rod McBan and his missus walked across the land of Doom to be

civil to their neighbors. This was indeed what inexorable custom commanded. She squeezed his hand a little tighter; he held her arm a little
more firmly.

After a long time they had done their formal courtesies. Rod pulled
Ted to his feet. "Hullo, boy. You made it. You know what you are?"

Mechanically the boy recited, "Roderick Frederick Ronald Arnold
William MacArthur McBan to the hundred-and-fifty-second, Sir and
Father!"

Then the boy broke, for just a moment. He pointed at Rich, who was
still laughing, off by himself, and then plunged for his father's hug:

"Oh, dad! Why me? Why *me?*"

APPENDIX:
Variant Texts

The material of *Norstrilia* has been published in several different forms: the original magazine editions ("The Boy Who Bought Old Earth" and "The Store of Heart's Desire"), the Pyramid editions (*The Planet Buyer* and *The Underpeople*) and the Ballantine/Del Rey edition (*Norstrilia*). There are several significant differences between the texts. While the text of this edition is based on the Del Rey edition, significant portions of other versions seem worthy of preservation. This appendix is not a complete variorum edition. We have made no attempt to note every difference between editions. Rather, we have included some of the larger blocks of text that were not included in *Norstrilia* itself, with notes explaining how the pieces were fitted together in the various editions. The notes are keyed to the appropriate pages in the main text.

Page 1, "Theme and Prologue." In "The Boy Who Bought Old Earth," this chapter is preceded by the following prelude:

Later, much later, people forgot how Rod McBan had bought the whole Planet Earth without even knowing that he had done it. They remembered the extraneous things, like the Council of Thieves chartering whole fleets to intercept Rod on his way between Old North Australia and Earth. They remembered the little ballad which had been made up for the Chief of Thieves at about that time:

Arson for the arsenal,
Money in the money-bags,
Parson in the parsonage,
And the girl for me!

(They even explained that a parsonage was a vital statistics computer and the parson was its input screen.)

The real drama remained untold.

What had driven a rich, mysterious boy to gamble everything—perhaps even his life—from the richest planet in the galaxy in order to buy Earth? What could he have possibly done with Earth if he did get it?

You have to understand something of Old North Australia (familiarly called "Norstrilia") to see how he did it.

You have to understand why a lot of the young died young.

Then you get the pitch of it and you have the real story, the inside story, the original history—not just a cartoon of a handsome yellow-haired boy standing with his arms full of megacredit papers.

He never held them, anyhow. He couldn't have held them. There were too many. This boy had bought Earth, Manhome itself, the Earthport tower, the oceans, everything. You couldn't get the paper titles of all that stuff into one person's room, much less into his arms.

So let's go back to the beginnings, and start with Old North Australia.

Page 3. In both "The Boy Who Bought Old Earth" and The Planet Buyer, *in Section 5, after the first 4 paragraphs (after the sentence that reads "We know the poor kid was born to troubles."), the remainder of the section is replaced by the following:*

He was born to inherit the Station of Doom.

He almost failed the Garden of Death.

The Onseck was after him.

His father had died out in the dirty part of space, where people never find nice clean deaths.

When he got in trouble, he trusted his computer.

The computer gambled, and it won Earth.

He went to Earth.

That was history itself—*that* and C'mell beside him.

At long, long last he got his rights and he came home.

That's the story. Except for the details.

They follow.

Page 24. "The soldier held out his hand." The four paragraphs beginning here are omitted in "The Boy Who Bought Old Earth." Similarly, on page 35, the magazine version omits the text from "Their faces still glowed with pleasure …" through "He went back to the table," thus deleting all mention of the wallet and its ticket to Earth.

Page 47. "Soon he would see it." In "The Boy Who Bought Old Earth," the text from here through "His own computer." on page 52 is replaced by the following summary:

Soon he would see it—the Palace of the Governor of Night, forever luminescent in the ultraviolet band. It was a Daimoni-built palace once, long, long ago. It had been built for the Governor of Night on Khufu II, where they used to raise the Furry Mountain Fur. But the Fur was gone and the Khufuans starved, and the palace had gone up for sale when there was no more a Governor of Night.

William MacArthur—"Wild William," they called him—had bought it for a prodigious price and shipped it to his farm.

It was a replica of the Temple of Diana at Ephesus, way back on Manhome Earth itself. Normal people could not see it, since it was visible only in the ultraviolet band. Sometimes, with a real mean dust storm, the dust outlined it and the palace then showed up in ghostly form ... mysterious, sacred, useless, but very beautiful—to ordinary people.

For Rod it was the front gate to his old family computer, just as the secret passage in the gap was the back gate.

Only relatives of the McBans, with eyesight which ran into the ultraviolet, could see the building at normal times.

And now it belonged to Rod McBan, and housed his computer. His own computer.

Page 89, "Traps, Fortunes and Watchers." In "The Boy Who Bought Old Earth," this entire chapter is replaced by the text that follows. (The Planet Buyer *contains the whole chapter except for the section "Ruth, on the Beach ..." on page 91.)*

That very night it happened.

They scunned him; they reduced him; they froze him; they dehydrated him.

The Lord Redlady arranged a relay with the special courier ship which would run him to Earth itself.

These things were supposed to be secret, but they could not be kept completely secret. We all know that no communications systems are wholly leak-proof. Even inside the vast networks of the Instrumentality, shielded, coded and protected though they were, there were soft electronic spots, weak administrative points, or garrulous men here and there. The old computer had not allowed for ordinary human wickedness. It understood the human rules, but not the temptations to break the rules. All the messages concerning Rod's vast speculations had been sent in the clear. It was no wonder that on many worlds, people saw Rod as a chance, an opportunity, a victim, a benefactor, or an enemy.

We all know the old rhyme:

Luck is hot and people funny.
Everybody's fond of money.
Lose a chance and sell your mother.
Win the pot and buy another.
Other people fall and crash:
You could win the pot of cash!

It applied in this case, too. People ran hot and cold with the news. On Earth, Commissioner Teadrinker wondered if he dared kidnap this rich man who was coming and hold him to ransom. It was illegal, but Teadrinker was so old that he had outlived mere legality.

At Viola Siderea, the Council of Thieves sent the Chief of Thieves in pursuit, spending hard-stolen money on honest lease of patrol ships, so great was their urgency.

At the heart of the underpeople world, an unknown magister invoked the seven logoi and the three Nameless Ones, hoping that the stranger might bring great tidings.

The Commonwealth Council of Old North Australia sat on the matter and decided to send along a full dozen McBan impersonations, just to throw robbers and interceptors off the track. They did not do this because they loved Rod, or because they had special regard for him as an individual citizen, but because it was against their principles to let any Old North Australian be robbed with impunity.

And Rod—

Rod woke on Mars, already reconstituted.

Page 95. "Vomact was a small man ..." In "The Boy Who Bought Old Earth," the text from here to "On their way back Rod said, very casually, ..." on page 101 is replaced by the single paragraph that follows. (The first two paragraphs of the Norstrilia *text appear in "The Store of Heart's Desire" at the equivalent of page 185, but as the description of the* second *Doctor Vomact.)*

Friends they became in the ensuing days. After several weeks, Vomact came to the plans he had—when Rod was well enough—for the disguise for a trip to Earth.

Page 103. "Hospitality and Entrapment." None of this chapter appears in "The Boy Who Bought Old Earth."

Page 114. "They all three spun around." The text from here to the end of "The Boy Who Bought Old Earth" is quite different, completely omitting the giant-spider incident and going directly to the interview with Lord Jestocost that also appears in The Planet Buyer *(see below).*

Page 122. "They walked toward a dropshaft." In The Planet Buyer, *the remainder of this chapter is replaced by an encounter with Lord Jestocost that appears nowhere in* Norstrilia; *essentially the same text appears in "The Boy Who Bought Old Earth." The text from* The Planet Buyer *follows:*

They walked only a few steps, then stopped short.

They all three spun around.

A man faced them—a tall man, clad in formal garments, his face gleaming with intelligence, courage, wisdom and a very special kind of elegance.

"I am projecting," said he.

"You know me," he said to C'mell.

"My Lord Jestocost!"

"You will sleep," he commanded A'gentur, and the little monkey crumpled into a heap of fur on the deck of the tower.

"I *am* the Lord Jestocost, one of the Instrumentality," said the strange man, "and I am going to speak to you at very high speed. It will seem like many minutes, but it will only take seconds. It is necessary for you to know your fate."

"You mean my future?" said Rod McBan. "I thought that you, or somebody else, had it all arranged."

"We can dispose, but we cannot arrange. I have talked to the Lord Redlady. I have plans for you. Perhaps they will work out."

A slight frowning smile crossed the face of the distinguished man. With his left hand he warned C'mell to do nothing. The beautiful cat-girl started to step forward and then obeyed the imperious gesture, stopped, and merely watched.

The Lord Jestocost dropped to one knee. He bowed proudly and freely, with his head held high and his face tilted upward while he stared directly at Rod McBan.

Still kneeling, he said ceremoniously, "Some day, young man, you will understand what you are now seeing. The Lord Jestocost, which is myself, has bowed to no man or woman since the day of his initiation. That was more time ago than I like to remember. But I bow freely to the man who has bought Earth. I offer you my friendship and my help. I offer both of these without mental reservation. Now I stand up and I greet you as my younger comrade."

He stood erect and reached for Rod's hand. Rod shook hands with him, still bewildered.

"You have seen the work of some of the people who want you dead. I have had a hand in getting you through that (and I might tell you that the man who sent the spider will regret very deeply and very long that he did it). Other people will try to hunt you down for what you have done or for what you are. I am willing for you to save some of your property and all of your life. You will have experiences which you will treasure—if you live through them.

"You have no chance at all without me. I'll correct that. You have one chance in ten thousand of coming out alive.

"With me, if you obey me through C'mell, your chances are very good indeed. More than one thousand to one in your favor. You will live—"

"But my money!" Rod spieked wildly without knowing that he did it.

"Your money is on Earth. It *is* Earth," smiled the wise, powerful old official. "It is being taxed at enormous rates. This is your fate, young man. Remember it, and be ready to obey it. When I lift my hand, repeat after me. Do you understand?"

Rod nodded. He was not afraid, exactly, but some unknown core within him had begun to radiate animal terror. He was not afraid of what might happen to himself; he was afraid of the strange, wild fierceness of it all. He had never known that man or boy could be so utterly alone.

The loneliness of the open outback at home was physical. This loneliness had millions of people around him. He felt the past crowding up as though it were alive in its own right. The cat-girl beside him comforted him a little; he had met her through Doctor Vomact; to Vomact he had been sent by Redlady; and Redlady knew his own dear home. The linkage was there, though it was remote.

In front of him there was no linkage at all.

He stood, in his own mind, on a precipice of the present, staring down at the complex inexplicable immensity of Earth's past. This was the place that all people were from. In those oceans they had crawled in the slime; from those salt, rich seas they had climbed to that land far below him; on that land they had changed from animals into men before they had seized the stars. This was home itself, the home of all men, and it could swallow him up.

The word-thoughts came fast out of the Lord Jestocost's mind, directly into his own. It was as though Jestocost had found some way around his impediment and had then disregarded it.

"This is Old Earth itself, from which you were bred and to which all men return in their thoughts if not in their bodies. This is still the richest of the worlds, though its wealth is measured in treasures and memories, not in stroon.

"Many men have tried to rule this world. A very few have done it for a little while."

Unexpectedly, the Lord Jestocost lifted his right hand. Without knowing why he did it, Rod repeated the last sentence.

"A very few men have governed the world for a little while."

"The Instrumentality has made that impossible."

The right hand was still in the commanding "up" position, so Rod repeated, *"The Instrumentality has made that impossible."*

"And now you, Rod McBan, of Old North Australia, are the first to own it."

The hand was still raised.

"And now I, Rod McBan, of Old North Australia, am the first to own it."

The hand dropped, but the Lord spieked on.

"Go forward, then, with death around you.

"Go forward, then, to your heart's desire.

"Go forward, with the love you will win and lose.

"Go forward, to the world, and to that other world under the world.

"Go forward, to wild adventures and a safe return.

"Be watchful of C'mell. She will be my eyes upon you, my arm around your shoulders, my authority upon your person; but go.

"Go." Up went the hand.

"Go ..." said Rod.

The Lord vanished.

C'mell plucked at his sleeve. "Your trip is over, my husband. Now we take Earth itself."

Softly and quickly they ran to the steps which went to unimaginable Earth below them.

Rod McBan had come to the fulfilment of his chance and his inheritance.

"The Boy Who Bought Old Earth" ends here. The Planet Buyer *concludes with the following brief chapter:*

EPILOGUE AND CODA

How Rod McBan CLI took his chance and enjoyed his inheritance is, of course, implicit in all that he had done and had been done to him up to his meeting with the Lord Jestocost. The details of how it all worked out are doubtless fascinating (and will doubtless be told later), but the reason for this chronicle ends now that the players have made the moves that will determine the outcome.

One piece remains to be removed from the board first, though.

This is followed by a section "Old North Australia, Adm. Offices of the Commonwealth" like that in the the chapter "Discourses and Recourses" (page 125). This is then followed by this section:

The Prediction Machine at the Abba-dingo

Jestocost was the only Lord of the Instrumentality who had bothered to put through a direct line to the prediction machine at the Abba-dingo, halfway up the immense column which supported Earthport. Most of the time the machine did not work at all; much of the rest was unintelligible, but Jestocost liked trying it anyhow.

The night of Rod's arrival he asked, "What is happening in the world?"

Said the machine, "What? What? Be clear."

"Has anything started happening in the world today?" shouted Jestocost.

There was a long delay. Jestocost thought of disconnecting, but finally the machine spoke, in the accents of ages past, "This-machine is cold, cold. This-machine is old, old. It is hard to tell. It is hard to know. But something has begun to happen. Something strange, like the first few drops of an immense rainstorm, like the tiny glow of an approaching comet. Change is coming to this world. It is not change which weapons can stop. This change whispers in like a forgotten dream. Maybe it will be good. Change, change ... at the center of it all, there is a boy. One boy. This-machine cannot see him. ..."

There was a long silence. Jestocost finally knew that the machine had nothing more to say. He cut the connection. And then, very deeply, he sighed.

Page 125. "Discourses and Recourses." At the beginning of The Underpeople, *this is preceded by the following chapter, which does not appear in* Norstrilia:

LOST MUSIC IN AN OLD WORLD

You may have seen the musical play which was written about the confrontation of Rod McBan, the boy who had bought Earth, and the Lady Johanna Gnade, proudest and most self-willed of the Lords of the Instrumentality. It was not a very long play. Indeed, among the many plays and ballads that were composed about Roderick Frederick Ronald Arnold William MacArthur McBan the hundred and fifty-first, this short drama was characterized by economy of form, understatement of the dramatic elements, and the generous use of music. People remembered the music even when they forgot which play it came from. (Then the Instrumentality stepped in and ordered that the play be withdrawn, gradually and imperceptibly, on the ground that the music was licentious. Unfortunately, it *was*. Old music from the First Space Age has a real tendency to corrupt people of our own time. You can't pick something out of a half-mythical place like ancient "New York" and turn it loose without people getting very queer ideas indeed.)

This is the way it happened.

Hansgeorg Wagner was one of the first musicians to be imprinted with the Doych language, sometimes called German or Teut, when the Rediscovery of Man began bringing the pre-Ruin cultures back into the world.

Hansgeorg Wagner had a neat eye for the dramatic. When the story of Rod McBan began to leak out, soon after McBan went back to his home planet of Old North Australia, Wagner refused to consider the obvious scenes: the boy gambling for Earth on his dry, faraway planet, and winning most of the available money in the universe; the boy walking on Mars; the boy meeting his "wife," C'mell, most beautiful of the cat-women who served as the girlygirl hostesses for Earth; the boy fighting Amaral for the life of one of them; the mystery of the Department Store of Hearts' Desires and what befell Rod there; or even the terrifying terminal scene with the E'telekeli. Wagner did not even want the dramatic scene in which Rod's companion, his workwoman Eleanor, parted from him on Earthport tower soon after C'mell had sung her own famous little tower song to Rod:

And oh! my love, for you.
High birds crying, and a
High sky flying, and a
High wind driving, and a
High heart striving, and a
High brave place for you!

In the Music Room: A Meeting with the Past

The passenger dropshaft from Earthport was like an ancient elevator shaft, except for the fact that if an actual ancient had seen it, he would have been surprised. It was ten miles deep, or more (it's hard to figure out exactly what *miles* were, but they were much longer than kilometers), and it had no elevators. The shaft was ornamentally illuminated. There were signs for information, frequent stops for refreshment, and curious sights to be seen. This was for people only. People put on magnetic belts, stepped into the shaft, and were carried up or down at the rate of about twenty meters a minute, depending on which shaft they had gotten into; shafts always came in pairs, an up shaft and a down shaft.

By contrast, the freight shaft had no signs, no refreshments, and no amenities. The down speed was considerably faster. Freight rose or fell, tied to magnetic belts; underpeople and robots wore the belts, unless they forgot them and swiftly became bloody pulp or mashed machinery far below. The freight shaft, like the passenger shaft, did have a warning in both the up and the down shaft, because if people got loose from their belts, they whistled downward to their deaths. Each set of shafts had interceptor nets, both for saving falling persons or objects, and to protect the other passengers below, but the nets did not work too well.

Wagner's drama has an initial scene showing Rod McBan and C'mell
pausing at the top of the freight dropshaft. She is carrying the small monkey-surgeon A'gentur, who has gone to sleep, bone-weary after the trip.
Rod McBan, standing a full head taller than most cat-men, is expostulat-
ing with gestures more coarse and more real than any c'man ever used.
His big bush of yellow hair had been made cat-like before he landed on
Earth, and the long sparse whiskers of this cat-moustache twitched oddly
indeed as he explained his emphatic desires with forthright Old North
Australian gestures.

After a short development of the scene, Wagner has both of them
singing the lyric refrain, "Earth is mine, but what good does it do me?"
from Rod, and "Earth is yours, but be patient, my love" from C'mell. A
touch of comedy is provided by C'mell's trying to get a magnetic harness
on Rod while he squirms. The scene ends with the two of them stepping
over the edge of the dropshaft (which looks bottomless) on their long,
long drop down to the surface of the Earth.

We know that the two of them dropped easily. The only difficulty was
caused by Rod's tendency to talk too much when he, the richest man in
the world, was supposed to be traveling in the disguise of a poor simple
cat-man. Torn between irritation and love, C'mell switched between hu-
moring him and shushing him.

Crisis came (and Hansgeorg Wagner catches it in his play) when Rod
heard the sound of unbelievable music.

It was like no music that he had ever heard before.

"What's that?" he cried to C'mell.

"Music," she said, soothingly.

He did not call her a fool, but he growled in annoyance and reached
over to seize a rung of the endless emergency ladder which followed the
dropshaft down. He climbed a dozen rungs upward and peered into a
pitch-black lateral corridor which led, apparently, to nowhere but from
which strange fierce beautiful music was certainly coming. He had climbed
against the gentle throbbing pull of the magnetic belt and he breathed
heavily with the double exertion. C'mell had dropped another ten meters
before she saw what he was doing. Wearily, but with no word of com-
plaint, she climbed up the ladder to him, carrying her own weight, that of
the sleeping monkey-surgeon whom she had tossed over her shoulder,
and the pull of her own belt as well. When her head reached the level of
Rod's feet, he stepped carefully off the ladder and took two very gingerly
steps into the dark lateral corridor.

The music was clear to both of them.

Throbbing, beaten strings made the lovely sounds.

She sensed his inquiry though she could not see his face in the dark.

"That instrument—it's a piano. They've started making them again."
Rod put his hand on her arm to quiet her. "Listen, I think he's singing."

Full-bodied and full-noted the music of the piano and a man's tenor
voice came clearly and fully at them from the corridor, hidden by the
darkness but not sounding too far away:

Ignoraba yo.
I didn't use to know it.
Ignoraba yo.
I didn't use to show it
       that I loved you, loved you so.

I love you and I love you,
Hoy y mañana.
There's nothing else in life for me,
Hoy y mañana.
You love me wild and use me up,
Hoy y mañana.
Was I happier or sadder when I didn't even know you?
Ignoraba yo.
I couldn't even show you.

The voice trailed away. There were a few flourishes of beaten strings, as
though the player were trying to get the arrangement just right.

"Part of that is Ancient Inglish," said Rod, "but I never heard the
other language before. And I certainly never heard that kind of a melody,
anywhere."

"I know most of the music which is played on Earth," whispered
C'mell, "and I never heard anything like that before. Come on, Rod.
Let's go on down the shaft. When we get to a safe place, I will send
messengers back to find out what is going on in this part of Earthport
tower."

"No," said Rod, "I'm going in."

"You can't, Rod. You can't. It might ruin everything. The disguise,
Lord Jestocost's plans, your safety."

"I bought this world," said Rod, "and I'm a ruddy fool if I can't even
ask for a piece of music. I'm going in."

"Rod," she cried.

"Stop me," he said, crudely, and walked boldly down the corridor into
the dark, just as though there might be no trap doors or electric screens.
C'mell followed him, carefully and reluctantly.

The corridor blazed red with letters of warning:

KEEP OUT!
NO PEOPLE ALLOWED
INSTRUMENTALITY WORK—SECRET

A recorded voice shouted at them, "Go away! Go away! No robots. No underpeople. No real persons. Lords of the Instrumentality, get individual clearance before you enter here. Secret work. Go away! Go away! No robots. No underpeople," and so on, in a sustained irritating shout.

Rod ignored the voice even though C'mell was plucking at his sleeve.

The red warning lights had revealed the outline of a door with a doorknob.

He took the doorknob, twisted it. It was locked. The door itself did not seem to be of steel or Daimoni material. Perhaps it was even wood, which was much too precious on Old North Australia to be used for anything as cheap as a common door: the Norstrilians used plastics derived from sheepbones.

Rod shouted, "Open up, inside. Open up."

"Go away," said a mild, pleasant voice from beyond the door, so near that it startled them.

The voice was so near and the door so fragile that Rod was tempted.

He stepped back until he was next to C'mell. He was sorry when he heard her sigh with relief—apparently at the thought that he had heeded the warning and was going to go back to the dropshaft.

Instead, he used a fighting trick which he had learned at home. He jumped with the full force of his body at the door, striking the door just above the knob with both his feet and putting his hands below him so as to cushion the fall of his body against the floor.

Results were startling:

The door yielded so easily that Rod plunged on through into a bright sun-lit room, landed on a carpet and slid with the carpet until his feet, firmly but gently, were stopped by a large beautiful upright wooden box, elegantly polished, which seemed to have a rudimentary console. A middle-aged gentleman, showing great surprise, jumped out of his way. Blinking against the brightness of the light, C'mell and A'gentur followed Rod into the room.

Their startled host spoke:

"You're underpeople! Do you want to die? Somebody will kill you for this. Not I, of course. What do you want here?"

Rod brought himself to his feet with all the dignity which he could command.

"My name is Rod McBan," said he, "and I take full responsibility for what has happened. I am the new owner of this planet Earth, and I want to hear some more of that music you were making."

"Ignoraba yo. That Spanish bop? What business is it of yours, cat-man? That is secret work for the Instrumentality. And all you are going to do is to die when the robot police arrive."

C'mell spoke up. Her voice had a calm urgency to it, which could not be ignored by anyone. Said she, "You have a connection with the Central Computer?"

"Of course," said the man, "all protected offices do."

"You are not a person?"

"Of course not, cat-woman. I am the dog-man D'igo and I am the musical historian assigned to work in this office."

"I am C'mell," said she flatly.

The dog-man was startled but when he spoke, his voice was very agreeable: "I know who you are. Anything here is at your service, C'mell."

"Your connection?" she demanded.

He nodded his head at one side of the room. She saw the speaker in the wall. A'gentur sat sleepily on the floor, while Rod had produced one single clear note by pushing one of the keys of the beautiful big upright box.

C'mell called, "Rod, come here."

"Right ho," he said, coming over to the speaker.

"Listen. Your life may be in danger, Rod. I'll call Central Computer and I want you to assert your authority over this room and this work. Demand to hear the music that you want. Tell the Central Computer the truth. That may keep the robot police from coming in and killing you before they find that you are not really a cat-man."

"He isn't a cat-man ..." murmured D'igo in wonderment from the side.

"Sh-h," said C'mell to D'igo. To Rod she said, "Speak now. Establish your rights."

"Centputer," said Rod, "take this name down. Roderick Frederick Ronald Arnold William MacArthur McBan the hundred and fifty-first from Old North Australia. Got it?"

"Affirmative."

"Do I own you, Centputer?"

"Repeat. Repeat."

"Centputer, have I bought you?"

"Apparently impossible, but this-machine will check. No, you have not bought this-machine."

"Can you tell where I am, Centputer."

"Restricted workroom of the Instrumentality."

"Do I own Earthport?"

"Affirmative."

"Do I own this room too?"

"Affirmative."

"I am in it."

"Re-state the instruction. This-machine cannot make your statement operational."

"I have taken this room from the Instrumentality and I will return it to the Lords of the Instrumentality when I see fit."

"That is not possible. The room belongs to the Instrumentality."

"And I," said Rod, "override the Instrumentality. Tell them to keep out till I am through."

"The instruction is impossible. This-machine has records that you own Earthport, and that the Instrumentality sold you all of it, including the room you are in. Therefore the room is yours. This-machine also has a basic programmed command that the Instrumentality cannot be overridden. This-machine must appeal to higher authority. The robot police will be warned away from your person until this-machine has been re-coded or reaffirmed by higher authority." *Click* went the speaker, and the Central Computer itself broke the connection.

"You're in for it," said C'mell. Her green eyes, which could look fierce at times, scanned him with soft indulgence: Rod could see that she was very proud of him, and he was not altogether sure of the reason. Her warning was ominous, but her expression betrayed no fear, only a new-found confidence that he would see them through.

A'gentur spoke from the floor to D'igo: "Do you have any cocoanut, raisins, shelled nuts, or pineapple, dog-man?"

"Forgive him, colleague D'igo, if he's rude, but he's very tired and very hungry."

"It's all right," said D'igo. "I have none of those things, though I have some excellent raw liver and an assortment of bones in my coldbox. My master, a Lord, has left a pot of cocoa which I could warm up for you, animal. Would you like that?"

"Anything, anything," said A'gentur cheerfully.

"Now I've seen everything," declared D'igo with a species of desperate composure as he put the cocoa on to warm it up. "My secret room is attacked, the famous C'mell herself pays me a visit, a cat-man gives orders to the Central Computer, and I have to feed an animal in my workshop. It's not often that this sort of thing happens, is it, Madam C'mell?"

"We came in here," said C'mell gracefully and quickly, "because this friend of mine insisted on hearing your music."

"You like it," smiled D'igo. "I like it myself. It's secret music and I'm not sure that it will ever be cleared for use. My master, the Lord Ingintau, wanted me to find the last song ever sung in New York."

"That was a city, wasn't it?"

"The biggest city on this continent. When New York was destroyed, there were various primitive electronic stations transmitting, some sending pictures and others relaying just words and music. The search-robots out in space have been recording all the salvageable messages from in that period of the First Doom, and I think that I have narrowed the choice down to three songs. You heard *Ignoraba Yo*—that was Inglish and Spanish mixed, in the style called bop. I'm not sure of the next one, because I have most of the melody, but for the words, only the refrain has come through. I got my helper, a dog-girl, to sing the part while I played the piano, and I spooled it just last week. Would you like to hear it?"

"That's what I burst in for," said Rod cheerfully.

The musician D'igo rested his hand against a blank part of the wall and said, "Forty-seven, please."

The room was immediately filled with the wild catchy music of the "piano," expertly played. The particularly musical melody was quick, startling, amusing and witty in its use of a tune. By Norstrilian standards, that song would be condemned as lascivious, thought Rod—but then, that wasn't Old North Australia. It was what Ancient Earth sang as Earth died the first of a hundred deaths.

After a preliminary *la-la-la la-a-a-la* a woman's voice came on and sang the catchy refrain three times in a row in perfectly accented Ancient Inglish, just as Rod had heard it spoken by the talking books in his family's storeroom of hidden treasures:

> *Only God can make a tree,*
> *But you can make a girl like me!*

"It's amusing, but there's not much to it," said Rod. "What's the third one?"

"That's a period piece, antedating the fall of New York. I think it may have had something to do with a collective entertainment which they called a square dance or a country dance. I can't imagine why. Or it may have been something translated from another language and another culture into the usage of the Murkins."

"They're the ones who had New York?" asked Rod.

"The same," said D'igo.

"The same ones who built those spectacular surface roads that people see everytime they look down on Earth from nearby space?"

"That's right," smiled D'igo. "They were a wild, gifted, wanton people. Do you want to hear the third song? I'll play that and sing it for you myself. I just finished arranging it myself."

He sat at the piano, played a few bars, and then sang:

Ring a bell
    and clap! clap!
Sing pell mell
    and tap! tap!
The wishing well
    will miss, miss.
Hug and tell
    and kiss, kiss.

Rod sighed, "I still like the one I heard outside your door."

D'igo smiled his full-faced, clean-shaven smile. Rod wondered that a dog could be made into so perfect a copy of a man. Except for his indoor pallor, D'igo looked as well-shaped and as well-spoken as any man that Rod had ever seen.

"What you heard out there," said D'igo, "was a spool of my own voice. Would you like to hear my assistant sing it? She is a very talented girl. She can sing either contralto or soprano."

"Soprano," said A'gentur promptly and unexpectedly. D'igo stared at him with astonishment and reproach, but since the others did not object, he said,

"Soprano it is, then," and he muttered under his breath, "For a talking animal, you've got a fantastic education."

D'igo called to the wall, "Thirty-one, third version," and then said to his guests, "Do sit down...."

Ignoraba Yo began to pour from the speakers with its full, hypnotic volume, carried by a woman's splendid voice.

Confrontation and a Half Challenge

This is the climax of Hansgeorg Wagner's musical drama. The four of them sat listening to the music: A'gentur on the floor, drifting off to sleep again; the two cat-people, C'mell red-haired and Rod yellow-haired, staring at nothing and giving their full attention to the music; the host, D'igo, sitting with a half-smile on his face and watching his guests. Wagner combines the thrill of illegal ancient music with some deft composition of his own.

His woodwinds represent the soft rustling in the corridor.

A quick light flurry of drums indicates the new arrivals:

A tall, pitiless intelligent woman with a vividly dramatic black and white dress of the most conservative cut imaginable, accompanied by two high-ranking robot soldiers, both of them with their bodies washed in silver and gold, their swimming eyes taking in all corners of the room at once, their heavy wirepoints already buzzing with potential death.

"I," said she, "am the Lady Johanna Gnade. *You* are D'igo, the musical historian. I have heard your work—"

Rod stood up and interrupted her. Though she was tall, he was several centimeters taller. "I," said he, in a perfectly composed copy of her own manner, "am Rod McBan, the owner of this room. You can sit down, Ma'am and Lady, if you wish. Your robots can sit down too, if they enjoy it."

For a memorable moment the two confronted one another: the tall, black-haired woman and the tall, yellow-haired youth in cat disguise. This was no meeting of individuals—it was a confrontation of systems, the trained power of the Instrumentality against the disciplined in-bred force of the Old North Australians.

The woman yielded, a little.

"You're a quick young man. Your name is Rod McBan and you have bought Earth. Why did you do it?"

"Do sit down," said Rod firmly and hospitably. "It's a long story and I would not want to tire a lady—"

Johanna Gnade snapped, "Don't worry about my being a lady. I'm one of the Lords of the Instrumentality. And make your story short."

"Please sit, Ma'am and Lady. And make your robots comfortable." There was a little more command than courtesy in his voice, but there was nothing at which she could take open offense.

"I've never had an underperson make me sit down before," she grumbled, taking a hassock and sitting bolt upright on it. "Lieutenant, captain, both of you, go in the hall. As a matter of fact, cut all outside connections with this room, but record the scene yourselves, so that I will have my own record of it."

The two robots turned off their wirepoints. They walked deftly around the room, touching the walls lightly here and there. The better-ornamented one said,

"Clear and secure, my Lady."

She did not thank them. She just nodded at the broken door. They walked out into the dark corridor.

The Lady Johanna Gnade looked at C'mell. "And you are C'mell. I've seen you before. As a matter of fact, I have seen you several times, almost always when there was trouble. Are you one of our confidential agents? You always come out innocent, no matter what happens."

"No, Ma'am. I'm just a girlygirl. I work at Earthport, welcoming off-world visitors and keeping them happy."

"I'm not sure I trust that word 'just,' " said the Lady Johanna Gnade. "Who put you on the job this time?"

"The Lord Jestocost," said C'mell, a little worried.

"Jestocost?" repeated the Lady Johanna Gnade. "If that's the case, it's really none of my business. Don't break into things any more, Mister McBan, without asking the Lord Jestocost to arrange it first. Old Earth is no citizen-commonwealth like Old North Australia. Often we kill first and ask later. I'd like to hear your side of the story before I leave, now that I'm here. How old are you?"

"Chronologically, I am about sixty-five years old. But I have gone back through a sixteen-year cycle four times, so that biologically I am sixteen."

"Are you a man?"

"Certainly. This cat stuff is just a disguise."

"No, I mean are you a grown man, according to the horrible customs of your home planet?"

"Citizen. Citizen, we call it. Yes, I passed the Garden of Death."

"Why did you buy Earth?"

"To escape, Ma'am and Lady."

"Escape what? I thought that Norstrilia protected every single one of her people, once they passed that awful survival test."

"Usually, yes. It just happened that I had only one enemy, and he was Onseck of the whole Commonwealth administration."

"Onseck? We don't have that word."

"Honorary Secretary. The man who runs the routine admin. for Her Absent Majesty the Queen."

"I've heard of that custom of yours. Why did he hate you?"

"We were both defectives, a long time ago. I was—am—telepathically deaf and dumb. Mostly. Can't *spiek* or *hier,* have to rely on the old spoken words, like outlanders or barbarians. He was a short-lifer, who could not take stroon, the drug which—"

"I know all about stroon," said she, "the immortality drug. As a matter of fact, my veins are full of it right now. I am near my six hundredth birthday."

"Congratulations, Ma'am and Lady."

"Never mind. What happened?"

"When I knew he was after me, I went to my family's computer. It's all mechanical, not a single animal brain or animal relay in it."

"I didn't know there was one left."

"I myself repaired it," said Rod.

In this part of Hansgeorg Wagner's musical drama about Rod, the music wears a little thin because he lets Rod and the Lady Johanna Gnade speak in normal voices, using his music only as an accompaniment. Now and then he lets the spotlight drift across the calm face and strong torso of D'igo the musicologist; when that happens, he brings in a fugue or two from *Ignoraba Yo*. Otherwise the music for this part of the show is rather dull.

"If you weren't so rich," said the Lady Johanna Gnade, "I'd like to buy that machine of yours for our Earthport museum."

"It's not for sale, Ma'am and Lady, not at any price."

"I can imagine that. What did it do?"

"It outcomputed the Commonwealth and I became the richest man in the universe."

"So you ran away again. First you ran because you were persecuted. Then you ran because you were rich. When did you get here?"

"Today."

"Where have you been between the time you left Norstrilia and to-day?"

"Mars, Ma'am and Lady."

"Do you have to keep using that double title on me?"

"Yes, Ma'am and Lady. It's our custom. We don't change our customs much."

The Lady Johanna Gnade burst into a friendly laugh—her first since their encounter. "All right. What's yours?"

"What's my what?"

"Your double title. You have one, don't you?"

It was Rod's turn to look uncomfortable. "It's 'Mister and Owner,' Ma'am and Lady, but you don't have to use it all the time. After all, this is Earth."

"But you own it."

"All right, you win, Ma'am."

"How are your parents, Mister and Owner McBan?"

His face clouded over. "Dead."

"How?"

"Their ship went milky while planoforming through space-two."

"Do you love anyone?"

"Yes, Ma'am, my servant Eleanor."

"Where is she?"

"Somewhere in this tower, Ma'am."

"What's she doing?"

"Pretending to be me, Ma'am, while I pretend to be a cat-man. They changed her into a young man when they scunned me down and then made me look like an underperson."

"Scunned? *You* were scunned? Frozen, dehydrated, cut up, boxed. You? Who did it?"

"That monkey-doctor there," said Rod, gesturing at A'gentur on the floor.

The Lady Johanna Gnade called directly to A'gentur, "You, there, monkey, wake up! He talks, doesn't he?"

A'gentur let one eye quiver open for a quick glance at the Lady Johanna Gnade. Within seconds he was snoring in deep sleep.

The Lady Johanna Gnade stared at A'gentur. She brushed the air with the right hand to keep the others silent. She even made a motion over A'gentur with both hands. The monkey did not stir or waken.

"I don't like this," she said. "I don't like this one bit. That being looks like an animal, but I can't tell whether it is an underperson or a human being. It went to sleep at me. I just threw the whole telepathic force of the Instrumentality at it and *it stayed asleep.* That's never happened to me before."

C'mell said, very softly, "He was sent out to Norstrilia at the request of the Lord Redlady."

"Redlady? Redlady?" said the Lady Johanna Gnade. "He's still working?"

"Yes, Ma'am," said Rod.

"Redlady at one end and Jestocost at the other! You couldn't find two more weirdos—more personalities, I mean—in the whole Instrumentality to match that pair. You're in good hands, young man. And what do you want out of all this?"

"A look at Earth, a bit of adventure, my life, and most of my fortune, Ma'am and Lady."

She almost looked as though she would lose her dignity and whistle in astonishment. "You're not asking much, are you? Not much by half!"

"I'll win," said Rod. "I'll win all right. The Norstrilian way."

"What's that?"

He turned serious. "Never plan too far ahead. Go from one immediate situation to the other. Never make a decision if you can put the decision on somebody else and still win for yourself. And most of all—"

"Most of all?" asked the Lady Johanna Gnade softly.

"Most of all, *never get caught winning.* Just win, but don't let it show."

"You're all right," she laughed, standing up. "You don't need my protection. And you aren't going to get my punishment. I'd hate to tackle you, young as you are. With those companions you have, you're practically an army. That girl of yours, C'mell—"

"Yes, Ma'am," said C'mell.

"She never gets caught. At anything." The Lady smiled. She went on:

"And that thing on the floor, that so-called monkey. I can't make it talk. I can't even tell what it is. You're in good company, young man. I'll speak to the Lord Jestocost sometime. Do you shake hands?"

Rod politely held out his right hand.

She stopped him with a wave. "I was being friendly. Is handshaking a custom on Norstrilia, Mister and Owner McBan—a custom even between men and women?"

"Indeed it is, Ma'am and Lady."

They shook hands cordially.

"Don't take too much of Earth home with you when you leave," she called to him as she entered the dark corridor, summoned her robots and dropped down the shaft.

D'igo said, "Come back if you wish, Mister and Owner McBan. Call on me to come out any time, Madam C'mell. Goodbye, monkey."

"Thanks," said A'gentur, wide-awake. "Let's go eat."

Page 125. "Old North Australia, Administrative Offices of the Commonwealth, The Same Day." As noted above, this section appears in the "Epilogue and Coda" to The Planet Buyer. *The remainder of this chapter is in* The Underpeople, *with the following omissions: pages 127–128, from "Aunt Doris started to get up ..." to the end of the section; pages 129-131, all of the two sections "The Assistant Commissioner's Office, Top of Earthport, Four Hours Later" and "Antechamber of the Bell and Bank, The Same Time." And on page 133, the text from "He started to explain who Redlady was ..." through "But go back to your story." is replaced by:*

... of all the civilized worlds. Directed and calculated by the ancient McBan family computer which, when asked by its new Mister and Owner how he could escape the sick enmity of Norstrilia's Onseck, had answered that the only way was to become the richest man in the Universe—and, in four hours, had brought it about. He unrolled as much as was necessary of the thread of Rod McBan's swift yet complex dispatch to Old Earth, overseen by the disgraced Lord Redlady—the disguise as a cat-man, and the nine Rod-doubles, the servant Eleanor and eight robots, to confuse thieves, kidnappers, and anyone else who might feel an unwholesome interest in the wealthiest man of all time ...

Page 141. "The trip was a vivid, quick dream." Here the text of the magazine version rejoins that of the books. "The Store of Heart's Desire" begins with the following prefatory section:

The animal-derived underpeople talked about it for hundreds of years thereafter. The story became a part of their legend, their balladry. Real people, walking innocently around on the surface of the Earth, some kilometers above, never heard anything about it. To most of them, Downdeep-downdeep was a place where robots and underpeople worked to provide the luxuries, comforts and pleasures of mankind. They knew nothing of the mysterious Aitch Eye or of its weird leader, the E'telekeli, and if they had known, they would have been very surprised to find out that a true man had penetrated the uttermost depths and had conferred with the Aitch Eye itself.

Very surprised.

But not interested.

Why should they care? Curiosity had died out a long time ago and the attempted Rediscovery of Man was awakening it only very slowly. A few officials knew or suspected the whole story, but then officials never talked much.

Only the underpeople cared and they were startled indeed.

A true man in Downdeep-downdeep?

How had that happened?

What could have gone wrong?

Nothing went wrong.

C'mell took him, and took him at the bidding of the E'telekeli himself. He was an offworlder. He had the odd pompous name of Roderick Frederick Ronald Arnold William MacArthur McBan the hundred and fifty-first and he was the richest sheep-owner from the richest planet in the galaxy, Old North Australia, which most people just called Norstrilia. He had gambled wildly, grotesquely, with help from his family's old computer, and he had won the largest fortune in the known or suspected universe. With this, he had bought Earth.

The name didn't mean much. He was no crabbed financier, no empire-builder in civilian clothes. He was a boy, blond, tall, athletic. His shortname was Rod McBan. Though he was a Mister and Owner and a full-franchise landholder in Norstrilia, he had been driven to adventure by mischance; he had not sought it for lust of power.

He didn't even go to Downdeep-downdeep in true-man form. The traps would have killed him if he had.

He had gone down disguised as a cat-man.

The cat-man disguise was not for the sake of Downdeep; it was to keep him alive while all the thieves in space and Earth were looking for him. He had escaped death from the weapons of an old enemy, the Hon. Sec. in Norstrilia; he had bought Earth; he had abandoned his cousin-sweetheart Lavinia on Norstrilia, at the urgent insistence of his own government; and he had arrived on Earth in a cat-body as the unwelcome but honored guest of the Instrumentality. The Instrumentality, which always ruled and never reigned, had even provided him the undergirl C'mell as his consort and escort for his time on Earth; and C'mell was the most brilliant, the most beautiful, and the most enticing of the girlygirls of Earth.

Knowing C'mell had been adventure incarnate. She had led him to things which he had not even imagined, including a knowledge of himself and of others. He had been places in the wet rich air of Earth, on the old streets and the complex cities, which no Norstrilian at home would ever believe; he had faced dangers, and now Rod knew that his time was drawing to a close. At last she was asking something of him and he could not refuse. All the time he had known her—days which seemed as long and busy as years—she had been giving: of herself, her time, the risk of her life. Now, for the first time, it was she who asked. He could not refuse.

He went with her down to a store. A commissary, run by a wonderful person called the Catmaster. Five hundred years old, and still allowed to live, and still allowed to run his store.

It was called the Department Store of Hearts' Desires.

Page 152. "The next section stopped him breathless." The text from here through the last poem on page 154 does not appear in "The Store of Heart's Desire," which also omits the text from "Rod cried out, ..." on page 156 through "Go on in." on page 157, and the text from "Thinking very carefully ..." on page 162 to the end of the chapter.

Page 163. "Everybody's Fond of Money." None of this chapter appears in "The Store of Heart's Desire."

Page 185. "Rod McBan was too weary to protest ..." In "The Store of Heart's Desire," the first two paragraphs here are replaced by:

Rod McBan went from the room of the stinkman to a place where a doctor gave him new smells to experience, smells of chemistry and of medicine and of heat and cold. The doctor's name was Vomact, and Rod would have enjoyed his company if he had not wondered where C'mell was and what she was doing.

This is followed by the two paragraphs from pages 95–96 (beginning with "Vomact was a small man ...") describing the other *Doctor Vomact (subsequent references to whom are also omitted in the magazine text).*

Page 206. "Rod tried to stammer his thanks ..." In "The Store of Heart's Desire," the text between here and "Rod made no move to leave." on page 208 is replaced by the following:

Rod tried to stammer his thanks.

The white giant took Rod by the arm and led him back to the visiphone, still trembling with the connection for Earth's surface, many kilometers above.

Rod trembled. Odd shards of dream-memory, coming out of his recently dreamed "life" with C'mell, pulsed through his mind.

The bird-giant showed him the surface of the Earth by borrowing a spying eye through the visiphone. They swooped through the streets of Earth one last time. Rod saw his rare postage stamps—Cape triangles, they were, printed before the beginning of time—being packed carefully into a metal box which had his formal address printed on it, very proper indeed:

Roderick Frederick Ronald Arnold William MacArthur McBan CLI
"The Station of Doom"
c-o Any Lawful Entry-port
Planet of Old North Australia

At last the E'telekeli sighed and Rod sighed with him.

"Enough?" asked the pale bird-giant.

"Enough," said Rod. He started to leave the visiphone and then stopped.

Page 211. "He waited for Lavinia instead." "The Store of Heart's Desire" ends here.

In addition, there were several places where text that appeared only in the magazine version appears to be necessary; the story makes more sense with it. In these locations (described below), the text has been reinserted into the body of Norstrilia. *This text is reproduced below. The text that has been added is shown in square brackets.*

Page 71. Note that this is the only place where Fisher states his title, yet after this point Rod knows it.

"You don't know who I am?" said Fisher.

["Silly games!" thought Rod. He said nothing but smiled dimly. Hunger began to stir inside him.

"Commonwealth Financial Secretary, that's me," said Fisher.] "I handle the books and the credits for the government."

Page 86. This text appears necessary to explain A'gentur's "hearing his name mentioned."

"Wait a moment," said the Lord Redlady. "Take your colleague."

["Colleague?" said the giant.

"A'gentur," said Redlady. "It'll be he who puts Rod together again."]
"Of course," said the doctor.

The monkey had jumped out of his basket when he heard his name mentioned.

Page 159. This speech appears needed for continuity.

The father was saying, "It's no use. Doris can watch him while we're gone, but if he isn't any better, we'll turn him in."

["Kill him?" shrieked the woman. "Kill my baby? Oh, no! No!"]

The calm, loving, horrible voice of the man, "Darling, spiek to him yourself. He'll never hier. Can that be a Rod McBan?"

The New England
Science Fiction Association (NESFA)
and NESFA Press

Recent books from NESFA Press:

- *Everard's Ride* by Diana Wynne Jones $19.95
- *Ingathering: The Complete People Stories of Zenna Henderson* $21.95
- *Norstrilia* by Cordwainer Smith $20.95
- *The Rediscovery of Man: The Complete Short Science Fiction of Cordwainer Smith* $24.95
- *A Bookman's Fantasy* by Fred Lerner (trade paperback) $11.95
- *The Passage of the Light: The Recursive SF of Barry N. Malzberg* (trade paperback) $14.00
- *Double Feature* by Emma Bull and Will Shetterly $17.95
- *Making Book* by Teresa Nielsen Hayden (trade paperback) $9.95
- *Vietnam and Other Alien Worlds* by Joe Haldeman $17.00
- *The Best of James H. Schmitz* $18.95

Books may be ordered by writing to:
    NESFA Press
    PO Box 809
    Framingham, MA 01701

We accept checks, Visa and Mastercard. Please add $2 postage and handling per order.

The New England Science Fiction Association:

NESFA is an all-volunteer, non-profit organzation of science fiction and fantasy fans. Besides publishing, our activities include running Boskone (New England's oldest SF convention) in February each year, producing a bi-monthly newsletter, holding discussion groups relating to the field, and hosting a variety of social events. If you are interested in learning more about us, we'd like to hear from you. Write to our address above!